THE TOO GOOD FOUNTAIN

D S ADAMS

THE TOO GOOD FOUNTAIN

This is a work of fiction. Names, characters,
businesses, places, events, locales, and incidents
are either the product of the author's imagination
or used in a fictitious manner.
Any resemblance to actual persons,
living or dead,
or actual events is purely coincidental.

Obligatory Trigger Warning
The story is set in USA in the late 20th Century. While the
characters and events should be considered fictional, the lan-
guage, dialogue, and attitudes the reader will find regarding
social activities, race, culture, and gender are a reflection of
that era and may be disturbing to some.

The "Max" series by D.S. Adams
is dedicated to my wife,
Ellen.
Free Spirit,
Strong Mind,
Good Heart.

A special acknowledgement
to Asuka Yow,
an inspiration to all who knew her.
Thank you Asuka
words to live by:
"Live a life that makes you smile."

NOTE FROM THE AUTHOR:

The memoir sessions of Harper Maximillan Wilson III, were transcribed and edited from recordings made at the Jersey Saloon in Prescott, Arizona. Harper or "Max" agreed to the interviews on the condition songs of his were to be included, that he would have an open bar tab throughout every interview, and no Karaoke would be involved in the process.

This manuscript also contains excerpts from the Arizona State University Department of Psychology program "Criminal Behavior: The Path to Prison Life" which was conducted at various Maricopa County Correctional facilities in conjunction with the privately funded documentary on Sheriff John Arnayo, "Arizona's Modern Territorial Justice and The Man Behind the Pink Pants."

Other interviews were then allowed for use from part of another Arizona State University program in the Journalism Department funded by a grant from the Scottsdale Institute of Body Sculpture titled "Gleaming Today's Teleprompter Stories from Reality".

NOTE: An essential part of this project was the interpretation of interviews into prose by select graduate students for movie and television. The author, through many Happy Hours of research, was able to procure the necessary manuscripts to tell the story and share it with you. Should anyone approach you with regards to this information, remember, it is to be strictly regarded as the facts.

Don't wanna glide in a dying wind,
or swim against a raging current.
It's no lie, I've spent time crying,
But now I'm confessing,
I need one more blessing.

Can I get a soul redemption?
Please, just give me
one more blessing.

On a breezy warm morning in North Las Vegas, Carter Benson slept beneath an overpass on Highway 15. During the night his cardboard blanket slipped below his chin, but he was still in the shade. He had managed to sleep past sunrise, but now disturbingly close to his ear, a woman's hoarse voice startled him awake.

"Hey mister, you got a smoke?"

Maybe she'd go away.

He pulled up his cardboard to cover his face, hoping to fend her off. He simply wanted to continue his hard-earned sleep in an attempt to forget about his life.

"C'mon mister, I'll make it worth your while. I know I ain't no Cleopatra or nothing, but I been around the sandbox a few times and I still know how to make a fella' smile."

Mollie wrinkled her nose and squinted at the cardboard over his face, then clenched her jaw, determined to give it another go.

"Hey mister, I got some fried chicken, too."

Carter was exasperated. He couldn't believe someone was hassling him in the middle of nowhere. He'd intentionally picked his spot, under this overpass, on this particularly desolate stretch of Highway 15 to ensure he'd be alone. It was a developmental zone where few businesses even existed. He planned to hide out until his trail went cold. Then he'd hole up at his last Las Vegas rental before he left on a journey to obscurity. He speculated he could fade into the remote wilderness north of Vancouver.

He heard her wheeze while she hovered over him and decided she wasn't leaving on her own. She was gonna be a hassle, though she probably just wanted some money, or a cigarette.

"I don't got no smokes..." he'd pulled the cardboard down far enough to peek at the woman. He shook his head, "and I don't wanna be bothered. Now go away! Leave me be."

"Well now mister, I was worried you wasn't even alive, sure was. I was scared you might be glazed over, like ole Jimmy was last week. You never know, sure don't."

Mollie got a good look at him, but still wasn't quite sure. She wanted to engage him a little longer. She didn't want to waste Veda's time, not with the temper she had, that would be a mistake.

She turned away and Carter peeked an eyeball at her. She wore an ill-fitted sun skirt over ratty dark leggings, her hair was dull ruddy blonde with black roots and gray blotches. It was hard to make out her face with the morning sun's halo blazed around her head, but it appeared she was missing some of her teeth and a dentist should probably pull the rest. She'd dropped her backpack at her feet and kept a comical yet concerned look while struggling to keep her balance. When she leaned over and got close, he smelled a robust mix of an old locker rooms, garbage, and syrup.

For a moment, she looked like a Medusa, her tendrils flailing about like little snakes in the desert wind. It gave him a start and he shifted his attention to the open road, looking in both directions for escape options. He was pissed she'd woken him up and wanted to dismiss her as quickly as possible. She was as an unwelcome busy-body in his personally staked out corner of concrete.

For a short time, she continued to stare at him with a furrowed brow and one hand on her hip, while her other hand tried to keep her hair out of her eyes. Satisfied she'd seen enough, she shifted into a comfortable slouch and looked around, before clearing her throat.

"Mister, you know you could get hurt out here in a heartbeat. Yes sirree, this here ain't no place to take a nap. Now I know a shelter about mile and a half from here. They got coffee and showers, and sometimes the kind folks there even bring round sammiches."

He didn't like her new pitch any better, and decided he'd use another tactic. Perhaps he'd read her all wrong. He let go of his cardboard.

"No thanks, that's ok... Look, I appreciate your concern, I really do, but I'm not interested. So, if that's all you wanted to tell me, you can go sleep over there."

He pointed to the opposite end of the embankment where an accumulation of plastic bags snagged on a run-off grate fluttered about. She gave the location a quick look then leaned her head to one side and squinted back at him.

"That's mighty kind of you mister. Really is. But you know, I think I'd rather take my chances back at the shelter, ...sure do. You change your mind, though, just go on up this exit ramp over here to the AM/PM. They'll direct you to the shelter, right near there."

Mollie wasn't a hundred per cent sure he was the guy, but she was pretty damn sure. Since he wasn't gonna go with her as she had hoped, she'd have to go back up to the AM/PM without him. She figured it would be ok because he didn't seem to be going anywhere anytime soon. If he did, this was such a remote spot it'd take him half hour to get anywhere else.

She'd call Veda the tracker lickety-split, after all Veda offered her a hundred bucks finder's fee. Veda'd pay up too, even if Mollie didn't have the guy in tow. As long he stayed put, Veda would find him.

She had to hurry up the ramp, she knew Veda rooted all around Naked City looking for the guy. That meant every thirsty bum Veda showed his picture to, would be looking for him. Mollie considered herself lucky, since Veda showed favor on her by seeking her out this time and giving Mollie her own copy of his picture. Then went a step further, telling her he might hang out by the highways. Veda knew those were Mollie's favorite hideouts.

She left the man without saying goodbye and hustled to the top of the exit, only stopping once to look back and make sure he hadn't left. When she finally got to the road, she stopped, smiled and lit a smoke. As she inhaled, she reached in her bra and pulled out the picture. She exhaled to the side and looked it over, holding it cupped in her palm. It was a black and white photo of a man with a beard penciled in over his cheeks and chin. Above the face, written in Sharpie was the name 'Carter'.

Yep, now she was confident it was him, and she was proud of herself. She'd played it cool and hadn't spooked him, didn't called him by his name or pull out the picture where he could see. Mollie knew Carter was hiding from someone. Stood to reason he didn't know Veda. Anyone with any sense would get as far away as possible if they had a clue she was tracking them.

Mollie couldn't wait for the finder's fee. She'd head straight to the Mini Mart. The 'Cleopatra' penny slot was fixing to hit any day now. She just knew it.

Carter went back to sleep easily, seemingly without a care, comfortable even on concrete. But after a half hour of his snore-fest Carter bolted upright from the sleep he'd fallen into. It'd been delayed, but he felt a jolt to his nervous system flash like a reptilian slash of tail up his spine.

"That deadbeat busy-body might be a spy!"

The message came from deep in his core where only survival mattered. Instinctively he checked his pocket, then remembered he'd put his driver's license in his left sock to feel it when he walked. He looked down at his sneakers. They were still laced up. He wiggled his tired toes and felt for the plastic rectangle. It was still there.

He hoped he was just being paranoid, the street lady has-sling him was too ragged to be connected to anyone he knew who'd be after him. However, the tingle in his spine and moment of worry reminded him he'd committed indiscretions that nagged.

One such concern was the wanton woman he tangled with at Dottie's Ditties. After the thrill subsided, he suspected it'd been way too easy to get laid, considering his current appearance.

Strangers in a bar, they made rapid acquaintance. She was suddenly and single mindedly attracted to him. She'd simply asked for a light, sitting next to him as they played video poker, attractive in a rough sort of way. He was lonely, and she started the conversation. He willingly followed her lead into a rapidly escalating game of seemingly spontaneous flirtation. He dove enthusiastically into the lust filled romp, racing ecstatically to her nearby hotel, believing he deserved the long overdue relief she'd provide.

Now he rued not vetting her at all and throwing caution to the wind. He reflected on how she'd been an absurdly enthusiastic lover. In fact, the whole thing was a fantasy hook up; he knew better, that wasn't how things really worked. He regretted getting off track, the escapade put him in danger.

"Way too easy..."

He'd said it out loud and decided to move ASAP.

Meanwhile, just before noon the same day at a Budget Suites not too far away...

"Richard, time to go!"

Larry Etrusco was pounding on the hotel door. When the pounding began, the occupant, Richard Boone, lay on the bed, head propped against the headboard, watching an Andy Griffith rerun, eating Cheetos balanced on his belly. He was making the best of it while waiting for their next move.

"Right on it, boss."

Richard responded quickly, he was used to it, Larry always wanted to leave in a hurry. Richard hated when they stayed in dumps like Budget instead of Caesar's and was ready to leave. Larry made the accommodations, and unfortunately Richard was used to staying in these low rent places when Larry was traveling on the low down.

Richard still thought it was stupid reasoning, Vegas was Vegas, who's gonna know? He threw the Cheetos aside, rolled off the bed and headed to the bathroom. When he stepped out on the second-floor walkway, Larry was there leaning against the railing, crushed cigarette butts scattered around his white Gucci loafers, holding his big mobile telephone against his head, waving a lit cigarette in the air, to punctuate his words.

"But I got it under control! .... ok, ...OK! ...Hey Louis, I gotta go, we're heading out. I'll call you later."

Larry looked Richard over.

"Man, I feel like a million bucks today, how 'bout you big guy?"

Larry looked up at the midday sky while nodding and turned back to Richard who hadn't responded. He really didn't want an answer.

"Nothing to say? Well, all right big guy, let's do this."

"Where we going today, boss?"

Richard figured something big was going down if Larry had a 'million bucks' kinda feeling.

"Don't worry, just a few miles, mostly highway. Then tonight we'll celebrate, long as everything works out."

"Sounds good, I got the Lincoln gassed up."

Richard was in a good mood, too. He liked it when Larry was in a good mood but knew it could change in a hurry. He preferred driving his older brother Louis. So far, he was more professional and predictable than Larry. Also, the new guy Joey, who was easy going. But, hey, a job was a job, and at least he was getting used to Larry's ways.

Richard reached into his left coat pocket to double check he hadn't forgotten his leftover sausage biscuit. Richard knew Larry didn't think about food the way he did. Now with biscuit in tow, he felt reassured it would be a good day, however, Larry stopped at the passenger side back door when they got to the car.

"Look Richard, I'm gonna ride in the back today. I'm expecting a visitor and he and I are gonna need to talk face to face."

They proceeded with Larry in the back giving Richard instructions when to get on the I-15. It was a few minutes after they got on the expressway, when he told him to slow down and be ready to stop. They spotted a man on the exit ramp ahead, and Larry had Richard corral him.

"Step on it, pull over and cut him off, but don't hit him for fuck's sake."

"You got it boss."

Larry smiled and rubbed his hands together. Richard made a show of stepping on the gas without squealing the tires, then pull over in front of the transient who was trudging along, lurching to a stop. The man halted immediately, standing by the passenger side holding his hands in the air. Larry leapt out, blocking the man's escape route and began talking in a welcoming voice.

"Hey Carter, it's me, your buddy Larry. Why'd you run out on us? Weren't we taking care of you?"

Carter attempted to side-step him, and Larry quickly checkmated his path.

"Look, I'm sure it's a misunderstanding. Tell me what you were thinking? We just need to straighten this out. C'mon Carter, whaddya say man?"

Carter was shocked by their abrupt arrival, and how quickly they'd trapped him, but he tried to remain calm. He didn't pretend he didn't know who they were, though his appearance was completely different than when they'd been together in Phoenix.

"Well, it just seemed like you guys were trying to squeeze me out. I guess I just lost my head. Uh, I think I understand now. It's nothing Larry, really. I'm just kind'a mixed up, that's all."

He stammered but surprised himself as he didn't panic and run. He started spinning his story about leaving Phoenix right away to Larry instead. Mentally, he didn't feel jumbled at all, the words slipped easily out of his voice box and across his lips. In fact, a weird sense of calm came over his mind and body. This was despite the inevitable slow tug of gravity occurring in his inner core. These internal biophysics had been with him since he left Phoenix, and never completely went away. Once he used to be able to escape these feelings but now they constantly lurked in the background of his soul.

He heard Larry continue to talk in what sounded like a voice he'd heard in dreams.

"Sure, I understand Carter. Maybe you sampled a little too much 'Huggy' and the world started closing in on you... Yeah, sure, it's natural, it makes people paranoid. No worry, let's figure it out."

"Yeah, I don't know. I mean, do you really need me anymore? I was thinking, since we started working with the younger guys and all, it seemed like I was being watched all the time. Maybe I am just paranoid, but I thought you guys might decide, you know, to make me the fall guy if something went wrong."

"Carter... Carter... Carter..."

Larry shook his head while scraping his white loafer in the dusty gravel, smiling like a dad making a point to his son still in middle school.

"I'm disappointed. You think we'd snitch on you? You think after all you've done for us, that we'd hang you out to dry?"

When Carter didn't respond he continued.

"No way! We're gonna take care of you, man. Now I admit, Louis was a little upset when you disappeared. I mean, you gave us no heads up. Didn't ask for time off or nothing. You know, just splitting like that, well, I figured you must have been losing it, buddy, ...But you should have known you could always come to us about anything like that."

Carter lowered his head and looked at his dirty hands. He didn't know how to get out of this right now. He'd have to play along and take his chance later when they were in a better situation to make a run for it.

"Hey, tell you what, come here. Let's walk around a little bit.... here, have some water."

Larry reached in the back seat and handed him a cold water. Carter took the water, handling it gingerly while he looked at Richard who had his head down while he fiddled with the dashboard, as if he wasn't even paying attention to their conversation. Carter opened the water and took a drink. Larry motioned to Carter with a friendly smile.

"Come on man, let's take a look at Vegas together."

The road on the overpass was still covered in dirt and gravel, its finishing touches were still to come. They walked to the railing together and Richard slowly pulled the car to the side, Larry's door still open.

Though it was miles away, they had a splendid view of the Las Vegas Strip, the sun glinting off the Strip Casinos' iconic shapes. There was no traffic at the time, and Richard could hear Larry talking thirty feet away, even though they faced the other way. As the two of them surveyed the Strip's skyline, Richard silently opened the trunk for Larry with the dashboard control.

Once the trunk was up, he opened his driver side window, and his door slightly then pulled his biscuit out of his coat pocket and put it on the seat. He'd double bagged it in Ziplocs so Larry wouldn't smell it and give him any shit about it. It seemed like a good time to eat and take a leak. He was sure they'd talk for several minutes. He scarfed down his biscuit in three bites then got out and walked quietly around the front of the car away from them, stopping by a small sage. After swallowing the last of his snack, he unzipped his pants. He could still just make out Larry's voice.

"It's so peaceful out here, just beautiful. Carter, you know Las Vegas is gonna be our next big operation. You're going to make so much money, you can retire, then go anywhere you want. You wanna live a thousand miles from anyone, and use a helicopter to get there and back, you can do it. You want a penthouse here or maybe Manhattan, you'll be set."

Larry put both hands on the railing and stretched forward. He shook his head while he admired the view. Carter relaxed, closed his eyes, and daydreamed of being able to leave his troubles behind. He felt a falling sensation and allowed himself not to fear it. He could do this. He could navigate Louis and Larry's moods and kneejerk decisions and get through this. He took another swig of water while the heat emanated off everything around them. The sky was clear, and the casino jewels of the strip shining bright. Behind them stood the red streaked, cream-colored rocks jutting from ridges, corralling the city's outskirts.

"Sure, this is all here for the taking, man. You just need to chill a little bit and embrace your good luck. This is your success story, Carter. Live it up."

Larry's voice had become a soothing refrain to a long day. Carter allowed himself to smile but didn't notice Larry had backed away from the railing and was quietly moving towards the open trunk.

"Yea, Larry you know what, you're probably right."

Sure, why not? He further embraced the thought as he gripped the railing. He could clean things up and get right back on the party horse he'd been riding before he panicked and fled. Louis had been the one who got him out of a big jam, so why had Carter gotten so uptight all of a sudden? He opened his eyes and looked out across the desert. He saw the Las Vegas horizon as a new beginning. He closed his eyes again and sighed, lightly bouncing his thighs against the railings. He didn't even react when he heard the rustle of Larry's feet, shuffling into position on the gravel for his home run swing.

Larry swung his aluminum bat at Carter's head with all his might catching him square on the back of his skull. Carter felt his head crack with an explosive jolt, crushing any possible new beginnings.

Instead, it was the end, the last sensation he'd ever know.

Larry rushed forward, immediately trying to push Carter over the railing onto the highway below.

"Come on Richard, help me for crying out loud!"

Richard was still taking a leak on the other side of the car. He heard the metal clang of the bat against Carter's skull. When the bat clattered to the ground, he froze.

"Oh shit!"

Of course, he'd known Larry's bat was in the trunk. He'd opened it as a standard operational procedure as Larry had other 'toys' in there as well. Usually though, Larry gave Richard some kinda warning, or a clue, like saying he was 'gonna play ball' or 'gonna go deep,' before using the bat in one of his 'conversations.'

Richard forced a quick finish, did a quick shake, and tucked himself in his pants. Without taking time to zip, he ran to the railing. When he got there, he grabbed Carter's arm and leg, and together they tried to hoist him over the rail. Unfortunately, on Larry's side the man's left hand still clutched the railing.

Larry let go of Carter.

"Fucking guy!"

Larry stepped back, picked up the bat again with both hands and raised it straight up and brought it back down like an axe on the knuckles of the offending grip. The sound reminded Richard of the Thanksgiving day's turkey popping when pulled apart for sandwich scraps. But even after the bat whack, two of the fingers continued clutching the rail. Larry wildly swung the bat back up in the air, and while he held it at its apex , he aimed, and with his face twisted in anger, he slammed it back down.

Even Richard was shocked by Larry's sudden savagery, as his boss looked like a horror film villain. Richard held tight to Carter's arm and leg, just in time to squeeze shut his eyes for the bat's impact.

Unfortunately for Larry though, as the bat came down, the two fingers clutching the railing let go before impact and the body slumped to the pavement knees first. Richard stumbled as Carter flopped against Larry's legs. Larry stumbled as he finished lowering the boom, and his grip on the bat faltered before impact.

It clanged loudly off an empty railing, subsequently bouncing free, and twisting up into the air. Before Larry was able to protect himself, the bat returned to glance off his head, inflicting a musical but painful 'doink,' then rattle onto the ground and roll across the dirty gravel a few feet away.

"Son of a bitch! I'm gonna fuck this guy up now."

Larry instinctively reached up to feel his scalp and backed up in rage while reaching down for the bat yet again. Richard sensed he better do something to stifle Larry's fit and rallied to shout at Larry.

"Hey boss, look!" he motioned with his head northward then pointed, "There's a car coming, we best drop him over the rail now!"

Sure enough, only a few miles off there was the sparkle of sunset kissed chrome with headlights heading their way. Larry's teeth were still clenched in madness, but Richard could see his mind working through it. He reached again for the arm and leg and raised his eyebrows at Larry hoping he'd relent. It took only seconds for what Richard said to become Larry's orders.

"Yeah, I got an idea, Rich, let's let the cars do the rest, and it'll look like an accident."

Richard was relieved. Larry dropped the bat and came back to the railing. Larry cussed Carter as he grabbed his loose limbs and together, they lifted the body. Carter's clothes were covered with blood and as they moved his torso onto the top railing, Larry stopped the process, letting his side sag.

"Hey, wait a second, let's get his wallet, then let's make sure he goes down headfirst."

Richard pulled an old wallet out of Carter's back pocket, then they scrambled to reset their grip while trying to turn him upside-down. They lowered him over the railing and Richard looked to Larry for a signal. Carter's blood was dripping from his matted hair, the red drips turning to dark dots as they hit the pavement below. Larry grunted then blurted out the signal.

"All right, let him go."

They released him but were a little out of synch so he fell slightly sideways towards the edge of the road and landed with a thud. They stepped forward simultaneously to peek as if there might be another movement. There wasn't, he was a motionless heap on Highway 15's outside lane. The remote spot where they stood became a noise vacuum, interrupted only by sparse sounds of the distant traffic. The two men gave each other a confirmative nod then Larry uttered an insult, instead of the dignified last rites Richard had expected from a former partner of the deceased.

"There you go you lying bastard, live it up down there."

Richard wasn't shocked but instead he was a little uneasy and waited to hear something more remorseful. Instead, Larry simply looked down and frowned at the mess on his beloved Gucci's.

"Get some towels from the trunk so I can clean off my fucking shoes, then we need to wipe off this railing and dump some water on it, too."

Of course, Richard knew by we, he meant Richard, as Larry motioned at the splotches of blood on the concrete. Richard went to get the towels and cooler and reminded himself doing things with Larry still beat hard labor or having another knee surgery. He shrugged and headed to the car.

When he turned around, there was Larry, visible to any car driving by, pissing right over the railing, loudly cussing Carter. Richard grabbed the cooler and some towels and headed back for clean-up. Larry's cussing turned to laughter and his voice became high pitched and maniacal, swinging his hips back and forth peeing wildly in a side-to-side arc. When Larry finished, his laughing subsided, and he began to hum some old 50's song. As he did his tone changed back to normal as if he'd just hosed down his driveway in a quiet Phoenix suburb.

"That'll give them Vegas cops a mess to work with."

He zipped up and beckoned at Richard.

"Hey Richard, when you're done cleaning up, get the wallet, water bottles and towels and shit and we'll drop'em in a furnace."

Richard reflected on how the afternoon had gone so far. It was almost a déjà vu of his high school days, drinking Bali Hai on a dirt county road with his football buddies, and taking turns peeing off an old bridge.

He thumbed through the wallet, no money, ID or pictures, just receipts. He tossed it into the bag as the useless piece of garbage it was, and never considered the significance of what was missing. Richard smiled as he loaded the bag into the Lincoln's trunk.

"Ah yes, the glorious days of my youth, High School... ...the Chickenhawks. Yep, those were good times."

He wasn't talking to Larry or even himself, it was just for the benefit of the Lincoln. After closing the trunk, he patted it like a good dog. All the while, Larry had been leaning against the side of the car intently wiping off his shoes.

Tacos and Sunshine

Sunshine, tan lines, tacos, and beer,
why worry when this is all here?
Clear skies above shaded eyes,
telling each other sweet little lies.

No matter if the lying ends,
we still party as friends.
We fall in love all the time
when there's tacos and sunshine.

I was back in Arizona, my resident zone, still recovering from a bullet wound I'd received in Atlanta, courtesy of their Zone 6 Department officers. I was in their 'zone' when I'd found myself at the end of my journey of tracking down an old friend's killer.

What would we do without old friends?

Well, it might not be good for me, because despite the occasional bullet along the way, friends seem to be the dots that keep my life connected.

My name's Max, and it's short for Harper Maximillan Wilson III. When this story began, I was in Tempe, Arizona, to be exact, accepting all the help I could get from friends. The roof over my head was provided via a luke-warm invitation from old friend, Billy Skeezer, a sound man who let me stay in his guesthouse efficiency. I used to rent the place as my own, but now it was his, as he'd finally taken over the lease and moved his stuff in, but he actually only stayed there between tours. It had running water, electricity, a phone, and a bed, though I usually slept on the well-worn couch. Fortunately, he was on the road again, so I could recover there while I tried to scrounge up some sort of gig, or job, or any type of money-making enterprise suited for my particular skill set. A recovery made necessary because I had been accidently shot by an Atlanta cop when I was tracking my friend's suspected killer.

My clothes were clean thanks to a new friend, Cindy Masters, who had kindly dropped by, picked up my laundry, and returned it clean, pressed and folded, a rare condition for my wardrobe. I would thank her properly next time we met, but with more than simple thank you's. I wanted to romance her, I was more than just fond of her, she had a special place in my heart. It was my intention to address my feelings towards her with more formal overtures after I recovered, as opposed to the amorous one-nighter we had. You see, previously we spontaneously drank our way into a grief-sharing embrace in the wake of a mutual friend's passing. The same mutual friend whose murderer's trail led me to getting shot in Atlanta.

As for money, the only viable lead likely to pan out any time soon was from my friend Jonesy. Jonesy had an Uncle Joey, who was a partner in some nightclubs and the two of them thought there was a job in it for me. They believed my booze slinging, key carrying skills would remain intact after recovery. I told Jonesy I was interested and within a week I received the following letter:

M r. Max Hamilton –
My nephew referred you with high praise of your talent and experience. Because of his high regard for your skills, I believe there is immediate opportunity for you in our company's entertainment division of Vettes' Nightclubs. You would be compensated generously if hired.

We understand you are recovering from injury, but it is our hope you would be available to work within 30 days. We would like to interview you at your earliest convenience.

Our Dance-Dance Clubs, LTD, are industry trendsetters we seek exceptional leaders who demonstrate a sense of urgency and foster quality teamwork. Our goal is to create a financially successful party every day.

Our Vettes Management Team Motto –
"Jamming like a Salmon swimming upstream,
I work at Vettes and life is but a dream."

Sincerely,
Joseph Spasula
Vice President
Dance-Dance Clubs, LTD

P.S. - Call us at 1-800-DAN-CING, to set up your inter-view.

So, I called the number several times and left messages for Joseph with his secretary, but nothing happened. Jonesy told me his uncle was quite a guy, and his letter sounded like they didn't beat around the bush. It sounded like they were anxious to meet, and I was intrigued. I had no idea what 'compensated generously' meant since it varied so much depending on who said those words, and what the job entailed. However, since nothing had happened after my calls, I thought I better have another talk with Jonesy.

I really wasn't supposed to be doing too much as of yet according to the surgeon who stitched me up. Thankfully, Eddie, my friend, confidant, and personal wizard of the newly paved internet highway, dropped by for a friendly visit and agreed to find Jonesy and bring him by. Eddie also agreed to pick up Jonesy's favorite beverage, Olde English 800, as motivation. They arrived late in the afternoon and after a few beers reminiscing about a recent trip to Mexico, Jonesy told me he and his uncle Joey had already talked. He claimed Uncle Joey would be getting in touch soon. He told me Joey's company had a club on the west side of Phoenix.

"Vettes! Yeah man, first class my bruthuuur. Big time! Neon everywhere, topflight DJ's, state of the art dance lights, and they got cheerleaders dancing on the bar. We gotta go some-time! I can get us in, no problem. We gotta wear our dress duds though, Vette's is choice stuff, man. Hey Max, I'm telling you, Joey's gonna hook you up, my bruthuurr."

Jonesy walked out first, and I whispered to Eddie asking if he could check Vettes out online and get me some information to be better prepared in the event something came of it. Screening them would give me something to do while waiting to hear back and coordinate a trip with Jonesy to the club. Another two weeks passed, with no call from Jonesy's Uncle Joey, and Jonesy couldn't be found, either.

My shoulder improved over those two weeks. It was supposed to be a six-week recovery window, but I could walk around with my arm in a sling and carry a bag of groceries or a six pack in my other. I whittled my pain pill regimen down to only taking Percocet twice a day and only small doses. As I'd begun to feel better, I started doing walk-abouts to neighborhood stores, using my remaining dwindling funds as prudently as possible.

One scorching Tempe afternoon I was on my way home after visiting The Palo Verde Lounge with a cold sixer of Pabst's annual Bock beer tucked under my good arm, my only grocery purchase of the day. As I approached my block, I heard the Martha and The Vandellas refrain from *Jimmy Mack,* behind me. Then I was accosted by two girls' giggling voices over the Motown beat.

"Hey Max! Whoo-hooo! Maxie!"

Alarmingly close, followed by the close crunch from gravel as the brakes locked, their car's tires slid to a halt on the shoulder just a few feet behind me. I shuffled forward a couple steps to avoid the flying gravel.

"Need a ride, cutie pie?"

My upper body was stiff, but my beer carefully cradled, as I turned around. There they were, Mira and Effie, the Tempe Town Bar Belles, in some low riding red Chevy Impala convertible. They were out on the town, jamming with the top down. Effie was behind the wheel, with a ponytail and tie-dyed bandana across her forehead. They were my friends, but my initial inclination was to berate them about reckless driving around a slow-moving pedestrian. But I took a deep breath, mine had been a long recovery and I really missed the Rock'n Roll escapades that were my life before I was shot, so instead of a reprimand, I welcomed their friendly ambush with a smile and tip of my cap.

"Sure, where we headed?"

After all, it was a perfect day for a joy ride with these legendary wild women and besides, what did I have to lose? There was no telling when I'd hear back from Joey or Jonesy about a job.

"We're headed over to a party at South Mountain and we got something we want you to try. C'mon Max, get in."

I ambled toward the backseat of the car but before I got there, Mira pulled herself up by the windshield in the front passenger side, jumped up to stand on the seat, and did an amateur back flip over into the back seat.

"You can have shotgun, Max!"

Her acrobatics made her hair fly around her head, while her pocket linings sneaking out from under her cut offs flapped on her thighs like splash guards. She landed on the back seat with a bounce, then wiggled down into a comfortable squat. Her reverse somersault left her peasant blouse pulled over her head and down her back, her collar caught under her chin. No fan of Victoria's Secret, her preferred au naturelle state now freely revealed her all over tan. She basked in the day's gloriously bright Arizona sun, raising her arms while twisting the hemline of her blouse over her head like a playful tourniquet.

As she twisted it tighter she laughed, "Hey Max, look. I'm a ghost! Yee-haw! Trick or treat!"

She shook her shoulders for maximum wobble, and Effie felt obliged to join in. Though clothed, Effie let go of the steering wheel and raised her arms to amplify her wiggles. Thankfully, her foot stayed on the brake.

With both girls twisting and laughing I negotiated my way into the front seat, with a halfhearted warning.

"Mira, if you don't pull your shirt down, I'm betting we'll have the whole town following us around wanting tricks *and* treats."

I knew they liked to flash their boobs and butts at every opportunity, but hell, it wasn't even Happy Hour yet and we were on Tempe's main drag. Just to make sure no offense was taken, I leaned back and shouted up to the heavens loud enough for all the neighbors to hear as Effie put it in gear.

"Nice tan, by the way!"

And with a wink, to make sure she knew I was still game for their hijinks, we took off with tires squealing, and spraying gravel. I held the sixer in my lap, pushed my hat and sunglasses on tight, and hoped I could survive Effie's driving without losing anything.

I opened three beers and handed them each one and took a sip of my own. Mira had unwrapped her head to show off her beaming smile, while ribbons of long brown hair and her blouse blew about without restraint offering continual random flashing boobs for the oncoming traffic. We were met with honks and shouts of approval, and she loved it. She didn't plan these things, but she was all for the world enjoying her play as long as she had a good time too.

We sang along with Martha, then the Supremes and then the Temptations, and the sun glared off our sunglasses and her tan. We enjoyed swigs of beer and headed past the Tempe Twin Buttes towards South Pointe Mountain Preserve. A few hundred yards after passing through the gate they pulled off to a secluded spot and stopped with a jolt, immediately popping open the trunk.

"C'mon Max, we want you to try some good stuff in private before we get to this party!"

Effie headed back to the trunk while Mira turned up the radio with the Stones' "Can't You Hear Me Knocking and hopped out into her interpretative spinning dance of the song. I got out and moseyed to the back and leaned against the car to watch. Effie produced a small bong she'd loaded with ice water, and some lumpy looking weed and walked towards me while she flicked a power lighter at the bowl. I heard it crackle to the flame and she made a seething noise holding in a lungful then handed it to Mira who'd spun between us at the perfect moment to intercept.

"South Mountain, baby! Super sunset, here we come!"

Effie nodded vigorously at her to not waste her turn so Mira stopped and bent over the plastic mouthpiece and began inhaling. I gulped, was I about to get in the deep end before I was really ready for it? I noticed Effie also had stuffed two huge American flag paper joints in her chest pocket, as red and white stripes poked up like strange antennae. These two didn't do anything discreetly.

"Max! What are you waiting for? It's your turn!"

Mira pushed the bong into my chest.

"Whoa, watch it now, my shoulder's still tender."

"It's ok, Max, take your hit. You know I can be gentle too."

She jumped in front of me and pulled my shirt out of my pants while I was trying to inhale carefully. Mira didn't stop with that either, as I held the bong out for Effie, she gave me a sloppy motorboat kiss on the stomach and stuck her tongue in my belly button to boot.

"Whoa! Ok, *easy* now."

As I spoke, I exhaled my bong hit and it swarmed around my head like a cloud of bees. I guess I sounded mistreated as Mira quickly changed her tone with me.

"Ok, Max, if you're gonna act like an old man, I guess I'll treat you like one. You old Humpty Dumpty, such a poor thing."

She gently cradled my free hand and led me back to the car with the careful gait of a caretaker helping the elderly. Once back in the car though, I began to see stars in the clear blue sky that were coming out of my head. Apparently from my toke on that bong's lumpy load. Effie managed a donut in the mountain's desert sand, and we got back on the trail and headed to their party.

The Warning:
Now this – tut, tut . . . tuh-dut
Is a warning - tut . . . tuh-dut
That the Chickenhawks – tut, tut . . . tuh-dut
Are coming on – tut, tut . . . tuh-dut

And we – tut, tut . . . tuh-dut
Are here to tell you - tut . . . tuh-dut
That the Chickenhawks – tut, tut . . . tuh-dut
Are kicking butt – tut, tut . . . some-butt

So, this – tut, tut . . . tuh-dut
Is just a warning - tut . . . tuh-dut
The Chickenhawks are gonna win
– tut, tut. . . tuh-dut
Work it out - Woo hoo!
. . . tut, tut . . .some-butt!

As Katy Kitts performed the Vettes' dance routine to *Blue Moon*, she indulged in a dreamlike flashback to her high school days. She remembered how she always got excited, maybe even lightheaded, and sometimes with a little flutter in her stomach when they got into the 'Warning' cheer. When the squad performed it, the whole student body fell under a spell, strong as the force she saw capturing the teeny boppers during the Beatles first TV appearance. Clapping and stomping along, it was the one time every one of the Charlton (Iowa) High students got rhythm, no matter how geeky and talentless they might be.

Then there was the night Charlton High star running back Richard Boone jumped on the school auditorium stage during the cheer. She lost it like many of the girls that day. He performed with exaggerated abandon, moving in ways she'd never seen a man move.

And he was a man!

Her pulse raced, and her body reacted so strongly she could hear each heartbeat. Her cheeks blushed so hard the blood vessels ached, and she got dizzy. It was too tantalizing to understand, she could only surrender to it. Her ears became hot, and the pit of her stomach stirred before the sensations crept even deeper. At first, she thought she might have an accident, then realized it was something else. It was a first-time thrill from her inner core, from the deepest fiber of her animal being and she knew the sensations were exactly the kind of feelings that made parents uneasy when asked to explain what the feelings were.

It was sex, the dark side of social behavior her friends whispered and giggled about. Most girls she knew spent their time wondering, and staying cautiously curious, but when a boy exhibited that much single mindedness in his approach, they protected themselves by staying away from any situation where they'd end up alone with him. To even flirt with a boy like him would be too dangerous for an inexperienced girl.

It was crazy having that reaction while in her cheer outfit at a pep rally, in broad daylight, with all the bodies in the student body there. She'd heard the gossip how Richard performed a still wet, fresh-from-the-shower, even dirtier version in the boy's locker room after the school's big win the week before the rally. Apparently, he'd used a towel and imitated the routine of two different girls on the squad. He'd done them longer, lewder and more provocatively than any other boy could replicate. Richard was, after all, four years older and looked ten years bigger. At the time Katy was certain his manhood was superior to the rest of the team as well, even if she wasn't sure what that might mean.

Rumors flew through girl's gym class like wildfire. He'd put a towel between his legs, one hand in front and one in back, sliding it back and forth in rhythm to the words. Katy saw Veronica, the most proper and studious girl on the squad, break down and cry when she overheard how he'd made fun of her with a falsetto voice while he wiggled his ass. Oh yes, and Linda Sue proudly strutted around with self-anointed queen like arrogance. Supposedly he'd mimicked her passionate pleas from a romantic backseat encounter, crowing loudly at the end, as he had strutted around doing her version. Katy wondered why he hadn't included her and wondered what she needed to do to be that cool.

She'd asked herself how she could get noticed. Of course, in the next minute, she realized that was nonsense. The cheer was a group effort the entire student body celebrated together. But Richard was special that way, and able to separate a student's body from the student body in so many ways. On the football field he simply ran over opponents, with a shrug of disrespect. When he strutted through the crowded Charlton hallways, the rabble of students parted like in the presence of approaching nobility. In the classroom he could interrupt the most enthralling lecture at its apex by asking to use the restroom and once there, simply smoke a cigarette, then casually re-enter the class in a relaxed strut, nonchalantly exhaling smoke, and stealing the attention from the teacher and reminding everyone who the Charlton High 'King' really was.

He was famous on his dates for his success rate screwing girls. He was actually in his fifth year but still needed to pass most of his sophomore and junior credits. As a cheerleader, Katy knew she couldn't go out with him on an announced date, it would be too scandalous. Any girl'd be naïve to think you could go for a joy ride with him on the nightly high school circuit by simply jumping in his car at the A&W and expect only to joy ride the circuit with him. No girl would, unless they were already willing to put out. There were even stories he'd spent time in reform school and perhaps jail, that he'd been shipped out of state and more. Apparently it was agreed he'd finish school, as long as he got to continue playing as a starter on the football, baseball, and wrestling teams. He also had two brothers coming up soon and the coaches hoped they'd bring success, too, and wanted to keep the oldest son happy.

True, due to knee injuries he'd never played an entire season in any sport, but it'd still been easy to get the Principal and Coaching staffs to agree on terms to allow him to play. Somehow, he'd get the credits to graduate, but details were murky and no one inside Charlton cared about the scuttlebutt townsfolk traded at coffee-stained breakfast counters in the neighboring counties. When he played on the Charlton teams, they performed at their best and drew the biggest crowds with brisk sales guaranteed at concessions and the nearby markets. In addition to being a bully and a lout he was an important economic engine to the town folks on game day.

Katy always wondered what opposing coaches must have thought, all this time at the same school! Charlton was undoubtedly his turf, and his status was legendary. At the end of the day, she knew he was of sketchy moral character, but Katy thought he was dreamy. He had power, he embodied manliness and was the source of so much excitement amongst her friends in her high school world. And after all, Charlton was the only world she'd ever known.

That seemed like so many years ago...

Now, when Katy danced in her red Vettes cheer uniform, it was fun and easy like those high school days on the sidelines at the stadium. The big difference was now she was much more confident, and it was the guests' attentions that gave her a real sense of satisfaction.

Her mind drifted back to the sideline stage. She loved to reminisce in a dreamlike state, her body easily remembering the Vettes dance moves she and the other girls knew by heart.

She would feel so groovy, imagining the high school stadium lights making trippy trails off the trombones and tubas, indistinguishable from the DJ's dance lights sequencing with the song. She could even see light traces off the helmets as the teams streamed by, the players full of testosterone, fresh out of the dressing room.

Reality faded in and out and she knew she felt remarkable, especially for this early in the night. When the song ended, she started to regroup, and tried to be present, remembering she was working and dancing on a bar.

Tonight, the DJ next launched the crew into a 'Vettes Shot Special' song. As the celebration began, a guy from the crowd pulled himself up onto the bar in front of Katy and twisted around to face the crowd holding his drink with an extended hand as he sang along. She suddenly felt a rush roll through her like a wave and for a moment it was like she'd left her body, her mind simply observing everything from a pillow-like cloud in the sky. As she finished her intro, a 360 twirl that raised her skirt, she abruptly halted. She felt the customer's head beneath her skirt against her legs as the skirt settled over him like a collapsed parachute after landing.

She was startled, uncertain, and dismayed.

She wondered, "My God, do I have on my panty hose? Did I remember to put on my blue bloomers?"

As the thoughts flashed through her mind, she grabbed her skirt with one hand and pulled it off him, backing away in a hurry, and losing her balance. Instinctively, she reached up and grabbed the metal tube part of a light fixture suspended from the ceiling above her. The tube was attached to the over-sized disc-like lamp, and as she fell, the force tore the tube's ceiling mount from the tiles above, sending fragments of tile and flecks of paint and dust into the air, showering down on revelers below. Amazingly, the crowd didn't notice, because the confetti cannon from the DJ booth signaling the shot special was firing away, all in the midst of the celebration as the arc of the song reached a crescendo.

The man who'd been between her legs tumbled over backwards with her, oblivious and euphoric, blissfully unaware of the chain reaction he'd fueled. Katy was stunned but realized she was free falling into the bartenders' well, with her hand clasping the light fixture and the man's right arm locked around her leg. Jocko, the bartender, noticed her and the fixture falling and jumped up on the beer cooler in time to grab her before the light's wiring snapped. He then quickly grabbed the man's arm and used it to shove him back down off the bar into the crowd.

"I got you Katy, let go of the light."

Jocko simultaneously cradled her and grabbed her fingers, peeling them from the wire-filled tubing, some of which were now frayed and exposed at the end of the tube.

Disoriented, Katy began to cry as Jocko helped her down. Moments later she was laughing. Her tears flowed freely with both emotions, and she haphazardly brushed debris from the 'V' on her chest. The light, swinging awkwardly, now flickered while pieces of dust and debris continued drifting down from the black crawl space the newly torn hole had created in the ceiling. Jocko led Katy to the service bar door and into the waitress service well, sat her in a chair against the wall, and poured her a soda to drink.

"Here Katy, you better rest a minute, you need to get your shit together."

"Thanks Jocko, I don't know what happened!"

She was sniffling, desperately trying to get her focus back. Other girls arrived in the service well after they'd climbed down from their dance posts. They gathered their drink trays and jockeyed for position in line to get their next drink order. Katy looked at them and started crying again.

"Can I go on a break? Can someone please cover me?"

She got up and headed straight to the ladies' room without waiting for an answer.

"Sure, I got you babe."

Abby answered her over her shoulder, while dabbing her neck with a wet cocktail napkin. It was not an out of the ordinary request from a fellow waitress on a busy night at Vettes, especially after a shot special started.

It was also not out of the ordinary for the Vettes bouncers to be hurriedly summoned into action to minimize or resolve a situation. Danny Boone, one of the dance floor station bouncers was on his walkie-talkie that very moment telling the team he was on it. He quickly headed toward the bar through the party crowd, his communication device pressed to his ear. He looked up to where the light still dangled.

"Un-fucking believable, what did this bitch do?"

Meanwhile, in the ladies' room two Vettes girls primped in the ceiling high mirrors behind the sinks. Throughout the night the girls sought these moments of relief in front of the mirrors to freshen their make-up and hair after the frenzied dance numbers. It was a busy spot; they didn't always have time to run back to their employee lounge at the far end of the kitchen.

The 'Drink Special' songs, aided by the stunning lights and gimmicks, created an electrifying atmosphere. As the night wore on and customers drank more, the scene became intensely addictive. The public consensus for partiers of all ages was that the vibe was greatly enhanced by the staff's unbounding enthusiasm and unabashed sense of play. In reflection, others would now tell you they believed the Jell-O shots and other house drink specials really heightened their buzz and the staff simply helped make them feel welcome to party their ass off.

The staff appreciated the status the club's consistent business brought, often playing it to their advantage. Vettes was full of potential suitors, and girls would go to great lengths to maintain their penultimate look for the entire night, which meant a multitude of mirror trips. You never knew when the next guest you wait would be an actor, pro athlete, comedian, drug kingpin, oilman, plastic surgeon, sports agent or maybe a federal agent. This was the Vettes scene on any given night.

Marni was working on her eyebrows but paused when Katy leaned into the mirror, reaching into her blouse for her comb and grabbed at the tissues.

"You look like you're just spazzed to the *max*!"

"Yeah, I almost fell off the bar, some guy got under my skirt!"

Katy furiously worked on tear-stained eyes.

Marni looked over at Jaylin who was sniffing her armpits and looked at Katy's reflection as she heard the story. Jaylin looked at Marni and mouthed the words silently and rolled her eyes.

"Country is *craazee*."

Katy noticed out of the corner of her eye, she often felt a heightened sense of awareness at work. A few of the girls here called her 'Country'. It didn't make her feel like she worked in her second home, in fact it made her feel quite the opposite.

'Country' was definitely a mean nickname, meaner than 'Kissy Katy' she earned in high school. Of course, 'Kissy Katy' was supposed to be a slur of shame when she'd gotten it as a junior caught by the cheer instructor kissing a boy from another school under the bleachers while still in her cheer gear. Katy realized later she had been trying too hard to get attention because of a dare from another cheerleader. Now she fondly remembered the moniker, as if a term of endearment. Well, at least she hadn't gotten caught doing something worse.

She lost almost all self-control her junior year before getting her act together as a senior. But she knew what 'Country' meant at Vettes, and it always seemed to come from one of the girls who'd simply been in Phoenix longer than her. The reality was almost all of them came from somewhere else they'd been glad to escape.

"I got bigger fish to fry than be bothered by any of you smack talking bitches."

Dismissing them comforted her and she continued working on her eyes. Her head was still spinning, and she wasn't sure why, but it happened a lot while working at Vettes. Thing is, she loved it and knew the crowd loved her. The enthusiasm she showed was encouraged and she seemed to reach new heights during dance routines. She even reveled in after work parties and couldn't be stopped by anyone when she was having fun, even if 'showing out,' as her mom would have called it. She didn't care either, she'd be better than anyone else in the Vettes' scene in no time.

After work this night after she pulled the ceiling light down, she was given bad news. Her boss Murray told her she would have to pay for the repairs to the light fixture and ceiling. When he told her, she started crying, and he simply gave her a tissue and sighed. But when she wouldn't stop bawling, he gave in a little and said he'd ask the GM, Dean, if she could work it off with the Vettes Community Promotions team or something. She could go with the other girls when they did their Vettes' dances at civic functions and passed out flyers. It might be a hassle to get up at 8 AM and dance "Blue Moon" at a pancake breakfast, but she didn't care.

"I don't care Murray, whatever you say, really. When that man put his head under my skirt it scared me. I don't know how it happened. I'm just so sorry."

Murray pulled a book out of his desk drawer, flipped it open to a bookmarked page, and made some notes. As far as Murray was concerned, Dean could figure it out. Dean always wanted to handle any damage control and people were always getting out of control, so it kept him busy, Murray figured that's why Dean made the big bucks.

When the Bar Belles and I finally got to South Mountain's observation point, our partying got serious.

Effie crawled through the straw-filled cargo bed of a flatbed truck where our merrymaking group had settled and leaned towards me with a smile. I expected a big wet kiss, but what I got was a lip lock and a well-intended blast of smoke she'd apparently sucked from one of her oversized doobies. As she blew into my lungs, I was too surprised to resist, and instead did my best to hold it in. I reckon I thought it would lead to more shenanigans as the night progressed back in my Tempe-town circle of non-stop fun.

However, things got hazy and crazy once the potent vapor was absorbed. I recall frantic stomping boots putting out a small straw fire. Once the fire was vanquished and tragedy avoided, Mira and I shot-gunned our beers in a celebratory drinking race. Later, as the sunset reached its peak, I remember falling off the rear gate of the pick-up, to the delight of the party crew. There are vague images of a group hug, with Effie and Mira topless among the gathered brethren in every stage of undress, in honor of another glorious sunset.

As more people showed I didn't recognize, my world began to unfurl, the images spinning round in a tinker toy sky. It was an early warning signal I needed a break from the party, perhaps delivered too late. I wasn't sure what to do and didn't want to be a party pooper by making the Bar Belles take me home. I considered my options as I watched them laugh and dance with their tribe and I began to withdraw.

I just wasn't my old party self but like some unwritten rule, I understood the fair thing would be to let them party themselves out a little farther before asking them to take me home. They would have done it for me, and I figured I'd be okay rolling with the flow a while. After all I was a pro, I could hang with the best.

While the South Mountain revelers savored the few remaining morsels of coral splashed sky, I crawled off to the side, unnoticed and dropped onto a blanket someone spread out on the desert sand...

...Instead of a desert sky above me, I looked up to see a glass bottom boat glide into place as I lay beneath the flow on a lazy river's sandy bottom. The water put ripples in my vision, but I could make out some activity on the boat. Tourists of all ages leaned over the sides or stared through the glass.

Were they looking at me?

As I peered through the ripples, I sensed another presence. Sure enough, a shadow twisted into place between me and the boat. As I began to decipher its identity, a wave of goose bumps commenced and I stared transfixed at a giant octopus, its form undulating ominously. The tourists pointed excitedly.

What was happening?

The creature began to rotate slowly. Its arms gradually straightened until pointing straight out and turned in a clockwise rotation. I tried to move away, but it followed as if mimicking my movements. The tentacles began to glow, the rotation picking up speed, with the arms bowing and rising. I reached for one of the illuminated tentacles, but my grip went through it like a phantom. The rotation continued accelerating, like a wagon wheel spinning in place. More in awe than afraid, I remained immobile beneath the strobe like effect. Plastered in place, I was getting dizzier by the second.

Enhanced by a rippling current, it morphed from the octopus-wagon wheel into a Tilt-A-Whirl at the fair. The tentacles' suckers became glowing lightbulbs while the arms transformed from seafood to metal beams. As the boat faded into the background, the carnival ride accelerated.

The lights began blinking rapidly, and my point of view changed from a river bottom into outer space. Weightlessly spinning around in tandem orbit with the carnival ride, the river had evaporated, and I was rising, my skin moist and clothes still dripping.

I felt flush, an itchy tickling covered me like ant bites, and I was uncomfortably hot, my body dangerously vulnerable to every degree of heat the desert night offered. I instinctively grabbed my stomach. A barre chord of pain shot through every bone in my body and down into my feet.

The sensation traveled up my legs, pinging joints on its way through my hips and bounding through my bladder, eventually racing through each vertebra of my spine. The intensity increased until the pain hit the top of my skull like a spinning top crashing into a wall.

The moment after impact, I thought I heard squealing kids, Tilt-A-Whirl engines, and side-show barkers. This overdose of Saturday night at the fair echoed in my brain.

I woke up with a gasp, and turned over to prop myself on my elbows while looking around. I tried to survey the scene in one jerky motion and let loose with an involuntary cry of protest.

"Hell no!"

It was all I could muster; I knew my stomach was unhappy and ready to prove it. I crawled off the blanket into the sand and over to the gutter's edge. Through my one open eye I spotted a South Pointe Park stenciled trash receptacle on a post ten feet away. I clambered over to it on all fours and tried to summon some wisdom from the cosmos.

"What the hell was that pot treated with?"

No response.

I couldn't stand but found a grocery bag next to the barrel containing an empty six-pack of bottles and used it as my South Mountain party-gone-wrong barf bag. After three heaves I twisted the bag's top shut and shoved it next to the can. I tried to crawl back to where I'd started but felt a gale force wind begin to blow through my body, whipping across my muscles, and surging through my veins.

It blew back and forth, head to toe.

I struggled up on my elbows and knees and reached a stanchion holding a set of Park Service Coin-Op observation binoculars. I wrapped my arms around the post and hung on for dear life, finally falling flat on my stomach, eyes squeezed shut. I braced myself, surrendering to the forces at work. If there was going be a storm, this pole would be my main mast. If I was going to fly, it would be as a freak flag in the desert.

I realized I couldn't feel my shoulder and suffered whole-body spasms that left me feeling like a tattered fluttering flag. Delusional, I wondered if anyone else spent their last moment on earth this way.

As the shudders subsided, I gripped the pole tightly in the crook of my elbow and pulled myself closer, straining till the pole pressed against my skull. The metal's coolness provided relief, perhaps even comfort, and I thought then if I could hold on, maybe I'd be all right. Amidst my internal turmoil, I flashed back on the flag papered joint we'd shared earlier. As if it was some sort of important message, the image held my focus, and I clung to the thought of 'broad Stripes and bright Stars' like those that survived the battle we sing about in our national anthem.

It was the psychic life preserver I needed. Once again, I told myself I could survive the self-induced tempest if I could just hold on.

I'd finally found the necessary faith to survive but was literally blowing in the wind. There was no brave left in me. Finally the only freedom I found was the blackness that eventually overcame me and left me unconscious at the end of the storm.

Pony got loose from the merry go round,
Now the pony wanders all over town.
He'd never gotten dizzy going circle steady,
Now he misses the calliope sound.

Pony got loose from the merry go round,
Now pony's friends dance all over town.
No more on a pole, he's in a noose,
Only when the rope is slack, can he lope around.

Got no compass, had to learn new tricks.
Happy to dance, but he's a little remiss.
He's learning life on a rope,
But the calliope sound is missed.

When the South Mountain sunset party festivities fizzled, Effie realized I'd been too long out of pocket and began looking for me. Unfortunately, once she found me, she left me in her fellow partier's hands while she tracked down Mira, also AWOL. My party handlers were no experts and launched an amateur effort to revive me. First, they dumped the icy dregs of their beer cooler on me without getting the desired results.

I didn't move.

Somewhere in the depths of my darkness I heard Effie's laughter. She returned, mercifully, to take over and attempt tried and true methods of resuscitation.

"Come on Max, wake up!"

She sounded like she was on a distant mountaintop. Another cooler with colder and icier contents was slowly emptied on my head, bringing a bracing shock of reality. I rolled over, sputtered, and wiped my face. Consciousness returned with an uncomfortable surge. When I first opened my eyes, a hand was waving in front of my face like a windshield wiper to get my attention. I pushed it away to re-establish sovereignty over my personal space.

"I'll be ok! Shit! Give me a minute."

I was spitting and blowing water off my lips. A man stood above me; his empty cooler tucked under his arm, still dripping.

He chimed in with a voice of false authority.

"Have it your way dude, but we need to get you in a car or something. If Park Security comes by, they'll hassle us for sure."

"Ok. ok, I got it. Just leave me alone for a second."

After taking several deep breaths while rubbing the sides of my head, I spit out some grit and struggled to my feet with Effie and Mira's help. I just wanted to get back to their car. I took it one step at a time, resting and reorienting for balance after each step. My shoulder hurt so bad I was just beginning to notice my knees were also gashed from crawling on the rocks. When I got to their Impala, I slid down beside the back tires, and pulled open the back door far enough to rest my head on the floorboard. I only meant to catch my breath, but I guess I faded out again.

I was awakened by Mira gently kicking my ass. I was grateful she was barefoot.

"Max, you party pooper, why didn't say you were ready to go."

"Umm, aww, no, that's all right, y'all were having too much fun... Owwww!"

I stretched my legs as I tried to stand while they helped.

"Just take me home now and I'll be fine."

They got me up slowly, and I turned painfully, before falling into the back seat. I tried to keep my bitching to a minimum but was truly exhausted. They were in a much better mood and Effie blew me a kiss with a wink at Mira. She pulled out with a scatter shot of dust, asphalt, and desert gravel, and quickly cranked up the tunes.

"You sure you don't wanna come over for a group shower?"

They giggled, obviously they were still planning to go all night.

"No, I just need to lay down and take it easy. I've done more today than I've done in quite a while. It was the most fun I've had since getting out of the hospital... just can't do it."

"Well, we might be easy on you, Max, what do you think about that?"

"Oh yeah, sure... Look, y'all been so good to me, don't think I ain't interested. And believe me, I'd love to take you up on your offer if I was in better condition... How 'bout we save your invitation for when I can give you my best. I'm still healing... By the way, what was with that weed anyhow?"

"It's called Righteous Mama Roux, ain't it dynamite shit?" Mira was all smiles, even with her eyes' half closed.

"Ladies, listen, I'm sorry, but you should put a warning label on it."

"Ok Max, have it your way spoilsport, you know we ain't certified nurses or nothing, but we still know some healing ways…".

Mira and Effie smiled at each other.

"We're always ready for a Happy Hour with you."

As if on cue, The Marvelettes started singing about my life: *Destination: Anywhere.*

But tonight, I was headed to my sofa…

I knew Effie and Mira weren't necessarily innocent, but they did approach life with a non-judgmental innocence. They were real free spirits, moving through life with a childlike wonder for experiencing anything and everything. They were treasures indeed, but hadn't they also been kind of lucky to avoid tragedy? I couldn't help but wonder if they realized how much darkness and ill intent lurked in the hearts and minds of so many of those they traveled amongst.

The Bar Belles deposited me on my couch with tenderness and apologies, no longer tempting me with their randy inclinations. They sat on either side of me and attended to my 'boo-boos', spending time cleaning me up with a bowl of water and a couple bandanas. Finally, as they prepared to depart, I got a nice two-sided two Bar Belle cheek kiss. When it ended all three pairs of lips were touching.

Then Effie asked me if I wanted her to read me the note.

"What note?"

"The one from your front door."

Unbeknownst to me, while I was getting trashed on South Mountain, Jonesy finally got in touch Uncle Joey, and arranged for me to meet with him. The Bar Belles grabbed the note he'd taped to my door as they brought me inside without me even realizing it. She held up the piece of paper in front of me.

"Let me see that."

I reached for it, but she pulled back her hand, shook it open and read it out loud in her sing song voice.

"Max – be at Little Naples Pizza 10am tomorrow to interview with Uncle Joey. – Good luck my brother! Jonesy."

"Unbelievable, you gotta be kidding me."

I dropped my head and shook it slowly.

"Max you got an interview!

"Yahoo!" Mira jumped up and clapped. Effie was more reserved, cocking her head and reaching for my chin with her hand.

"You sure you don't want us to help fix you up for your big interview Maxie?"

"Oh.... Oh! ...no, I'll manage. I'm gonna rest first, it's still early, you two go on ahead."

I couldn't risk being in their company any longer if I wanted to get my head together.

"Ok, Max, it's your loss..."

And just like that I was sitting on my couch contemplating my future while Bar Belle party possibilities slipped away into the night

After resting quietly on the couch for a half hour, I dragged myself into the bathroom and looked deep into my eyes. There was no miraculous revelation to be found there, so I simply told myself to give it my best shot. I managed a warm shower avoiding any direct spray on my shoulder. I patted myself dry, got out appropriate clothing for the next day, and set my alarm. After taking half my prescribed Percocet dosage, I decided to set a second alarm just in case and rolled onto the couch.

I had ten hours till the interview.

Next morning after shutting off my second alarm, I faced the day but was too stiff and sore to get moving without getting under some water. I got up and took a shower, quick but painful, hot first, then cold. While in the shower I experienced a full body shudder flashing back on the Tilt-A-Whirl. I managed to push it down into my subconscious and focus on the task at hand. Toxin induced dreams could wait another day for critical analysis.

I dried off, took a Percocet, and put two more in my pocket. I got the Blazer started, then stopped and grabbed a coffee and a Bear Claw to inhale on the way. Luckily, the meeting was in the East Valley close by.

A few minutes later I parked the Blazer in the three-sided strip mall parking lot. Above the front door a small hand painted sign with broad vertical swaths of green, white, and red hung from the awning, 'Little Naples Pizza' written in ornate gold braid.

The door was unlocked, so I let myself in. There was a register on the counter behind a three-foot plexiglass shield extending from the register all the way down past the counter opposite the pizza ovens. In front of the ovens, two guys tossed pizza dough in a casual practiced manner. One had a cigarette hanging from his lower lip, the other had an hourglass tattoo on his forearm. Both men's aprons were well decorated with red sauce and flour and folded over one third their full length then tied around their waist, leaving their tight t-shirts against their chests showing off their pecs and short sleeves rolled up to show off their guns. Any splatter ending up on the muscles was worth it to these guys. They gave me a 'What's up?' eyebrow salute with a jut of their chins and went about spinning as nonchalantly as twirling a key ring on a finger.

A tall young lady with an inky black bob, wearing an equally tight undersized Breton T and tighter green shorts rose up from behind the register.

"Hey mister, welcome to Little Naples. How can I help you?"

She wiped her hands on her shorts, then pulled her shirt down in an attempt reconceal her midriff.

"I'm Max, and I'm here to see Joseph Spasula."

I hoped there'd be no snafu and she'd know about my appointment. She turned and looked at the spinners.

"Anybody know what's up with Joey?"

They exchanged uncertain looks with the practiced carefree shrugs of guys who knew it wasn't any of their business unless certain people asked and that didn't include me. They both shook their heads with stuck out lower lips. She turned back to me and looked me over.

"Mr. Max, I'm sorry but he's not in yet, but you can wait in the lounge through that door," she pointed to my left, "he usually takes his meetings in there."

I turned to look, unable to avoid pursing my lips in disappointment, thinking, 'What the hell, might as well stick around, I got nothing to lose.'

I thanked her and headed in. The lounge was dimly lit by candles placed in randomly punctured tomato cans giving a cheery catacomb welcome. I grabbed a seat and surveyed the walls covered with common Italian pizza parlor décor straight from the universal playbook. Mr. Spasula, being Jonesy's uncle, was probably a character. Jonesy once told me his Uncle Joey was a real 'wheeler-dealer.'

The tables were scattered around two connecting rooms with only two windows. The windows were small, and each contained a neon sign wholly visible from the street but obscured in the lounge, as pizza box shields only allowed fragments of light into the dining area.

I went in the Men's room to check my appearance, finger comb my hair, and straighten up. The bathroom walls sported an unfinished paint job while a partially installed uptake fan dangled from the ceiling over the sink. It looked like something one might see in a hastily built spring break bar in Mexico, except for the Italian decor. Well, at least there was a mirror.

While I enjoyed *Mambo Italiano* by Rosemary Clooney, I gazed at my profile, a face in pain. I tried to plaster on a permanent smile for our meeting and just in case, I took another Percocet as catalyst. I had decided if I looked the way I felt, it might scare him off hiring me. I felt obliged to change the way I felt.

When I was done, I looked out through a sliver of window on the side of the Moretti sign and saw glimpses of car headlights as they passed. I picked out a table where I could catch little bit of the view of the entry area and after a couple of minutes, the cashier came in to check on me.

"There you are! By the way, I'm Janet. Sorry, you're having to wait, I came in a minute ago but didn't see you. I'm glad you didn't leave."

She shared a flirty smile that helped me relax.

"Can I get you something to drink while you wait? We got soda, tea, coffee, wine, beer..."

"Nice to meet you, Janet. Sorry, I just dipped into the men's room. I will have some water, thanks. By the way, you don't have to call me sir, just call me Max."

"Ok, Max. I'll be right back with your water."

She returned and was so tall and the table so low, she had to bend her knees just to set the glass down. She gave me a con man's sheepish smile as our eyes met.

I sipped on the water and shifted around in my chair too many times. Even with the meds, I was unable to get comfortable. Finally, I heard a car pull up playing loud music with noisy brakes and slow to a stop. From the shadows it cast through the windows' pizza box slits, it must have been some kind of land yacht. I could hear the one-line refrain by The Reflections from *Just Like Romeo and Juliet* blaring from the sound system when the car doors opened. Men's voices laughed and sang along.

The Little Naples front door slammed opened immediately. I heard a man called out from the car.

"Hey paisano, cosa sta succendo?"

The man who'd opened the Little Naples door responded.

"Hold on a minute, cuz."

Then Janet spoke.

"Joey, you got some guy named Max waiting in the Lounge."

Once again, I heard a man yelling outside but I couldn't make it out, but I heard the man at the door.

"That's it for me, boys, I got work to do. A dopo!"

The car pulled away, the Little Naples front door shut, and Joseph Spasula came into the lounge. I stood up as he worked his way to me, while he insisted I do otherwise.

"Hey, it's Jonesy's man, Max! No, don't get up. Relax, man."

"Mister Spasula, glad to meet you."

He turned and yelled into the other room with a wrinkled brow of concern.

"Hey Janet, get Max a beer or some wine. Come on, show our friend Max some Little Naples' hospitality."

Then he turned back to me and smiled.

"Max, please, just call me Joey."

"Thanks Joey. And uh, don't worry Joey, she's been taking care of me so far," I held up my water, "I'd rather finish the interview before having anything stronger."

It appeared he had not waited to start his day drinking. His cheeks were flush, and his eyes sparkled with Happy Hour highlights.

"Oh, a serious guy, huh? Ok, suit yourself."

He pulled his chair from the table at a forty-five-degree angle and slouched with his legs and coat spread open. His shoes were shiny and pointy while he sported three gawdy rings on both hands. He had a tanning bed tan and a short perm, dyed coal black in tight curls, a half inch off his head. Wearing a dark blue Adidas velour tracksuit with the top zipped only to the middle of his chest over a gray silk crewneck with a gold chain and a diamond studded 'J', I could only guess he was somewhere between forty to seventy years old. He beamed and pulled his hands together, lacing his fingers and resting them on his lap.

"So Max, Jonesy says you're a slick operator, but he also tells me you're also recovering from a cop's bullet you took... So, how you doing?"

"I don't know how slick I am, but I have lots of experience in bars and restaurants and I'm healing fine, thanks."

"Yessir, them cops can mess you up Max, I've seen some shit, lemme tell you."

"Well, it was all a misunderstanding but I'm gonna be fine."

"You need a good lawyer? I can fix you up with a good one, you know."

"No thanks Mr. Spasula, but I am interested in the job, and I'd would like to know more about it, if it's still available."

"Don't call me Mister, Max, just Joey, ok?"

Thankfully Janet showed up right then with his drinking regimen: a glass of ice, a glass of red wine, a glass of ice water and a bowl of limes and lemon wedges.

"Here you are Joe, need anything else, you let me know."

She stood at attention for a moment, then he winked at her. She flashed a professionally forced smile before turning and walking away.

"You know Max, now my nephew Jonesy speaks very highly of you."

He reached for his limes and lemons and started squeezing them into the glass of ice while continuing to talk.

"I'm gonna have you train with the top-notch people in my organization. They may give you some tests and stuff but if there's any problem with anything, you let me know right away, you hear?"

He poured the red wine into the glass he'd been prepping and looked at me for a response.

"Well Joey, I won't let you down. Where do you want me to go?"

"You'll start right here in Phoenix, then we might send you down to Memphis or New Orleans, maybe Dallas, too."

He took a big swig of his cocktail and smacked his lips.

"You sure you don't want a drink? I always say when you put it on the rocks and squeeze in a little juice, red wine's a real health tonic."

"And it does look good, Joey, but I better wait. I wanna get my business together about working before I start drinking."

"Well, you gotta stay and have some pie with me while I fill you in on some of the details."

He hollered at the crew in the other room, "Hey, you guys start my Joey special yet?"

"Yea boss, be ready in 10 minutes."

"So, thing is Max, I don't want you to go into these joints and be a hard ass. I need you to go in there and keep'em running smooth and get a feel for what they're about. Learn what key goes to what lock, and who has which key to what. You gotta find out who touches the money and when. Find out who orders what, who hires the girls, who hires the boys. You need to know who trains who, and if you think there's any funny business, you talk to me before anyone else. You got me?"

"Sure, Joey. I can do that, no problem."

"Well, I want you to show them what you know, but don't go trying to reinvent the wheel. We got plenty money going in the bank and so far, money's coming back to me. I don't want that to change, understand?"

"Absolutely."

He leaned towards me a little and wrinkled his brow.

"There's another reason I want to bring someone new into the company right now. I'm getting all these official reports from the GM's, but I need someone on the inside to be my direct line of information. Someone I know is looking out for me. We're getting busier by the day, and there's crazy things happening, a lot of money involved. I'm not sure I can follow all this money too good. I need to make sure it's either going in the bank or coming to me."

He winked at me.

Janet backed into the room and turned around after passing through the doorway. She had two hands under an enormous pizza pie loaded with double handfuls of green olives, pepperoncini peppers, and chopped green onions on top of steaming cheese. As she got closer to the table, I could smell fresh basil and anchovies, too. Somewhere underneath all the greenery my nose detected sausage, pepperoni, bacon, onions, mushrooms; pretty much everything in the walk in.

"Max, you should come with us to go see Janet here perform. She dances with her doves at Little Angels!"

He looked her up and down as she set the tray next to the table. In a flash she'd cleared a spot and set down the pizza with plates, silver ware, crushed red pepper and Parmesan shakers. He watched her intently, flaring his nostrils while he stared at the lower half of her figure.

"You really get their wings flapping, don'cha Janet?"

He snickered and tucked a napkin into the collar of his shirt while mimicking bird motions with his elbows. Then he motioned for me to have some pie. She made a point to smile at his joke, but then I swear I saw her roll her eyes as she turned away after she grabbed the empty tray.

"Sure, whatever you say, Joe."

She was polite and cheery, but Janet didn't appear as excited about his build up for her as he was. Maybe she was just embarrassed about a stranger finding out she was a dancer at Little Angels first time we'd met.

Just as quickly, she put me at ease and surprised as she flashed me a quick smile with a little eye twinkle before looking back at Joey again.

"Do you need another drink, Joe?"

"Sure sweetheart, how about you Max, you ready?"

He was on a second piece of pie already.

"Well, if it's all right with you, I'll have one of those Morettis?"

I pointed at the neon in the window like that would make a difference. I decided the toughest part of the interview was over since he'd apparently already given me the job. Joey answered before Janet could speak.

"Sure, we do... All right, Max, you're ok!"

He swung his hand in Janet's direction with his first two fingers and thumb touching.

"C'mon Janet, get our drinks over here before we die of thirst. Max, you're gonna love this pie."

She left after he finished his request, and we both commenced eating pie. In less than a minute she came back with our drinks and left them on our table without saying a word.

Suddenly Joey threw his slice down on the table and shouted.

"What's this crap, you goombas burnt my pie!"

He picked up a piece with dark crust and hurled it through the doorway into the other room where the crew was working. I heard it hit the side of the counter. I was startled but tried not to show it, my Percocet was kicking in, so it wasn't hard to stay relaxed, but I did take note of Joey's sudden temper. Janet came running through the door and stopped with her hand on her hip.

"What the hell? What's going on Joe? What if there'd been a customer in here?"

"Well, there ain't, and I want you bums to see the burnt pizza, so's it won't happen again."

"Ok, Joey, I'll make sure they don't burn anything else today."

"Better not or I'll tell their probation officers what they really do after work."

He smiled, then winked at me and waved her off.

"Go on, go on, already."

After we finished what we could of the gut bomb pie, I took a box of leftover slices to the Blazer at Joey's insistence. Each piece could feed two people, so I was set for food for a few days.

As I drove back to my place, I considered how Joey didn't share much information about the job. He told me how when he was a kid in Detroit, the Reflections recorded *(Just Like) Romeo and Juliet*. He'd hung out with the band and been at some of the recording sessions, getting to sing with them at a gig when a band member was ill. His memory of them and his lifelong love of the era's music fueled his passion for the Vettes' concept. He told me to report to Vettes corporate office on the westside of Phoenix, the following Monday morning at ten. He made it clear my cowboy look had to be cleaned up, starting with a haircut.

"Max, you know, something classy. You gotta look like you're somebody that runs the joint, ya know?"

I was pretty psyched about everything except the haircut, but I knew hair would grow back. Of course, I was also relieved to have a few days to recover from the South Mountain sunset episode. I was still reeling from The Tempe Town Bar Belles and their killer joints.

I'll play a fool at the follies.
If they need a fool, I'll play the fool.
I'll put myself to good use,
So all can be amused.

I had that shiny car,
And traveled sea to sea.
Wondered what I learned
And let my money burn.

I'll play the fool at the follies.
They need a fool, I'll play the fool

I reported to Vettes corporate office, where they explained I'd be provided with a hotel room and be restricted to staying there during training; 'sequestered for reasons of company security'. That was an odd surprise, however, the Hide Away Court was on the west side of Phoenix and conveniently near the club. This was a part of the valley I'd never considered my stomping grounds and had never really explored. Told the arrangement was standard operating procedure, I signed the paperwork. I didn't expect this twist, and they apologized as if it was an inconvenience, but it was sort of a bonus for me as my current accommodations were temporary anyhow. I welcomed the idea of daily maid service and a per diem for meals.

The only downside of being sequestered was I'd be unable to see friends. This would include Cindy Masters, who I was determined to woo, but was impossible to reach except in person when at her home or work. Our courtship would have to wait.

After the first two nights I decided the hotel would've been more accurately named the 'Wide Awake Inn.' My room was in the most remote part of the building and the furthest spot possible from the road which would seem perfect for peace and quiet. Nonetheless, I still heard all-night pool partying, the constant racket from the soda and ice machines, and hourly comings and goings from the room next to mine, all of which made it difficult to get much sleep. I was convinced the Hide Away must have been renting rooms by the hour and my next-door neighbor was either dealing drugs or running an escort service. I wasn't spying mind you, but I never saw the same man or woman enter or exit a second time.

Of course, it didn't matter. I wasn't going to investigate, I had too much on my plate to add another investigation of illicit activities beyond what I'd already signed up for. I couldn't help but wonder why they would be so adamant on keeping tabs on me and then put me somewhere that didn't seem vetted? Later, I wondered if perhaps it was an arrangement of financial convenience and I'd been put there only because the Hide Away was part of some devious business arrangement.

For two days, I spent mornings at a corporate office taking various aptitude or screening tests from third-party personnel company contractors. I wasn't used to their corporate way of training.

Joe had warned me they were gonna cram a full month's training into two weeks, so I expected a grind. He'd said not to worry, he'd have my back if I had any problems with the process, so I skated on some of the reading. All their paperwork had me itching to get out of there and into the Vettes' live nightclub action.

I mean a dishwasher manual, really? I could wash dishes, wait tables, and tend bar in my sleep, so I simply skimmed through most of the training manuals.

It was nice to know Joe wasn't worried about me, but as I got deeper in Vettes' minutiae, and interacted with more of the corporate staff, I realized I needed to be diligent. The shop talk in the corporate office, was any new guy hitting the floor so soon after being hired would be heavily scrutinized. Not only by the people I'd be responsible for, but also every other manager and owner not named Joey Spasula.

Ultimately, I had to keep in mind there might be something going on, and Joey believed I'd find out if there was, so he'd hired me. He certainly didn't admit to having any knowledge of mischief, but I sensed someone must be doing something sketchy, and so it was my job to find it.

On the fifth day I reported to the corporate offices I was told I was no longer being sequestered. I was told to work the night shift with the Vettes' managers at the club. I'd possibly get a training session with the Director of Entertainment, Frank Fortuna. I was warned I might be the last person to leave so I better show up rested. I arrived earlier than scheduled and I'd been given a key, but when I approached the 'Employees Only' entrance in the rear, it was already open.

This was a real déjà vu for me. In my previous caper I'd found the corpse of my friend and co-worker Jerry Roseman, in Baxter's Bar walk-in during my ill-fated attempt at a bit of self-employment. When I'd arrived at Baxter's there was no one there in charge and it had been unlocked. From that day on I promised myself to check out everything and anything amiss or out of order before stumbling into another unnerving surprise.

I checked around the outside dock, around the dumpster and by the storage shed. The shed was already open as well, and its lock dangled from the door latch. There was a plumber's pick-up parked by the dumpster with a display on the toolboxes that read 'Drumber the Plumber – We Love Jams!' The truck looked like a proper working vehicle with toolboxes mounted on the sides and plumber's junk in the back bay. I poked my head in the storage shed and saw nothing out of the ordinary. I pulled open the door to the building, entered and checked out the kitchen.

"Anybody here?"

No response.

In the kitchen everything appeared to be shut down in good order from the night before. Some of the lights were on, so someone was inside somewhere, but the walk-ins were locked, which was a relief. I wasn't looking for any keys other than the one I had. Someone else could unlock the walk-ins.

I headed to the right and passed a small office with a mini basketball goal on the door and a small look-out window covered with a Bugs Bunny's poster. I knocked, but no answer, so I continued down the unlit hallway which ended at the server side of a service bar at the end of the bar.

Behind the main bar was a giant scripted lit pink neon *VETTES* sign, behind a three-foot tall wall of box glass built along the back bar. In the middle of the room was a raised platform surrounded with more box glass where the DJ performed. My eyes adjusted to the pink glow of the neon, and I was able to see well enough to find a door. I stepped behind the bar and checked out the eight bar wells for making cocktails. To me it looked like the ultimate operational set up for first-class, high-volume cocktail service.

When I walked past the neon *VETTES* sign, I could hear its buzz. Even though I was walking on rubber safety mats I noticed a weird sensation on my neck from the sign's static electricity. When I finally exited through at the end through the swinging service bar, I noticed a heavily bolted door in an indentation along the wall to my left. It led to a room behind the boxed glass *VETTES* sign.

On the door was posted, 'No Access!'. What was so special?

I turned and surveyed the main room. On the other side of the dance floor was another, smaller bar. I was impressed by Vette's sheer amount of cocktail-making fire power.

Jonesy was right, with this set up they could throw quite a party. I'd never worked anywhere that had more than six bartenders working at the same time, and I'd witnessed a lot of high-volume debauchery.

When I retraced my steps, I realized I'd missed a beautiful pink Corvette Stingray on a round platform situated near where I'd gone behind the bar. I guess I'd been so awed by the bar set up, I looked past it. The Corvette sealed it, I was sure this job was gonna be quite an adventure.

I saw lights blinking in another room up off in the corner, so I headed there. As I got closer, I could see through an oval portal a row of old pinball games against a slightly curved wall. The game lights were on, and I heard their enticing percolations, all calculated to draw potential players like me. Maybe someone was already in there playing. I took a leap up the steps and dipped into the arcade.

Looking around, I surveyed an incredible Pinball Hall of Fame line-up. The games were in mint condition and seemed to be winking with preprogrammed chirps and clinks.

I'd been a Pinball aficionado in my younger days, so I walked over to the Gypsy Queen, planted my feet, and took up my pinball playing pose. I put my middle fingers on the flipper buttons on each side and gently pressed my palms, forefingers and thumbs against the lockdown bar that held the glass top onto the machine's body. I closed my eyes and remembered the rhythm of the game and pushed my left hip first against the cabinet, then my right, lifting each of my shoulders in tandem, while bending at the elbow. Kind of like giving a gentle nudge of bootheels to the sides of a horse.

I remember spending hours throwing hip checks to these four-legged glass covered attention addictive beasts in middle school. It was a rite of passage trying to influence pinballs to go where you needed them to, and score points without making it tilt. I loved the older games. They allowed more physical interaction, their design and structure more mechanical with less digital electrical circuitry.

I felt a twinge in my shoulder from the bullet wound, still a reminder of what could happen when I stumble into a strange place alone. I pretended it was my cowboy badge of courage and smiled. reaching into my pocket to see if I had a quarter to relive some childhood memories. Before my fingers found a coin, I heard a noise from behind me, like heavy equipment being moved.

At the time I still didn't know if Joey's concerns were gonna end up being real, but the noise sounded like something I should investigate. Keep in mind I'd found the place unlocked and still had not found anyone in charge. My pinball flashback would have to wait. I retraced my steps back through the kitchen to the hallway and headed to the sound.

The hallway was only partially lit, but at the end I saw three doors. On the right, close to the floor, a person's rear jutted out from behind a drinking fountain, and it shifted about. Peeking out where their clothing had parted I could just make out a prominent slice of butt crack, framed by shirt, jeans, and cheeks. Whoever it was, was busy working on something out of my view while squatting and leaning forward.

Pleasantly surprised it wasn't a plumber's hairy ass that greeted me, I stared. There was a smooth, tan, top of a woman's derriere, with a bongo drum tattooed on the top of each cheek. I moved closer. I noticed a faint tan line on naturally dark complexion, and healthy hips with a fetching feminine curve. She wore a tool belt high on her left hip while on the right side the belt hung below her tan. She squatted on formidable thighs bulging under tattered blue jean cut-offs. An unusual tramp stamp rose was scripted above the bongos. I leaned in to get a better look while she reached behind the fountain.

'Let all that you do be done in Love.'

Was that Corinthians?

She leaned back, so I pulled back, too. As she rearranged her posterior to return comfortably back in her squat, I took notice of the heavy construction boots beneath the white strands of thread dangling from her shorts. Impressively, she maintained her balance on the toes of her steel tipped boots, which accentuated her muscular legs. Just as I started to ask a question, she turned her head and beat me to the punch.

"You like what you see junior?"

She had a deep-rooted voice smothered in good humor. She smiled and turned to face me; her bronzed crow's feet delightfully framing her mischievous sparkling eyes as she showed off some solid muscle standing up effortlessly out of her squat. Built as sexy as a rodeo clown's hourglass barrel, she was compact and possessed a world's full of attitude.

"Well, that depends on what you're up to," was as witty a comeback as I could manage after a gawking awkward pause.

"Well, I'm five-foot, half-inch, and can play a guitar with either hand. And you're welcome to play my bongos if I decide you're nice enough, but before we get to any of that, I gotta ask *you* what *you're* doing here."

With my height advantage, if I leaned forward, I could look straight down at the top of her head. Her shiny Elvis cut shined but up close I could little white streaks sprinkled in.

"I'm Max, reporting to Vettes to work my first shift. I walked in because the back door was open... so... what is it you're doing?"

"Well Max, I'm Olga Drumber, you might'a seen my truck out back. Anyway, I'm working on this water fountain," she waved her wrench toward the 'Boppers' and 'Bobby Socks'ers' doors behind her and continued, "this here's the Vettes' employee lounge," she chuckled as if it was an inside joke.

"Were Dean Unato or Frank Fortuna around when you got here?"

"Yeah, Dean went to run some errands, I haven't seen old crazy Frank though. He supposed to be in town to meet you or something?"

She wiped her brow with the back of her hand that held the wrench, then dropped it to her cocked hip and waited with interest for my answer.

"Well, I think he's getting here tonight or maybe tomorrow. He's supposed to do my DJ training... so, do you work for Vettes often?"

"Work here, work it out here, get worked here, yeah sure, I know my way around Vettes."

She winked and extended her hand for a handshake. I shrugged apologetically as I shook her hand. Tattooed up both her arms were musical notes spilling out from her loose sleeveless denim shirt with the 'Olga' name patch. Across her left shoulder was a crest with roses cradling a guitar. Underneath it read, *'I Got The Blues & The Blues Got Me'*.

"Well, sorry if I startled you, I guess I heard you moving this fountain while I was checking out the game room."

She saw me admiring the tattoo and turned so I could see it better, lifting her eyebrows for approval.

"That's nice, so are you a fan?"

I wanted to know more.

"No baby, I'm a player. I use my wrench all day, and my axe all night, and sometimes I get lucky and get some bongo action in, too."

She gave her hips a one-two shake then held up her wrench with the end of the handle balanced on her palm to stand it straight up. Then she let the wrench head fall slowly into the palm of her other hand like a felled tree. She cocked her head to the side and gave me the once over after that little trick.

"And I'm wondering how you fit in with all of the above."

She paused long enough for me to look around uncomfortably, then burst out laughing.

"Sorry Max, I'm a little crazy, too. I got some Havasupai blood. Don't worry though, I won't do nothing you don't wanna do first."

"I'm not sure what you mean by that, but I'm damn glad to meet you. I'll be grateful for any help you can give me while I'm here."

I was trying to keep it business like for the time being. She had a lot more going on than I could ever guess in just one meeting. Who knows, eventually she might be someone who could get inside information.

"Well, Max, I am always eager to help a Vettes' newbie, whether you need it here or anywhere else. Here's my card."

She reached to her back pocket and produced a long brown leather wallet on a chain. She opened it, exposing guitar picks of various colors lining one side, and ID's and a Rough Rider condom showing through the plastic on the other. She reached in a fold, grabbed a rainbow striped business card and handed it to me.

"Thanks Olga, I appreciate it. You know where I might get my hands on a good but cheap guitar that stays in tune? See, I play, too, but they've had me under lock and key during training, and I didn't bring anything to keep my chops sharp."

"No worries, Max, just give me a call. I'll fix you up. I'll want collateral, though. My mobile number and beeper are on there. Don't be afraid to call, no matter what. I know how hard it is for a stranger to get started and I'd be lost without my axe."

"Well, I've lived on the east side for a while, working at Baxter's and the Brashcan Club in Tempe, but never worked over here before."

"Baxter's, you? Huh, I thought there was something familiar about you. I used to take one of my girls there to watch Vikings' games."

She gave me the once over again.

"You know, I heard through the grapevine you tracked down a killer. Is that true?"

"Well, I tried to help, that's all."

My natural inclination would've been to say more, but Judd, the guy I tracked to Atlanta, hadn't gone to trial yet, and I wasn't supposed to discuss any details. She nodded and let her eyes wander up and down my torso in an intimidating but flirtatious manner.

"Yea, Max you're gonna be all right, but you let me know, if you need anything, OK? ...and call me about a loaner if you want."

She turned back around to the job at hand. At the time I didn't realize how much our meeting would mean.

The Seeds...
Chasing money
to keep dreams from slipping away.
We used to sow seeds for tomorrow,
now we barely get through today.

If you'd have told me where I was headed,
Going `round and round in circles,
I would never have believed.
Now, I have to wonder:
What will grow from these seeds?

Let's go back eighteen years earlier to what most folks around these parts referred to as a 'Gentlemen's Companion Boarding House' in northern Mississippi, half-way between Arkabutla Lake and the Tennessee state line...

Angorra flushed the toilet as she stood up, pulled up her panties with one hand and reached back for the robe's sash with the other before opening the door. There was no sash, so she pulled the lapels together and crossed her arms, then pushed past the white girl she didn't recognize leaning and waiting her turn by the door.

The leaner had a shoulder on the wall with a hand on her free hip. Sticking out from her fingers, a sad little ornament of an ash dangled from her menthol cigarette. Her dark painted eyelids were closed, framed by a tousled blonde shag, and delicate wisps of smoke circled her head. A frayed purple negligee hung off her shoulders at an absentminded angle still looking like it was picked off the floor, as she waited for the bathroom.

Angorra swiveled her hips past the cigarette, paying it more mind than the girl's attire.

"Wake up sunshine, it's your turn."

'Sunshine' was slow to respond and didn't earn another glance as Angorra shuffled down the hall towards the kitchen. Her worn out hotel slippers caught on nail heads poking out of the pinewood floor, but their soles were so shredded her gait was unaffected. She smelled the Community Coffee Maddie the 'House Mom' brewed and Angorra inhaled the balmy bouquet in anticipation, hypnotically drawn to the kitchen by its aroma.

She stepped in the kitchen and brushed the back of a white dude sitting at the table hanging his head with his chin on his chest and his John Deere hat barely on. His hand clutched a white ceramic cup filled to the brim. She knew Maddie insisted the girls use their own cups, but those cups she provided to the visitors.

Across from the hungover houseguest sat Bayou Beatri and Arkie Annie. Beatri's distinct skin was a wonder of God's abstract handiwork, her blotchy complexion resembled the topography of our planet; random shapes much like the planet we live on. Pale skin like the earth's oceans reflected light and the pigmented land masses like earth's continents, absorbed it. Always regal in her bearing, Beatri proudly sported stoplight-red lipstick and a bright floral tignon crown. Anyone not already familiar with Beatri would definitely have to do a double take.

The morning coffee was one of the few daily customs allowing girls a chance for casual conversation. Most of their nicknames came from remarks made around the kitchen table. Angorra knew it was only a matter of time before she'd get a nickname, too. She'd been there long enough but mostly kept to herself.

Beatri blew a rolling smoke ring at the guest before turning to Angorra with her piercing gray eyes. They captured Angorra's gaze immediately, with her usual disarming intensity.

"Good morning, Angie, you ready to join us, gone get some wake up juice for dat cute little head of yours?"

Angorra opened her mouth but was too slow to respond. Beatri nudged the stranger with her foot and pointed her chin his way.

"Mon ami, you better drink up and get your ass done outta here before de boss come."

This roused the fellow and he lifted his cup with noticeably shaky hands, raising it for a noisy slurp. Annie grunted, pulling down the bill of her camouflage cap and leaned forward.

"Hun', you gonna need more than coffee to cure that full bottle headache. You want some Black Beauties?" she asked, then leaned back in her chair tugging at her ponytail sticking out the back of her cap and nodded knowingly.

Maddie came in the screen door with a towel covered pot and set it in the sink. She turned and looked over towards the table and smiled at Angorra.

"Good morning, Angie."

Meanwhile, Beatri reached over to Annie and began whispering in harsh tones.

"Hush your hillbilly ass up, me gonna get him right, don't you bother about it none."

She motioned at Maddie with the side of her head and wrinkled her brow sternly at Annie to shut up. Nobody was supposed to give guests drugs; *that* would cut in on house sales. Annie mouthed "Sorry," back at Beatri and reached in the middle of the table for her rolling papers and her Bugler pouch to roll another cigarette.

"Angie you just gonna stand there and stare or you ready for a cup?"

Maddie either hadn't heard Annie or ignored it. She had pretty good ears but was also sympathetic to the girls.

"Yes ma'am, Miss Maddie."

Angorra grabbed her cup off the wall from her one and only trip to New Orleans. Purple with a gold fleur-de-lis, she admired it as she walked over to the stove. She poured herself a cup, then pulled out the chair closest to the sink and sat down. After a sip, she grimaced.

"Damn y'all, I got to have some cream and sugar for this shit."

Maddie let out a hearty laugh. She was becoming fond of Angorra even though still fairly new to the house.

"Child you gonna have to learn to drink it straight someday, cuz I ain't suppose'd be using all my cream for your coffee."

She winked as she set down a jug of cream next to her cup while Angorra reached for the sugar by the stranger's cup. He didn't seem to notice, and Maddie couldn't help but comment on Angie's coffee preparation.

"Young'en, you be making a damn milk shake like dey serve up at Borroum's over in Corinth."

The other girls laughed too and smiled kindly looking her way. Maddie and pretty much all the girls loved having Angorra in the house. They taught her and teased her with equal measure about how they believed their way of life was best pursued.

'Sunshine' leaned into the kitchen while holding the doorway for balance with her cigarette bearing hand. She ran her fingers through her hair with the other and forced a hoarse but quiet greeting.

"Hey y'all."

The girls turned to face her silently. She was newer than Angorra, and they weren't sure of her future. Only Maddie, standing at the stove, answered back.

"Missy, you ok? You know we got coffee here, but the house rule is you gotta put on a robe or something', no nighties 'llowed in here, sugar."

Angorra discreetly pulled her own robe together tighter. She knew she'd better make sure Maddie didn't see she was still only in her bra and panties.

"Oh, ok, yeah, let me find something, I'll be right back." She looked around nervously.

"Miss Maddie, can I take a cup with me?"

"Tell you what, girl, I know you ain't got no cup yet, so I'll give you dis visitor cup, but you gotta promise you gonna bring it back when you dressed proper."

"Yes ma'am."

After the girl left with her freshly filled cup, Annie asked.

"Maddie, is her name Missy or you just call her that?"

"I call her that cuz I don't know if she is staying. Miss Jackson says she from Glory Falls near Fayetteville and dey call her Gloria. Miss Jackson the boss, and I don't usually call y'all by y'alls names till I get used to you... usually after 'bout a month and half. But y'all be nice to her, and get this fella on outta here, cuz I gotta fix y'alls lunch and we gonna need dat spot."

The guest set his half empty coffee cup down with both hands and tried to get up, groaning as he struggled to steady himself.

"Unnhhh, I'm going, I'm going."

"Hold on cowboy, I'll help you."

Beatri was up and around the table in a flash and grabbed hold of him.

"Annie, get my bag and gimme a hand."

She nodded her turban towards the back of her chair and Annie stood up, grabbed the bag, and circled the table with it. They helped him around the table and out the door while Beatri rummaged through her bag with one hand. The screen door slammed behind them when they departed. No doubt, the Black Beauty treatment was in play for the hungover guest.

Angorra sipped her coffee by herself for a moment and thought about her journey so far. She'd given her Mawmaw her own baby girl to raise after a tumultuous eighteen months of motherhood. Her daughter's birth took her out of high school and landed her on the streets of Memphis where her boyfriend Jerrod never came up with the money for a second month's rent. She guessed it hadn't mattered; it was apparent none of their neighbors wanted them there anyhow. She'd been so naïve in the ways of the city and had been lucky to find solace at her Mawmaw's house in Jackson.

However, after three months of ever rising tension, Mawmaw tired of Angorra's baby mama screw-ups, and told her she could either take Pearlie and go, or just go, without Pearlie. Mawmaw told her if she left, she'd see Pearlie was raised right until Angorra could come get her.

The twenty-one months since leaving were a blur, but at least for the last one she'd found a way to make something of herself working at Miss Jackson's 'Boarding House' as a professional 'Gentleman's Lady."

She figured she'd eventually be allowed to escort men to events outside the house. Maybe even get to go to new places around the world, something she hungered for. Some girls told stories about their travels during morning coffee and in the wee hours of the night, and she hung on every detail. For the first time in her life, she dreamed about who she could be. When there were no clients and it was slow, she daydreamed while flipping through picture books Miss Jackson kept on the parlor shelves. Fact is, she really hadn't thought much about Pearlie lately. She'd been caught up learning the ropes and daydreaming about a world she'd never seen.

She got up and went over to the sink. She looked down into the sink and gasped. Filling the pot was a monstrous hog's head staring back at her, gnarly, and pink, and yet to be properly prepped and dressed. It seemed to be sneering, its empty eye slits and wrinkled snout jutted upward. Random black hairs bristled around the slits and sides of the snout, while the jaw hung slack beneath the head. The crooked, discolored ears were hollow, firm, and pointy. The whole thing had jumped into her point of view like a spook at a haunted house.

"Oh, my gawd!"

She dropped her empty cup on the counter with a clatter, breaking the handle and sending it skittering across the counter onto the floor.

"Damn-it-all Maddie, what the hell are you doing with a nasty thing like that in the kitchen?"

"Lord child, ain't you ever seen supper before?"

Maddie laughed, shook her head, and shuffled over to the pantry. She ducked in for a second before backing out and turning to face Angorra, extending her hand.

"Here you can have this cup for now, I got an extra."

In her hands was a white cup with 'Mardi Gras' in tall letters with a purple, green, and gold mask underneath. Angorra bent to get the busted handle off the floor, so Maddie just set the loaner on the counter by the sink. Angorra stood up with the piece of ceramic handle between her thumb and fore finger and a frown.

"Damn-it, I can't believe I busted this! It was my good luck cup."

"Well now, your good luck gonna be you gotta go back to Nawlins' and get another."

Maddie raised her eyebrows and shuffled over to the stove, lifted a lid and stirred a pot.

"Now get you another cup of joe and get outta my way, so I can start fixing y'all's supper."

"Don't be fixing none of that hog on my account, I don't want none of whatever that gonna be."

Angorra scooted past Maddie and reached for the coffee pot. Maddie kept stirring but began laughing at the ceiling.

"You done had it a couple times already, child, and you gobbled it down like The Last Supper."

Angorra stared down into her coffee in horror.

"Yuk! Damn, Maddie, you gonna give us all some kinda disease cooking that nasty kinda food."

Angorra grimaced at the thought, which was aggravated by the bitter taste of her second cup. Annie and Beatri were just stepping back inside and Beatri heard the last remark.

"Oo-ee Maddie got yummy stuff working for the dinner table tonight. Angie, you ain't gonna get no disease from Maddie. You best be checking close them boys you like, or stick to the old men like me, you wanna keep in good health."

Annie giggled, covering her mouth with her hand.

"You keep playing with them boys you gonna end up seeing the Diddle Doctor, Angie."

They got back in their chairs, Annie refilled their cups, and picked up her half-smoked home roll from the ash tray and re-lit it. The two of them smiled and nodded while looking at Angorra who was still shaking her head in disbelief about where her dinners may have originated. Maddie, who was at the sink spoke with her back to them.

"Y'all get that trucker on his way?"

"He ok, and he gone now. He gonna have trouble sleeping tonight less he drink another pint of whisky, but he be all right."

Beatri blew on her coffee with a satisfied look, while Annie nodded in agreement and stubbed out her last bit of cigarette with her fingernails then got up and stretched. She walked over to the sink, looked down at Maddie's working hands and hollered.

"Damn Maddie, you crazy old woman, you used my razor on that damn pig!"

"I got to shave off the eyebrows and such Annie, you don't want none'a that in your food."

"That just ain't right. I use that razor to shave my coochie."

She grabbed her crotch with her right hand while shaking her left fist at Maddie, then stamped her foot for emphasis.

"You can't do that! That just ain't right, Maddie."

"Well, it was sitting on the table in the hallway, so I thought you's done with it."

"Well, I'm done with it now, that's for damn sure!"

Beatri and Angorra started laughing and Beatri tried solacing Annie.

"Don't worry I got an old arrowhead somewhere, but you might need to sharpen it up."

She winked at Angorra whose mouth was hanging wide open in astonishment before she received the wink.

Annie turned and leaned back against the counter and folded her arms.

"Very funny."

"Beatri, just give me one of yours, I know you got razor's stashed and don't even use'em, I seen you. You got enough Cajun bush on you to fill a queen's jewelry box."

"Oh Cherie, you's just jealous. I'm a delicacy only the finest men earn de right to try. You know since you helped me with de trucker boy, I'll find you some razor to keep dat poody hair off."

Beatri was beaming, she knew she knew many things and always kept the rest playing catch up.

"Beatri, you gotta give me a new one now, and I ain't drinking dem potions you take neither, they's nasty."

Annie exhaled with determination.

"Yea baby, but them's Mama Roux's special charms and they keep them critters and them bad spirits off'a me."

Maddie raised her voice.

"That's enough of that kinda talk y'all! I don't need to hear none of it, and y'all gotta start getting ready for dem lunch visitors."

She shook her head with a slight hum as she checked the stove then moved back to the sink.

"Y'all all ridiculous! Now go on Annie, check on Gloria for me, she been gone too long, and she got my mug she needs to give back. If you don't get a razor from Beatri, I'll get you one from Miss Jackson."

Maddie wrestled with the pig's head and had the snout pointed straight at the ceiling.

"Oh, don't bother Miss Jackson Maddie," Annie shook her head for emphasis.

Beatri grabbed Annie's hand and stroked it gently.

"I'm gonna get you one Annie, don't you worry. I even help you shave you self."

She gave Annie an inviting look... "if you want."

"Oh...ummm, oh!"

Annie blushed while trying to figure how to answer, but not before Maddie was done with all of them.

"I said GET!"

She raised a ladle above her head.

"Annie, either come back with Gloria or the cup."

Maddie was hot and started fanning herself with her other hand, lowered the ladle and began muttering.

"Dese damn girls are sweet, and I love them so, I can't help wondering sometimes why God's grace don't bless 'em with no more sense than an ole hog...".

She stared in the sink then out the window and shook her head.

"...Mercy me."

S ignals & Rattles...
      Birds call at morning,
crickets call at night.
Winds shake the trees and
hearts pound out love.
Signals... nature's rattles all around.
Shake it baby!

We're having so much fun,
Babies with new rattles.

Look in the mirror,
Eyes sparkle with fire and dazzle.
Well, it sure looks good on you.
We're bold, and we're gonna roll,
like babies with new rattles.

After seeing Vettes and meeting Olga the plumber, my ex-
pectations were sky high. I left her to finish her work, and
continued snooping around, even tried to turn on some of the

lights to get a better look. After I messed with a few controls, I heard a raspy voice from behind.

"Hey cuz!"

I turned to see General Manager Dean Unato come around the corner of the bar. He was moving fast, waving papers in one hand. His glasses were perched at the end of his nose beneath his free-for-all salt and pepper hair while his coat and tie tossed around like in a mini tornado.

"I'm Dean, how are you doing buddy, it's Max right?"

He extended his hand as he approached me while his chin seemed to be twisting to the left with a little jerk of the neck. His eyes blinked, and he sniffled.

"Hello Dean, it's great to meet you. I was just looking around a little."

His handshake was vigorous, but after a few seconds he swiveled his head around to look at the lighting I'd turned on, then looked back into my eyes.

"I see. Well, we'll get to all that in good time. We'll have your head spinning before you know it. Tonight, we need to see what kind of short order cook management skills you can dazzle us with. Ha, ha, ha!"

He snorted while he laughed, jerking his neck and rolling his shoulders, showing off a toothy smile.

"We got a no show from one of our Hobart boys."

He seemed to be expecting a negative reaction from me, but I was ready. I remembered Joe told me Dean liked his team members to show a 'can do' attitude.

"Let's do it. I'm ready to rock'n'roll."

I tried to mirror his toothy smile.

He led me back to the kitchen, handed me a menu, pointed to the linen closet, then demonstrated how to turn on the flat top, char-broiler, and fryers, before unlocking the walk-in and freezer. I naturally moved over to the walk-in to check it out. Just to make sure there were no surprises.

"Awright Max, your Vettes training is *live*! Show us what you got. Oh, and make sure that anything you cook, you get a ticket first. I don't need another rookie in here giving away all my food."

Out of pure selfish curiosity, I took a tentative step into the walk-in to look it over but when I turned around lickety-split, he was gone. Without giving me a chance to get another word in, he'd abruptly exited. I didn't see him again for a couple of hours.

I was disappointed but hung up the clothes Cindy Master's washed and pressed for me and put on a pair of checkered chef's pants and a white bus coat from the pantry. I made an effort to introduce myself to the staff as they arrived for work, but most of the girls raced by in street clothes to change in the employee lounge. A few introduced themselves.

"So, you're the new cook?"

Whenever I tried to explain I was a manager in training, they glazed over and lost interest. They were simply looking for a free meal. Eventually, one of the girls coming back from the lounge in her cheerleading uniform started talking to me while she adjusted her collar.

"Hey, you're new here, aren't you?"

"I sure am, my name's Max."

I walked over to her, and she turned her back to me and reached behind her head with both hands. She lifted her hair, holding both ends of a necklace with her thumb and forefingers.

"Well, here you go hun', you can start by helping me get my good luck charm on."

"Oh, ok, sure. Here you go."

I fumbled with it at first, surprised by her casual approach. To get it connected required her to bow forward slightly pushing her back end into me, and then straighten back up. I finally fastened it and realized I'd blushed.

"Sorry, that was a little tricky."

"It's ok, honey, it always does that. You're sweet. We got anything special tonight. I'm starving."

She raised her eyebrows and looked at me expectantly. She had curly brown hair and freckles and looked like the All-American midwestern girl, with 'Katy' on her name tag surrounded by sparkling pink hearts.

"Well, I'm gonna try and make everything special, Katy, but it's my first night, so go easy on me. How does the employee meal program work anyhow?"

I knew I'd read about it in my training but couldn't remember the details and thought it might be each Vettes location had their own version.

"Well usually for me it works really well, I get hungry, and you fellows feed me. Say, you don't seem like one of the Hobart guys, what's your deal anyhow?"

"I'm here to train as a manager. I'm just helping out tonight cuz someone's not gonna make it and Dean asked me to cook."

"Well don't do too good a job or you might not get out of here! Hah, hah, hah! They seem to go through a lot of cooks here."

She seemed to have been imitating Dean's laugh, but I didn't ask, instead I wanted to let her know I was a team player.

"I don't think that's a problem for me, but I'll do whatever they ask."

"Well, I'm just saying, you might wanna burn Dean's food or make it real hot and spicy or something to make sure you don't get stuck in here again, that's all."

She winked at me and strutted off with a few shakes of her hip, showing off the color panels in the folds of her pleated cheer skirt. She looked over her shoulder to catch my eye and smiled as she turned the corner. It was the kind of smile that never got old.

So, without much guidance I faked my way through the action in the kitchen. As the night wore on the staff would come through in a hurry to pick up their orders or get to the employee restroom or grab bar supplies. Otherwise, it was pretty boring.

When Dean finally came back to see me, he caught me off guard, "So, Max how was the opening inventory, did it look ok?"

"Uh, I didn't see an inventory sheet."

While I did a quick once over of the kitchen from where I stood to see if it was in some obvious spot I'd somehow missed, Dean strode right past me to the pantry door I'd left open. With one motion he slammed it shut, spun around on one shoe and held his palms out with his fingers extended like a game show host, pointing at three clipboards hanging on the front of the door.

"Ha, ha, ha, looks like they were hiding in plain sight, cuz."

Then he snorted and squinted while laughing and twitched his neck some more.

"Well shit, I guess I better get right on that. I'll let you know... Sorry 'bout that, man."

I walked over and grabbed the clipboards.

"No biggie Max, just make sure you don't lock yourself in the walk-in, especially with any of my gals. They might bite! Ha,ha,ha!"

Then he was gone, again.

I got a little frantic as started on the inventory, trying to find each of the items in the kitchen listed on the sheets. I didn't get very far with the inventory, because while I was looking into a cooling drawer, I heard a hoarse sing-songy voice approach from behind.

"Shoo be dooby do, my baby boo, I'm here to crank the bank, so come on now and walk the plank with Far-Out Frank."

I turned around and met Frank Fortuna. He had a pale pock-marked face and wore red wrap-around shades, bobbing his head as he adjusted his collar. He sported a blond flat top, in a loud plaid coat with matching slacks brightly broadcasting 'I'm yellow, I'm red, I'm orange!' while on his feet were regal red and beige saddle oxfords.

I must have looked a little dazed as I took his presence in, but he continued in his raspy voice before I could say a word.

"It's ok man, I get that all the time. I know it takes people a minute to know how to deal with greatness. How are you doing? My name's Frank Fortuna."

He extended his hand and showed me a huge smile.

"Hello Frank, I'm Max and I'm glad you're here. This is great!"

He exuded energy, but in addition to his splendorous attire he exuded an aromatic blend of cigarettes and Aqua Velva to match with his blood shot eyes and thoroughly chapped lips.

"Yeah man, that's what I like, enthusiasm. Well, hey, I'm here to train you on our Vettes' entertainment program. I didn't expect you to be in the kitchen. In fact, I was only checking in with the kitchen first because I just got off the road and I'm starving."

"Well, I was told to get a ticket for anything I cook by Dean but I'm sure you're allowed to have whatever you want."

"You got that right, so you got any lobster?"

"Unnhhh, lobster... well..."

I must have looked confused.

"Just jerking your chain man, hah! Yeah, I just did fifteen hours straight, no chaser, with a coke bottle for a pisspot, heh-heh. You know what, just make me a double cheeseburger, no pink but not burnt, with onions and well-done fries. Grill the bun but don't put anything green or any tomato anywhere near my plate, ok?"

His raspy voice was like Rod Stewart's but rougher, like he'd smoked two packs of non-filtered cigarettes on his trip.

"You got it, Frank!"

I was excited that my training was actually gonna get on track.

"Sure thing Max, now after I eat, we'll have a little show-stopping session right here where the feedbag happens. I'm gonna go find Dean and say hello to the troops. I'll get you a ticket too, hah-hah."

He winked before walking away.

"Hey, why don'cha throw something on the grill for your-self man, and we'll chew over Vettes biblical history with dinner."

But as it turned out, just before we ate, Dean popped into the kitchen with his takeout from Greasy Tommy's Subs in hand, and corralled Frank.

"Frankie, I need to have a private consultation with your holiness in my office. How 'bout it?"

"Sure, Dean, ok if I bring my burger, Max made my special and I'm starving."

"Bring it on, Frankie, we'll eat together. Sorry Max, you'll need to stay and man the line. I'll turn the kitchen's main speaker on so you can listen to the action out front. Don't worry, you ain't gonna miss nothing, I'll make sure of that... Hah, hah, hah!"

Frankie grabbed his plate and drink and followed Dean around the corner to the office. I gobbled down a couple of sliders and a lemonade and went back to inventory. After I finished marking down what I could find and faking what I couldn't, I walked out to the service well to take a look at the crowd. I could hear the music clearly, but I was itching to get a look at Vettes in action.

The crowd filled the place even though it was early. From my vantage point, all the bar seats were full, and people stood in the spots where there were none. It was a booze swilling line up all the way to the other end of the room. The dance floor was full, but mellow. The DJ was playing *Little Deuce Coupe,* about one hundred beats per minute, and only good for the Twist, and some older couples were giving it a go. There was a half dozen people hanging around the pink Corvette.

A cocktail waitress leaned into the well and put her elbows on the spill mat. She poked her head under the hanging glassware and over the glasses waiting to be filled and shouted at someone behind the bar.

"Hey Bobby T, you gonna go up to the booth for *Hand Jive*?"

The service bartender in front of her, who apparently was not Bobby T, was visibly annoyed.

"You gonna get an eye full of booze you keep poking your head in here. If these aren't yours, go to the back of the line."

He motioned to two girls leaning with their backs against the wall, their cocktail trays full of empty glasses balanced on one hand while the other arm braced their elbows, waiting their turn. They both stopped chewing on their gum as soon as they saw me. One of them was Katy. The girl in the well withdrew her head and backed out a step.

"These *are* mine! You don't have to get all huffy, Warlock."

The girl put both hands on her hips, obviously annoyed, and stared at the service bartender.

"Look Cindy, my name's Warren but you can call me whatever you like if you're nice about it. Just remember to stay on your side of the bar, ok?"

"All right *Warlock Warren*! You know you cast a spell on me when you smile!"

She turned and winked at me and the two girls.

"Course that probably won't be till the next full moon, right?"

She grabbed the tray of drinks he'd poured quickly while shaking his head, before she lifted and turned in one motion, laughing at her joke. She extended her arm to lift the full tray above her head as she passed and headed around the corner into the crowd.

"Cocktails! Coming through, cocktails everybody!"

Then the girl next to Katy spoke to me.

"Hey, we heard you're training. Is your name, Max?"

"That's me."

I stuck out my thumbs and pointed them at my chest. Katy, who was leaning on the right, winked at me as she pushed off with her foot, and moved into the service well. The other girl instinctively slid into the spot Katy vacated. The bartender grabbed the ticket from the printer and looked at Katy's tray of glasses as he reached to the right for the bottle without looking. You could tell they had their work ballet down pat and I was anxious to see them do one of the famous Vettes group dances.

Before that could happen a pair of girls came out of the crowd with empty trays at their sides and rushed by me towards the kitchen and I realized I better get back to my post in case there were any food orders.

There was nothing in the kitchen except the trail of perfume as their skirts disappeared around the corner to the lounge. As I passed the office, I heard Dean and Frank. A few minutes later Frank leaned his head around the corner with one hand on the wall.

"Max, we're gonna go out front for a minute then I'll be back to start your training."

Then I heard Dean's voice after Frank disappeared.

"A couple of shots ought'a wrap this up, whaddya say Frankie my boy? Ha, ha, ha!"

When Frankie returned, there was a fresh bounce in his step, a bright sparkle in his bloodshot eyes and bourbon on his breath. He got right down to business.

"So, Max you understand our BPM dance programming?"

"I get the gist of it, but I'm glad Vettes has the beats listed by each song. You see, when playing guitar I stay on beat, but it's hard without the guitar in my hands. I'm sure I'll get used to it."

"Oh, so you're one of those. It's OK, the thing you should always remember is in the DJ booth, the crowd can only see you from the knees up, same on the go-go stands. So just memorize the triggers in every song and keep your moves in synch with the DJ. It's easy, because nobody can see your feet. Now when you dance on the bar or the floor to our Vettes Top Twenty-Five, you need to know the moves by heart, because Max, and this is *important*, you're the leader of the pack. You gotta be able to show your team those moves same way you teach'em how to make a Margarita."

When he finished his spiel, his mouth was half open with a strand of spit linking his top and bottom lip, his bulging bloodshot eyes quivering slightly.

"Got that?"

He'd told me a lot about Vettes, but I still wanted to find out more. I figured I should get him to keep his groove going. So, I decided to egg him on.

"I'm ready, let's do it!"

He jerked his left leg up so his saddle oxford was at his knee and began to spin around on his right foot with his left hand clutching the bottom of his lapel, he shot his right hand in the air and bent over just a little for momentum and started to yell.

"Jamming like a salmon, baby, and we're swimming upstream."

His whipped his arm around as he straightened up, hand cocked like a pistol. He thrust his gun finger within inches of my nose as he finished his spin. I had to uncross my eyes but was able to finish the Vettes' mantra without him having to ask.

"I'm working at Vettes and life is but a dream."

His smile let me know it was what he wanted to hear. I was glad I'd remembered the company motto from the manual.

I'd passed my first test.

Dancing on a greasy cloud.
   If it was so easy, there'd be more in the arena.
But it's not so hard that you're all alone.
Call me crazy when I'm lazy,
call it not worth a try,
But tell me - ain't it worth a lifetime?

Sure, I have to smile like a clown
for the real clowns.
Cry like a fool with a frown,
for the really sad,
But it's the only rainbow I can climb,
and besides who knows?
Maybe you can eat fool's gold.

Frank got intense with training, immediately taking two steps over to the fryer and pushing the rubber floor mats out of the way with a kick swipe from his fancy shoe. Then he grabbed two fry baskets that hung over the hot grease. One of them still had a handful of fries in it, but instead of dumping them out, he kept moving, tossing the baskets back and forth by the handles like a juggler, one over the other, deftly catching them after each toss.

I stepped back and gave him room as he called it home, "Come to Poppa!"

His trick left a splatter of grease where I'd stood seconds earlier. Then he reached above the fryers, and while expertly holding the handles, chin high and loose, he dropped them. The front lip of the baskets fell into place perfectly, catching on the holding bar. He'd let go with dramatic flair, and the baskets bounced rhythmically into position. Pleased with the results, he put his hands on his hips, and pushed back his jacket. He was ready for his next trick.

"Awright Max, it's your turn!"

"Frank, whoa! ...wait a minute. I think I'm gonna need some practice in the parking lot first or someone's gonna get hurt. I'll try it if you really want me to, but you gotta take responsibility for whatever I break in Dean's kitchen."

I ended with a nervous laugh and considered the absurdity of the idea, not to mention my shoulder wasn't a hundred per cent. I didn't wanna raise my arm that high if I could avoid it. I looked at him apprehensively and he dropped his head.

"Awww come on man..."

He sounded truly disappointed, but when he finally lifted up his head, he wore a crazy smirk.

"I gotcha didn't I? Don't worry, everybody knows you can't possibly do what Far-Out Frank does without years of practice."

Turns out, instead just showing off with the baskets, he was lubricating the floor. That way we could slip and slide through our dance moves with ease. He had a special technique for teaching a newbie like me the ropes. Somehow, in the limited space between the pass shelf and the cook's line, working side by side, we danced the *Harlem Shuffle*, the *Slide*, and the *Hully Gully*. He easily reduced the dance steps to simple routines for me.

Occasionally in the blink of an eye, while nimbly landing on one foot, he'd grab his flask for a slug of whiskey, and slip it back in his pocket, without missing a beat. He grabbed a mop; threw me a broom and we played air guitar to the *Dirty Water* by The Standells wearing cleaning towels on our heads for wigs. He seemed to really enjoy that number and during it he handed me the flask and winked.

"You're starting to get it."

I had to wonder how many years he worked in the kitchen before he landed this corporate DJ gig. For a guy that looked like a high school math nerd, he harbored an array of unexpected talent spurred by a bottomless well of whiskey'd inspiration. He had a ton of patience with me, no matter how awkwardly I started each dance he showed me. He used his raspy voice sparingly, usually to alert me to an upcoming move. He was always spot on lip synching every single word of every song, even the back-up singer's lines, while adding amazing facial expressions and body english.

He explained to me if you were good, you lip-synched, you kept moving, you welcomed the staff in the booth, and never lost the trajectory of the playlist while you spun, dropped, and hopped. The weird thing was your inner world often became the solitary dance of a mime, only using your voice to talk to your teammates or make announcements. You never actually sang. Well, I guess it could depend on how many shots you had, but it's not like anyone would hear you over the music.

The Vettes DJ should never forget to give a flirty wink to a lady on the dance floor or the bar, but never stop lip-synching. Also, when guys made eye contact give them the wink of party time encouragement and keep them in the groove. He drilled the ole Vette's dog and pony show into me that night while he filled me with half his whiskey. The booze amplified my meds and kept things rolling.

But to where?

I'll admit time flew learning the tricks of the trade in the cramped confines of the cook's line beneath the unglamorous glare of kitchen lights. I barely noticed the staff's comings and goings to the employee lounge, though he enthusiastically acknowledged them by name. The few orders I prepared didn't cause me to miss class on a single dance step or word of advice.

At the end of *Rock Around the Clock* he looked at his watch.

"Max, you can close the kitchen and come out to the deep end of the pool now, its midnight. You brought your Vettes' duds, right?"

"Sure did!"

I nodded and looked at what I had to do before I could join the crowd out front. He pulled out a pair of the black rimmed Ray Bans, slid them on and left on a parting note.

"All right, you got me one more night. We'll do it again tomorrow in prime time, but now it's time for Frank to crank that bank and show the kids out there how it's done."

Soon as he left, the kitchen got quiet. I cleaned as fast as I could. Frank's training was full of surprises, but I sensed it was only the start of what I could learn. I was buzzed and anxious to watch him in action with the crowd.

After I changed, Vettes was in full on party mode. *Hand Jive* was playing, waitresses and bartenders were interspersed with the guests who were lucky enough to get a prime spot on top of the bar. The scene around the DJ stand was outrageous when Frank was in charge. The Vettes' staff synchronized versions of *Hand Jive* with more suggestive and exaggerated moves, wearing masks, wigs, fake tits, and sequined capes. People wore million-dollar smiles, slapped their thighs and waved their hands, high-fiving anyone within reach. It was beautiful, organized chaos.

It was also a far cry from what I'd experienced working with the Baxter's sports bar crowd or the Rock-N-Roll roadshows at The Brashcan Nightclub. They were amazing party places, but what Vettes did was on a whole other level. Truth be told, most anywhere paled in comparison with the sheer energy and intensity of this place, with the crowd whipped into a feverish frenzy. Very impressive, especially when you consider the Vettes crowd was a little older, a little straighter, and more flush with cash.

It didn't take long before I was flying with the rest of the flock. True, I'd had a headstart with the Percoset and Frank's flask. I watched the staff's rendition of *Stop! In the Name of Love* and was glad I was seeing them in action before I took the floor as a manager.

I turned to signal for another drink but was hooked by the arm by someone with other ideas. Katy had grabbed me on her way to the DJ Booth.

"Let's do '*Gimmie*' Max, it's easy!"

"Whaaaaat?"

I didn't know what she meant but we were on our way, me stumbling to keep up. She had a firm grip of my hand and pulled me into the booth when the organ intro for Spencer Davis Group's *Gimmie Some Loving,* started.

"Don't worry, it's easy!"

"Why not?"

What else could I say?

Resistance was futile, she wasn't stopping. We piled into the DJ oval. The giant jukebox was front and center and elevated platforms rose above the dance floor, glowing with a kaleidoscope of colors. Frank was the conductor surrounded by drawers full of 45's, and bins full of props while he tended to the mixing board and turntables. He could see over the jukebox to the dance floor with just a glance, while he masterminded the chaos. The staff clamored past him to get on the platforms or any available space, girls perching on both sides of the jukebox.

"Just follow me, Max!"

Katy started spinning, taking two steps to the right then spinning back in time with the music. I shuffled my feet to get in synch while trying not to step on her feet. After a couple spins, she handed me a shocking blue-sequined wig.

"Here put this on!"

She grabbed a pair of two-foot-wide sunglasses with wiper blades and started nodding her head while I pulled the wig down over my eyes, accidently stepping on her foot. She stepped back on mine to counter and didn't miss a beat while she spun away nodding with a smile letting me know it was just flirty fun. It was spontaneous craziness but looked well-rehearsed to the dance crowd. I knew because I'd already witnessed several songs with similar antics. Still, it seemed like the energy level was off the charts. When *'Gimme'* was over, we dismounted from the booth, hyperventilating, I thanked

Katy before I headed back to the bar. She gushed a compliment back.

"You did great Max! We busted your *'Gimmie'* cherry. Hah-hah-haaaah!'"

We did a high five and she gave me a friendly hug. She squealed, then disappeared into the crowd like a spoon into batter before I could get in two cents worth but felt like I passed some sort of test.

I tried to move politely through the crowd, but half the people were leaving the dance floor for the bar, and the other half were pushing onto the dance floor from the bar, and everyone just mashed into each other like human bumper cars.

As I calculated how many drinks must be misplaced by guests at any given time I knew the club was a gold mine in ways most never considered. Everything was in constant flux. I moved sideways, and stopped, started, and excused myself repeatedly, and kept looking beyond the crowd to make sure I was headed to my drink.

When I finally got to the bar there were three napkins on three glasses labeled 'Max'. I'd only left one drink when Katy grabbed me. The bartender caught my eye and raised his chin at me.

"You got some admirers Max," then motioned to my right.

I looked over several people to see Olga the Plumber with another girl in tow. They smiled, standing side by side, their eyebrows raised expectantly. Olga had slicked down her pompadour and faux sideburns, and her friend had a tall bouffant, of course both their hairdos were black as coal. They looked like they were Elvis and Priscilla at a Halloween party. I must have had a dumb look on my face because they both laughed at me. I regrouped to show off my waiter chops, grabbed all three drinks and negotiated through the bodies between us. I set down the drinks and leaned on the bar to make eye contact.

"Thanks Olga."

I turned to her friend.

"Hello, I'm Max."

I extended my hand to the bouffant wearer.

"Hi Max, I'm Darla."

She lifted her hand, palm down like an offer for a kiss or curtsy. Olga grabbed her by the waist before I could do either and squeezed her against her own side and got a wiggled giggle for her effort.

"We decided you could use some support on your first night at Vettes, Max."

"Well, I appreciate it, but I don't really need these extra drinks."

I waved my hand at the drinks.

"Max, you were up there dancing and missed out on the super Jell-O shot special, so we saved you some. We'll help you if you need it. Don't worry..."

They lifted mine to me, and we clicked and tossed them back. The mix of gelatinous hooch was purply and pink and looked like glitter was in it.

They took turns dancing with me to the next few songs until *Shake A Tail Feather* started. As soon as it began, they each grabbed me by an arm, and we plowed through the crowd until we reached the dance floor.

The staff was doing a Vettes routine to the song, but Olga and Darla had their own special dance. They bent over, wiggling butt to butt and waved their hands above their ears. They were outrageous. I was laughing so hard I could barely clap in rhythm. They grabbed me by the second chorus, sandwiching me between their rear ends. Their bouncing buns knocked me around, so I instinctively reached down for balance and grabbed hold of their waistbands. Once they realized I had them in a rodeo grip, they started spinning around like a giant clock. That left me in the center, holding on tight to their britches.

It seemed like they'd been through the whole routine before and I knew they were playing me when they managed to jump up to attention before I could let go. They pushed against me, reached back, and gave my hands, still in their pants, a slap. Then they spun loose and collapsed back into me for a group hug as the song ended. I looked around but no one seemed to be paying any attention to us at all.

"You ladies are too much!"

"Maybe we're just enough, huh Max?"

Olga and Darla were laughing freely.

"Tell me you've never done that before, and I'll call you both liars!"

"Oh no, Max, we've never done that with a *man* in the middle, have we Darla?"

Olga reached over and gave a playful tug to the back of Darla's pants and got a wiggle in return.

"Not a straight one," she winked for emphasis. My first thought was I was in a little too deep hanging out with these girls. It also occurred to me something else was happening. I started noticing the same spine-tingling sensation I'd felt the night of my South Mountain episode.

We went to the bar for a few more rounds, then back to the dance floor for a few more songs. I began to worry where it was going, so I didn't drink anymore. I was positive I was receiving a much different buzz than just the alcohol we were drinking. The next slow dance I excused myself and went to the restroom. Once inside, I had a moment with myself and the bathroom attendant, nametag 'Bopping Benny'.

I asked, "Do people get this high at Vettes every night?"

"Sure mister, those Super Shot specials puts the devil in some of them! They have an awful lotta fun."

I tipped him a dollar but didn't introduce myself. I decided I better get out of Vettes while I still maintained a shred of Manager dignity. I announced I was gonna take a cab, but the girls insisted they'd take me home.

I wanted to pick Olga's brain, but because I just met her and Darla, and didn't know the dynamics of their relationship I figured it would have to wait, unless they brought something up in the normal course of conversation. They asked if I wanted to go to their place for a joint, but I deferred, telling them maybe some other time as it'd been a long day and I was exhausted. So, we made small talk, and I guaranteed them we'd do it again soon.

"You're damn straight we will."

Olga was adamant but Darla looked at me inquisitively.

"Why don't you wanna come to my house?"

I reiterated how tired I was and assured her I'd enjoyed my time with them. She said she'd try to forgive me. Finally, I offered to pay for gas, but they turned my offer down. When we pulled into the Hideaway Court they were whispering.

"What's with all the whispering?"

"Max, we've had some crazy times at the old Hideaway and wondered whether you were gonna be safe here, or if you'd be better off at our house, that's all."

"Don't worry, once I get in the room, I won't be getting out of bed except to piss, until I go to work tomorrow."

"Ok, Max, well, you know you gotta kiss us *both goodnight.*"

With that Olga threw open her door and scooted around the outside of the cab while Darla grabbed my cheeks with both hands and kissed me on the lips, muffling any attempt to stop her.

"Wait, mm, mm," she was a good kisser, so I relaxed and let her lead. She found my hand and squeezed it while we kissed, but then Olga opened the door and tugged at my sleeve. She grabbed my hand away from Darla's.

"Time's up there, cowboy. Damn, Darla, you gonna wear him out, you heard him say he was tired."

"He's all yours."

Darla relented and playfully shoved me out the door into Olga's arms.

"Whoa!" was all I managed.

Olga pushed me down on the running board so she could lean in and lay a whopper on me. She was way more aggressive with her tongue but not as graceful. When we finished, we both wiped our mouths, me on my shirt sleeve, Olga on her tattoo'd bicep.

So, life at the west side Vettes was gonna be completely off the charts. That's the last thing I remembered thinking as I flopped onto the bed.

That's also when I noticed more of the same tingle along my spine. It seemed like the same tingle I felt crawling in the desert as the one I felt as I bounced around the dance floor. I was sure it was the same weird buzz I had at the sunset party. I got up and scrounged around my room for a pen and jotted

down some words on the back of a loose page of my Vettes'
training manual...

I once woke from a very deep sleep,
Stumbling through the gutter
underneath the trees.

It was clear as ice,
I knew everything would be all right
I could play the fool...
...the midnight clown.

I'll play the fool at the follies,
If they need a fool, I'll play the fool.

It suits me fine and to a T,
I'll play the fool for bread and butter.
After being in the gutter,
Being the fool's like being a celebrity.

Where did I go wrong?
I never thought I'd do the things
I do now every day.

Never ever thought things
Could turn out this way.
I never meant to be this far
from my childhood dreams.

I want to get on a fast train,
fly away on a jet plane,
leave this cloudy reputation behind.
Land in a new land, try a new plan,
Somewhere where my skies are clear.

The dead man's body found on Highway 15 in Las Vegas, Nevada, was identified by the driver's license in his sock. And to be fair to Carter Benson, his corpse was a pretty big bite in what otherwise was a trail of crumbs in a larger investigation. At first his death appeared to be just another homeless man's tragic passing, but there would be more to his life story than the authorities would ever have guessed when they first found him...

Carter fell hard long before he landed on Highway 15. Three years earlier, he was dating a cover girl. He fancied himself a mover and shaker in the Scottsdale party scene, hanging with the coolest crowd at the clubs. His upstart business, CB Products, pulled in six figures and he drove a baby blue convertible Beamer. He lived in a stocked bachelor pad with multiple jacuzzis, and an edgeless pool with a Camelback Mountain view.

When his parents passed, he went back to Iowa to close out the estate and while there he recommended his niece Katy come visit. She came out, visited, and eventually got a job on the west side at Vettes. She seemed to be doing great, but with their age difference, they really didn't have much in common, so after her initial arrival in Arizona they seldom saw each other throughout the next two years. He was fond of Katy though, and with her future in mind he convinced her to agree to be his beneficiary. They both estimated it would be in the far-off future when he passed on. This was of course unless he married, which he pointed out might change his situation. No matter, he didn't, and they never really dwelled on it, so for the most part it was a forgotten matter.

His luck began to change, and he started having glimpses of his possible demise. Finally, he began to see his life, at least as he knew it, ending sooner rather than later. By the time he reached his hiding place on the concrete abutment of I-15 in North Las Vegas, and holding a cardboard blanket, he knew he could no longer contact anyone he knew in Phoenix without putting them in danger. He was looking over his shoulder every waking minute.

He called his niece Katy from a hotel lobby guest service phone and left a casual message saying he was going on a trip overseas. He explained it had been a lifelong dream and would get in touch with her later, maybe send a postcard.

He sifted through his recent past, searching for a clue, something he might use to bolster his plan in hope it would help him survive after fleeing his predicament.

Carter Benson first met Louis Etrusco at Jetz in Scottsdale, convinced their meeting was a godsend. Carter was going broke at the time and needed a quick fix to get his finances at CB Products in order. Louis had offered to help him by buying in as a business partner. This would enable Carter to balance his books and cover up his mishandling of funds. Plus, there was Louis' enticement of a seven-figure contract for CB Products. He just wasn't sure how to present it to Barry.

Carter had realized too late he'd crossed a line in living too large. Approaching his mid-forties, he'd finally worked his way into a profitable venture. He might have gotten his affairs in order if he'd dialed it way down. However, when the moment of truth arose, he declined to give up the lifestyle he'd grown accustomed to. He'd worked too hard and wanted to finally have fun.

Carter understood his business partner Barry was willing to do the same thing day after day, content to raise his family. To Carter that was boring and knew eventually the time would come for them to cut ties. When Barry wanted an independent audit conducted, they had a falling out. Carter knew his lifestyle splashed red ink on the books he'd hidden from Barry.

When Barry confronted him to finally begin an audit, Carter blurted out an offer to buy him out. He was shocked when his partner accepted.

There was a problem though, not only was Carter in debt to the company from innumerable ill-advised advances, he also made them without Barry's consent. Plus, he didn't have the additional funds necessary to buy out Barry.

Then, as he struggled with less than a month to come up with the money, one of his girlfriends recommended he talk to Louis Etrusco. She said she was tired of his whining and knew Louis could probably help him out. Many of their party scene friends knew Louis. He'd been involved in helping several club owners in the area and had his fingers in lots of businesses around town.

The offer seemed too good to be true, so Carter spent a few days asking around, and visited some of the places Louis owned. He figured it was the only due diligence he'd need, and never actually hired a professional investigator to check out Louis. Carter personally verified Louis' investments in night clubs and a strip bar, all still in business. The owners and general managers vouched for him, albeit cautiously. After explaining himself, he received their confirmations with minimal elaboration, as if bothered by his interruption.

Louis was also involved in industrial park businesses that looked like mini strip malls with garage door fronts. They were all legit, or at least listed in the phone book and open for business. He did the vetting himself, saved their business cards and they seemed okay to him. They ranged from print shops to massage parlors.

The night he waited for Louis at Jetz to sign their partnership deal he repeatedly felt for the cards in his pocket. He'd fantasized beforehand he would grill Louis card by card just in case one of his inquiries might uncover some reason to back out of the deal at the last-minute.

Louis was slick but stayed relaxed and appeared impressed Carter had personally visited the businesses. During the final negotiations he lauded Carter's business sense.

"Now that's what I'm looking for, a partner with a good head on his shoulders. You know Carter, I like to keep moving forward. I like to make a list and check things off. Get it done, that's how you get ahead. I think we're gonna get along great. Just tell me what kind of help you need!"

As soon as Carter heard what he wanted, he was smitten and began to daydream he could right his ship and get back to living the life he wanted. He forgot his own fantasy to grill his suitor. He realized later he'd never asked anything of substance about Louis' businesses, instead Carter greedily pivoted to how soon he could get the money. In fact, when he drove away, he felt lightheaded from what he believed was a successful deal. The Louis deal would enable him to buy Barry out. He was so pleased with himself he celebrated till last call.

In only nine months, the lightheadedness was replaced with the undeniable pain which tugged at a person's heart and soul as if weighted down from making their life's biggest mistake. Every day little triggers reminded him of the ever-burgeoning karmic weight. Eventually the burden grew into helplessness. It engulfed him and he began to believe his fate was spinning out of his control. The barhopping gave him only brief relief in delaying the inevitable. He always awoke finding himself returned to a soulless reality where he struggled to escape his personal maelstrom.

He'd gotten into deep shit and needed a way out.

How did this happen?

For the first six months, Louis brought him different formulas, simple treatments for plexiglass and window tinting, the basics of his auto body workshop product line. Then he brought him a formula for a chemical anticholinergic to produce. Louis said he would be shipping it to a company that manufactured women's PMS treatments. Carter later figured out it was likely a designer drug they were making, but at that point he was happy with the fruits of their arrangement and told himself it was too late to change course. Besides, it was a minor amount compared to the volume of auto products.

However, when the new chemical's production began Louis brought in his nephew Larry Etrusco to work on it. Carter was reluctant to accept him as Larry was fifteen years younger and undisciplined in the lab. Larry came and went at all hours without ever communicating with Carter. Louis explained Larry was also on salary with the body shop and he wouldn't impact CB Products' payroll. Louis told Carter to be patient with Larry.

"Don't worry, Carter, good things are on the horizon. Soon you'll be swimming in a pool full of money with the hottest girls in town."

Louis explained the chemical would be very lucrative, and for Carter to go ahead and hire any staff necessary as volume increased. Louis authorized Carter to make lab improvements needed to keep up with volume of orders and maintain product safety as he requested. Louis had even kicked in more money than required to make it happen, but then, without waiting for Carter to act, awarded the contract to a construction firm Louis stated had won the bid to get it done.

When Carter balked and shoved a stack of plans with a five-figure number for the work on the table in front of Louis, Louis didn't blink, instead echoed his favorite refrain.

"That's what I like, moving forward, making a list and checking it off. I like getting things done. Of course, they can build this stuff, too."

Carter sat speechless and stunned, unable to comprehend what was happening. He could only stare back at Louis while Louis just smiled.

"Hey, let's go get some pizza at Little Naples, I got a friend who makes the best pizza in Arizona, my cousin Joey."

They took a Lincoln Town car with a driver and watched rock videos and porn on the way. They spent four hours drinking and eating pizza and met several men and women. He felt exceptional, even euphoric the whole time, but the next day couldn't remember the names of the new acquaintances he'd made. It took him most of that next day to get his brain to work at all, so he kept his door locked at work and hid behind his computer. He watched the clock all day desperately waiting till he could leave for some basic hair of the dog.

In order to keep his balance as he left, he had to look at the ground for every step then drove with one eye shut until more liquor finally touched his lips.

He was sinking fast, being pulled down little by little with each new twist of Louis' partnership. Each day brought a new layer of concern, like a shovel full of rocks being added to the soles his shoes. Each new step seemed heavier than the last.

Three months after Louis introduced the anticholinergic, Larry hand selected a crew to begin making various gelatin compounds in small batches. Eventually, Louis said Larry found a formula he wanted produced in bulk and put Carter in charge of it, telling him Larry would now oversee production of the anticholinergic powder.

Carter responded he had to bring on three more people and Louis said it was fine as long as he approved the new hires. Before Carter could fill the posts, Louis sent him a dozen people, eight from an ex-inmate probation program. Louis said he'd used program enrollees at his body shop, and they were loyal, hard-working, and very affordable. Several were not qualified, but Carter liked the fact it would keep the profit margins' fat and juicy. In spite of all his concerns he received a hefty financial reward.

After the gelatin production was kicking out smoothly, Carter took some time to study the books and saw Louis was steadily reducing automotive orders and increasing production of the powder and gelatin.

He noticed new clients dropping by to see Larry who were never introduced to Carter. Often, they didn't seem like genuine prospects for auto refinement *or* over the counter remedies. In fact, they seemed to be coming or going straight to a party.

One night they brought in a rich frat boy, who talked loudly and carried a Corona full of mashed lime wedges. The guy was buzzed, and Carter realized things were getting too out of control for his comfort. When he asked, Larry explained the Corona toting frat boy away.

"His daddy's a big buyer back east. I'm just gonna show him around a little to get some extra cred with his pop, don't worry about it. We got this."

Carter didn't protest but left his office door ajar while they wandered around the warehouse and heard the kid's remarks.

"So, this is where you make the huggy shit, huh?"

And other things unrelated to Larry's spiel about the client...

"We gonna have some amazing parties at the house now!"

And finally...

"You know if you can get this batch in time for our Sonora Smash Party, I'll kick in a few extra grand. It's gonna be a desert demolition! It's only three weeks away. We've already slammed major coverage, but I'll triple my flyers if I can score for that."

Carter had not only lost control of his company but was convinced what they were doing was even more illegal and careless than he'd previously allowed himself to imagine. He knew Larry wasn't being careful. He was certain they were approaching production levels that couldn't help but attract law enforcement. He'd had suspicions before but had enjoyed the ride so much he hadn't let it bother him.

He felt the flutter of too many red flags waving in his subconscious. He tossed and turned every night when he tried to sleep. He worried what Larry and Louis might do next, and what it might mean for him.

Carter's plan to get out was to lead a double life until he could jet. It was the only way to keep from ending up in the ground or in prison. These were forces he couldn't control. In his work life, he kept everything cool with the Etrusco's, and the rest of the time he began moving any money he could, money they didn't monitor closely went into secret separate bank accounts. He did both for a while, and remained careful not to raise suspicions, but knew sooner or later they'd find out and he'd have to stay focused and ahead of the eventuality.

Louis had often given him cash in lieu of checks, so he'd got the cash out of his safe deposit boxes, depositing it in secret accounts he could access when on the road. In addition to that, he started faking invoices to CB Products to write checks to fake companies, in order to obtain even more funds for his secret accounts.

He knew it increased his risk but was determined to build up enough capital to start over again, somewhere far away. He projected Vancouver as his eventual destination but would head north to the Pacific coast before crossing into Canada. He decided to hide first in Las Vegas, then Reno and on to Portland or Seattle to let his trail die out. Then move to Vancouver.

He wondered about his niece Katy Kitts who worked at Vettes but was afraid to contact her other than leaving a message. He wanted to ensure no one at CB Products knew of her existence. He decided to leave something for her and contact her later. There was really no longer anyone else in Phoenix he was close to. The girlfriends he went out with only wanted his money and he had failed to cultivate a meaningful relationship with any of them.

He hadn't talked with ex-partner Barry in over a year but despite their time apart still felt he could trust him. Barry had been fully paid and things between them were on relatively good terms for a dissolved partnership. He decided to send Barry his 'in case of emergency letter' in an envelope with two sets of instructions and a safe deposit key. One set in the larger envelope with the key and some cash for his trouble, the other in the smaller envelope which was to remain sealed unless deemed necessary based on the first letter's instructions. The letters were a rush decision and felt a bit dramatic, but with his paranoia and fear peaking, he couldn't think of a better plan.

When he got to Las Vegas he first tried hiding out in dumpy hotels near the Strip, but the big casinos he went to had too many cameras, and he got paranoid and headed to the outskirts. He had rented four apartments and still had one near the North Las Vegas Airport he hadn't used but was waiting to make it his last Vegas stop. It didn't take long before he no longer felt safe going to the other three. He was sure those were already being watched.

He reckoned his Vegas time was growing short. So, he went to the streets rather than the last residence, a trick he'd learned to live with. He felt it let his trail go cold. He picked up cardboard from dumpsters. He learned quickly on the streets, occasionally between his apartment moves, cardboard was essential to protect him from flying rocks and debris when he slept beneath an underpass. He didn't like hiding in the homeless scene but decided it took desperate measures to stay in hiding. Carter's paranoia imagined Etrusco tentacles lurking everywhere.

On this day, he was coming to grips with his previous night's decisions. He'd let his partying get the best of him. During his manic spree, he spent hundreds to change his appearance and going to casinos to let off steam and try to get laid. He'd finally gotten laid, but not when acting like a high roller, where he'd simply blown wads of cash in the finest casinos. No, the previous night he was in a local dive wrapping up what he thought was another lost night when he scored.

He'd been playing bar top poker at Dottie's Ditties on Washington, spilling nachos on his lap when he found himself in an increasingly friendly conversation with a chain-smoking biker chick. She was a shapely woman, who presented a weathered but striking profile framed by coal black hair with blue streaks and gray roots. It didn't take long before they shared intentions to leave together. He was so excited he didn't bother to screen her, and she didn't seem concerned about vetting him either. After a lively and acrobatic consummation of their carnal desires in her bare bones' hotel room, he heard her snorting drugs while he used the restroom. He didn't really care, but it brought a wave of uneasiness to his mindset, and he worried she might be a hard-core user and difficult to get rid of.

When he stepped out of the bathroom, she was still undressed, nonchalantly asking him if he wanted to go again. She offered him a toot, but he declined, and turned on the charm, expressing his joy regarding her delightful performance in, on, and around the bed. He'd already made up his mind to ditch her and change locations before he'd heard her snort-fest so he offered her dinner instead, suggesting they would have another go afterwards.

He was proud of how he manipulated her, glowingly praising her skills. He told her she was so spectacular he'd worked up an incredible appetite. Turned out the offer of dinner and drinks before another round of demonstrating their newfound attraction for each other appealed to her. She took a long turn in the restroom, and he just assumed she was having another boost, then they left in their separate cars.

When they got to DT's Pub for their no tell hotel 'Halftime' party, he excused himself to use the men's room and caught their waitress in the hall by the kitchen. He stuffed a wad of twenties in her hand, telling her he'd be right back. As soon as the server went in the kitchen, he slipped out the emergency exit to the back of the building where he'd purposely parked his car, as there were no windows on that side, allowing him to drive off unnoticed, only five minutes to his favorite overpass and ten minutes from his last apartment.

He was paranoid and sinking, thinking the crazy drug whore was after his money. Maybe she even knew Louis or Larry! He started to panic and threw the current apartment's key out the window when he hit full speed on the highway. It meant one more night at his favorite underpass spot, this time for the last time.

C ome down off the mountain
    Tell us what you know.
Give us a little information
On which way to go.

Heard you got a tiny little mind,
But drive a big car,
that your wallet's diamond lined.
There's no use
asking you a favor,
It's better to catch you fading,
or use a big persuader.

Carter hadn't grown up in Las Vegas. It was a place where on the back streets and in the back rooms *'What have you done for me lately?'* didn't apply.

Veda Disht knew. In her Las Vegas world, and it was truly her world, it was *'What have you done for me today?'* Unless of course, someone could top your offer. And yes, both mantras were ones Veda Disht lived to the fullest.

Veda suspected Carter would flee after their impromptu no tell tango and had enlisted their waitress at DT's, who was an old friend. After stuffing Carter's wad of bills in her apron, the waitress kept an eye on Carter with the help of the Jägermeister mirror on the wall. Soon as he rushed out the fire exit, she slipped into the Ladies room where Veda Disht waited, smoking a cigarette and leaning against the sink. Veda dangled a small brown bottle of white powder on a silver chain at her side. The instant the waitress entered the restroom, Veda held out the vial, and dropped it in the girl's hand. She gave her a kiss on the cheek and lovingly touched her chin with her thumb.

"Thanks, babe."

Veda slipped out the bathroom and headed to the same fire exit Carter used at the rear of the building. She pushed the door open slightly, just in time to see Carter back up to the dumpster behind DT's. She quickly shut the door. Once she heard the crunch of his hasty gear change, she reopened it with a 'gotcha now' smile and watched his dingy green Toyota Camry lurch out the parking lot exit. Carter was hunched over the steering wheel as he sped away.

Veda rushed back to the table they'd shared. She reached over the brass rail and grabbed her purse with her mobile phone. Without pausing, she hustled out the door into her red Camaro IROC-Z. She jumped in, jabbed her key in the ignition and started it all in one motion, then headed down the street in the same direction.

At the first red light, she was already three cars back but felt comfortable hanging there. She pushed the button on her mobile phone and called her Phoenix contractor. Even if she lost Carter for now, she knew he'd stay in some nearby dive or sleazy nook on the streets. She couldn't help but slap herself on her thigh and bite her lower lip.

The job had been easy and easy money was her thing. Carter Benson had been her perfect mark. After she'd accepted the job from Larry Etrusco, she looked for Carter in all the regular places people thought they could hide in her Las Vegas. After a couple of calls and a little cash, she found his Social Security number, got his Arizona Driver's license number, and started a serious search. Turns out he had a Nevada Driver's License too, but that just made for a little extra cross checking, both showed up in her research.

She didn't find him researching area home purchases, so she tried apartment and time share rentals, but no luck there either. She spot-checked used car dealerships, vehicle rentals, pawn shops, bed and breakfasts, small airplane companies, and strip joints. She began calling hotels and checking into their rewards programs.

She finally found action on Carter while searching the Casino rewards programs. He had been to the MGM. Carter had been tricky by utilizing ghost LLC's for renting the different apartments and buying vehicles, but he'd made the mistake of using his casino reward benefits card while playing the Casino machines to get the reward's benefits. Of course, Veda was able to hack their databases. The only problem was no recent activity at the big casinos. Now that she knew he liked to gamble on the machines and utilize rewards, she took time to run through the records of the smaller pub operations around town.

There was old activity at DT's Pubs, so she tried pulling their records and checked in person at their locations. After two days with nothing, she decided to look into the remaining smaller bars with similar programs. There he was, he had made a recent stop at Dottie's Dittys.

It was time to switch and stake them out instead. There were only three locations, but it would require a lot of driving, and she wanted to work without stopping or sleep. To prepare for nonstop surveillance she procured more meth from her truck stop dealer and mixed it with coke she'd gotten from a boy toy. It created her favorite boost for a weeklong chase.

She knew the first week he was on the run was the most crucial, as you best catch someone in seven days. Usually after a week in Las Vegas marks like Carter typically went into deep cover with a bunker mentality. They might head for the Nevada mountains or hit the road into someone else's territory.

So first she started with a stake out on the Washington Street location. She waited in her car parked behind a hedge at the Circle K across the street giving her a clear view of the entry. It was a calculated risk but maybe he'd come back to the same Dottie's Ditty where she got the hit. After eighteen hours and two adult diaper changes, she'd spotted him getting out of his car.

She grabbed her bag, crossed the street, went in the back of the club, and hid in a corner by the pass shelf. She stepped out of the shadows when she caught the eye of a cocktail server she knew and gave her a come-hither look. As the cocktail waitress slid up next to her, Veda whispered her the arrangement. The dye was cast, the girl tucked the bills from Veda in her bra, smiled and nodded.

Veda took her bag and headed to the restroom and into a handicap stall, immediately doing a thick line of coke off her make up mirror while leaning against the door. She cleaned up with alcohol wipes then slipped on a slinky black dress you could fit in a soda can, doused herself liberally with perfume, and took a couple hits of speed for good measure. She stepped out of the stall, pushed up to the sink, looked in the mirror and gave herself a knowing nod. She loved herself the most when she circled her prey. Not only was she going to make some money, but she would get laid, get buzzed and play Carter the way a cat tortures a field mouse.

When she was done with him, she would turn him loose and over to Larry, the steel bomber.

After Richard Boone settled in the Valley of the Sun, he'd run out of career options. He'd doubled down too many times in his youth. He used up his chips in his glory days playing high school sports, and now he couldn't find anything else to do. His skill set was greatly diminished and was terrible at job interviews. He couldn't get a job in Phoenix with his name the same way he had ridden his high school fame during his Iowa years.

Of course, eventually he'd messed that up, served time, then worked construction on work release. After a few months of that, he decided he didn't like hard labor. He'd blown out both knees and had too many aches and pains. So, he ended up in Phoenix where his brothers Danny and Dave worked security jobs at a shopping complex. Then they'd gotten a gig as part time bouncers at Vettes Nightclub and met Louis Etrusco, one of the owners. Louis was looking for a driver with a physical presence who could take care of 'stuff,' so Danny and Dave recommended Richard.

They knew Richard needed a steady job, and instead of being the big brother and mentor they'd grown up with, he'd developed into a brother who was a lech and a bother. He was getting drunk too often and wasn't the 'High School Hero' he used to be, now becoming a burden; lazy, broke, and constantly complaining. To their detriment, they'd never learned how to say no to him as he'd been the family's winning status symbol all their lives. But to Richard's detriment he never got his high school degree, much less college. Since then, he'd gained weight, aggravated his sports injuries, and after arriving in Arizona, he started borrowing money and crashing at their apartment.

Luckily for them, things turned around after they recommended him to Louis, who hired Richard as a driver. At first, he was only working a few hours, a few days a week. Then he started running more errands, driving both Louis and Joey Spasula around, sometimes being the silent strong tough guy on collections and things changed, Richard's career arc turned around.

Richard learned to 'hop to' whenever Louis or Joey called. It wasn't hard for them to figure out what type of carrots motivated him. The tasks quickly became more varied and less passive in nature, but nothing he couldn't handle and that he didn't find some satisfaction in. He was a good intimidator and fortunately for him he didn't have to get physical very often.

He knew he couldn't afford not to do their bidding as they'd been very generous with extra cash and other amenities. His id was the same as a high school freshman on steroids except nowadays he cared more about food and less about sex.

As the job continued Richard got drive time with Larry, Louis' little brother. Larry didn't have as much class as Louis or Joey but started off treating Richard with the respect of an older relative. But then there were times, Larry made Richard uncomfortable, especially when he lost his temper or got fucked up. Also, it turned out Larry was prone to spontaneous fits of violence.

Richard still remembered the day Larry called him on the Motorola Cellular phone they'd given him to keep at his side.

"Hey Booner, get yourself ready, we're going to Las Vegas."

Richard thought about it but then decided to call back.

"Hey Larry, are we gonna eat?"

"Hell, yeah, we're gonna eat, but first we're gonna drive to Vegas. How soon you gonna be here?"

"Uh, gimme thirty minutes boss."

"Ok, great, I'm ready when you are."

Richard had less than twenty bucks in his wallet but knew better than to ask for money for food when picking up Larry. He'd already driven Louis, Larry, and Joey to Vegas several times but keeping Larry by himself in a good mood would require effort, especially since Larry was already rearing to leave.

Richard did a quick wash over the sink and got chicken biscuits on the way. He knew their smell would annoy Larry, so he tried to hide it. He kept air freshener in the glove compartment and his toiletry bag had various body sprays. He decided to pack his suit bag and a couple ties, too. He'd heard stories about Larry running loose in Vegas without Louis around to keep him in check. He was now familiar enough with Larry to know he'd be less forgiving than either Joey or Louis if anything went wrong, especially something Larry didn't like.

He tucked a napkin in his collar and drove with the windows down, chugging down two chicken and biscuits and a tall coffee on the way, taking care to not get any crumbs on his coat. He stopped, used the rest of his cash for gas and fumigated the car again, brushing the seats, and using wipes on his face. He swished some mouth wash and spit while the gas filled. He was supposed to keep the tank full, though it was a little short, even with what he added. He knew he'd have to stop in Kingman and use the company's Terrible Herbst gas card to make it all the way to Vegas and hoped Larry wouldn't complain about having to stop.

The ride was uneventful, and Larry was feeling pretty good, singing along with 50's and 60's radio. Richard wasn't much for conversation, something his bosses liked. It was a little unnerving that Larry hadn't told him anything specific about their Vegas business, because Richard liked to plan his meals in advance.

"Don't you worry about it, Booner, it's just business."

They stopped for gas in Kingman, took Route 66 and at Larry's suggestion stopped at Mr. D's Diner for lunch. He'd stayed in a good mood singing along with the music playing there while they ate. Catching Richard off guard, Larry tried to strike up a conversation during their lunch.

"So Booner, got any girls in Vegas?"

"Huh? Uh no, well maybe, like what do you mean. You need one?"

"No! What are you, gagootz? Why would I ask you for a girl? I ain't looking for a girl, I'm asking you if you got some tail there for yourself?"

"Oh, sorry, boss... I dunno, let me think about it. I brought my little black book with my girls' numbers though... so... how long we gonna be there, you know?"

"As long as it takes Booner. That's all, just as long as it takes. And don't worry about it, you need a girl while we're there, I'll take care of you. You just lemme know."

"Thanks boss!"

It troubled Richard how he never knew what to expect from Larry.

"The hell you keeping numbers in a little black book for anyway. Why don't you use that car phone we got you?"

"Yea boss, thanks for that, it's really cool and all, but I'm afraid if I take it out of the car except to charge it, it might get stolen."

Actually, he was more afraid he'd lose the damn phone, he thought it was a burden. He kept it close by wherever he went, even using the bulky harness when doing something that required two hands. He felt the mobile phone was really just a trap he'd been given, and he'd get caught in it, if he ever failed to answer when called.

The only time he was totally able relax around Larry was when Larry and Louis took the whole gang to Mexico. For the last two years they'd paid for him and his brothers and some other associates to go to Rocky Point, AKA Puerto Penasco for fun in the sun on the beach. Larry didn't give a shit about anything when they were down there, as long as everyone had a good time. This trip to Vegas, however, Richard knew to stay on his toes, Larry was definitely on the hunt.

Thankfully, Larry was snoring when they got to the outskirts of Vegas. Richard pulled in the first Terrible's he saw as quietly as possible and gassed up again and got some snacks. The next day they found Carter Benson, the business Larry was going to Las Vegas for.

Playing catch up,
    A fast skate on thin ice.
A debris filled domain,
on fool's golden pond.

Sky diving through decades,
Pretending eternal youth.
Never checking the proof,
But sure to spend the loot.

Always drinking double,
And always doubling down.
Surviving with passion,
But not the lessons learned.

The trail overgrown,
and littered with victims,
like greeting card poems.

Years earlier when Angorra lived in Whitehaven, a suburb near the Mississippi state line, she returned from a trip to

Phoenix in July. Stepping inside her apartment she gasped and immediately turned on the air conditioning before glancing at the blinking light of her answering machine. She pushed play, and heard her Mawmaw, so she fast forwarded to the next message - Mawmaw again! She repeated the sequence over and over, but each time the tape's squeal stopped, she got the same result.

The AC was slow to cool her place down. It was so hot, with local humidity, even more uncomfortable than Phoenix where it was simply scorching. It didn't matter either way, she left the air off to save money when she went out of town. She stripped, left her clothes on the bed, slid into a slip, and went to the fridge. She put a full tray of ice into a pitcher, filled it with water, grabbed a glass from the cabinet, and turned to the pitcher of ice water. As she reached for it, she looked at the message machine and stopped and sighed, closing her eyes. She knew she needed to listen to the messages and put the pitcher and glass on the coffee table, next to a stack of mail. She sat back down to organize her bills, while her glass and pitcher stood in a growing puddle of condensation.

In Arizona, Angorra called Mawmaw, and Mawmaw had gone on the offensive right away about her relationship with Pearlie. How Angorra had not been honest with her daughter.

"So, when you gonna tell her?"

Angorra knew from the way Mawmaw exhaled, though she wanted to be supportive, she was running out of patience. Angorra struggled to respond quickly enough, so Mawmaw continued.

"She starts high school next week, you know."

With her eyes clenched tight Angorra nervously changed hands with the phone and took a deep breath. She'd thought about this but still wasn't ready to be a mom yet, not if she could avoid it. Being Pearlie's big sister worked out pretty well, she was able to be in Pearlie's life, yet live her own life the way she wanted.

She would give Mawmaw money, but money wasn't the problem! She didn't want to think about unveiling the truth to Pearlie. She felt if she kept things this way, she could do her part and still be there for her. She'd let Mawmaw deal with the day-to-day trials and tribulations of raising a daughter. After all, Mawmaw was better at it. Angorra didn't know how she could have gotten Pearlie through her first eight years of school herself.

She told Mawmaw something she thought would calm her down.

"I was thinking sometime in the next couple years of school I'll have her move in with me. Then after she's settled, we'll come for a visit, and I'll get it all straight with her. That way you'd be there too, to help it go smooth."

She held her breath and waited.

"Well, I reckon everybody's different but high school's a tough time to be changing schools. Ain't no telling what all she'll get into or what kinda friends she'll have. She's likely to quit. Un-huh, but y'all don't do that shit. Just cuz you didn't finish, don't mean Pearlie gonna be that way."

Angorra's schooling had been incomplete, and her Mawmaw was never gonna let her forget it.

"I know, I know, but I might just move *there* if I have to."

"Hah!" Mawmaw blurted out in disbelief, then her voice went high pitched as she continued, "Ooo-eee, you are making up some tall tales now, girl."

"Well mama, I'm working on it, don't I give y'all enough money? Maybe y'all can move here?"

"It ain't about the money, don't you see? It's about being here for her every day. Even if she don't want you here. Hell, I already saved over half what you give me for her college or for whatever she may need when it's time for her to get out on her own. You want it back? I'll give it to you, but I ain't moving myself nowhere less'en I win a big damn house from Publisher's. No, Angie, we're staying put."

It was no use, she was no match for Mawmaw, who was so set in her ways.

"All right, Mawmaw, I understand. Sometime soon, while she's in high school, I'm gonna make it right, you'll see."

"Baby there ain't never gonna be no right time and there ain't gonna be no wrong time, either. Don't you get it? Look, I just know one thing, she deserves to know the truth, and I ain't gonna be around forever, so you best keep it top of your mind till you do set it straight."

"Mawmaw, I gotta go, I'm working, I'm a hair stylist now and I got an appointment. I promise I'm trying, *really I am*, and I'm saving money. I'll talk to you soon."

"Ok, Angorra, you better be smart and better be safe. Call back when you can talk to Pearlie, Ok?"

"Ok, I will. Bye, Mawmaw, I love you."

Angorra rushed out of her South Scottsdale apartment, jumped into the cream-colored Mercedez convertible her client lent her and rushed to her appointment.

"Thanks, sweetie."

Mrs. Lauderdale discreetly palmed a fifty to Angorra.

"You know you always welcome ma'am."

Angorra slipped the money into her purse and gathered up her scissors, combs, and dyes, and put them in her Ophidia Gucci tote she used for appointments or luxury resort 'dates'. She'd almost forgotten the jade necklace Ms. Lauderdale gave her. Ms. Lauderdale had offered it casually, holding it up behind her, while Angorra dug around for some foil to do her highlights.

"It doesn't go with any of my stuff, but it's still in style, and I think it would go so great with your skin, don't you?"

Angorra answered before she saw it.

"Yes ma'am, that's nice,"

Then as she turned into it her jaw dropped.

"Oh, *Ms. Lauderdale*, thank you."

"Angie, I told you before, please call me Julie."

"I'm sorry... Oh my! Miss Julie, the necklace is so beautiful, I forgot myself. Are you sure?"

Later, as she organized her stuff, she slipped the necklace into the bag's zipper pouch. It probably would look good with the right dress, but more likely would fetch good money at a pawn shop.

Angorra knew she was playing with fire working for Ms. Lauderdale. Why? Well, because she also saw Mr. Lauderdale from time to time. Probably a half dozen times, total. She'd only entertained him at her apartment, wearing little more than a robe, and she didn't cut his hair. She figured it wasn't safe to work for either of them much longer, soon she'd have to make herself unavailable.

She'd served dutifully as Ms. Lauderdale's hair stylist and bedroom counselor. She knew the missus went to top-notch salons for coloring and regular cuts. Thing is, Miss Julie Lauderdale had put a monetary value on Angorra's advice for the romance in her marriage. The suggestions Angorra gave her always seemed to get results. Naturally, it was easy for Angorra to make recommendations; she'd drawn out a variety of maneuvers to satisfy her husband's appetite during their sessions together.

Once her bag was packed, she decided it was time to go.

"Let me know when you need a freshen up, Miss Julie."

Miss Julie went into the kitchen to feed her dog as soon as they'd finished her hair.

"I will. You can let yourself out dear, talk to you soon."

Angorra closed the door on her way out and rushed to the car.

Meanwhile, in Louisiana, Beatri's life was at another crossroads. She'd been released from city lock up and returned to her one-room efficiency in Marigny near the river. She'd been careless, got set up, busted, and charged with solicitation. She knew she'd probably be able to get the charge reduced to a $500 fine as an unlicensed masseuse, even though she was not working in a parlor. The court wouldn't care about that. Once she paid it at least she could avoid jail time. She was barely hanging on to a life in the Crescent City. It didn't seem like she got to enjoy the Big Easy glamour the Crescent City offered, but she sure ended up with plenty of the Big Easy's dark side.

Her dreams of glamour had faded in a few months. Whether it was the oddness of her vitiligo patchwork skin or her equally odd personality, she'd never gotten past the point of 'almost making it'. Seemed like she was swimming towards shore, but the beach kept moving further away. This week had been more of the same, she landed three big clients then got busted. She was still determined to stay in the city, though only a few people she met really touched her heart, those who scared her the most, the ones from the VouDou Krewes.

She saw the tip of a letter poking out from under her door. The landlord probably slipped it there and it was probably bad news. If it'd been a government check or a package, the landlord would never notify her, instead he'd wait for Beatri to track him down and then want to barter before turning it over.

It was worse than bad news.

Her Auntie Brake, her only surviving family member had passed. Beatri'd gone to visit her a few months earlier. Since, she'd been saving money to get Auntie in a home in New Orleans or Alexandria. That way Beatri could visit and more easily care for her. Now, it was too late.

According to the letter, she only had a week to go back and take care of things, before her own court appearance in New Orleans. As she read the letter, she held her breath, but after the word 'deceased' the air poured out of her lungs, and she crumpled to her knees.

At that point she simply became a vessel for the powers that be. Some part deep inside her, long held in check, awoke, and took hold of her and her actions. She had the fleeting thought she was watching herself from the ceiling but was too overwhelmed to be able to stop and figure out what was happening.

Her mind's eye watched every move.

No time to clean off her lock-up grime, instead she catapulted into another gear like a fast-action automaton in a zombie-like state. She sprayed herself liberally with Confess cologne, grabbed a stashed roll of bills, threw together a travel bag and left for the bus station. She took it to Alexandria; she would figure out her way from there. There was no anxiety or doubt from her normal consciousness to hold her back, she was now without worry.

It was never easy going back to Coochie Brake and once she got on the bus, and napped her human frailty brought her worst fears for her Auntie to the fore. There weren't fifty people living within hollering distance of Auntie's place in the swamp, but Beatri'd never been able to convince her to leave. Last time they spoke it became obvious to Beatri even a mule team wasn't going to drag her Auntie out of there.

This final ordeal exhausted her. They spent most hours in Auntie's sweltering shanty, the rooms buzzing with flies. Outside was the continuous call of God knows what in the moss-covered trees and from below in the muck which sustained them. While Beatri tried to reason with Auntie, both kept busy fanning and slapping bugs.

The heat and humidity were too much for human life. Her shack smelled like damp rot. The only way to dry laundry was when the sky was clear with several hours of sunshine. Even then, once dry, you had to pick the bugs off, lest their shells and stingers nick your flesh. The only good news was after a couple hours of sun the bugs died too before they could lay eggs in the fabric. Though Auntie and Beatri used to beat and brush the sheets, in time the linens became dotted with black specks of insect remains.

Those sunny days! They pinned you down worse than gravity. Most folks used moonshine, but any elixir that helped your soul bear it was welcome. A person had to find something in order to breathe the muck filled air each day and be able to block it out enough to sleep at night.

Beatri's Auntie knew she wouldn't be able to receive the proper care to live the longest and easiest life possible, but it didn't matter. She was staying put, committed to staying true to her first freed ancestor's staked claim.

To Beatri however, the land felt like a ball and chain. As dreamlike as her childhood might be in her memory, the present reality was more of a nightmare.

When Auntie Brake got feverish at night, Beatri pressed a wet cloth to her forehead and fanned her with her other. There were times when Beatri nodded off in the rocking chair, only to be awakened by Auntie's delirium and the sad slow, song they joyfully sang years before...

"Tingalayo,
Come little donkey come.
Tingalaaaayo,
Come little donkey come,
Me donkey fast, me donkey slow,
Me donkey come; me donkey go..."

Beatri's head rolled against the bus window, while rare tears rolled down her cheeks. She remembered the song which resonated so powerfully again. When a toddler, they'd owned a little donkey, one folks called an 'Easter Sunday Donkey', named Tingo. As Beatri grew older, she and Tingo became inseparable and of the same mind, to the point where she could lay prone, balanced on his back, her feet clutching his neck, with tufts of his mane between her toes. Her head rested beside his backbone and between his hips. She watched the sky while he moseyed about.

Even when she got taller, she could rest her head on Tingo's hips and rest her feet on his cross marked shoulders, rubbing her heels into the sides of his neck and give him the caresses he loved. Tingo would eat carrots right out of her teeth till his whiskers brushed her cheeks, but he wouldn't allow anyone else to saddle him up or ride him bareback. Yet Tingo allowed Beatri to roll around on his back like a kitten in the grass. Her Auntie insisted Tingo was Beatri's twin spirit. Schoolmates and friends said a girl shouldn't carry on in such a manner with a donkey, her Auntie told her to ignore the teasing.

"Keep him sacred in your heart and treat him like your brother."

A brother! Beatri would never know what a brother was, much less what it was like to have a mother or father. But Tingo was special, and she taught him to give the other kids rides. One day feeling too lazy to let a boy who stopped by ride on Tingo, the boy offered a dime, so she relented. This fortuitous exchange grew into a regular routine. Beatri began going around Coochie Brake on Sundays after church offering rides for spare coins the other kids collected. She saved the earnings in a small pouch her Auntie gave her and kept them in her keepsake box.

Growing up was just her, Auntie Brake and Tingo.

As it was now, it was just Beatri, and the process of gathering and delivering Auntie Brake's body to Alexandria and filing the paperwork to the state for the land proved spiritually exhausting. After the two-week tribulation ended, the only thing she felt she'd accomplished was she owned her Auntie's ashes and the urn to carry them. The paperwork from Auntie's passing seemed to grow daily, but never reached a final resolution.

She decided to leave and gathered up Auntie's few pieces of jewelry, her hunting knife, a vulture's claw, and the keepsake box containing Tingo's tail tuft and the remaining old coins in the keepsake pouch. She put it all in a burlap rice sack Auntie decorated with swamp feathers and shells and she used as a purse. Auntie had saved Tingo's tuft as a charm after he was shot and killed by a gator hunter after Beatri had moved to Mississippi. The hunter claimed it was a mistake but never offered anything in return or showed any remorse. Auntie claimed she got even with him, but Beatri never heard the whole story.

Auntie Brake beamed when she presented Beatri with the little wooden box containing Tingo's token legacy. Beatri couldn't bring herself to take it, instead hid it under her bed.

Now the box with Tingo's tuft and the bag of coins would go to New Orleans. She now had no doubt, his token and spirit would be her partner wherever her journey led. As for her estate, Beatri would have to finish working it out when the magistrate was done with the official business of county and state. She left the rest of Auntie's belongings in the shanty for any human and animal scavengers to work out on their own terms.

She headed back to New Orleans anxious to get on with her next chapter of life. She vowed to seek out the ones she feared most and turn herself over to them. It was time to let the Voudou Krewe teach her how to tame the power she held inside. She somehow understood she held inside a force stronger than any desire she ever felt or any doctrine she had ever followed to this point in her life.

"Cosmic Cowgirl"

I've been a Cosmic Cowboy,
and a hobo on the run.
Always looking for the Cosmic Cowgirl,
who doesn't care
about things in the past I've done.

I worked long, long hours
for low, low pay.
Quit my job when it got in the way,
but never quit the search for
a Cosmic Cowgirl.

She could be the one, my only one.
Not just a girl who takes
my loneliness away only when
my chips are piled high.
But one who'll stick with me
when all I own is my smile.

The rest of training after my first night at Vette's was more like I expected. I was told the lock down at the Hide Away Court was over, I could leave and stay where I wanted as long as I got to work on time. With barely enough time to get four hours of sleep and keep up with work, I decided to stay at the Hide Away for the time being. The weekly rate was less than the cost of gas to drive across Phoenix twice a day.

When told my sequester was over, the first person I wanted to see wasn't Olga, it was Cindy Masters. We'd had a promising encounter that left me wanting more, and something longer, but we hadn't really been together since I was shot. Though she did me a big favor when my arm wasn't mobile, delivering food and doing laundry before I started at Vettes. Unfortunately, she worked the whole time while I was recuperating as she was a lifer bar Manager. Now that I was mobile again and working, we still hadn't connected.

We played tag, never getting a chance to explore if we could turn those initial sparks into fire and know for certain if our attraction was real. I wanted to take up where we left off and thought about her often, while wondering whether she felt the same. In addition to our potential romance, it occurred to me she might have heard scuttle butt regarding Joey's business. She'd been in the restaurant scene a long time, and on the west side, where I had not.

After my shift, I was in my room alone, staring out Hide Away's dusty windows when I had an epiphany.

"Why don't I just drop in on Ms. Masters?"

After all, even if she had company, at least I had a valid reason to drop in. Hell, my Vette's stories might even impress her. So, I went by her bungalow, but she wasn't there. It was after eleven and I was pretty sure Macho's restaurant might be closed, but maybe she was still there. I decided to stop by and see. If she wasn't, I'd check her after-work watering holes. I wasn't sure how, but I was determined to track her down, and common sense doesn't rule the little head in such matters.

I pulled in Macho's past the decorative donkey cart in front and around to the dumpster near the kitchen exit and parked. I knocked on the back door, but no answer. Then I tried the buzzer for the intercom used for deliveries.

"Hello, anybody still working?"

"Arnie, I told you I put your backpack in your car!"

It sounded like Cindy yelling into a tin can.

"Hey, I just wanna get some chips and dip and a free side of advice."

Not my cleverest line.

"Oh, I thought you were uh, *hey*, who is this?"

"It's me, Max!"

"Max you've got horrible timing, I'm working on inventory tonight."

"Well, if you need a hand, I'd be happy to help."

I heard someone on the other side of the door undoing the deadbolt and deactivating the panic bar. I stepped back and she pushed open the door.

"Well Max, nice to see you out and about... *and* sober!"

She gave me a friendly hug but no lips.

"Ouch! I've been wanting to catch up with you since I started getting around again, now that I've got a job."

We instinctively clutched each other in a light embrace and looked into each other's eyes. What was there and how it made me feel scared me, and I think maybe scared her, too. We simultaneously broke eye contact, lifting our heads and hugging a little tighter before leaning back and looking each other over again.

"Cindy, you look great. You're a sight for sore eyes."

"I appreciate that Max, but I know better. It's been a long night and I'm beat."

"Well, I want to see you, so what can I do to help you out with inventory, then maybe we can get a chance to talk?"

"Well, hell, I guess there's some things you can count. Sure, follow me...", she took off through the kitchen.

"So, you still got the job, Max?"

"Yeah, well I had this connection, so they've got me at Vette's on the west side. I've been training..."

I had to cut my spiel short to keep up with her pace. We went through the kitchen and turned down a short hallway by the office, where she paused, reached inside, and grabbed a clipboard off the desk, then continued around the corner to a door standing half open. She stopped and pushed it the rest of the way open. She barely acknowledged my job announcement.

"Good deal, Max, now these two sheets are for the liquor room. It's pretty straight forward."

She flipped a few pages on the clipboard loudly with her thumb and forefinger. I stood in front of four shelves of liquor, bar mixes, papier-mache' piñatas and other junk. The two walls on my right were blocked by chin high stacks of boxes of 'Macho's Home Style Tortilla Chips'.

"Just count what's on the sheet, it's basically only stuff you can eat or drink."

She handed me the clipboard. It had a pencil taped to a string, tied to the hole in the metal clip at top of the board.

"It's the end of the quarter, so I'll be in the office crunching numbers. I already counted the kitchen, and bar, but haven't done this room yet.

"So, you want me to circle all the whole numbers, right?"

"Yea Max, it's inventory, goofball. You sure you got this?"

"Yeah! It's like riding a Harley, you never forget!"

I smiled at my witty remark, but she just rolled her eyes and turned away.

"Ok, Harley dude, but I don't wanna have to do any of it over, so ask me if there's anything you don't understand."

She turned her head to look back at me and raised "Know what I mean?" eyebrows for emphasis, then turned and quickly went back to the office. I was disappointed I didn't get more recognition for working the Vettes' job but was happy we'd sparked when we hugged.

I started counting the top shelf to my left, moving right. I had to grab the wooden supports and lift myself up and put my foot on the second shelf to pull myself up with a chin up to see items stored on the back of the top shelf. It was just like old times at Baxter's Bar, where I'd done inventory many times.

I missed that job but had walked away from it to travel and when I returned, instead of a job, I found a dead friend. The same friend and manager who'd covered my shifts while I was gone. And now I was enamored with the woman who'd been his best girl, Cindy. Whether she really liked me or was just lonely, only time would tell. If I thought about it too much, it was not a perfect situation, but it was what was happening.

So be it, things change.

Inventory, however, is always the same, you just count what's there.

At Machos that night I had a fun time perusing their collection of pinatas while doing pull ups to see the top shelf. I couldn't help but admire all the ornate Tequila bottles and my mouth watered surrounded by one of the biggest Tequila rosters anywhere. I kept hearing Johnny Winters' *Cheap Tequila* echo in my mind. Sure, none of this Agave was cheap, but I always smiled at the song's sentiment, *"Wake up and be happy..."*

I pushed the cases of chips apart so I could get a look at the shelves behind them. It took a couple minutes to forge a path, as the boxes were bulky and took up half the floor space. Luckily, they weren't heavy. While I was wedged in between two sets of boxes stacked three high I heard Cindy.

"How're you doing Max?"

She'd snuck up behind me. When I turned, she was standing with a big smile and a surprise. She held a shot glass and lime wedge in each hand and asked a question.

"Are you ready to sample some product?"

She glowed with a naughty smile, and an enticing shine in her eyes. A blue bottle with a skinny twelve-inch neck rested at her feet.

"Well, sure." I was not afraid.

In fact, I found her offer irresistible. I tossed the clipboard on the shelf and reached for the shot glass and lime. As soon as I did, she reached down for the bottle, uncorked it with her thumb and poured us both a messy shot. We clinked our glasses and threw the shots down.

"Whew, that's nice...", my throat had lit right up, and I barely got the words out.

"Yeah! It's pretty good, it's called 'Manny's Moonshine,' from a Tequileria down in Rocky Point."

She was close enough for me to reach her waist. All the yearning and dreaming I'd done for Cindy swelled in my chest. I put my left hand around her and leaned in.

"How 'bout we seal it with a kiss?"

"Oh! ...OK, Max."

She closed her eyes and presented her lips in an accommodating manner for a lady who usually took the lead. We shared a feverish kiss, which got longer, as after I thought it was almost over and had begun to break away, she pulled me in tighter. I sensed she held feelings for me the way she moaned while squeezing me. I also suspected it wasn't her first shot of Tequila that evening.

I remembered her back brace as soon as I felt it and sort of lost my balance. I didn't want to fall into her, so I held on tight, and shifted my weight to my heels, which caused us to both lose our balance. I fell backwards onto the cases of chips behind me and took her with me. The sounds of bending cardboard and crunching tortillas followed, as bags of chips inside the boxes popped as the cases collapsed.

Not so gracefully, she ended up on top of me, laughing a crazy laugh.

"Max, you are so clumsy, good thing these aren't cases of Margarita glasses."

She grabbed my shirt, pushing her hand inside through the buttons and began kissing me. Bags of chips from a box above us slid out, glancing off her back and the side of my head, and adding to the fun. Suddenly, it dawned on me we might not be in such a discreet situation.

"Hey, are we here all alone?"

"Yes, you got me all to yourself, Max. I told Arnie he could leave earlier, after he finished in the kitchen."

We disrobed to the sounds of crunching tortillas, rustling chip bags, and heavy breathing. Next thing you know our underwear was at our knees, and our shirts open. She slammed her fist to the floor as she adjusted her posture which popped open a bag of chips and added more salty corn aroma to the Tequila and the passion. Our hasty reunion was not a champagne celebration, it was a backroom cantina smashup and now that one-of-a-kind bag of chips being popped open sound will never be the same for me.

Just when I thought we were finished and began to button my shirt, she grabbed another bag and swatted me upside the head.

We weren't finished.

"You're not going anywhere! We still have to extend the inventory, but first we're gonna extend this party. I'm not done with you."

She grabbed another bottle of Tequila off the shelf and pulled out the cork with a giggle. It was a fancy ceramic jug and surely an expensive one, but we swigged straight from the bottle, and never looked for our shot glasses. Hopefully the 'Tequila Gods' forgave us. After all, we were having a special moment.

It was after three in the morning when we finally stood in the office to finish off the bottle and hang up the clipboard. Per her instructions, I cleaned up the liquor room, took the bags of crushed chips to the pantry and dumped them in a large plastic storage container. She had explained they used the crushed chips to make crust for their 'Loving Key Lime Pie', so I was not to throw them out. After she set the alarm, we stepped outside. She looked at me and giggled, then walked over to her van and looked at her reflection in the window and laughed.

"We both look like we've been dragged around the block in a drunken donkey cart!"

"You know what they say, making key lime crust keeps the doctor away, but there's no guarantee 'bout any donkey carts."

"Max, you know what, our pies always had love in the name but now with your help we got pies made with love…". Then she gave me an insane woman's smile and whispered, "…crazy love."

She gave me a hug and a peck, and we had a good laugh. We stood by the dumpster and let the night sink in and mellow our glow. Finally, my attraction to her stirred me to suggest we go somewhere to talk and maybe have a nightcap to share our feelings on where we thought this thing was going, and she laughed.

"Max, you think I'd go to last call looking like this. I got what we need right here."

She reached in her purse and pulled out a bottle of some fine Agave squeezings, then quickly dropped it back in. She reached over and grabbed my hand with her van's keys still in hers.

"I got limes at my place but I'm hungry, can you pick up some munchies on the way over? I'll take a rain check for a night out if you manage to stick around town long enough."

She gave me the ball is in your court now expression, then let go of my hand, stepped back over to the Macho's van and unlocked its door before adding, "No Mexican food! I've had enough beans today."

What? Did I say Mexican? No, she was taking the ball back into her court.

"Ok, sure, see you in a few minutes."

My mind sorted through the nearby food options available in the wee hours, and decided Panic City was the place. I pulled the Blazer door open, hopped in and waited for her to leave, then headed for late night take out. We would be eating greasy sliders on Hawaiian rolls with a side of Pimento cheese fries.

As it turned out, the desire to stoke our passion was stronger than my intentions to quiz her about the west side bar scene. So that's what happened, and it was worth the wait. Not so much the food, I don't really remember savoring the food. But I savored the memory of being in each other's arms twice in one night, and once even in a bed.

In the morning I scrambled to get back to the west side of town, barely making it to Vettes as fashionably late.

Cindy and I said hasty Tequila-tinged farewells. I had every intention of seeing her again as soon as possible and wanted to quiz her about Vettes' owners.

I wanted to keep our fire burning, I was young, but I'd already learned one thing about life and love.

"Cook while the skillet's hot."

Of course, I was in luck, there's another undeniable truth: The anticipation of being in your lover's arms will keep you going even when the previous night's Tequila bangs on your brain screaming "No!"

CHAPTER

13

Pollen, powder from the flowers.
    Everybody knows.
Heads are buzzing like bees
Smelling higher than a rose.

Share the wealth, share the pollen,
share the cane.
Feed the fever, let the candy
from the fountain
load into your brain.

I hurried into Vettes that night putting on my coat, still savoring the memory of Cindy and my hasty farewell kiss. I headed straight to the Employee Lounge and pulled open the 'Boppers' door and looked in the mirror and inhaled deeply. I could still taste Tequila, a tinge of Cindy's perfume and a dash of chips. I felt a need to freshen up, so I took off my coat, rolled up my sleeves and splashed cold water on my face. I hoped it would do the trick, wiping my face with a brown paper towel and looking at what was probably my best condition for the night, day after roughage.

I put my coat back on, shrugged my shoulders and stepped out, and stopped for a long gulp of water from the fountain. As I stepped away, there was a déjà vu zinging in the back of my brain, familiar, but something I couldn't quite put my finger on. The realization I should know what it was made the hair on my arms stand up, but I was moving too fast to give it further thought.

The evening turned out to be memorable for several reasons. First, for Happy Hour, we had a special guest. Yep, there he was, Sarge, better known as Sergeant Bob Growler of the Tempe Police Department. Even in his civvies, trying to be undercover, he was obvious. Accompanying him were a couple off duty officers I didn't recognize. Just the same, to me and everyone else in Vettes, their looks shouted middle-aged cops playing undercover cops. He and I'd gotten acquainted during Jerry Roseman's murder investigation, but I'd never met his companions. After I finished circulating and touching base with my Vettes' crew for the night, I approached Sarge and put out my welcoming hand.

"Sarge, how's it going? What brings you to the west side tonight?"

He recognized me, but immediately sent mixed signals.

"Oh hey, lemme see..."

He looked around to see if any of his group were listening, "...it's Max Wilson, right?"

"Come on, Sarge, don't act like we're strangers."

He pulled my extended hand to his chest and me with it. As he got me uncomfortably close, he leaned in to whisper in my ear.

"Listen, Max, I'm on duty here with some west side officers, so I can't really talk, ok? Just keep it casual and quick, no referencing our history, got it?"

He gave me a big smile as he pushed away and tried to act relaxed as if he were a Vettes' regular.

"We love your place here Mr. Wilson, thanks for having us."

He stared a hole through me as if he was trying to put certain words in my mouth, and I played along.

"Our pleasure sir, any time. Let me know if there's anything I can do for you and your group."

"Well now that you mention it, we'll take another round, thanks!"

"You got it!"

Of course, he wanted something for free!

I went over to the service well and asked who had the cops, that I wanted to get a round on the house for them.

Abby raised her hand.

"You mean the middle-aged beer bellies who keep staring at my pooper? They're mostly drinking soda with lime on a credit card..."

Then she moved in closer for just me to hear. "...But doing shots on the down low for cash."

She winked at me and wiggled her behind. I laughed with her, she had a way with words and could really hustle a sale.

"That'd be them Abbie, get'em a round on a separate ticket and I'll take care of it..., ...and Abbie, don't let'em get too mucked up in here."

"Ok, Max but *you* better keep an eye on'em, too."

"Oh, don't worry, I will."

It wasn't half an hour later when Sarge snuck up behind me at the DJ booth while *Rescue Me* played. I was strutting along clapping to the beat when I heard his distinctive growl.

"Pssst, Max, meet me out back at the black Ford Explorer with the silver ski rack in ten minutes. Don't turn around! Just stop and nod if you got it."

I followed his instructions, cruising past my Vette's door staff on the way out, announcing I was doing a perimeter check, and carrying a clipboard to look official. It was cool to think he might need my help with his investigation. When I found his Explorer, he was seated inside on the driver's side, his visor down to hide his face. He pushed the passenger door open as I approached.

"Well, well Max, you're in the big time now working at Vette's. It's like you have a real job, isn't it?"

"Gee Sarge, thanks, I guess. You know, I might just surprise you sometimes with my talent."

"Max you never fail to surprise me, but mainly it's how you manage to stay out of jail."

He let out a short laugh.

"Well, it's not like you haven't tried."

I wasn't gonna let him forget it either because he had. I'd come to see him during the Jerry Roseman investigation and his front desk locked me up overnight. He must have approved, though he never confessed. No matter whether he approved it or not, he enjoyed it. Me, not so much.

"Hey, sorry about that, not sure how it happened but you probably deserved it. Anyhow, you're ok by me now. We all right?

I just nodded. What could I say?

He continued, not waiting for me to speak.

"Look, I'm here on official business. There might be a tie in with one of your regulars at Vettes. I can't tell you too much, and don't breathe a word of this, but I wanted you to know why I'm here. Look, if you see or hear something, I'd be forever grateful. Those other lunks I'm with are from other jurisdictions with the same problem, but with the ASU campus in Tempe, I need to be the first one to get on top of this. If one of them breaks it first, well, it'll make my work hell."

"I don't understand Sarge..."

His stern expression didn't change one iota, so I tried again.

"Well, what's going on?"

"Again, Max this is strictly police business, so don't go blabbing. There are weird incidents being called in and a couple drug related deaths. They seemed to be connected to some street drug called Huggy. At first, it was a small problem, you know, only showing up at overnight dances in the desert and off campus after hours' bars. Now it's a priority because it's showing up all over the place and in such large quantities, well...".

He shook his head.

"...It's very dangerous, being pushed all over Phoenix. We haven't figured out where it's coming from or who's behind it. Damn shit went statewide real fast. Whoever they are, they're ambitious suppliers, it's a no-nonsense operation, making big bucks now. And Max, whoever's behind it is ruthless. We consider them very dangerous."

"Why Vettes? This is an older crowd, we got a dress code, an age limit, and we don't play any of the music like at the parties you mentioned, we –"

He cut me off.

"Look, I wish I could tell you more. We had a few leads that brought us here, that's all I can say. There are other places we'll have to check out, but right now we think one of the people involved with the source of this Huggy, frequents Vettes."

He smelled of Vodka, but he was concerned about the case. He wasn't just blowing smoke. Of course, I should have guessed before I asked, he wasn't really interested in my questions.

"So, what should I be looking for? A man or a woman? You have any other clues you can tell me?"

"Max! *You're* not looking for anything! We didn't have this conversation! Listen, if you see or hear something about Huggy from a customer, cocktail waitress or *anyone*, just listen to what's said, and get in touch with me right away. Don't start asking a lot of questions like you know anything..."

He shook his head like he might have made a mistake talking to me, "...cuz you don't! Just get in touch. I gotta go back inside."

"Ok Sarge, I just wanna help is all. Let me know—"

"Don't worry I will, and hey, thanks for the drinks. We gotta get out of the vehicle. You go first, I'll be in shortly."

He flashed his lights after I got out and held up my clipboard, opened the door back up and handed it to me shaking his head.

"I hope you're better at watching the company's booze than their clipboards."

What could I say to that? I just muttered to myself and shook my head. I walked around the rest of the building and tried to shake off my frustration at being Sarge's whipping boy again and scribbled on my clipboard as I looked at the walls.

That wasn't the only surprise though.

Once inside, I received a call from my running buddy Crazy Eddie over in Tempe, whose research helped me considerably during my Atlanta trip on the previous case. When the call came in, I was behind the bar but rushed back to the office and shut the door to pick up. I told Eddie what transpired since starting at Vettes. Eddie was familiar with Huggy by name but hadn't experienced the effects. He said he'd research it on his end. He told me the Blue Phantom Fender guitar I'd swapped him for a cash advance was in good shape, full of blues and birdcalls.

It made me yearn for the feel of it in my hands. Any axe I could get my hands on would have been welcome, and I wondered again why I hadn't heard back from Olga. While we talked, he did some internet research for me about the Olga, aka Betty Bongos. He told me she'd won a Beale Street Blues Guitar competition, and I should take her musicianship seriously.

Wow, who'd a thunk it? I mean she said she was a guitar slinger but, hey, people say all kinds of things.

I told him I'd try to drop by and see him before leaving Arizona. I told him the rumor I'd be transferred to a different Vettes after training. Then Katy Kitts started tapping on the office window, so I let Eddie go. It had been good to talk to him, he always had my back. He was really the only person I knew who knew how to use a computer for meaningful research.

Dean called toward the end of the night. Straight away he told me to go to the office. When I picked up in the office, he told me the news.

"You're headed to Memphis tomorrow!"

"What? You're kidding me."

"Heh-heh, no brother, you going to Mempho-town. You gotta straighten up that bunch of wild ass Delta girls, heh-heh."

He was using his weird obnoxious Amos'N Andy voice.

"Well, I've always wanted to go there, but this is kinda sudden."

"It almost always is, Max, my boy. Now make sure you don't let them give you a big send off at the club. You know how my crew likes any excuse to party. I want you to clean up the joint like a Marine barracks inspection is coming in the morning, got it?"

Shit, there were ball busters everywhere I turn!

"Sure Dean, you got it, thanks for everything."

"Ok, good, because there will be inspection tomorrow, this is not an idle threat! Now, go to my desk and look in the filing cabinet on the right. In the bottom drawer there's a file 'Transfer Travel.' Pull it out and make a copy of the sheet labeled 'Manager Flights.' There's a number for booking flights and you need to call first thing in the morning, and they'll get you on a plane to Memphis. Oh, heh-heh, you better pack your bag before you call, they might put you on a plane within an hour, heh-heh."

He was snorting and laughing at the same time.

"Ok, I got it. Anything else?"

"Well, put everything in the file back when you're done. And don't forget to pack some condoms with your toothbrush, you don't wanna end up in a shotgun wedding while you're there. Hah, hah, hah, heh-heh!"

"Pretty funny, Dean, don't worry, I'll be careful."

"Well Max, and another thing, stay out of West Memphis after dark if you know what's good for you. They got different rules and too many truck stops. You won't stand a chance there, ain't nothing there you need anyhow, take it from me, heh-heh."

"I'll try to remember that."

As I was digging out the file, I accidently set several other papers in the Manager Flights file into the copier feed. Copies printed of all the pages, and when I saw what happened, I just grabbed the whole stack of copies and folded them in half without looking. Then I took them all and left them in my Blazer so I wouldn't forget to take the ones I needed.

Dean was right to warn me about the staff's tendency to party. As I started the rounds with staff throughout the club and work through last call, they started in on me.

"Hey, Max are we doing some bon voyage shots after we close?"

"You gonna take your farewell fifth with you or are you gonna share it with us?"

And so on, till I finally laid it down for them.

"Look, Dean's doing an inspection, so we ain't doing no partying in Vettes tonight, ok?"

But it turned out I couldn't leave it at that. After another long thirst-quenching drink at the employee fountain during deposits, I wiped my mouth across my sleeve and looked over the remaining crew waiting their turn. They'd been good to me so far and now they put off an air of disappointment.

"Look, if y'all have any suggestions for anywhere else to party after work, I'm game."

I was starting to feel a little high-headed and maybe up for some boogie time.

"All right Max!"

There were some 'Woo-Hoos' from the lounge bathrooms too.

"Hey, we can do Freddy's Dive In. It's in Tempe behind Panic City! They got Raidyo Luv playing tonight, and they're outta sight. Katy knows the bouncer if we need to get in. Max, can you bring a bottle?"

Marni looked at me with sad puppy dog eyes. I remembered how Murray told me during training we could requisition a bottle for 'Emergency Manager afterhours use'. So why not? Since I couldn't bear any more Tequila so soon after inventory with Cindy, I grabbed a bottle of Ketel One. I did a spontaneous 360 on my heels and scanned the liquor room shelves and decided to grab a bottle of Jager, just for party insurance. You never know how thirsty the crew might be, and from what I'd heard, Raidyo Luv was quite the show.

They cleaned Vettes with a feverish urgency I'd never seen before. I even inspected their work with white gloves Dean kept in his office lock box. I was feeling a buzz and wanted to give them show. I ran my fingers underneath the bar top, behind the tea machines, along the soda gun hose, and on top of the frozen drink dispensers. I pulled out the sliding doors from the tops of the reach ins and ran my index finger along the plastic edges. All tricks I'd been shown by Dean himself. I had no luck finding cleaning fouls, as they'd done a great job. Just to keep the upper hand, I took all the cocktail trays out of their holding rack and ran a finger around the cork. A little smudge of Kahlua stained my fingertip.

"Aha!"

I looked up at Jocko who represented the bartenders on the final walk through with me.

"C'mon Max you did more checks than anyone. What the hell? We busted ass, and you're gonna pass inspection tomorrow with flying colors. We did you righteous, man. It's better than we ever do Murray. Come on..."

Jocko seemed genuinely hurt by the smudge I found.

"All right, all right, I know."

I relented. They had cleaned spectacularly, but I didn't want them thinking since I was a rookie who'd shown his ass on the dance floor a few times and still stumbled through dance routines, they could take advantage of me. I wanted to show them I could bust them if I really wanted to and I made my point, so it was time to go.

"Let's hit Freddy's, I got the hooch."

I reached behind the bar and grabbed the Ketel One and Jaeger and held them up for show. They hooted and hollered their approval.

"You ain't half bad, Max, no matter what Dean says!"

Boy, they really know how to hurt a guy even when they salute him.

"Ok, who's driving me to this hoedown?"

I wasn't about to drive across town, and I knew it was hard to find a place to park near Freddy's in downtown Tempe, I figured, 'I have the booze, I get to ride shotgun'.

Katy and I rode with Jocko and after a thirty-minute drive and several swigs of Jager, we pulled up in the alley behind Panic City. Jocko told me to get out, he'd park, and make sure his name was on the guest list.

Katy got out and poked me in the ribs.

"What're you looking for Max?"

"Well, Freddy's for one, where the hell is it? I only see a dumpster and some trash cans."

"Over here."

The rest of the group had arrived and was headed to the other side of the dumpster. There was a lone blue light bulb over a brick arch with a sketchy sign painted in glowing colors above the door: 'Freddy's Dive In'. Right away, a large man, steroid muscles rippling beneath his wife beater, stepped out to receive the hugs and adoration of the Vettes' girls. He acknowledged them with stiff snuggles of his own and let them in, smiling at each as they passed. His smile turned to a frown when I walked up with bottles in my hands.

"What's your problem dude?"

He posed his query as he turned away and surveyed the alley.

"I'm not trying to be a problem, man, I'm trying to bring you some business."

He'd grabbed a brown bag out of a box behind him and stuck it in my face then blocked my view of the entrance.

"Well, you gotta have your booze in a bag, it's the law. Here you go, bag it up, old man."

So, I did. He tilted his shaved dome at me and gave me the sideways stink eye.

"Good thing you got some hotties with you, man. Try and keep it cool inside, all right? I don't wanna get no shit for letting you in."

"I'll try to behave, big fella."

I gave him a wink which got a frown and a pissed squint. I was starting to feel a little tilt-a-whirly and dipped inside without starting any more scintillating conversation with my host. I really needed a drink.

Inside we entered a descending hallway in the revived tunnel system dug by previous settlements of Native American tribes, shopkeepers, outlaws and bootleggers who once conducted their affairs beneath Tempe's downtown. Once upon a time the local sheriff used these hidden holds to keep prisoners and corpses from the public, whether they be lynch mobs full of blood lust, or loved ones seeking their guest of honor for a family burial. These underground cavities were now forgotten by most until recent Downtown renovations re-revealed their existence.

The hallway entrance had been a chute, designed for a quick stash or hideaway into the underground bunker. When we got to the bottom, we entered a large chamber where the main bar was. We stopped and looked over the beverage selection, when a trench coat with a head of slicked back hair and garish eye make-up approached. I was still getting my bearings when he introduced himself.

"Will Campen. Glad to meet you, Max."

I recognized the face from somewhere. He reminded me of a character who frequented The Brash Can nightclub where I'd previously worked.

"Hey, aren't you the same Will who came to The Brash Can every Sunday night?"

I waved my hands over my shirt, and around my head to reference his memorable 'do and wardrobe.

"That's me, the one and only."

I *had* met him before. In those days he wore a three-piece Italian suit with his hair blown out like a surfer and dark blue glasses, even at night.

"You don't look the same."

He'd undergone an amazing transformation since our last encounter. Maybe it was a daily occurrence.

"I wear a different hat for different scenes, my man. Tonight, my amazing band Raidyo Luv is gonna make magic music for your enjoyment."

"Oh, this isn't your place? You're not in charge here?"

"Hell no, but I'm flattered. I just rent the place out for artists I'm promoting. Freddy probably won't show tonight, but you never know. If you need anything just ask Freida, she'll take care of you."

He pointed to a tall blonde behind the bar in a strained black bustier and a pin-curl crew cut, with visible high main-tenance attitude. I saw a heart tattoo on her neck from across the room, but my guess was most people didn't get past her weaponized chest.

"Ok, Will, you're the man. I will, thanks. I look forward to being amazed."

The Vettes crew gathered at a few tables and did some shots while the place filled up. I was antsy. Knowing I'd be flying out the next day, my pulse was racing from booze and the weird sensation that kept hanging on. I didn't want to mess up my departure, but I wanted to pay tribute to Vettes' dedicated party animals. They'd tried hard to impress me and wanted to give me a proper send-off. I felt nervous and jumped up to cir-culate. Maybe there were others here I'd recognize. I noticed a dark hallway curving away from the main room through an unmarked doorway. Moving forward I noticed a wavering light in a smaller chamber. I approached and heard excited whispers behind the door. I moved carefully, sticking my head around the door just enough to snoop. I heard someone plead-ing.

"What's she saying?"

"She wants a Margarita and a straw."

I recognized Will's voice. From where I stood, I made out Will with a younger dude sporting a green mohawk and between them was a girl in a weird upright stance, pink feathered starbursts of hair on her head and duct tape over her mouth. It was not well lit, but I could tell her upper arms were bound behind her back and she was tied to a pipe coming from the wall. An odd arrangement. Her forearms were extended, and her hands free, holding what seemed to be an Etch-a-Sketch. Her fingers worked the knobs while Will leaned over the screen and studied it, a loving hand resting on her shoulder.

Quite a scene! I stepped back for a better angle and sharpened my gaze. I realized the girl wasn't being held captive, regardless of the odd situation. I didn't really know what to make of it, so I watched and listened, trying to be a sponge.

She wore a modest bikini and from neck down was wrapped in shiny pink plastic. Her legs were attached to the pipe too. She was tied up but complicit. When the green mohawk guy returned with a fishbowl sized Margarita and a straw, she carefully handed Will the Etch-a-Sketch. With practiced expertise he used a thin blade to carve a small hole in the duct tape over her mouth and held up the drink. She lowered her head, pushed the hole over the straw, and proceeded to drain the colossal Margarita faster than I can down a shot. Once gone, she raised her eyebrows up and down repeatedly. Will sent the green mohawk to get another.

I heard a woman's voice come through the cavernous hallway on the PA.

"Now, Ladies and Gentlemen, from the depths of the Pima canal system, beneath the earth's molten core…, the one and only Raidyo Luv!"

Seems band members were already in the main room and started dabbling in random arpeggios. Will waited for his willing captive to finish her second Margarita, then reached behind her and removed her restraints. Once loose, he reached up and cradled her head in his hands. She put her hands over his, and he quickly ripped the duct tape off her mouth. Her eyes ballooned and her body shook but he quickly covered her mouth with a bandana. The two collapsed into a couch against the wall as she shuddered to hold back a scream.

Will stared in her eyes.

"Are you ready?"

She nodded and held out her hand in which he placed a small vial. She promptly twisted off the cap, shook it, and shook it into her mouth. Closing her eyes after the powder fell, she pushed the vial back into Will's hand with a smile and a wink.

"Huggies and kissies, my lovely. Time to jam!"

Will shook a little of the vial into his hand and licked his palm. He helped her up then strategically tore at her plastic wrapping till it hung in tattered trails. Before disappearing, Will pulled off a few excess pieces, as she stretched. Finished, his hands on his hips, he smiled adoringly as she exited the room, leaving a fluttering trail of cotton candy-colored tatters in her wake, and slipping through the door to join her band.

I was intrigued, and full of questions, but decided not to confront Will, and instead headed to the main room to catch the show. My brain searched a lifetime of experience for a point of reference to what I witnessed but there was nothing like it. For some reason the scenario reminded me of *Love Potion #9,* and its reference to the kitchen sink concoction, but this scene was more unbelievable than any sixties ditty.

Raidyo Luv's band had noodled around while I was witnessing their singer's release from her pink cocoon, but as soon as she joined them, they dove into a highly charged electric techno-funk that simmered and popped with frenetic energy. It reminded me of a Tangerine Dream mash up with Sly & The Family Stone. As she jostled among her bandmates, they continued into a heavier beat, and they put on quite a show.

We could have been at the Ritz in New York City or the Roxy in LA, but we weren't, we were in a downstairs back alley underground hide out turned rave dungeon in Tempe, Arizona. It didn't make sense it was happening, but it blew our minds anyway.

She had an incredible high falsetto; Yoko Ono-like screams paired with guttural exhortations reminiscent of Nina Hagen, soaring over the bands driven, funkified jams. We were transported into her unique musical universe; magical but always flirting with danger, like a thrill ride at the carnival hastily reopened after a crash closed it down. We wanted to go on this fun ride with her, but once it started, weren't sure if it was a good idea to stay on board. It's the only way I can describe the dicey element of chance her performance raised in real time in our collective psyche.

Where are these musicians now? Who knows? This type of sound would be polished and taken to new heights by artists like Nikka Costa, Bush and later even Prince at a much more refined level.

Years after, I spoke to Will. He told me Raydio Love had damaged her vocal cords and needed surgery. His story was instead of taking time off until fully healed, she wanted to keep playing, though she'd been warned to stop. So, she created a unique self-care program. She stopped singing *and* talking altogether, except for the onstage performances. The bit with the gag and the Etch-a-Sketch was her idea to keep her from using her voice. He claimed she liked being tied up and got a rush from being released when time came to take the stage. I had to wonder if there was more to it than he told but never heard otherwise.

My state of mind began to wobble during the show, spurred on by the band as they transported me into the unknown. I decided I should get fresh air and went to the bar to check in with Frieda to make sure I'd get back in without a hassle from Mr. Steroid at the door.

"Freida, you don't know me, my name is Max and Will said you're the one to talk to if I need anything."

"Hi, Max who I don't know," she responded while twisting off a bottle cap.

"Yeah, unh, hello. Hey, I'm gonna step out for a minute and wanted to make sure I'm good to get back in."

She looked over at our group and nodded.

"If you're going out to get high, it's better to use the john."

"No, I'm good, just wanted to check on my car."

A little white lie. As I climbed the ramp to the door, I wondered what the ghosts in this place could tell me. Surely there were some stranger-than-fiction tales from its past. Even without hearing from any ghosts my mind was fuzzy. Little gusts zipped around and through me, like on South Mountain with the Bar Belles.

It occurred to me, "Wasn't this teasing déjà vu the same as the evening at South Mountain? Could this be the same noxious ingredient that makes this happen to me at work?"

It dawned on me it was likely true, at least to some degree. I took a minute to consider, have I done permanent damage to my brain? Was there something still in my blood from that night? Or had something new been added? Was I missing something critical that was happening right in front of me?

I felt good about my training and in general about the job at Vettes. I mean I wasn't gonna make a career out of it, but it was a good way to get back on my feet and help a friend. I wasn't overjoyed at having so many responsibilities with so many tasks to perform at work, but the old tunes Vettes played were fun and so was the dancing. Still, it was no substitute for a good live jam or working all night sculpting a new tune.

I realized I'd been pacing the alley with my hands in my pockets of my coat, and perhaps this night wasn't the time to solve the ruminations percolating in my brain. I would be in Memphis the very next day. I best enjoy the send-off but cut it short and get safely back to my pad.

When I got back to Freddy's entrance there was Freida talking to the cops. They had their backs to her, leaning into one another and whispering. As I got closer, I saw how one of her areolas was peaking above her bustier and realized the officers were struggling with the appropriate tact to take to correct her wardrobe malfunction. She seemed oblivious to the nip slip and lit a cigarette, exhaling into the night air above the men in blue while they exhibited obvious consternation.

Instead of introducing myself I decided to dive right in.

"Hello gentlemen, can I help anybody with anything?"

The cop closest to me turned nose to nose with me while Freida looked on with more amusement than surprise.

"We're gonna have to close Freddy's down for the night if we can't get some compliance."

He must have been the officer in charge. I immediately moved towards Freida.

"Let me help you out here, OK?"

She gave me the 'What have you got to do with this?' look, but I persisted.

"May I?"

I reached past the cop closest to her in spite of her resistance and grabbed her bustier.

"Hey, wait a minute..."

Her response was to lift a knee to my groin, but I shifted to the side and gave a quick tug to her bustier, pulling it up over the offending nipple, and whispered in her ear.

"Forgive me for being so forward before properly introducing myself to your guests, my dear."

She shook her head.

"Oh, is that it? These damn uptight cops!" She gave me an appreciative wiggle and glance.

"Thanks, m'love."

Disaster averted. She quickly relaxed and began teasing the concerned visitors.

"Officers, I do apologize. I'll go back inside and double check my attire. But while I'm there, does anyone need a soda or a tamale, or anything stronger?"

She let the words hang in the air as she looked over the men in blue. She gave a brief shoulder shake just to show she'd complied to their wardrobe concerns and the city's moral standards. One of the officers' walkie-talkies started squawking, and they all stiffened up, taking on serious looks of concern, like the RCA Victor dog on alert. Finally, the one who'd threatened the closure spoke up.

"Thanks for the offer, young lady, we will be back to take you up on that some other time, we got to get going right now."

The rest of the night was me treading water trying not to drown or get any higher. After our party started scattering into the night I pleaded with Jocko, and he delivered me back to the Vettes west side parking lot. My good fortune got me to the Hide Away in my Blazer.

That night my dreams were filled with images which didn't make sense. Screeching bats swooped into tunnels, then crumbled into rainbow-tinted white powder, falling and tumbling in snowflake shapes, only visible a moment before dissolving into swirling pools where octopi hovered in place. All the while cheerleaders danced on the dock pilings above the water.

I tossed and turned and finally opened my eyes. I was desperate to halt the cinematic madness and got on the floor and prayed for a safe journey to dreamland that night and the next day to the home of the blues. A quiet calm surrounded me, and I crawled back into bed, slowly closing my eyes. Far off in the distance, barely audible, I could hear the Cicadas' buzz. Then like a balm for the soul, Coyote howls layered a woeful lament on top of the cicadas.

As I drifted off, the cosmos unfurled and my dreamscape welcomed the sound of a six string twelve-bar blues, sweetly soothing the pain of my restless night. While sorrowful cries of guitar licks and bending notes of joy blended together, my mind's eye bore witness to neon signs reflecting off a giant Fender Stratocaster, its neck caressed beneath a sky of billowing clouds by calloused and blistered hands.

The image and song brought solace somehow and allowed me a deep sleep. The old sweet song soared in my soul. The melody was new to me, but not to countless souls who'd scaled the progressions over and over, summoning their own version of its call. This celebration was how men and women found re-lief for their restless spirit while they struggled and toiled in the Delta.

Over the years it's lament had beckoned many in much the same way.

It spoke to the fiber of my soul.

"Can you feel my power in your hungry heart?

Memphis waits for you."

S ugartoes.
  Riding out the night,
on Sugartoes.

Bouncing till the buzzer goes,
dancing on our Sugartoes.
Dance heavy, dance light,
doesn't matter,
as long as the current flows.
Sugartoes.

Twirl it till the buzzer blows,
Dancing in your dancing clothes.
Fancy steps will follow,
dancing on those Sugartoes.

Shame on those Sugartoes!
I'm not talking about the dancing life,
I'm talking about the appetite.
So hard to control them Sugartoes!

Almost a year before Carter Benson's body landed on the interstate, Pearlie sat in the Candy Canes' dressing room. She looked at her side view as she applied her make up for her spotlight dance. She was confident she was an attractive full-grown woman, no longer that petite girl people considered 'cute'. She got second looks from men *and* women now. She was small-boned, blessed with a beautiful facial structure and possessed a tawny tone like her sister Angorra, whom she called Angie.

Pearlie knew she'd end up shorter than Angie, and with wider hips but decided it was an advantage. In fact, she'd heard her sister's friends joke how Angie's slim hips made her look like a boy.

"She's lucky her butt sticks out so much."

It was true about Angie's hips, and her butt stood out nicely when viewed from the side. She'd quickly learned to show it off. Otherwise, she might not get a second look. Pearlie wouldn't have that problem. She had a round butt, and it stuck out all over. The men noticed.

Angie often emphasized to Pearlie to never underestimate the power of their family heritage and gave her an important tip while she matured into a woman.

"You're a high-spirited redbone, it runs in our blood. Don't you ever forget it."

Pearlie still remembers the day she found out she had a sister. It was before she started school. Ever since, Pearlie believed Angie was different than anyone else she would ever meet. A stubborn independent spirit, Angie went out of her way to stay connected during Pearlie's early school years. As Pearlie grew older, she learned about the life Angie led. It was never really hidden from her, but when Pearlie took on responsibilities of her own, she grasped the challenges Angie's lifestyle created day-to-day.

Her older sister often said, "I gotta make up for lost time with my little sister, so you're always welcome to hang with me."

Angie mellowed as time went on, but they were apart for longer periods of time. As Pearlie got to middle school, Angie began to lean more towards Mawmaw's rules. When Pearlie had disagreements with Mawmaw, Angie suddenly began siding with Mawmaw.

In her teen years, Pearlie became increasingly uptight, her inner voice bolder. She wanted things in her life in her own way and in her control. In time she learned she had a shorter, quicker temper than her sister and unlike Angie, she liked to follow a schedule. She didn't have the patience for the back and forth of running around without a plan.

She didn't understand Angie's choice to be on call for so many different jobs and people. Pearlie loved and respected her sister. She was proud how she kept her head held high no matter what anyone said, amazed Angie always had energy to do whatever she needed to do to make ends meet.

Mawmaw would not have approved, but Angie helped her get set up in her apartment after she moved out from Mawmaw, and showed Pearlie the ropes of living alone.

But in time, Pearlie wanted independence from Angie too. She studied herself in the mirror now and considered their differences. She didn't have Angie's energy to go-go-go all the time, and she could only relax when alone. She preferred the company of her dog, Able, and her cat, Cain, to her coworkers. She had only a few friends she'd hang out with and liked it that way. Pearlie liked to dance and preferred to strip at a reputable club or as a concert stage Go-Go dancer. She got jobs doing both.

That night she danced at Candy Canes near the Memphis airport as on most weekend nights.

As she got ready, she applied toner to her stomach and thighs and gave herself an approving look. She stuck out a stern bottom lip, and reflected on how she learned not to fall for the bogus party offers from those promoters anymore.

"All party favors will be provided and maybe tips, too."

Yeah, right.

They still tried pitches to get her interested, but she'd had enough. Why spend her time fighting off rude, doped up creeps from tours? They just wanted sex. She didn't care anything about being a groupie or partying the night away with the girls who were into that. She certainly wasn't into any guy who thought he was cool just because he got backstage.

Things were going fine until her awful accident. She had suffered injuries to her eyes and ears and believed the incident caused permanent damage. So far, no doctor or healer she'd visited had been able to fix how her eyes saw the world and ears heard sound. She was resigned to her situation but didn't believe she had to be ok with it.

It happened after she'd moved out of Mawmaw's and was unable to afford her own place, so she stayed with Angie in Memphis. She was brand new to the dancer stripper scene and party girls for hire. Angie had invited her along for what would be Pearlie's second decent paying job. Angie told her it was more involved than the first gig, but still easy. It didn't matter to Pearlie, first time all she had to do was pop out of a cake on the side of a helipad at a Corporate Office Airport for in a special welcoming party for a Chinese investor. They put Pearlie in a giant wooden cake and wheeled her out on the runway.

Dressed as a Sexy Lady Cop she'd held a boom box on top of the small platform inside the cake. When the cake stopped rolling, she heard the signal, and pushed open the top. She set down her boom box, raised her hands above her head and carefully stepped onto the dance platform. As the boom box played, she did the *YMCA* dance to the glee of the visiting entourage.

Angie and other girls handled the after party at the visitors' hotel suite that night. Angie told her about it when offering the runway gig.

"You're still a little green for the hotel party, baby, but you can make a little cash when they land out on the runway."

It was easy and Pearlie pocketed two hundred bucks. Pearlie never asked Angie what she and the other girls made for the night, but she knew Angie well enough. It would've been a lot more money, and a lot more other stuff probably happened Pearlie didn't want to be part of. So, as far as she was concerned it worked out fine for her.

The night she got hurt was different.

Described as a surprise birthday party for Louis Etrusco and his entourage, it was sponsored by Larry, Louis' brother. Pearlie was told the guys flew into town exclusively for the party and requested five girls to strip and a girl for a cake dance. It would take place at a private clubhouse owned by Candy Canes.

Angie and the other girls had previously worked parties at the clubhouse, saying it was in a fancy apartment complex a couple blocks from Candy Canes. No pool, but some rooms had Jacuzzis, and there was a large wet bar in the clubhouse with glass doors overlooking a large patio bar playground. The eight bedrooms in the rear of the clubhouse lined a single hallway set up like a small dormitory.

Pearlie and the girls met Harry at Candy Canes. Harry was the chaperone, bouncer, and supervisor for the night. He explained the evening's party plan while driving. The girls were to get in their outfits and stay in the bedrooms and wait for his signal after he returned with the guests.

Black Velvet, a favorite song of Louis, would be the signal to dance out to the main room. If they weren't prompt, Harry would be pissed. If anyone missed their cue he would be pissed, and it would cost them part of their cut.

The cake was on the patio, out of view, with the curtains drawn until the cake dance for Louis. Pearlie was to get in the cake as soon as the girls got their *Black Velvet* cue.

The girls would strut their stuff for a few songs and when Bar Kays' *Rump Shaker* started, they would open the curtains. Harry said there would be party games and fireworks. After Pearlie heard the plan, she decided to get in the cake as soon she could. She knew from the last gig; she could see through its cracks when she got inside. She didn't plan to visit the Jacuzzi rooms where girls earned extra money, and Angie told her she didn't *have to* do anything else at all. In fact, some girls would probably just dance in the main room for extra tip money.

Pearlie knew some girls would take advantage of the back rooms, but she trusted Angie it would be a safe gig, and also Harry was there. As wild as these parties were, some guys just hung out and got drunk, buying table dances, same as at the club. So, she'd be able to make money doing the same thing she always did.

Pearlie asked Angie to explain everything before she agreed to the gig, and Angie let her know Harry's position.

"Well, Harry's ok if you get an offer and you want to take it, because he gets a cut of our action, so best price yourself accordingly but he'll stand by you if you don't want to."

Turned out she never got a chance to make that decision…

After Harry left to pick up the partiers the girls took advantage of the open bar and did shots. They grabbed a bottle of Spiced Rum and moved into the largest Jacuzzi room. They worked on their make-up, compared outfits and took turns passing the bottle around. One girl lit a joint and saying to blow the smoke up the bathroom ceiling fan.

Angie had to laugh, "Yeah, like one of these hoods gonna care if you been getting high? We be lucky they ain't already all full of blow when they get here. If you're smart, you best think about where you gonna hide your stash *and* your money, cuz they likely try to steal both."

The girls murmured their consent and got serious about getting ready. That's when Pearlie felt the first twinge of uncertainty. She clutched her treasured MC Sha-Rock picture bag, determined she wasn't going to let it out of her sight thinking how at Candy Cane's she had a locker and lots of bouncers around to protect a girl's stuff.

When music started, the girls did one last primp, doused their cigarettes, checked the mirror for close ups, and turned to admire their butts. Pearlie gathered her purse and headed to the patio. She climbed up the side of the cake and into the open hatch. She stayed halfway in facing the drawn curtains inside.

As it turned out, Harry showed up with a much larger group than predicted. There were almost two dozen guys and additional girls. The clubhouse sounded chaotic from the moment they arrived. Pearlie smoked a Kool, looked up at the night sky, and enjoyed a slight breeze as she waited for her cue before she ducked down inside.

At the proper time, she popped out of the cake no problem. She didn't have to deal with a boom box, since the music came from the patio speakers. She started her dance slowly rising one step at a time, teasingly stripping off her Cop outfit down to her string bikini.

Beforehand she'd been told to climb down for a lap dance with Louis. As it turned out, Louis was sitting by the cake as planned, but there were already two girls with him she didn't know. Each one rode a leg like a horse, facing him and bouncing around. They were oblivious, their backs facing Pearlie and holding Louis full attention. She figured they were all coked out of their minds. The girls leaned into Louis, their hands in his shirt as they kissed his neck.

Louis wasn't waiting for Pearlie's lap dance.

However, there were other guys behind him at the patio bar who saluted and hooted, so she continued her dance on the top step. When they beckoned her to the bar, she decided if she wanted to make any extra dough she might as well try them. No additional tip would be coming from Louis anytime soon. She ducked down to get her bag, but as luck would have it she inadvertently knocked it off its perch.

She squatted, saw it wedged between boards in the bottom section of the cake and decided she better retrieve it before she got out. To reach it she lay on her stomach and bent her legs at the knees supporting her feet against the top. Then she was able to reach down through the beams for the purse with one hand while holding onto the ladder with the other.

While in this position, she heard fireworks. She gripped her bag and carefully lifted it towards her chin but was startled by an explosion next to the cake and lost her grip. Luckily the purse didn't fall all the way to the bottom, instead it caught on a closer beam.

She reached again and easily nabbed it.

"Damn, this shit's starting to be work!"

Once her bag was in hand, she rose on all fours. That's when the cake shook violently, and there was shouting and laughter on the outside right next to her head. She clutched her purse to her side and let out her breath.

"What the hell? I need to get outta this thing!"

She stepped on a ladder rung with her bag on her arm and poked up her head out to see what was happening. Two guys were running around the yard shooting roman candles at each other while a third stood on the edge of the patio lighting firecrackers and throwing them in the air.

She looked over at the bar to make sure the guys who'd waved at her were still there. She went up another step and waved until they noticed her and yelled back.

"Come on honey, we're waiting for you."

She climbed another rung and felt something hit her in the back causing an immediate burning sensation. She reached around but dropped her damn purse again.

Right then she heard a voice from behind.

"Oh shit! Get out of that cake, girl that was an M-80!"

The boys in the yard were yelling, too.

"Shit, Danny! Whatcha trying to do? You're gonna hurt someone!"

Different people were shouting different things, and Pearlie heard conflicting instructions amid typical party whoops and hollars. The guy on the patio stepped up onto the side of the cake.

"Girl, get down from there, right now!"

She could smell whatever hit her in the back and heard it sizzling below. She wasn't sure what to do but wasn't leaving her bag. Before she fetched it, she looked around for Angie or Harry, and yelled for him.

"Harry!"

The guys at the bar looked around, shrugged their shoulders but didn't seem aware of her situation.

She yelled for her sister, "Angie, get out here!"

But she didn't see Harry or Angie, on the patio or through the glass doors.

"Girl, I said get your ass down outta there. Now!"

The guy in the yard who'd yelled at the guy on the cake, was suddenly screaming and waving frantically at her.

That guy on the cake, now behind her, was Danny Boone. Next he jumped on bottom section of the cake, and was shaking the chassis so hard Pearlie had to grab the sides not to fall back inside. He yelled as he tried to climb towards her.

"I'm gonna drag you outta there if you ain't gonna leave by yourself!"

The guy yelling at Danny hollered at her.

"Jump, girl!"

It was the last voice she heard as she didn't heed his warning, instead, ducked down to grab her bag. That's when Danny's knee came crashing through the side of the cake's walls and knocked her off balance. Before she could stand again to climb out, the world exploded around her.

She went blank.

A sober guest went to find Harry.

Angie heard Harry's frantic knocking on her Jacuzzi room door.

"Pearlie's hurt! Stop what you're doing and come help!"

Angie was sitting on a man's lap in her panties. She'd unbuttoned his dress shirt and pulled it out of his unbuckled, unzipped pants. She heard Harry's panicked plea while pulling on her guest's belt. He was kissing her neck. She pushed him away, jumped up and grabbed her top all in one move.

"I'm coming, Harry!"

Her client, shocked and scared, stood up and rearranged his clothes.

"Hey! What's going on here?"

"Sorry mister, youre just gonna have to chill!"

It was all she took the time to say before following Harry. When they got to the patio, Pearlie lay curled up on a beach towel, a wet bar rag on her head. She was sobbing while holding her hands over her ears. Angie tried to comfort her and find out what happened while Harry took charge shooing the crowd back to the bar. Most of the party guests continued to rage, indeed, most guests were oblivious to their situation.

"Listen, Angel, we gotta get her outta here. We can take her to a clinic or whatever, but we gotta get her somewhere safe and outta this place. We can't stop the party."

Danny was at the bar complaining to his brother, Richard he'd hurt his leg. Richard got Danny a shot of Whiskey and asked the bartender for ice.

Harry barked at Richard.

"Come on, man, get some ice for the girl too!"

Richard stepped behind the bar and returned with two cold beers, and a wet towel filled with ice, and handed the towel to Harry. He didn't pay any more attention to their situation, instead turned back to the bar and told Danny to man up while handing him one of the beers.

Finally, Harry carried Pearlie on a lounge chair through the side gate and placed her in a Limo. Angie got in, too. Pearlie began to talk but refused to be taken to a hospital. Finally, Pearlie got Angie to agree to have the Limo driver take them to Angie's apartment.

After that night, she would never see the world the same or hear music the same either. For a while she blocked out thoughts about her injuries by trying to party, but she wasn't much of a party girl.

After seeing her struggle after the accident Angie gave her some advice.

"We redbone's don't make good party girls 'cause we like it too much. We forget to take care of ourselves. And when we get like that, then nobody else gonna care about us or take care of us either one."

Angie tried to cheer her up with tough love. "Don't pout Pearlie and don't party! Use your blood line! You already got the power to get yourself right."

For months Angie's talk seemed silly but one night after she drank electric punch at a party, she tripped out. Once she started feeling the psychedelic effects, she had to get away from everyone as she was afraid she would completely flip out. She left her car at the party, got a cab to their apartment, and locked herself in her room to ride it out. She stayed shut-in for a week, without company, alcohol, or drugs. She only left her room for food, and the bathroom. She finally allowed Angie inside, but not to talk, she simply thanked her for her food.

Angie checked on Pearlie every day.

Pearlie knew Angie felt guilty about getting hurt and so she didn't bug her. What she didn't know was the guilt was compounded for Angie because she was keeping the truth about their relationship secret and all the while fending off Mawmaw.

Pearlie committed to use her pain to make herself stronger. She was lucky to still have her good looks. She'd met girls who went to great lengths to hide injuries, from unfortunate damage to their face and more from car wrecks and bad relationships. Her wounds were a constant reminder of how precious every gift she received at birth was. Now she knew these natural gifts could be taken away at any time without reason.

Angie continued to tell her not to worry, they'd get even someday. But at the beginning of her recovery Pearlie thought it better to not focus on revenge. She had enough to do just learning her way forward.

When she sat before a mirror to do her hair, she often lowered her head, letting her hair fall over her face to hide her tears. No one else needed to know she cried.

Unlike many tears we shed, hers no longer came from the emotional well of self-pity, instead her tears poured forth from an inner source like a badge of courage. The streaks of her tears like little ribbons of achievement.

Pearlie's heart grew hard through brave sweat and tears. Eventually, deep inside her heart the first seeds of revenge did sprout.

The Party Flag.

Make no mistake, it's our escape -
We live for the party.
And there's no out of bounds
when the party flag comes 'round!

Ladies wave their scarves
side to side, smiling wide.
Toasts!
The gentlemen lift them high.
Ah yes, when the party flag goes by.

I landed in Memphis, grabbed my luggage, and headed to the passenger pick up. The Vettes welcome wagon Vettes didn't take long to spot, a '59 Pink Fleetwood Cadillac convertible. Two young men in Ray Bans, white button-down shirts, and red suspenders sat in the front. *Any Day Now* by Elvis blared from the car speaker. Seated atop the back seat a Vettes' cheerleader waved a Welcome Max sign over her head while she blew an impressive balloon-size blue bubble gum bubble from her lips.

I was embarrassed yet impressed. Maybe Sarge was right, now I was really in the big time. As a bar manager, I used to slip through the back door unnoticed for work before Vettes. This was a brand-new way to meet the crew.

Doing General Manager Nash Hollister a favor they were driving a borrowed car from a local tour service, and it made me feel special. I was beaming when they pulled up. Paul 'B.T.T.' Bone and Adam 'Shady' Shades with Beatle haircuts were bar-backs and Kimmie 'The Shimmy' Rhodes was a six-foot server who specialized in roving stand-up service. Shimmy brunette mane had a mid-part perm that mushroomed above her neon blue headband. She wore overkill eyeshadow above disarming freckled cheeks.

They were pretty amped up and I was bone tired from my previous night's escapade, so I let them do the talking as we drove away. They engaged in good-natured horse play, ribbing and shoving, abandoning all concern for the land cruiser's lane position or other drivers. But they knew the way by heart, and though I stayed nervously alert, the car didn't require much steering.

Shimmy laughed loudly, sometimes leaning over me and poking her head between the two boys in front, gleefully swiveling her head face to face with them while constantly working her jaw preparing an array of impressive bubbles. After each exchange, she pushed back over me like a kid on the monkey bars, lifting her legs over my shoulder and kicking her heels against the driver's headrest.

Conversation soon turned to shop talk, bragging about their team dancing, showing lots of Vettes' competitive spirit.

At one point Shady received a left-handed punch in the arm from Shimmy when he mentioned an after-hours pool party incident.

"You better hush!"

A bursting bubble accompanied her fist, and he changed the subject. She gave him the evil eye while readjusting her skirt, and pulling down for proper coverage before smoothing it out in an exaggerated lady like manner. When they started arguing about their favorite barbecue joints, it got so heated B.T.T. pulled the car over and stopped in a parking lot and re-counted the awards of Gridley's, his favorite, versus Shady's favorite, Leonard's.

"Lawdy, I swear I don't care as long as y'all are buying!" was Shimmy's contribution, clearly exasperated by their circular conversation.

She confided in me that though she'd bounced around, she'd had a boring childhood in rural Kentucky and subsequently loved the hell out of the sights and sounds of Memphis. The three of them were young and fun and I looked forward to working with them, but I was beat and wanted to get settled.

"So, are you taking me to my place or the to the club?"

"You gotta get your keys from Nash and we'll take you from there, unless you wanna see the sights."

Turned out Nash had left the keys for me at the club in an envelope with a message on the outside.

"Welcome to Memphis Max! See you tomorrow at 2p."

Since Nash wasn't there, they dropped me off at my designated residence after getting the keys. They were familiar with the company rental and past visitors sent by Vettes Corporate office. B.T.T. even offered advice.

"Don't break any windows or Nash'll be pissed."

"Or pass out on the porch in the buff!" Shimmey offered this tidbit with a giggle and another punch at Shady, who shot right back at her as he pushed her away.

"You're one to talk."

"Oh, just shut it, you're only jealous."

Shimmey's gum smacking retort seemed to put Shady in his place. I was ready to crash and wanted to cut things short for now.

"Hey, don't worry about it, I'll take care of the place and make you proud. Thanks for everything, really. You did great, I'll see you tomorrow, ok?"

I was too beat to yuck it up or take them up on any offers to hit the bars. Plus, I had a Memphis connection named Chris, who I left a message with the night before. If I did anything later, it would be to try and look him up.

The Vettes' Midtown guest house apartment was a sweet deal, and the place was mine for ninety days. After that, I had to figure something out on my own. Conveniently located within walking distance of the club, it was smack dab in the middle between two entertainment districts: Overton Square and Cooper-Young. The scene felt similar to Virginia Highlands in Atlanta or Mill Avenue in Tempe. I felt certain if there was spare time for carousing, I wouldn't be bored.

Situated behind a large manor on a tree lined boulevard my place was originally a garage apartment next to an alley. The two floors were on the side of the hill. You entered off the sidewalk into a screened porch, originally the garage. That connected to the living area with couch, desk, empty refrigerator, and a water closet. Upstairs was a bedroom with an angular ceiling and compact bathroom with a triangular shower. An upstairs door opened to a flagstone path in the main houses' sloping back yard and up to the backdoor.

It was hot and humid, so I fetched the box fan from the porch and placed it on a chair to pull the AC window unit's air stream to the bed. I put my clothes away, showered, and lay on the bed to rest. I quickly fell asleep, even at four in the afternoon. At 8:30pm I was rudely awoken by an obnoxious buzzer bell. So, I got up in my t-shirt and boxers and went to the door.

No one was there, but the buzzer went off again. Then it dawned on me I'd have to traipse downstairs to the downstairs door. I stubbed my toe turning the corner and limped down the stairs. I looked outside, and saw a guy with a scruffy blonde beard, his dark eyes squinted at me from beneath a khaki felt Pork Pie hat.

"Hello?"

"Hey Max! I'm Lehigh, friend of your buddy Chris. He told me to guide you around town."

He held a five pack of sweaty Schlitz, so I figured he was a friend of mine, too.

"Well okay then, why don't you come on in."

I opened the door, and he stepped inside. He had on a Bambu logo t-shirt under his wrinkled seersucker jacket, faded jeans, and black loafers with pennies in the front and lightning bolts on the sides.

"Those are some classy shoes, Lehigh."

I reached for his hand, and he set the Schlitz on the couch and reached out with both hands to grab mine.

"The pleasure's all mine. Chris told me you're a real Rock'n Roll desperado."

"Well, I don't know about that. I'm just hours into Memphis, and still trying to keep my nose clean."

"Yeah, he told me you were a slick talker, too." He winked.

I grabbed a beer and popped the top and took a long swig. I'm not gonna lie, it was nasty, like something my friend Jonesy would drink. Nothing like the Mexican beers I was used to, but was cold, and I was thirsty, so I choked it down.

"Kinda rough, huh? Well, it was on sale, and I haven't tried it in a while, thought I'd give it a try. I usually drink green bottle brew."

"It's fine, it's cold and I need one."

"Well, we can go out cruising and get something different if you want."

"I wasn't planning on doing too much tonight, but I guess it wouldn't hurt to look the town over."

"Whenever you're ready."

"Lehigh, I only got a little pocket money until I start working..."

"Oh, don't worry, this one's on me. Anybody Chris vouches for gets a least one free night on the town."

"Have it your way. Have a seat I'll go up and change."

I finished my beer and grabbed another, popped it, and headed upstairs. I forgot about my toe and winced on my first leap, while trying two steps at a time. I realized a Percocet might be in order after a few beers.

Down to the last two beers, we jumped in his yellow 69 Volkswagen Beetle stick shift convertible and took off. He'd covered his bumpers with more stickers than a college freshman's wine bottle candle holder art project, including 'See Rock City.' It sputtered loudly in first gear but smoothed out by the fourth, just in time to gear down again for the next stop. We looked at each other and laughed in unison the second time he put it through the gears.

"Max, what do you like to hear?"

He reached under the seat and grabbed a Peaches bag of cassettes and handed it to me between gear changes. I selected the 1970 Charlie Musselwhite's *Memphis, Tennessee*, held it up for show and got his rousing approval.

"Charlie, hell yeah! Let's jam to that."

He nodded vigorously, pushing it in the player.

Eventually we cruised Riverside Drive, and I got my first look at the Mississippi River up close. By the time Charlie was huffing on *Arkansas Boogie* we were parked on the bluff overlooking the Big Muddy as it rolled by. I saw felled trees, cowboy boots, picnic coolers, and two by fours tumble along in its churning muddy mass. The trees were easy to spot, but most things only stayed visible an instant before disappearing back into the muddy murk.

Sometimes it was only a guess as to what the rushing water was pushing downstream. It swirled and surged as it passed, a majestic mass of America's mud, sweat, spit and grit, rolling to New Orleans and the Gulf of Mexico. After we finished our beers, Lehigh wanted to hit the road.

"Some other time I'll take you down to Mud Island and you can look at her at eye level, but tonight we're gonna make a pit stop, then hit Beale."

Lehigh drove on back streets till he came to Ernie's Body Shop. It looked closed to me, but Lehigh pulled into an alley behind it. He crept the Bug along the perimeter fence at a crawl. When he turned off the music I could hear him breathe. A building sat fifty feet inside the perimeter fence, after we passed it, we parked. I was puzzled.

"What is this?"

Lehigh stared at the building and spoke in a whisper.

"Max, this is a pit stop."

Between us and the main building I could see several vehicles scattered around in various states of repair. Barely visible from where we sat in the alley, a dim light was on.

"I'll be right back, just sit tight. I'll leave the keys in the ignition, if someone drives down the alley move the car, then circle back for me after they're gone."

It seemed an odd request if he was going to be right back.

"Ok, no problem..."

I said it but wondered if it was a good idea for me to be in such a situation. I was certain something sketchy was in progress.

He walked alongside the fence a couple car lengths, then lifted a portion of pre-cut fence. He stooped and stepped through, quickly disappearing behind the parked cars on his way to the building. It was quiet at first, but then I heard Lehigh, and he was loud.

"No way! No fucking way."

It wasn't a humorous response to a joke. He was pissed. A bright light came on, then off again. I heard another voice.

"C'mon Lehigh, that ain't the deal!"

"It is now!"

After Lehigh's 'now,' a door slammed, and I saw Lehigh reappear coming fast through the cars.

The other voice shouted out.

"You're going to regret this, Lehigh!"

But Lehigh didn't miss a beat, he ducked down, duck walked under the fence and shouted to me with an update.

"Get ready to roll, Max, we're gonna get some real beer now."

I was concerned about the shouting. I didn't need to be involved in any disreputable incidents before I'd even worked my first shift in Memphis. After he jumped in, I asked what was happening.

"Is everything ok, man?"

"Oh yea, just a difference of opinion, that's all."

He flashed a big smile but drove out the alley a lot faster than we entered. When we reached the street, he gunned it. This all made me nervous, and without thinking I squirmed and rubbed my chin, but caught myself and stopped. I didn't want him to think I was uncomfortable, so I looked over and beamed at him, faking a big smile so he'd think I was cool.

Meanwhile, I wondered if my real work might have just begun.

He turned the music up, and we picked up speed. He glanced at me again and gave me a 'don't worry' look and nodded in time to the music. We soon pulled in at a Stop'N Go and he asked me to help choose the beer. When we got to the beer cooler, he looked at me and smiled like someone about to have a big night on the town.

"Lowenbrau or Heineken? I'm buying."

"Why not do both?"

"I like your style!"

Lehigh grabbed a six of Lowenbrau and six of Heinie dark. When we got to the car, he opened the front trunk and grabbed a small cooler filled with icy water and put it in the back seat. He put four of each in and opened the remaining four on the door jam. He grabbed a paper bag off the back floorboard and pulled out a couple Big Gulp Squirt plastic soda cups.

"We'll pour'em in these for camouflage. Don't want no cops thinking we're drinking and driving at this hour."

He winked.

"Sorry I ain't got nothing swankier, but it's best to look natural."

He waved the cups at me.

"Let's mix'em up over here."

He set a cup in the folds of the convertible canvas top and simultaneously poured each in the cups like a mad scientist in the lab. I must have looked skeptical because he looked back at me like he was disappointed in my reaction.

I shrugged.

"It's ok, Lehigh, I'm cool, like they say, when in Rome…"

He handed me my cup after he drained the bottles, and I took note he walked over to the trash to disposed of the empties. He might have some sketchy business in hand but was no litterer.

We hit the road again, enjoying the night air with our jumbo beers in hand. He took me down The Memphis Parkways and I marveled at the trees and greenery. There seemed to be more vegetation in the median and on the sides of these beautiful proud streets than in the whole city of Phoenix.

"I gotta see a man about a dog up here in a minute."

Lehigh had given me the scenic tour for sure. We cruised by several blocks of convenience stores and fast-food places while cruising Jackson Avenue. The convenience stores seemed very popular. One, Mae's Market, hosted a craps party just to the side of its 'Block Ice' cooler. I craned my neck for a second look, surprised to see it obviously going on so out in the open.

"What are you gonna do?"

Lehigh offered a shoulder shrug as his critique when he saw me crane for a better look. Eventually we pulled up to the front door of a building with 'Club Robot' painted on the side. A buxom female robot was spray painted next to the name and a very large and live black man in a black tank top stood at his station as bouncer by the door. His biceps bulged and his muscular neck was adorned with gold chains. He lifted his head slightly to acknowledge Lehigh, who returned the greeting with a question.

"Hollywould in tonight?"

He answered with a shake of his head.

"Thanks."

After speaking, Lehigh did a quick about face. I sensed there really wasn't a dog involved with our Club Robot stop. We left and after a few miles, pulled into an abandoned lot. I could see some neon lights a few blocks away and Lehigh quickly reached back and grabbed the cooler.

"Let's fill up before we head to Beale."

He concocted another round then put the cooler on the floorboard and threw a dirty towel over it. We pulled the VW's retractable top up and secured it.

"Just follow me."

And off we went.

Our cups were full, though I managed to only spill a little keeping up with him. We moved down an alley and slipped in between two buildings. There was a gate at the next alley where he reached over the top and opened it from other side.

"Hurry up, we need to do a quick dip through this place."

I followed, walking through a dumpster area with a bunch of empty kegs before coming to an emergency exit, stenciled on the door was 'Jugbands - Exit Only'. He reached in his pocket, and pulled out a pocketknife, stuck it into the crack between the door jam and door and pulled the door open just far enough to grab. He turned to me with raised eyebrows.

"Pretty slick, huh?"

He didn't wait for my response. I followed him inside. I heard pianos, drums and people laughing as we passed the kitchen and restrooms. We stepped down into a room full of picnic tables and drunken students waving souvenir pink plastic funnel cups, with giant straws dangling from the tops. Disco music played from a DJ in the corner.

"We'll need to get back on the street A-SAP, just follow my lead."

We threaded between tables and slipped into another room full of stand-ups with an older crowd. As we entered, we passed a stage where a rowdy female singer who wouldn't have looked out of place steering an eighteen-wheeler, playing her piano side-straddle from her bench. It was dark, but she wore sunglasses, belting out *Hit The Road Jack* like there was no to-morrow.

On the other side of the room was a main bar with a mirror running the entire length with 'Jugbands' scrawled in gold leaf, bookended by a cartoon of a couple old prospectors playing jugs. We made a fast path along the bar stools, when over the piano player's best Ray Charles imitation, a voice called out.

"Leeee-High!"

I looked over to see a short young bartender in a sequined vest and a gold star in his front teeth. He aimed his pistol fin-ger at Lehigh. Though it seemed like a casual greeting it caught Lehigh off guard, and he grimaced like he'd been caught sneaking around. To his credit he recovered with a quick pivot, flashing that big party night smile before heading to the bar.

I followed.

The bartender patiently waited while swaying on the balls of his feet.

"Whassup, Mr. High?"

"Mr. Doomuch, it's good to see you."

Lehigh leaned over, and they did an elaborate handshake where both aimed their thumb pistols at each other, then blew on their fingers and crossed their arms, with a side eye glance for as a finish.

"I was looking for your brother earlier, Doo, but he wasn't in."

"Well, whatever he needs, I need too, my brother," he gave Lehigh a quick wink, "especially since you didn't call before using the VIP entrance."

He leaned in and raised both eyebrows.

"What's up with that?"

"I know, I should have called first. How 'bout you set us up a couple cold ones with some Jack Knives on the side."

"Now you're talking."

Wearing a big smile, Doomuch went to work on the drinks. As he pushed them towards us, Lehigh leaned over and they exchanged words so no one, including myself, could hear. As Lehigh pulled away, he got loud.

"I think it was black but might have been some other color, I appreciate you checking on it."

Then Doomuch scooted to the end of the bar, lifted the service bar flap and disappeared into the crowd as he headed to the back. I turned to my guide.

"Lehigh, listen, can we put this on my tab?" as he nodded I asked, "Where'd he go anyhow?"

I didn't want to be a freeloader and wondered what was up, after all he said we were in a hurry. I knew we could walk around on the street with our drinks, so I didn't understand why we stopped.

"I might have left a bag here last visit, so he's checking on it."

We clinked glasses and downed the Jack Knives with a grimace, washing them down with the beers. Pretty soon, Doomuch showed up carrying a baby blue Smurfs knapsack.

"Here you go, Mr. High, I hope little High hasn't been too sad about it being lost."

With a wink he handed the bag over the bar to Lehigh.

"Yeah, well lemme see if this is his."

He dropped it to the floor, knelt down, unzipped it, and reached into his pants pocket and pulled something out. I could still see clearly but tried not to stare. Whatever it was, it was wrapped in a brown paper bag and Lehigh put it in the knapsack, then zipped it back up and stood up while shaking his head.

"Naw, it ain't his, but thanks for checking,"

He handed the bag back over the bar to Doomuch.

"Ok, well, I'm sorry, it was all we had in lost and found like your bag. I do hope you find it soon."

"Yeah, me too."

With that Doomuch opened a cabinet behind the bar and tossed the Smurf sack deep inside and slid a box of bar mix in front of it. He slammed the door and turned around as the song ended and yelled to the crowded room.

"Cocktails, y'all, we got kick ass cocktails right here."

I guess that was our signal to leave.

"Let's go!"

Lehigh headed for the door that emptied onto Beale Street. The drinks must have been on the house.

"Hey, you must be connected."

I knew something else was happening, but it didn't require an explanation right then.

"Yeah, I'm sure I'll end up paying for them as well as most of Hollywould's share."

Lehigh exhaled while shaking his head.

"Oh, that's the brother of Robot Club dude you were looking for?"

"Yeah, yeah, hey we're not gonna worry about it, let's check out the crowd on the street tonight."

I realized I would need to cut the night shorter than Lehigh may have had in mind. We headed down the street and stepped into Rum Boogie Cafe where the bouncer waved us in as soon as he made eye contact with Lehigh. A band was jamming on stage right behind the entry. We ducked in, but the bouncer stopped the group after us.

"Whoa now. Y'all know it's five bucks a piece or two for seven. Lemme see them ID's."

Right away we found a place under the stairs and leaned on a stand-up table and Lehigh ordered beer. The music was pure and from the heart. All the players were different ages, and we listened intently to each, as they jammed through each measure. The beer went down easy, and we clinked glasses over guitar riffs and sax solos, and I began to feel better about the welcome tour he'd put together. At some point they announced they had a special guest in the house about to sit in.

"Ladies and Gentlemen, all the way from the Grand Canyon State of Arizona, welcome Betty Bongos."

The stairs above us jostled as someone bounded down them then up to the stage.

There she was, Olga Drumber aka Olga Drumber the Plumber, apparently aka Betty Bongos, dressed in a red leather miniskirt and black sequined top with plunging neckline. The band's guitarist handed her a solid body Blonde Fender Strat. She put the strap over her head and turned to face the crowd. It was a good thing she didn't see me with my mouth open so wide and my shocked bloodshot eyes.

She launched into *Wham* by Lonnie Mack to get the crowd's attention, and they responded with whoops and pig hollers. Then she keyed it down and the lead singer took over vocals, while Olga filled in the gaps and more while they glided on *I Believe I'll Dust My Broom.*

When she spotted me, she gave me a wink while the singer 'dusted away' and I raised my glass in return. She looked much different in her stage outfit and with her guitar wailing. I was intrigued. When the song ended the place went wild again.

Olga handed the guitar back, blew a kiss to the crowd and bent over to collect up two shots sent to her in appreciation. As she did, I got a better glimpse of her Bongo tattoos, not that I ever doubted they were real or that it wasn't her. The way she clowned, smiled and grimaced on stage showed me she was the same playful troublemaker I met at the Phoenix Vettes. She did both shots and toasted the crowd, but before she could step down from the stage, a server delivered another full tray which she passed around to the band and downed one more for good measure.

The next song was kinda loud and as I leaned over our table to try to tell Lehigh I had met Betty Bongos in Phoenix, there was a tap on my shoulder.

"Hey stranger, are you following me?"

Olga grinned, unashamed and visibly sweaty from her boisterous performance. I flipped into flirt mode.

"I could never follow that performance, Olga. That was impressive, I loved it."

"You flatter me Max, or should I say Mr. Tailfeather," she wiggled her behind for emphasis and continued, "Hah- haaah! You know Max! How long you gonna be around?"

She swung her hips, one-two, and bit her lower lip, waiting for my answer.

"We're about to leave here now because I start at Vette's tomorrow, but I'll be in Memphis awhile I guess."

"Well, I'll just have to drop in and see you then."

"Well, I can't wait. Maybe you can find me an axe, too... I'll pay you."

I held up my glass and tilted my head.

"Don't worry Max, I'll take care of your 'Zona cowboy ass."

She slapped her thigh for emphasis then bowed while backing away then headed back up the stairs.

Lehigh took stock of my newly acquired Beale Street cred.

"Well, well, Max my boy, you're in some deep and muddy water now. I'm impressed. You and Betty Bongos on a first name basis. Hmmm, I'm wondering how you did that."

My status had just been elevated in Lehigh's mind, but I wasn't going let him know she was also associated with Vettes after what I witnessed during his guided tour. I was new to Memphis, and to be honest I didn't know why Betty was here other than playing her music.

I realized my world might be moving a little fast even for me. Pretty soon I might have to learn to use the brakes.

The Grandest Lure

You must understand,
the river water dance.

We sing our songs,
We laugh in our whiskey,
While the lights on the water dance,
the river water dance.

Deaf to the mosquitoes,
I hear the voices of home...
How I loved that girl
with the freckled nose.

And the stars dance upon the water...
The world, the stage,
the grandest lure.

Lehigh got me back to my place around 3am. Jet lag worked
in my favor, allowing me to sleep in the humid Memphis air

till noon. I woke refreshed and strutted into Vettes at 3pm for my shift. Nash was the manager on duty, greeting me with a big smile and a vigorous handshake. He gave me the fifty-cent tour and I took note how it looked much different on the outside, while the floor plan was much the same as Phoenix.

After an hour familiarizing me with nuances of the Memphis Vettes, Nash took a break and said he'd be back around nine. Things went smooth without him, B.T.T. and Shady bird-dogged me for an hour which made me uptight. I felt obligated to tell them to keep their nose out of my butt and just do their job. They were pretty bummed after my bitching, so I cornered them later and revisited. Declaring they were my righthand men, but let me figure things out on my own, unless I ask for help.

Shimmie was there and handled things like a pro, she wasn't as green in the scene as the boys. Indeed, she was even cockier, ready to bust out to Cali and be a star within a week.

When Happy Hour started, I pivoted around the DJ booth ready for our first group dance. I spotted Olga in her plumber's duds at the front door. She saw me and waved me over in her own special way.

"Come over here and give your plumber some love, Mr. Max."

Slouching in a grubby jumpsuit soiled by grimy hands, her tool belt hung over her hip on one side and below her waist on the other. I couldn't resist having a little fun with her.

"Good evening, are you the plumber we called?"

I grinned at her like I had just told a funny joke and was waiting for applause.

"Oh, we're sorry your pipes are backed up mister, but I'm here to report a broken heart."

She grinned back. She grabbed my hand and guided me out of earshot of the staff at the door and along the sidewalk.

I was puzzled.

"What're you doing?"

"The broken heart thing..." she looked up sweetly, "see, thing is, it's what you'll have if you don't join me to meet a very special friend who's right here in Memphis."

She gazed in my eyes waiting for a response, then whispered in her husky baritone, "...Tonight, after work."

"Well, ok, ...but I don't get off till three. When's this gonna happen?"

"Oh, Max, it'll be prime time then. She's a legend and goes all night. She really wants to meet you."

"Oh ok, so how's it gonna work?"

"It's gonna work fine is how. I'll come by in my red truck and park out back and wait. If I get here before you close, I'll let them know at the front door. Otherwise, I'll just be here, don't worry."

Sure enough, as I finished check outs, I poked my head out the back door to see if she'd show. I saw her truck and there she was leaning against the door, blowing smoke rings, gazing at the moon. She didn't see me, and I didn't let her know I'd seen her.

Once I finished up, I could have snuck out the front to avoid her. I knew she was a distraction from my focus as manager. So why didn't I slip away? Truth was, my interest was piqued. Seeing her perform at Rum Boogie left me more than ready to make a risky decision in her honor.

I stepped out back after setting the alarm and turned to see her leaning back on the roof of her truck watching me.

"All right Max! Let's get a move on, your door's unlocked."

I jumped in the passenger side as she jumped to the ground and into the driver's seat. She'd changed from her plumber's threads to some short cut blue jean overalls with metal studs spelling Ziggy Starbuster across the front. Underneath she had on a sheer black sleeveless hoodie full of holes connected with safety pins.

We were a perfect mismatch with my button-down collared shirt and tie, khaki slacks, and saddle oxfords. She tossed a black bundle at me.

"Here, I brought you a shirt, so you won't mess yours up."

I unfolded it to see Romeo Void plastered in white from one shoulder down to the opposite corner. I wrinkled my brow and wondered about the meaning, she just smiled.

"Just consider it a gift, here, have a listen..."

"You didn't have to...".

She cranked the tunes before I could finish thanking her and we left the lot with Debbie Iyall's unbridled vocals shouting over Romeo Void's crunching guitar work. Windows down, we headed downtown with beers she pulled from under the seat. She turned off the music as we climbed the riverside bluff near where Lehigh and I'd been. We reached the crest, and she held up her hand.

"Listen Max, I can hear her calling you now."

I wasn't getting the message and strained my senses to pick up the sound of a voice and Olga started laughing sweetly.

"Aahhh, Max it's Miss..., Ms. Sippi calling you, the Big Muddy, *the River!*"

I smiled back.

"Oh, okay, I get it, so lead on, Miss Betty Bongos."

We pulled into the Church On The River parking lot then took a lesser used driveway round the berm next to the levy, eventually parking on part of the bluff near what's called the 'Old Bridge'. She recommended we get a closer look, so we scrambled down to the river's edge close enough to hear the ripples as the river water rushed by. It was impressive and scary, no doubt about it.

"Max you wanna see my special place?"

She looked up at me gently grabbing my hand with a little girl's 'please, please' look.

"Sure, where's it at?"

What else could I say?

"Follow me."

She took off like a kid at recess. She had two beers in a pouch tied to her belt and they bounced off her butt. The refreshments didn't affect her progress as she rambled up the hill to the bridge mounts and I followed. The brushy levee gave way to a gravel clearing, then narrowed to a path on the underside of the bridge. When I caught up, she had one hand on the bridge's iron span, and the other pointed where it reached across the mighty river towards Arkansas bottom lands.

Her instructions were brief.

"Just follow me and go slow. Use both hands all the way to the hide out."

She didn't give me time to argue, instead she turned and climbed onto the bridge, scooting along the iron frame of two six-inch parallel beams.

Crisscrossing iron rods rose from under the beams and connected to the top. We were next to and a little below the actual railroad bridge. I saw a service walkway grate two foot wide to our left.

Nervous about our route, I offered a question. "Why don't we use the walkway over there?"

"Because we can't get where we wanna go from there."

She shook her head at my concerns.

"Don't worry, just follow me and don't think about it."

I followed on hands and knees and watched the soles of her boots moving back and forth. She wasn't trying to exaggerate her hip movements but framed by her cut offs' ragged edges her derriere swung wildly as each knee centered on the narrow tract. She looked back occasionally to see my progress and I tried my best to flash a smile. We got to the second piling on the pile cap and stopped. She pulled herself further beneath the bridge and into a cubby hole. She scooted around till she was cross legged facing me.

"Come on, Max!"

Struggling not to look down, I tried to keep my eyes on her as I followed her moves. When I finally arrived at her little nest, she leaned over and pulled me onto the platform. She pointed to an inch-thick wire just above my head.

"There you go, now keep a hold of that wire if you feel wobbly. By the way, I saw you checking out my booty."

She gave me a wink and a big smile like the one the first day we met.

"Betty, I was just following your instructions."

I admit she was fun, and I was grateful she'd taken the time to bring me on this special adventure.

She pulled the beers off her belt and popped a top. As she turned it up for a drink, foam ran down her chin and into the night air along the pilings rising below us from the depths of channel. It was funny, and she chortled, but I didn't laugh. I was transfixed as I watched the foam disappear into the backdrop of the river's turbulent surface.

I settled and started looking around, shocked at what we'd just navigated. We were directly over the center of the Mississippi River's fastest current, fifty yards higher than anything I'd ever jumped off of in my life, diving board or cliff. As I looked back to where we'd crawled, the return trip looked impossible. I was mortified, but when I turned to her, she looked back at me with moon pie eyes and a smile to comfort me.

"It's gonna be all right Max, I'll get you back in one piece."

"Yeah, I can't believe we just did this. I'm gonna need to rest a minute."

"Just lay back and watch it flow Max, my man. Just let it flow, it'll be all right."

She lit a joint while I stared at the swirling water rushing by. I instinctively took a hit when she passed it not thinking about the crawl back. I noticed how clear the sky seemed, and I realized I hadn't felt this cognizant after a Vettes' shift since I started.

What was different? Could it be because I didn't drink anything at work on this night other than a carton of Orange Juice?

Uncertain of the answer, I chilled and let it flow, the two of us stared out at the river as it moved downstream, disappearing into the southern horizon. We closed our eyes and immersed ourselves in the subtle but powerful sounds. As it rushed past the pilings there were random ripples and splashes, sublime accents softly layering this river's low rumbling grind. The river's never-ending song was occasionally interrupted by eighteen-wheelers, their tire flaps slapping, bridge slats and joints croaking from their weight as they rushed past. Like percussionists joining the bridge's band, the big rigs chassis rumbled and jumbled, their beats coursing off the bridge's rattled frame.

I took time to scan the western horizon where the waters spread out across the Arkansas flood lands as far as we could see. The moon and stars sprinkled little glints of light on the water's surface, with splotches of errant vehicle lights amid accents from the Memphis skyline.

I admit after a while I became more relaxed but realized I would have to pee. I didn't want to say anything, but started to get antsy, worried about the crawl back to the riverbank with the disadvantage of a full bladder.

"I think I need to go back now and find a bush, know what I mean?"

"Aw Max, you gotta piss? Go right here, don't be shy, if you pee in a bush it'll end up in the river anyhow."
"Hah! uh, yeah... Well, really that's not what I was worried about. It's just that I didn't wanna just whip it out to whiz in such close company."

"Oooh," she laughed sarcastically, "you're such a gentleman! Tell you what, I'll turn the other way. You go ahead, I promise not to look if you promise to go *with* the wind. And please hold onto the wire so you don't fall."

"Uh, okay, I guess that will work, but I don't know about standing up..."

"Oh. come on Max you're in the Delta now, we don't care, you can piss from your knees if you're worried about that. You gotta go, you gotta go."

"Okay, okay, I'll try."

I rose gingerly on unsteady legs, careful not to hit my head on the structure careful to keep my left arm wrapped around the wire. I undid my belt, unbuttoned my pants, and lowered the zipper with my right hand. Because of the wire's location I couldn't reach my left arm over to hold my pants. Once let go, the left side of my pants and belt buckle fell to my knees. Something slipped out of the pocket with a clink and jangle, hitting metal one last time on its way down to the pitch black Mississippi current.

"Oh shit! No! Those were my Vettes' keys!"

I almost let go of the wire and had to steady myself when I realized what had happened. Olga reached over and grabbed my shirttail just in case.

"Careful now, Max!"

"Shit! I'm so screwed!"

I thought I felt the first pangs of a heart attack when I realized how final it would've been had I lost my balance and fell. No chance in hell I'd have survived.

"It's ok. Just relax, Max. I got some Vettes' keys, and I can make you copies. Go ahead. Just go ahead and piss... don't let go of the wire and don't drop anything else."

I stood for minute in a daze, my heart pounding. What a strange situation. I was really nervous.

"I'm not sure I can do this now. I'm too freaked out and self-conscious."

"It's all right, Max. Tell you what, close your eyes, and listen..."

At first, I thought she wanted me to listen to the river again but to my surprise, she began to sing. Her voice was deep, but smooth and sugary like black strap molasses. Her higher notes came out easy, but never lost the smooth thickness she started with. It sounded like a field hand song written on velvet.

"Don't leave me on the levee baby,

Don't leave me all alone.
Please take meeee...
to the higher ground
Where I-I-I-I can rest my soul."

I'm calling on you moon
Oh Oh Oh
I wanna rest my soul
Oh Oh Oh
I want you to know
Oh Oh Oh
I wanna rest my soul.
Ohhhhh, please baby, let me rest my soul."

With her behind me, and her song in the air I was peeing freely by the time she started the next verse. I took joy in the relief, as it flowed into the wind and darkness beneath the belly of the bridge and into the current below. I don't remember the rest of her lyrics, but I do remember her soothing voice and the ever-present roar of the Big Muddy bringing special joy to the welcome relief of emptying my bladder.

In the distance a large barge appeared heading our way, it's search light beaming back and forth on the riverbanks. It looked like a robot cyclops, or one of the alien spaceships from *War Of The Worlds.* As it got closer, it scanned the bridge and the beam hit us full blast before I shut my eyes.

"Wow! I hope I can see to crawl back. Holy crap, that was brighter than any strobe I've ever used."

"You might be stoned, Max. Just don't let it hit you again, when the beam turns toward us, close your eyes. You don't wanna sort out a bunch of spots when we head back. When I close my eyes I try to feel the heat of the beam. Try it."

I have to admit, I couldn't really feel it but instead of blackness I saw brilliant red as it hit. Eventually, we heard the engine and hissing curl of the wake as it passed beneath. Olga started hollering, encouraging me to join in.

"Woo-hoo! Hey there you river rats! Where ya going? Woohoo!"

We shouted a couple Woo-hoo's, in harmony, and the tug belched out a Toot-toot back. A riverman stood on the tug's bridge and looked up. He gave a friendly wave, relaxing against the railing around the wheelhouse. I couldn't help but think if his crew had saluted my friend Betty Bongos before and wondered, is tug life on the river something I'd ever be ready for, and how different was it from mine?

"That was cool, it's awesome out here when barges come by...".

I was staring off into space, but she kept focused.

"So Max, just let me know when you're ready to head back."

"Yeah, thanks, this is cool. You know, I still got a blind spot from the beam, but it's getting smaller, it won't be long."

When the spot finally dissipated I let her know. As soon as we started back she scrambled like a monkey, no longer turning and looking back to see I hadn't gotten too far behind.

In fact, she needed a reminder. I had to rest and catch my breath, I was dizzy.

"Slow your Bongos down, Betty, I need a second."

"Oh, so you did notice. Don't worry Max, I ain't running off."

I didn't have the energy to acknowledge her flirting, instead I filed it away for later. It seemed to take an eternity to crawl back. When the riverbank finally came into view, I was covered in sweat and my arms were rubbery. We jumped off the trellis into the gravel clearing, and she stepped towards me, reached up and wiped my forehead with a giggle.

"First time's kinda scary, huh? My knees are killing me, how are yours' doing?"

I reached up and intercepted her hand gently as she wiped the sweat from my forehead running down the side of my cheek.

"I'm great. I wouldn't have missed it for the world and yes, my knees are killing me. We ever come out here again, though, I'll just watch. Right now, I'm happy just to say 'Been There, Done That.'"

"That's fine, Max, I'm glad we did it, too."

Our arms relaxed and settled between us, and we held hands. She stared at me, beckoning without moving, and stood perfectly still with moonlight beams in her eyes.

I leaned into her.

We both waited to the last second before we closed our eyes and kissed. As we came together before the actual kiss it was weird to see her open eyes so close. But she hummed her approval, and it went from weird to fun.

"Ummmmm..."

Then almost just as soon as it started, we separated. Our hands on each other's hips, we stared at one another, and just when I thought we were going in for another kiss, our mouths transformed into comedic karmic smiles. We both began to chuckle faster than we could stop ourselves.

Our chuckling broke spontaneously into joyous, tension free laughter. It was from deep inside our souls, and a very special moment. And I'll be damned I'm not sure why it happened.

In between the laughs, we still snuck glances at each other, and continued to enjoy the natural, nurturing goodness of the moment without letting any animal impulses take the reins.

I swear it happened, the simple pleasure of two people arriving at the same place, present with each other and in concert with their feelings. Not something you can fake. It snuck up from deep within from a place neither one of us really understood. Our fingers slipped down to grab hold of each other's belt loops, pulled and leaned forward, pushing back and forth against each other's bodies in tandem, until she put her hand on my shoulder.

And we stopped.

"What were you laughing about, Max?"

"Me? What about you? I'm laughing because I wondered whether we'd crash into each other sooner or later and if we'd be friends or foes."

"Oh, you did?"

"Well, you were pretty flirty first time we met, but I wasn't sure. I mean I thought I might just be fantasizing or even flattering myself, especially after witnessing you burning up that guitar on Beale."

"Really? ...well, I'm glad you did. You best believe I won't crawl around on my knees over the Miss'ippi with just anyone in the middle of the night."

"Well thanks, I really appreciate you... and this, I mean, this is great..."

"But?"

"But you know I'm really tired, and dirty right now, and..."

"And?"

"I think I'm in trouble, I lost my Vettes keys..."

"Dude, you are *high* maintenance."

She laughed at me and winked and tugged at my hand. "Let's go take care of some of your issues."

**I'm the Daredevil Clown,
  Bellboy for the town.
Tight roping down the line,
Tickling every heart I find.**

**Friends and neighbors,
Please come laugh with me.
Life's too serious for you,
Don't you see?
A lot of living
is a fun time to me.**

**So, come dance!
Come dance with me -
the Daredevil Clown.**

When we got back to Betty's truck, she insisted she take me by her place where I could shower, while she washed my clothes. She had spare overalls, and a guitar to play, so I accepted. She explained the house rules while we walked up the wooden stairs.

"We need to be quiet cuz the neighbors are asleep. We've got most of the second floor. It's actually a sweet set up."

I wasn't sure if she meant me and her as 'we,' or if there was someone else, but I just wanted to get cleaned up and try out the axe. The place was a cool combination of funky art, luggage, Plumber's tools, musical instruments, Mandala prints, magazines, and hanging plants. She dug around in some boxes behind a drawing table and pulled out a guitar case. Once open she handed me a hollow body Ibanez electric. Pearl inlay of 'Bongo B' on the fretboard.

"I don't have an acoustic handy right now, but you can hear this well enough."

"Wow, that's nice, thanks Olga... er, uh Betty."

I took the guitar by the neck and began checking it out.

"Yeah, this will definitely work."

I started strumming my Mill Avenue barre chords and forgot about everything else. She disappeared while I was soon consumed with my new acquaintance. She reappeared later with a towel and some overalls.

"Hey Max, you got some hillbilly chops."

"Are you giving me a hard time already?"

"No, it's cool, I'm more into the blues, but that sounds like some real Tempe trash you got there. I like it."

"Well, hell, maybe some of this Memphis stuff and your friends will rub off on me. I could use some new tricks."

"Here, take these, and gimme your clothes for the wash. You can use the bathroom over there to shower."

She tossed some clothes my way and waved the towel towards a short hallway to the right of the entry.

"Yeah, I better get cleaned up. I need to get home and get some sleep."

"You can crash here too, if you want…"

She gave me a mischievous smile.

"Well, no, maybe another time, it's awful late. I'll just clean up."

I set the guitar against a chair and took her overalls and towel while she gave me a comical frown. I went to the end of the hall, stripped and tossed her the clothes from around the corner.

"Here you go, thanks again for this."

"No problem, Max."

As I closed the bathroom door, I heard her continue to herself in a softer voice, "Around here most would call it still early…".

She may have said more, but I started the shower and gauged its readiness. Afterward, I dried off enough to put on the overalls, and finished toweling my hair off while walking out to the main room.

"Hey Max, I'm in here."

Olga's voice came from the other end of the hall, so I did an about face. When I got to the door, I peered in to see a washing machine and dryer next to a breakfast table. Across from the table Olga was laying upside down on an L-shaped couch with her legs up over the back, reading a Rolling Stone, a box of chocolates on her stomach. She had on a Kimono and some gym shorts.

"Betcha feel better now. I know I do; cuz I took a quick shower, too."

Her hands were raised as if conducting an orchestra, but her head was upside down over the side of the couch while she spoke. I sat down on the other side of the 'L' and continued drying my hair. With the towel over my head, I heard her re-arrange herself, then lean in behind me using a sweet tone.

"You need to relax your neck and shoulders. Here, let me help you Max."

She began rubbing my back and collarbone, and damn if it didn't feel good.

"Just be careful of my shoulder Olga."

I didn't have a shirt on, just the overalls, so there wasn't much covering my back, and I knew she could see my scar, so she had free reign to work on the few muscles I had. Then she pushed up against me and her kimono must have opened. I felt her points graze my back as she pressed in closer. Then she seemed to slowly melt into me, and we were connected in a layer while she kneaded my neck and shoulders.

"Ok, that feels better than it should."

She didn't pause or respond with words, so tried being more direct.

"Olga? Or should I say Betty?"

Always the prankster, she didn't break stride...

"Tell you what, Max, you can call me whatever you like as long as you call me."

She gave a short deep purring laugh.

"Ok, it's a deal... you know what? Feels like you're enjoying it, too."

I moved my torso back and forth just enough to have an effect.

"Mmmmm," was her only response.

I kept the towel in my left hand and reached down behind my back with my right to feel for her thigh.

"Oh Max, I like the way you get into your back rubs. Now let me finish and then it'll be your turn to work on me."

But then someone else showed up.

"Hey, what's going on?"

The woman's voice was groggy and puzzled. I thought I recognized it.

It was Darla!

Darla stood in the doorway, in her terry cloth robe, one hand propped against the wall, squinting and holding her hair above her eyes with her other hand.

"Daaaarrla, baaaby!"

Olga said her name surprised at first, but then changing into a tone like she had expected her.

"Come over here."

I was more than surprised by the unexpected company. I bumbled to my feet, which caused Olga to rewrap her Kimono. I blurted out my best most obvious line.

"Darla, I didn't know you were here. How's it going?"

I dropped my hand with the towel over the front of the overalls. No need to display my excited response to Olga's successful attentions.

"Apparently it's going on without me, I reckon."

Her voice dripped with sarcasm while she crossed her arms and tilted her head. Darla, bemused, raised her eyebrows, and stared at Olga while waiting for her response. I wasn't sure what to expect.

"Baby, you were asleep when we got back. I didn't wanna wake you. I guess we're getting a little carried away. You know I'd want you to join us if you were awake."

"Well maybe that's the way it was, but I sure ain't in the mood now."

"I'm sorry, Darla, baby. It's not like it's a date or nothing. We're just cleaning up after a Mississippi bridge party."

Olga moved over to Darla and tried to comfort her, but she put up the universal stop sign with her hand. She looked at me next, so I tried to settle things down.

"Yeah, she took this here rookie on a bridge tour and I was dirty and sweaty after... uh, well, anyhow, the shower did me good. I, I mean we, didn't mean to disturb you. And it's great to see you again. I'm really sorry we woke you."

I gave her the warmest smile I could muster in my bare feet and overalls, still nervously holding the towel.

"Eww - whee! You should see both your faces! Got caught with your hands in the cookie jar, didn't ya? Hah, hah!"

The sophisticated goth girl suddenly sounded pure country then slapped her thigh and gave Olga a kiss.

"My Bongo baby, you know to always wake me up whenever you're showering and giving out back rubs. I'll sign up for that every time."

"Well in that case, you wanna join us?"

Olga was something else.

"No, no, I'm hungry now. I passed out early and never got dinner. Let's go eat."

I wasn't really hungry, but of course I can always eat, and felt guilty at the time, ready to do whatever Darla wanted. I didn't want her to feel shunned.

"What have you got in mind? Want me to cook? I'm a pretty good cook."

Olga looked disappointed body rubs were no longer on the table and turned to Darla who squinched her nose at the idea of me cooking in her kitchen.

Instead, she had another idea.

"I don't wanna stay in. I don't wanna mess up the kitchen, besides we ain't got time to cook what I'm hungry for. We can go to the Old White House, they'll be open. Y'all get decent. Let's fly in a flash,."

After settling it, Darla headed back down the hall, "ain't much of nothing in the kitchen to eat anyhow."

Olga winked at me as Darla's voice trailed off.

"Well Max, you can't blame a girl for trying."

"Well, I don't blame you and I sure wasn't putting up much resistance."

Honesty is often the best compliment.

"Well, if we ain't gonna kick it, let's go eat. I'll get you a shirt." Olga lifted her hands from her hips and gave me the 'whaddya say?' gesture.

"Yeah, yeah, thanks, probably a good idea you've outfitted me with some pretty cool duds so far. Are my clothes dry?"

"Aww, thanks, Max. I'll check, if they are, we'll take them with us, and we can drop you off on the way back."

Olga turned and followed in Darla's footsteps, disappearing into the one room I hadn't visited.

At first, it was awkward, but Darla's incredibly good nature kept us calm during the drive. She sat in the middle, never bringing up the situation she'd found us in. Instead, she smiled and plugged in a tape of It's A Beautiful Day. Darla made full smile eye contact and sang along in perfect harmony.

White Bird played and she slowly moved her head side to side with the music.

I found out later Darla gave up her career as a bibliophile after becoming smitten with Betty Bongos before she even knew Betty was Olga the Plumber. Darla followed Betty around and eventually became promoter for Betty's musical career.

Her unique skills originally got her hired at libraries and museums restoring documents long before she met Betty.

She'd worked for US Navy publishing, as The Civil War Times, and Old West Magazine. She later worked with The Mississippi Blues Foundation researching the Historic Beale Street District. That's when she ran into Olga while she was performing on Beale Street. The rest was history.

The Old White House was a red brick building with dusty old aluminum awnings, and cobweb covered windows next to a used car lot on Summer Avenue. There was no sign on the street, just a small, recessed entry on the side of the building. On the door in small red letters was 'White House,' underneath, 'Please Knock.'

Olga began knocking as soon as she got to the door.

"Hey Ray, open up, we're hungry!"

"Easy, Olga, we don't want to get him cranky, or worse, we don't want Mabel thinking we're troublemakers."

"All right, but hell, they're both hard'a hearing."

I was enjoying the show and wondered what the heck someone served in a place like this at 4am.

"Oh shit, I almost forgot, there's a new knock."

Olga began tapping out morse code for S–O–S on the door. As she started the second time, a slot below the sign opened and two pair of eyes behind thick lenses peered out.

"Whaddya want?"

"We came for your famous bacon pizza, Ray."

"Well why didn't you knock right the first time? Come on in."

The slot slammed shut and the door opened, though he stayed behind it as we entered. Once inside, a short little man with a crooked slicked back toupee emerged in his white shirt, and black and brown striped suspenders. He stepped towards us while bolting the door shut and did a quick adjustment of his hairpiece.

"Welcome to the Old Whitehouse folks, please follow me."

He nimbly walked towards the back past a table of diners who looked like two roadies slouched in their chairs out with their ladies.

Ray took us to the back of the room, and we had an amazing time. The girls ordered bacon pizza, which came covered with chopped thick brown sugar, black pepper coated bacon, smothered with sizzling extra sharp cheddar. We took turns grinding the card deck hunk of fresh parm onto the pie then oohed and aahed with every bite.

The girls also ordered cheeseburgers which arrived halfway through the pizza. The burgers were piled high, the bun crusts distinctly smashed with Ray's signature thumb prints, stacked high with roughly torn head lettuce, a thick lipstick red slice of tomato, American and Swiss cheese, and a ton of mayo. I didn't think we could possibly eat it all, and we didn't, but we came close. Darla wrapped the two remaining slices of pie in a napkin, and we passed around the last half of burger, bravely taking little bites till it disappeared.

They dropped me at my bungalow with cutesy waves and girly goodbyes. We'd all gotten past the early weird vibes. In fact, way passed it, as they pawed each other at every stoplight.

I stumbled through the screen porch and made it onto the first-floor couch just in time, passing out from food overdose. It was a roaring, snoring sleep interrupted only by two cats howling outside. Once awakened, I stumbled upstairs to my bed.

I never saw the note from Eddie on the floor of the porch until late the next morning. On the backside of the envelope.

No, it wasn't from a mysterious superhero, it was Eddie reminding me he still had my favorite guitar in his possession, it read:

"Call home! The Blue Phantom."

Before I ever landed in Memphis, a young man I'll never meet found his world crashing down around him. Hollywould, an aspiring young musician and entry level jailbird, did six months in county after an arrest for simple possession unfortunately while on probation. Later, he was arrested again and charged with possession of a controlled substance with intent to sell.

He'd been given a choice by a MPD Lieutenant Delmonico to give someone up further up the drug supply chain in order to avoid a lengthy prison sentence. Boxed in by his earlier convictions and a probation violation hanging over him, he also owed over two thousand dollars in fines with more due at the end of the year, and late payment penalties were growing. Delmonico warned him they'd get a hanging judge for his next hearing, too, because he took Hollywould's recent bust personally.

You see, Delmonico claimed he vouched for him on the last sentencing which allowed Hollywould to get off light. Hollywould's public defender said it was standard procedure, but the truth was Hollywould's folder was growing thick. He didn't know who to believe and couldn't see his own decline. Truth was he'd gotten into dealing and let his music career flag, resulting in fewer gigs. He got plenty of promises from musicians who wanted to buy dope, but gigs never materialized with the sales. He hocked his drums figuring he could turn some deals then get them out of hock. After he took care of that, he'd find someone to turn over to Delmonico.

He went to the Club Robot often but didn't have the leads for Delmonico. He continued to sniff around but failed to meet anyone with a big enough stash. One night while pretty loose at an afterhours party, he tried a new thing called Huggy. Ever since he was having an even harder time getting back on track.

He ordered a quart of Colt 45 and stared at the bubbles, Atlantic Starr's *Freak A Ristic* jammed around him. He noticed two hotties writhing to the music in the far corner of the dance oval, doing their best to live out the song.

When the tune ended, they came over and asked him to join in. He thought, maybe my luck is about to change. Sure enough, it had. Before long they were at a house party, and he was six sheets to the wind, sunk into a bean bag chair the size of a couch. He wasn't sure where the two girls were, though he tried to focus. Topless girls danced around the room as if it was a Love-in. He kept one boot firmly on the floor to prevent the spins. When he squinted through the bay window, he saw a hospital in the distance beyond the trees. He hoped he wouldn't end up there but just couldn't shake his disorientation.

Eventually, Cherry, one of the girls from Club Robot, came over, pulled him up out of the chair and led him to the bedroom. After undressing him, she asked how he was feeling. Normally he would have dismissed such an inquiry, and done his macho music rap thing, but overcome with anxiety and full of malt liquor he became introspective. Instead of being the best pretend version of himself, the soul stripping drugs had inverted him, and like a child he spilled his guts to Cherry.

All of it!

Especially things he was most anxious about and should have kept to himself.

When he awoke, naked and alone on the bed, he tried to recall what he'd said. It was a night of confusing words and images. Worse part was for some reason in his over marinated condition, he thought he'd found a soul mate to help him with his problems. Then he spilled his soul to them. This person he knew nothing about.

Had he told her about Delmonico's offer?

In Phoenix at CB Products Larry Etrusco picked up the phone in his office and called his brother Louis.

"Louis, you know I got a call today about some son of a bitch in Memphis who's talking to the Narco squad?"

"Yeah, what's the problem, he one of your guys?"

"Nah, his brother is, but it's all taken care of. I got someone on it. He won't bother us anymore. When he goes to get his big score, he'll get a surprise he can't handle and that'll be the end of it."

"Good job, keep a tight lid on it. Listen, if there's any loose ends, send someone else to smooth it out, don't you go down there. Send someone who don't know shit about it, alright?"

"No problem, see you at Naples later?"

"Hey, don't worry, I ain't gonna miss my pie, ciao."

"Ciao."

Parlor Dreams.
    In the parlor,
In our birthday dreams
We cut the cake
And lick the blade.

But when they've offered
you their neck
Should you still slice away?

Angorra slipped through the downtown Memphis lobby of Hotel 'M' confident she'd be noticed but not recognized. She wore red Versace sunglasses under a Diana Ross wig, with Jordache jeans and a Chanel blouse, and carried a Birkin knock off. She'd done an escort job at the 'M' before but was unable to explore as it was rushed. Entering incognito gave her a chance to check it out, and she could gaze and graze, as it were.

She looked around and wondered what Mawmaw would think of the place. No expense was spared showing off the glitz and ghosts of the Delta. Gold Records earned by the Musical Stars of the Mid-South hung on the walls, while mannequins in plexi-glass cases donned their most memorable stage outfits. Some were just cool; Rosetta Thorpe's floral print dress, Tina's Turner's sequined Mini-skirt, and BB King's Blue Tuxedo coat. While others were outrageous, Isaac Hayes' gold chains, or Bar Kays' white leather fringe snake handling diamond stud jumpers. Perhaps the ultimate was Rufus Thomas's fire engine red hotpants trimmed in mink with matching knee-high patent leather platform heels.

In the past Mawmaw only hinted at her younger days and club life glory and now wouldn't admit to any such goings on. Angorra knew Pearlie's arrival was why. Mawmaw was happy to raise Pearlie for Angorra but her daughter's wayward lifestyle tarnished the joy she may have had in recalling her memories. They both knew Mawmaw never wanted Pearlie to know about those wild times.

Angorra's mind began to wander while she looked at the local legends' outfits. For a moment she allowed herself to feel that spark of her younger self's dreams.

An elevator chimed and brought her back to reality. She considered the incident with the Boone boy and realized she'd never taken revenge on anyone who wasn't a client. When younger, she always considered pay back something reserved for lovers who spurned her, then as an adult, for clients who mistreated or shorted her. Her guilt was buried so deep she couldn't identify it, but she took her daughter's injuries personally.

She never expected to be spurned by a lover again. She decided she would never be in a relationship again that wasn't part of a negotiation. The dream of finding a sweet man to share her life barely existed in the seldom-explored back of her mind. And that was only because of Mawmaw, who always tried to steer her towards finding such a man.

She'd always said, "A sweet man ain't your best bet in an alley fight but he's your best friend come daylight."

Mawmaw would know, she probably witnessed more alley fights than Angorra ever would, and that was fine. Angorra remembered her early childhood when they lived in a hotel behind a Go-Go club Mawmaw worked. Though memories were sketchy, she remembered they persevered, surviving sirens and flashing lights, and cops and jealous lovers busting down their doors, with many frantic late-night getaways and desperate mornings scrounging bail.

She owed her Mawmaw plenty but didn't want to continue a personal inventory of their past as there was too much to think about now. She had to pay back the man who took away her little girl's God-given sight and sound. She suddenly found revenge easy to embrace. It was great motivation and simple to understand.

Through the grapevine she heard the Etruscos were planning another party. She wasn't sure if the Boones were invited but knew there was a good chance they'd be there. If not, she'd fly to Arizona, as she also learned Danny worked at the Vettes there.

She rode the elevator to the roof of the M. Happy Hour overlooking the city was in full swing and on the east side of the rooftop a business group gathered at the bar. On the west side was a faux patio area with umbrellas and potted plants. Nobody was there at the time, and the sunset on the river view made her feel like she was on the set of a movie.

She decided to chill, got a wine spritzer from the bar, and picked out a lounge table as far from distraction as possible.

With the area to herself, she put her purse on the chair and walked over to the rooftop's rail on its edge. She took a couple hits from a hash loaded cigarette, just enough to catch a buzz but not attract attention. Then she relaxed in her chair, sipped her drink, and daydreamed. Misty eyed, she watched the sun descend over the Arkansas wetlands, as the hash lolled through her veins and tickled her synapses. By and by she lapsed into a startlingly realistic dream.

Following the Boone brothers on their trip to Mexico with Louis; Angorra plotted her own road trip hell bent for revenge with the unknowing help of Phil, a regular client in town for a conference. As their paid rendezvous began, her thoughts were focused on how to parlay their trip into revenge for Pearlie and while they discussed their arranged encounter Phil sensed her brain was in overdrive elsewhere.

"What's on your mind, Angel?"

It was her chance.

"Let's go to Rocky Point for some fun."

She expected him to decline, but when she realized he was considering it, she pushed on.

"Well, you said you're finished with the important conference stuff and wanted to play. If you take me there, you can play me anyway you want."

Angorra's intent was to find the Boones, but Phil played along. Soon as they finished their cocktails, they threw their bags in his car and left. They stopped a few miles south of Ajo, where Angorra paid her respects to a friend 'Gloria,' she'd lost earlier in life.

Gloria flipped her Miata there, and never made it home. Angorra offered a small tiara, a bouquet, and a framed picture of

Gloria decorated with red bows. They took their place among a collection of dusty plastic flowers, costume jewelry and pictures of saints, all sun bleached and worn though lovingly arranged. At least the newest tribute would shine bright for a while. Like her old friend.

"Gloria, I will never forget you, darling. I hope you're resting easy now."

Grief swelling inside, Angorra couldn't stop the tears rolling down her cheeks; their salty sadness sparkling in the desert sun as cars whipped by. The tailwinds lifted her blouse and tussled her hair, the loss spurred forward her growing determination for revenge. In one motion she wiped her tears, sniffled, and pushed her hair behind her ear.

"Listen, Gloria, I gotta go, you know the world don't wait for us that ain't gotten even yet."

The rest of the drive was uneventful, though when she got back in the car, Phil sensed she was in pain, and reaching over, pulled her close. She took comfort in the compassion of human touch. His radio played Jimmy Cliff, "You Can Get It If You Really Want," and the reggae helped her smile. When the song ended, she threw back her head and shouted.

"You better believe it brother. I want it and I'm gonna get it!"

Phil reached over, placed his hand on her thigh and joined in, thinking he understood and smiled with anticipation.

"Yea baby, Rocky Point here we come!"

Once there, they checked in off the main drag into the very discreet Hotel Palma. She'd stayed there before. They signed in as Bill and Gloria Wilson.

Immediately after entering the room, Angorra made good on her guarantee to Phil he would have a great time. They made love on the bedspread, with the late afternoon light casting *shadows on the wall and the clock radio playing Mariachi songs. Instead of lingering, they went to the pool afterwards. She left him there and told him she needed to - "Do some girl shopping on her own."'*

First, she went back to the room, put on shorts and grabbed an M9 Beretta and a silencer from her suitcase. She put them in her beach bag, slung the bag over her shoulder and put on a red poolside coverall. Indeed, it covered everything, including the bag. She put on a floppy beach hat with an oversized brim to hide her face.

She pulled out her weapon, held it against her chest and looked at her get-up in the mirror. She convinced herself she could have been anyone. Her heart raced though, and she felt lightheaded. She leaned back and took a deep breath.

"You got this, Angie..."

She waved to Phil from the other side of the pool when she left the hotel property to head down to the beach. When she got to the Princessa Del Mar, where Louis preferred to stay, she weaved through the beach chairs over to the pool. From there she could see the palapas and lounge chairs set up in rows between the bars where guests had set up base with colorful umbrellas and towels.

She scanned the palm shaded areas on the beach, and the water inflatable playground in the water for sign of the Boones. She finally spied Louis' group near the edge of a nearby palm line. Four guys and five girls with beach toys in hand ambled down to the water. She didn't spot Danny, so she decided to get closer for a better look. She slowly zigzagged towards their area.

That's where she spotted Danny in a row of chairs laying in his at a very relaxed angle. Wearing Laguna jams, and a pink souvenir T-shirt, his straw pork pie hat covered most of his face. She *meandered closer, looking as if she was watching the tourists at play in the water. Thirty feet from his row she slipped into the aisle that ran behind him. She saw no one within three rows.*

She knelt when she got behind his chair and pretended to adjust her shoe. The plastic pineapple souvenir cup on his table ice had melted, and the cup sat in a puddle, the condensation running off the table, dripping on the sand. He must have passed out. He was motionless and she heard him snore. His face was hidden, but not the silver necklace around his neck.

"Danny."

He was a sitting duck, served up on a platter for whatever she wanted, while his fellow partiers were over a hundred yards away.

She calculated how half the distance between her, and his friends was the waist high water where they played on the inflatable slides. She could barely hear their laughter; they were at least three minutes away.

She reached in her bag and lifted the gun while checking the silencer was still attached. She positioned the weapon through a gap in her cover all, and carefully leaned into the back of his chair. She pulled her garment just enough to expose the nose, angling it between his shoulder blades at a downward angle. She quickly squeezed the trigger twice, shooting into his back. She hoped the bullets would go into the sand if they passed through him. He jerked but settled quickly.

His hat tumbled onto the ground while she hurried the gun back into her bag.

"I'm sorry sir, let me get that."

She instinctively reached down, grabbed his hat, and carefully placed it over his face. His body jerked again, and it startled her, but she didn't stop.

She couldn't waste any time. Her heart raced; her body filled with adrenaline. She stood up and backed away. Through the chair's plastic slats she saw blood blossom on the back of his shirt. She turned to leave when it puddled at his waistline and drops found their way to the sand.

She sucked in her breath and tried to remain calm while walking at a quick pace, with no one within twenty yards. People hollered and clowned at jet skis buzzing by.

It had been perfect timing.

Still, she found it hard not to panic. She passed hundreds of chairs until she reached an opening and strode towards the gift shop. She heard a scream but didn't stop, telling herself it was just someone going down a slide.

She decided to take a cab to Cholla Bay and dump the gun, then go back to their hotel. Before she could hail a cab; she felt a turbulent swirling in the pit of her stomach and someone touched her shoulder. She heard a stranger's voice in her ear...

"Are you ok, Miss? You need another drink? I thought I heard you call me."

The 'M' rooftop bartender was checking on her. As she awoke, she felt nauseous and struggled to answer.

"Uh, yeah, uh, you gotta wet towel and some ice water? I think I'm having a bad reaction to some food."

"Yes, ma'am, I'll be right back."

He turned and left, and she tried to get her head together. When he returned, she put the towel on her forehead and took a sip. She felt her stomach flip and got up while holding the towel in place. She passed the bar and pointed straight ahead, barely able to speak.

"Ladies' room?"

"Yes, ma'am, right over there."

She unfolded the towel and quickly refolded it over her mouth and hurried into the bathroom into a handicap stall. She shook uncontrollably and started to retch. She was sweating profusely and squeezing her eyes in pain.

When she was through emptying her guts she heard her old friend Beatri's voice inside her head.

"Angie, you ain't cut out for this James Bond shit."

She wiped the perspiration from her forehead and cheek and looked in the mirror. She saw someone she barely recognized wiping spittle from her chin.

She may have been changed by her dream but knew what her next move needed to be. Like Mawmaw use to say, "Get the right tool for the job."

She didn't have any idea what that 'tool' might be, but knew she needed help to get proper revenge. She was certain for the revenge she sought for Pearlie she would need Beatri.

S he's a rattling rabbit,
      a flapper, an expert in flooze.
A cartoon mystery,
so charming,
never rude.

When she asked for a light,
 I thought I might
join in her courting dance.

You know the crazy little lady,
 Cray-crazy little lady,
You know she might turn out,
Might turn out to be,
A great big bunch,
Great big bunches of fun.

Once guests filled the Memphis Vettes it was a funkier, looser vibe than Phoenix. The surf music wasn't as popular in the Delta, most all were eliminated by Memphis DJs, replaced by songs culled from catalogues of extraordinary and often little-known artists. The common thread being they created their groundbreaking styles in hot sessions in local studios. Hearing these different songs seemed odd at first; as specific song sequences were drilled into me in training, but these different tunes with local groove brought a new carefree rhythm to my work.

The house DJs harvested their stuff rummaging through used record bins, random yard sales, and even found some limited issue 45's at estate sales. In their heyday these were only sold out of the trunks of musicians' cars. Nuggets like these became anthems igniting the Memphian's spirit. It didn't take long before the songs juked their way into my heart as well.

I was particularly fond of Ben Cauley's *Sweet Soul Medley*, and Thermos Greenwood's *Who Gave the Monkey A Gun?* Of course, nothing could top Rufus Thomas and *The Funky Chicken*.

My third night, Mr. Rufus Thomas came in Vettes and conducted an official full blown, full throttle *Funky Chicken*. A king and a jester, his presence was irresistible. He jived his way through the crowd, gray mutton chops wrapped round his shiny dome, the crown above the electric pink, fur trimmed cape. He topped his outfit off with matching pink shorts and knee-high patent leather stacked heel boots.

Our DJ immediately slapped Rufus' strutting music on. Anyone who didn't know before, was alerted by the horn intro and clucking, he was in the house. The DJ handed Rufus a microphone and the place went nuts. People scrambled onto their chairs and climbed onto the bar to catch a glimpse and strut their stuff. It was quite a sight, five hundred goofballs partying away: Elbows flapping, butts bouncing, feet scratching, heads bobbing to the beat.

When a local hero came in the club it was routine for the staff to break out the special Jell-O shots shipped from Vettes Phoenix headquarters. The staff caught a buzz while passing them out to the crowd. People didn't need additional encouragement to celebrate when Rufus showed up, but it was another example of the Vette's team party appetite.

I felt like this city was a place I could call home. I wasn't sure about a long-term career with Vettes, but I dug the Memphis vibe. Deeply rooted in its soul was an innate, river-town party attitude. A deeper connection than the pool partying desert scene I'd departed, but I wondered if I could thrive. Would I be able to make my own music and pay the bills? That was something I'd have to figure out later, I was deep into Vettes, and it took everything I had to keep up. The job had more bosses and paperwork than I'd ever dealt with, and those things were not second nature for me by a long shot.

Rufus' conducted his impromptu dance clinic of *Walking the Dog* as an encore, then, like a pro, with the crowd at its peak, he deliberately strutted out the front door, his entourage in tow.

Meanwhile, as I did my rounds, I sensed a familiar presence, there was a 'blast from the past' energy in the house. I zeroed in on a woman at the bar in the rear of the club. She had her back to me so I wasn't sure at first. Her hair looked completely different, but her essence was familiar pulling me in like a magnet. Fabric was spun into her Fulani braids, and her locks were dotted with glimmering beads cascading down her back. As I approached, her caramel skin and stunning profile struck an old familiar chord. I had to remind myself though chances were slim it would be Angel.

I hoped it was. You see, I had a fling with her when working at Baxter's. The memory was exciting but painful. I fell hard for her then. Recalling the emotions gone by, I considered leaving the situation alone, just might be better to keep it a mystery, but before I could turn away, the excitement of the night and Memphis vibe spurred me on.

"Angel? Could it be? Is it you?"

She made a slight movement but didn't turn around. The bartender raised his eyes to check if I needed anything, but I waved him off. I leaned in next to her and faced her.

"Hey, you look like someone I used to know."

She gave me an 'oh really?' look while lowering her red cat eye shades to look me over. Her her eyes were stinging memories, but her response put my confidence off balance, and for a second I thought I'd made a mistake.

"Oh, I'm sorry, I thought, well, I didn't mean to bother you..."

She pushed the sunglasses back in place and tilted her head to the side. Just as I pushed off from the bar to back away, she reached out and put her hand on top of mine.

"Yes, Max you got me, but listen baby, I'm Angorra tonight. I don't answer to Angel around here."

She looked around as if checking that anyone might identify her. I was speechless.

"I'm very surprised to see you here, Max. What'cha doing in my neck of the woods?"

"Whoa, you're from around here? I thought you were from Arizona..." I shuffled my feet, " I, I work here now."

"Oh, I'm just passing through. I'm originally from these parts. Just visiting family right now. But my, what a pleasant surprise to see you."

"Yeah, me too. You know I think about you all the time."

I was excited, and well, it was true that I used to. In fact, it took me quite a while to get her out of my system after our adventures.

"Ah, Max, you're sweet. Sorry, I don't have time to catch up more. I gotta head down to New Orleans to see an old friend on the overnight train. I just dropped by cuz I heard through the grapevine Rufus was coming in."

"Well, damn, it's great to see you. I just started working for Vettes and got in Memphis a few days ago..., still learning the ropes."

"Well, you'll do fine here, Max." She smiled at me and tilted her head adding, "Uh huh, I bet the ladies be sweet on you."

She reached over with her thumb and forefinger and grabbed my lapel. Moving her hand up and down while humming, she lifted an eyebrow and smiled coyly. I must have blushed.

"Well, I don't know about that, I'm working a lot, but it's been fun so far."

"Uh-huh, I bet it has. I mean you're all spruced up in this fancy club with Rufus doing a floor show and all."

"Yeah, well, I... uh, it's something all right. That was my first-time seeing Rufus. I do like the city, it's a lotta fun."

"Hey, you have any openings for dancers? These girls got great routines."

"All the girls you see dancing are hostesses, servers, or DJs, I've never heard of Vettes hiring professional dancers."

"Hmmm, well my sister Pearlie's a very pretty girl and I know she'd go over big here."

Something about her way made me self-conscious in such close proximity. There I was in this crowded bar I managed, and I was wishing there was a way to leave and talk to her privately.

"You sure know how to get to a guy. Hey, I don't know the hiring situation here yet, but we're always interested in any applicant you recommend."

I smiled and did a goofy 'hubba-hubba' with my eyebrows. She smiled back and lowered her eyes, then let go of my lapel. She stood up and put her arms around my waist, presenting herself with parted lips and pressed her body against me.

"Well, I gotta get going. I'll let you know if she's coming by."

"Ok, do you want to get together later, maybe?"

She raised her head and lowered her eyes.

"No, Max, but I'll see you around, baby."

I looked around to see if we were being watched and decided I didn't care. I leaned into her, and we shared a sweet little kiss. Then she pulled back her head slightly while still holding my hips and brushed past my cheek and whispered in my ear.

"Max, you and I were good together, I hope we can be that way again... sometime soon...".

With that she slipped out of my grasp and turned away, quickly sliding through the crowd. Every muscle and joint in her was well-trained to entice the viewers. She held her head high while her slender frame moved with deliberate stealth, like a jungle cat on the prowl. Her pace was just slow enough so anyone who picked up her vibe would see the show the way she intended them to. Every subtle movement, and every cell in her body was full of unmistakable attitude. As she continued out the door her eyes remained focused straight ahead never wavering.

The rest of the night I tried a few times to reach Eddie in Arizona but couldn't connect. Still hyped with excitement, I left him a crazy chicken call on his machine, "Bawk-bawk-bawk!" and signed off with my best, "Rock-a-doodle-dooooo!"

After the last bartender check out, I declined late-night house party invitations and walked home with thoughts of days gone by.

My time with the girl I knew as Angel really didn't seem like all that long ago...

In my early days at Baxter's, I first noticed a sultry single lady, who always traveled solo. Angel's eyes and skin were caramel, her disposition casual and sweet. She sat at the bar, drank iced tea and stood out in a crowd of sports enthusiasts, graduate students, and hopheads. Her clothes, subtle yet stylish, seemed painted on, and her eyes moved with lethal grace. Angel never stayed long but was the target of many advances, deftly handling them all in good humor.

The main course of our affair was a spontaneous trip to the Texas Gulf Coast. Originally, I planned to go to Austin to work on a stage crew for a couple of concerts, but my plans fell through at the last minute. As I remember it, I got off work ready to begin the week vacation the following day without a backup plan.

Angel showed up that day when I finished my shift. As I stood at the bar drinking a beer, and considered the change of plans, I leaned into her making room for a server with a tray full of beers in one hand and a pizza in the other. When I apologized to Angel, she gracefully reintroduced herself, and we began a pleasant conversation. It wasn't long before she offered a solution for my plans gone awry.

"You know Max, a trip to Texas might still be a lot of fun with the right traveling companion."

She moved her hand to a place below her neck and tilted her head, looking very alluring.

I tried a little charm.

"I appreciate your kind encouragement. You might be right; do you know where I might find such a 'right' companion?"

I wasn't taking her seriously because I figured it was just bar talk. She smiled demurely.

"You're sweet Max. I thought you already knew. I'm referring to myself, of course."

Then she went from seemingly shy to truly interested in a heartbeat. I was at a loss for words.

"What do you think?"

"What do I... I mean, do you go to Texas a lot or something?"

I was intrigued our conversation might be something other than bar talk.

"I get around sometimes, and it can be a nice place if you know where to look. You said your original plans got dashed, didn't you?"

She shook her head like 'Why not?' as she took another sip of tea.

"Well, it's true, suddenly I've got no plans for the week."

"Well, guess what? I got a brand-new Mustang convertible just itching to travel."

She uncrossed her legs and leaned in a little closer, "now Max, if you filled my Mustang up with gas..."

She moved her eyes and wrinkled her brow in a 'You never know' look. As she waited for my response, she smiled. She pushed her tongue out to gather her straw, and delicately gripped it with her lips. As she took a sip, her pert cheeks showed off her dimples while she raised her eyes again to meet mine.

And she waited, and her sly little smile grew bolder, while her pert little Angel face continued looking straight into my stare.

I was smitten, emboldened and loved the idea.

But was it crazy to leave on a spree with such a vibrant mysterious woman? She was much different from the girls I usually met in a sports bar or the music scene.

I was willing to bet it was crazy but worth it.

"Why not? I'll need to grab some things, but I can travel light."

"Me too, Max, you just let me know when and where."

"How about tonight?"

As I remember, we didn't leave that night. First, we went to her apartment. Once there, she pulled a joint out of her bag, lighting it soon as we stepped inside. The door closed behind us and she offered the joint to me before she even turned around.

"Oh, uh, ok, don't mind if I do."

I tried to play it cool, taking too big a toke and holding it in. My eyes got big and as I handed it back, I exhaled sooner than I wanted with a cough.

"Hey, how strong is this? I wanna be able to help you drive."

I tried to wave the smoke away to get it out of our faces.

"It's all good baby, take a couple of hits and you'll feel ok. I want us to get comfortable with each other."

She squinted, took a long effortless toke and gave me a sweet sexy smile, and slid her bag off her shoulder. She pulled some long matches from a vase and began gliding around the room lighting candles.

"Make yourself comfortable, baby. Tonight, I'm in the mood to get to know you better. We'll leave in the morning, and we'll get your stuff then."

With the candles lit to her liking, she started to shed her clothing, and encouraged me to do the same. It didn't take long before all clothes were off, and she put her hand on my chest as I tried to embrace her.

"Wait, let's get in my bed, I got some new satin sheets. You know Max, just like the song."

I was high and happy, and totally taken in by her graceful yet powerful guiding ways, her caramel skin like candy in my eyes. With a smooth swing of her head, she tossed her hair over her shoulder. Her eyes locked on mine, she pushed forward, grazing my hip with her hand and leading me into the sheets. Side by side, we kissed in a test of tongues that could only end in mutual surrender. With my face in her hands, she pulled back, and while still close enough for my lips to feel each word as she spoke, she made a proclamation.

"Max, don't you know I'm just a horny little redbone?"

She laughed so freely, I had to join in. She'd succeeded in getting me more than comfortable.

"Angel, all I know is you're really something."

We rolled around in the sheets until our lovemaking left us sighing. I watched the candle's shadows dance off her hanging beads and 1920's French Postcard posters. While I surveyed her pad, she dragged her finger down my chest, and drew circles on my stomach. After she traced infinity on my chest, she lay her head next to her hand. We let our bodies hum and glow before dozing off.

It was early when she roused me, and we hit the road while still dark. We carried on like honeymooners as we traveled to the Texas coast, bar hopping in Houston and disco dancing in Dallas. To end the nights, we grabbed a cheap hotel room and shook the sheets, heading out a little later with each new morning.

Eventually, I was popping Lone Stars as we cruised from Corpus Christi along South Padre Island Drive with the Mustang's top down and our hair blowing free. There without warning, a smattering of dollar bills, apparently caught in the causeway's tailwinds, burst into our car. We tried to snatch them while they danced in the air currents, and she began to swerve. We laughed so hard she pulled off on the sandy shoulder and stopped.

"Max! Baby! Stop it! I'm gonna wet myself if I don't stop laughing. Lordy mercy!"

"Whooeee, it's raining *money* today."

While she gathered herself, I grabbed another beer from the cooler and chugged it in celebration.

In the trunk she had a pup tent, and we bought cheap beach towels and inflatable rafts. We slept on the beach with the tent open to the water and watched the moon settle in the ocean. The waves caressed our ears while we caressed each other, all the while our passion stayed cranked up to ten. After a few days, all smiles, we finally hit the road back home.

I was smitten.

Strange thing was, when we got back, I never corralled her again. She made appearances at Baxter's from time to time, but we were never got our schedules to sync. At least that's what I thought.

I mean she seemed open to more dates, but it never happened. I got the feeling I had seen a side of her on our Texas trip she usually kept locked up. The enjoyable whirlwind had been a time of salacious companionship without judgement, and given the trials and tribulations of life, it's true it would've been hard to ever duplicate again.

But hell, you can't blame a guy for wanting to. Nevertheless, whenever I saw her afterwards, she was always on the way back or on the way to somewhere and had only stopped in for tea.

When she finally gave in to another date, we met in Scottsdale, Angel telling me in advance it was a one-nighter, as she was leaving the next day.

I hung out by the potted palms on a Scottdale patio anxious and hungry. I spotted her as she glided along the building wearing movie star sunglasses and had a white shawl over a low-cut coral top, with skintight floral print pants. In the crook of her arm with a gold chain hung a small white purse.

The Grateful Dead's familiar refrain began to play in my head, *"She had rings on her fingers and bells on her toes…"*.

I repeated the words under my breath, the excitement in my heart rising. Her skin's caramel candy tone still glowed from within. When I stepped out from behind the palm her smile curled bewitchingly.

"What are you doing hiding in the bushes?"

"I was looking over the menu."

"Seems like you always hungry, Max."

"I guess so," she had me shrugging already.

"You look really nice, Angel. Hey, why don't we sit out here?"

"Wonderful."

She stood by a chair and looked at me expectantly.

"Oh, here you go."

I clumsily pulled the chair for her, and while scraping the concrete moved my chair nearer. When the waitress arrived, we ordered and Angel didn't even look at the menu, she simply said she'd have her usual. I ordered the special, unsure what it was and didn't really care, I was excited just to be with Angel again. I ordered two House Margaritas, too, but when they arrived, Angel declined hers and stuck with tea, so I drank both.

As we finished lunch, Angel rather oddly dropped her lip gloss. It rolled over near me and she quickly spoke up.

"I'll get it."

She held up her hand to stop me as I struggled to scootch my chair. Before I knew it, she'd stood up, stepped towards me and knelt down slowly. She reached under the table and grabbed the shiny cylinder, while carefully placing her hand on my knee. She lifted her head and grinned slyly. 'What do you want me to do now eyes' shined at me.

"Did you get it?" was all I could muster.

She slowly slid her hand along my jeans without changing expression and held up the lipstick setting it on the table. Suddenly, the intensity of the moment became a thing, and she looked deep into my heart as it raced in response to her touch.

"Max, we sure had fun in Texas, didn't we?"

I remembered all right; we had experienced an intimate paradise in our open tent on that Texas beach. The moon had winked from the waves in tandem with rush after rush of our heartbeats. We took it slow and easy; the nights chocked full of ecstasy.

Once we got to her Scottsdale apartment, Angel told me her story, explaining she owed it to me to let me know she couldn't be in a relationship. She really enjoyed our sex, it was an easy way for her to enjoy its gifts, but the thing was I needed to understand it was also a way of life for her. Among other things, she told me she was unable to pleasure herself, saying she found out when she tried to give up men.

Later, when she was sharing an apartment with a woman named Gloria, they'd double-teamed clients for big money, and in time the two women got close. But Gloria kept going through one horrible client turned lover relationship after another. Since Gloria kept falling in love with clients, they broke up the friendship. Angel just couldn't bear to be around Gloria and witness her pain or endure the drama that came with it. Angel believed falling in love with a client was never worth it.

She knew all clients weren't bad people, but often they weren't the best folks, either. She and Gloria had fished in shallow waters. Angel wanted to go deep and catch bigger wallets. She learned tough lessons aplenty when she started 'the life', and never wanted to learn any a second time. The lifestyle often dangerous, could be a vicious cycle, and the money inconsistent. Getting busted was constantly a risk. Now she rarely accepted jobs from someone she didn't already know.

She only booked preferred clients, men who paid the highest fees. She would never work with a pimp again. She'd done fine now for years without and was determined to stay independent. According to Angel, clients wanted dependable results and variety, usually something they didn't experience in their normal day to day lives or bedrooms. She'd developed her business herself claiming she knew how to stay safe. So far, it was working.

Something came undone that night and she opened more than her body to me, indeed unfolding her heart and soul. Instead of her usual tight-lipped ways, with her cards held close, she laid the deck out face up. I was only able to quietly acknowledge with my eyes while she poured out the details of her life.

And I was in shock; I'd done a similar thing as Gloria only with the tables turned. Instead of a 'fallen Angel' in love with her client, I was the lovesick schoolboy who fell for his teacher. Only she wasn't a teacher, she was an escort.

In retrospect, she opened her heart to me on a whim. The romance I thought we had had simply been an education. For me it had been a blessing to know her briefly, even if only as a paramour. More importantly, in the big picture and perhaps as an even bigger blessing, she warned me not to pursue her for any type of relationship.

Of course, I didn't find out about her career until after I'd been smitten. Once she'd opened up, her revelations had been many. She explained how she had peddled herself for dinner dates, couples healing, aromatherapy, any intimate encounter that could showcase her charm and love of courtship. In truth, she'd never exactly hidden it from me, I just didn't see the telltale signs, and of course once smitten, I never thought to ask.

"I guess I'm in over my head, huh?"

Propped up on an elbow I looked over to her while she stared blankly at the ceiling.

"Max, you're an OK guy, and you and me, we get along well enough..."

"But you'll never let it be a relationship is what you're saying..."

"Listen baby, this is my life, and I could never drag you into it."

Looking back, I simply didn't play in the same world she did. When I was playing, she wasn't. Her life was in a completely different world with a much sharper edge. After that last night together, I finally understood. She was way more than a survivor. She'd developed a virtuoso's capacity for her lifestyle, and I was certainly out of my league.

In her kindness and as a courtesy, she confided in me. She didn't do relationships; she was only for hire.

Since that night, I always expected to find out she had a Sugar Daddy. It turned out except for tough life lessons, she'd made her way on good looks, street smarts, and determination, always keeping her heart locked up.

As much as she turned me on, she made her point. Now I realize she wanted to protect *my* heart, too. Basically, on our Texas trip, she made an exception.

Over those next few months, I met a couple of her acquaintances, never knowing if they were clients or friends. I never would out her to anyone who didn't already know. As far as I was concerned it wasn't any of their business. Not just because of the respect she'd earned and deserved, but hey, even the chance of another road trip was good enough reason.

It took time, but I was able to let the longing for her fade from my heart. I would have denied it, but I also knew she had ability to turn a dying spark into a blaze if she wanted, so it was lucky for me she stayed away. I told myself another road trip was probably more fantasy than possibility.

So, now I'd met her again in Memphis, and though she quickly slipped away, I wondered if I'd ever see her again. I'd never forgotten how she drew infinity on my chest holding on to it as a delicious memory. I never imagined I would feel her presence or join in her journey before we touched again.

I like to lap up a little dew,
   And get a little buzz.
Don't put away the honey jar
please don't make a fuss.

Don't let the lights go dim,
Or have my candle snuffed
I don't have to tell you
There's never ever enough.

Hollywould was in a jam, his grace period from the Memphis Narco Squad was running out. He needed to rat someone out. They believed he was stringing them along and were out of patience. Soon they'd pull their offer, push him to trial, and recommend the max. Lieutenant Delmonico issued the ultimatum.

"Get a big fish or go to jail."

Hollywould couldn't tell anyone about his dilemma, including his brother Doomuch. If word got out on the street, it would be too risky, he wouldn't stand a chance satisfying Delmonico much less staying alive. The only time he dared mention his plight was in anguished prayers. Prayers unfortunately lacking the focus or devotion to bring relief or results.

He spent sleepless nights contemplating his next course of action. Unable to find a credible dealer, he fell into an extreme panicked funk, and deciding he best go on the lam.

After aimlessly wandering around his apartment, unable to decide what he needed to pack or where to go, he went to Club Robot. Perhaps some liquid courage would help him decide his destination, maybe he'd even get lucky.

Sure enough, an attractive and unattached lady introduced herself as Eden and asked to join him. Said she was a friend of Cherry and was flirty. Their conversation conveniently led to her saying she knew a supplier. Someone he should meet, who had just arrived in town looking for someone to distribute their goods. It seemed too good to be true, so Hollywould held back and played it slow. But as he hesitated to show a real interest, she quickly rescinded the offer.

"My friend Cherry said you were a good man and needed a haul, said you were reliable and could raise quick cash with the right stuff..."

She stood up as she pulled her bag to her shoulder. "...I'm sorry, maybe you're not the man she thought, or maybe I've got the wrong man..."

She turned to leave adding, "Don't worry, dear, I didn't mean to bother you, forget I said anything at all, I'll be on my way."

"Wait, baby, now hold on, you're moving too fast. I'm your man, let's just take it slow. Tell me what you got for me."

To his surprise after returning to amicable discussion Eden simply turned over her contact to Hollywould. She said a Ms. Rita would call for him at Club Robot the very next night. Eden had to leave in the morning but told Hollywould he would be in good hands.

He had never met her before that night, but he was charmed by her; she oozed confidence and cast a spell on him. It immediately bolstered his courage and amplified his ambition. Before leaving, Eden gave him a little sample to try, warning him not to nose around Club Robot concerning Ms. Rita or the deal wouldn't happen. He knew better and figured she wanted to avoid competition between runners, as high-volume dealers used more than one runner to unload a big haul.

He felt a special thrill, a new type of rush. Now he could escape the tightening noose. He had a chance to score, and though it would be tricky, he could satisfy Delmonico, pay off debts, and maybe even stash some cash. Most importantly he wouldn't have to go on the run.

He did the line of Huggy. It gave him a new sense of urgency, as the world filled with vibrant sounds and colors. His heart beat a little stronger. He heard his breath course through his lungs. He knew he didn't have time or intention to waste. It would be his only shot and if it didn't pan out, he would have to hit the road running for his life.

The next night he waited at Club Robot for two hours for instructions, but Ms. Rita never called or showed. Desperate, he decided to find Lehigh to front him a little something to sell for travel money. He called Lehigh and placed an order. After the call, he was despondent and kicked absentmindedly at the bar stools as he shuffled out the door to his Toyota.

However, when he opened the car door there was an envelope on the driver's seat. To his surprise there were instructions with a vial of powder. He touched it to his tongue; it was the same Huggy he tried with Cherry and given by Eden. He was re-energized, full of optimism and snorted the rest of the vial's contents off the back of his hand without hesitation before he started his car.

The note directed him to meet at Ernie's Body Shop. He realized she was being oddly cautious to leave the note in his car and not come inside, but it really didn't really matter. He was at a point of no return. He was all in with this one chance.

Ernie's was where his brother Doomuch had scored though Doomuch had never been. Even with the knowledge a deal there might affect his brother's connection he couldn't worry about that now. If she was the main source for Doomuch he really didn't care, Ms. Rita was the big fish Delmonico wanted. He had to deliver Ms. Rita to Delmonico, it was his ticket out.

First, he had to make sure she was legit. Things would shake out in the end. As he drove, he told himself Hollywould wouldn't get arrested since he was too small time.

He followed the instructions at Ernie's. After checking there were no other cars, he pulled in the alley and turned off his lights. He was high and riding the thrill of meeting a big-time dealer, like on a secret mission holding the promise of freedom.

He lifted the fence, ducked under and checked around after each step, tiptoeing carefully all the way to the front door. It was dark inside the shop. The door was unlocked as expected.

He backed in the room, closed the door and per the instructions started to set the lock, but when he pushed in the bolt, he was grabbed from behind.

His arms were instantly pulled behind his back and hands zip tied.

"Hey!"

A plastic bag was pulled over his head and squeezed tightly at the neck before he could utter another sound. Too stunned to mount much resistance he was tripped while being pushed headfirst and crashed to the floor. Pungent fumes in the bag had him out before his head registered the impact on the cement.

When he regained consciousness, it was dark, he was bound to a chair, and the bag was replaced by a cloth blindfold. Unable to close his mouth, he found his jaw painfully propped open to one side, as if a patient at the dentist. A nasty chemical taste coated his tongue and back of his throat. He struggled to make a sound but heard a woman's voice.

"Well, hello Mr. Hollywould. Listen, my dear, I want you to swallow now or you're gonna choke." Her hand gripped him by the jawbone.

"Oh, but don't worry, babe, this'll make you feel *really nice*. And after you swallow nothing will hurt at all. Then we can get down to business."

Veda patted his thigh, then slowly wiped her bare hand across his forehead to relax him. Her other hand sported an industrial PVC coated glove and held the sheared end of clear tubing. She jammed the tube in his mouth, covering his gape with her gloved hand, and gripped his jawbone with the other. She stepped on the switch attached to the aquarium pump set up in the sink.

Liquid streamed into his mouth, as he choked trying to stop the flow. He swallowed and swallowed some more as he tried to keep up. As he gagged on the noxious cocktail, it rushed into his stomach, the chemical stench attacking his sinuses, leaving a trail of numbness. The liquid sprayed through Veda's fingers, running down his chin onto his chest. He panicked then convulsed until the convulsions became unmanageable.

His body rocked so violently Veda tired of struggling to steady his head. She let go and backed away.

"You're on your own now, Mr. Hollywould."

Still bound to the chair he fell over on its side, which pulled the tubing and pump from the sink and in turn jerked the cord from wall socket.

When his head hit the concrete floor, he didn't have time to for any more prayers.

Veda collected her personal belongings and headed to the alley. She changed her Arizona plates to Nevada, did some crank while cranking up Larry's loaner vehicle and left on a non-stop drive back to Vegas.

Across town Lehigh waited in unlit parking lot next to Club Robot for Hollywould, already an hour late for his urgent score. Lehigh wondered where he could possibly be especially after Hollywould had been so adamant, calling at the last minute to set it up. Even saying Lehigh owed him as much. Lehigh was pissed and told himself it was his last favor for the dude.

He was right.

Memphis Vettes' was jamming like a Salmon swimming up-stream and I was having the time of my life working and play-ing. However, there was an unexpected problem keeping DJs healthy enough to work their shifts.

The very first week I had a no-show for a closing night shift. Needles was there but scheduled to get off at nine and leave for another gig. So, even though he could stay a little longer, I still needed to hustle to fill the gap.

I rushed back to the office and called off-duty DJs but had no luck, seemed like at Vettes when I needed an open phone line, they were always all tied up. Right after I hung up after leaving another message, I punched in a line to make another call, but someone was already on the other end of the line, so I gave my standard spiel.

"Memphis Vettes, your Rock N Roll heaven, this is Max, are you ready to party?"

Silence....

Before I even had a chance to get frustrated, I heard a familiar voice.

"What the 'Brack-brack-braaaaack' is going on?"

The Rufus Thomas' chicken voice from Eddie was perfect comic relief. It reminded me how crazy my life had become.

I told Eddie I only had a few minutes. He gave me a quick rundown over what he'd dug up on Vettes and CB Products. He'd been unable to locate a Carter Benson, the man who started CB Products, but he found out Carter's company had been later absorbed by a group of nightclub owners among other things. It included Vettes with partner Joey Spasula who hired me, and the Etrusco brothers, Louie and Larry.

He believed there was money behind the brothers from other sources but couldn't identify them yet. He confirmed Sarge's statements, there were a rash of overdoses at hospital emergency rooms in Phoenix, Tucson and Flagstaff. Many were college age, and most of the first responder reports originated from parties near campus.

Unfortunately, our conversation was cut short when Marni started tapping on the office window. She was trying to let me know I was needed in the DJ booth.

"Oh shit! Gotta go Eddie, bye!"

I dropped the phone in the cradle, and hit the door with my shoulder while I turned the knob. I ran down the hall, slipped on a spill but stayed upright, and eventually slid to a stop by the service well before heading to the booth.

Johnny Unato stared at the phone on the wall in Ernie's Body Shop, the Valvoline clock reading two twenty. He was beyond worried, the front door was bashed in, his equipment was in disarray and some packages sent from Vettes and CB Products were opened. By far the most disturbing problem was the dead man on the floor in the storage room.

It was a real mess.

One of the ripped open packages on the floor was full of white powder, and its dust was scattered on the floor. A chemical smell hung in the air.

Johnny found the man's body lying face up next to a chair, the lower half of his torso twisted unnaturally. Pasty vomit covered the bottom half of his face, neck, and shirt which one hand still clutched. He was black, thirtyish, but someone he'd never seen. He appeared to have been beaten, his lips swollen and a large knot on his forehead. When Johnny first tried to deal with the situation, he grabbed a towel, and wiped the man's face but couldn't bring himself to perform mouth to mouth resuscitation, though he did notice a gold tooth.

He tried half-heartedly to revive him by pounding on his chest but realized he really didn't remember his CPR training. It didn't matter, he knew it was too late. He stopped after two attempts.

He found keys, a switchblade, and wad of cash in the unwelcomed corpse's pockets. As he looked him over, he searched for more information before calling his brother Dean. There was no ID, so he decided to check the Toyota he noticed in the alley after looking through his shop.

When he first pulled up, he noticed the car in the alley and how the safety light was on in the storage room. When he got near enough to see the door ajar, he knew something was amiss, but never expected anything like this.

He tried to collect his thoughts. He couldn't call the police. He had to contact Dean to find out how to handle things. He decided to make some notes first, then call Dean from a pay phone. He would tell Dean to call him back there, so before going over details, Dean would be off Vettes's phones. The call back system would be enough of a head's up to alert Dean it was serious business. He scribbled down the time, a brief description of the man, and the addresses of the open packages, then went to look in the car.

He looked at the keys he'd taken off the body. On the key chain was a metallic gold 'H' with a Toyota car key, a house key, and what looked like a lock box key. The car was unlocked, there were no registration papers or driver's license in the glove compartment or under the seats, so he checked the trunk. There was no trunk light, but he could see an aluminum briefcase. He tried the lockbox key, and it fit. There wasn't anything inside the briefcase but a book of matches from Club Robot.

He put the matches in his pocket and went back inside. Before he left, he put combination chain locks on the storage door and front door. He then rushed to his car and headed to the pay phone at the Stop'N Go near his shop.

He pulled up close enough to the payphone to block the view from drunks hanging out by the dumpster forty feet away. They were drinking quarts and flipping coins. He wanted to be able keep an eye on them while he remained screened. He grabbed some coins from the console cup holder and got out, hoping no one else would show up to use the phone. He knew his first call would be quick, but also knew he'd need to wait for the call back.

He never thought if he ever found a dead body anywhere, he wouldn't be calling the cops first, but here he was. He felt the clock inside his head ticking, he knew every second counted.

He got through to Phoenix Vettes and a girl's voice answered.

"Hold, please."

"No!... ...Shit!"

Then he remembered it was two hours earlier in Arizona; still prime time at the club. He'd have to be quicker when she picked up again.

"Rocking your world at Vettes, this is Jaylin, how may I help you?"

"Yes, please don't hang up! This is Dean's brother Johnny, and I need to talk to him, it's urgent. There's a family emergency!"

"Oh, hi Johnny, I'm sorry 'bout the hold. Let me get him for you. I hope everyone's all right. Hang on."

It didn't take long.

"Johnny, what's going on man?"

Dean sounded worried.

"I'm on a payphone, Dean, you need to call me back. We gotta talk real soon. *Tonight.*"

"Well, were busy as shit right now Johnny, can't it wait till tomorrow?"

"Listen Dean, I wouldn't bother you or tell you it was urgent if it wasn't serious, just call me back at this number as soon as you can. I got notes."

"Notes? Ok man, give me fifteen minutes. What's the number?"

Johnny gave him the number and hung up. He really wanted a cigarette; his heart was pounding. He left the receiver dangling as if he was still on the phone and reached into the car's glove compartment and grabbed his Malboro Lights. They were old, but he wasn't going inside the store for a fresh pack. He lit one with the Club Robot matches and looked around nervously, the receiver to his ear and his hand over the cradle holding down the switch. The drunks had spotted him, but so far hadn't decided he was worth approaching.

Finally, the phone rang, he released the switch and pulled his notes out of his pocket. He leaned in as close as he could while a semi pulled to the light on the corner on the other side of the store. Its brakes released and the chassis creaked, drowning out all the other sounds of the night.

"Dean, listen, can you hear me?"

"Yeah, go ahead Johnny, I ain't got much time."

"Listen, someone broke into the shop tonight and they're dead."

"Did you kill them?"

"No man, I found him like that..."

"So, what's up?"

"What do you want me to do? Listen he ain't got no ID, it's a black dude about five-six. Looks like he was in a fight and must'a OD'd or had a seizure. There's a '78 Toyota parked in the alley with no registration or nothing! I don't know what the fuck I'm supposed to do!"

"Why do you think he OD'd?"

"He had puke all over him, and his eyes were bugged out. Plus, there's a couple packages open and some of the shit's scattered all over the floor."

"Ok, he must'a had a heart attack, but the Huggy wouldn't kill him like that, less he did some other shit first..."

"Yeah, well, maybe... There's a package tore open for F&A Salvage that's something different. Is it smack? Y'all sending smack now? I tasted it but couldn't tell."

"F&A Salvage...hmmm..."

"C'mon man, whaddya want me to do? I got a dead man in my shop!"

"Sorry, man. I'm sorry... Ok, listen...stick the body in one of your sink bins. Get some bags of ice and put'em on top. I'll call you back noon tomorrow at your shop. Don't leave the shop, keep your lights off and don't let anyone in. You hear me? Nobody! And you gotta stay there till I call. Got me?"

"Huh? You want me to keep the body? Man, I don't know...".

"Listen, Johnny, just trust me on this, I gotta call someone. I'll make sure we get this straightened out. I gotta go, don't fuck this up!"

"What the fuck! ...Shit, ok, ok, tomorrow, but I can't keep this..."

Dean hung up before he could finish. Johnny mulled over why he didn't mention the tooth or the matches. He decided it was stuff that could wait, maybe forever. What did it matter, his whole world was upside down.

As he headed back to the shop, he remembered a song a bluesman at Peanuts, a nearby bar, used to sing. Unbeknownst to Johnny, the song was written by Leroy Carr back in 1929.

"Early one mornin',

the blues came falling down

All locked up in jail,

and prison bound…"

When he discovered the bluesman at Peanuts, he fell in love with the man and that song. It made him feel he was soaking up the authentic Memphis blues scene. Eventually though, it made him sad, so he quit frequenting Peanuts.

He smiled at the memory like reminiscing over a childhood scar. He had escaped the song, left the sadness behind, and dismissed the memory. His thoughts quickly turned back to the vigil he would have to stage at the Body Shop.

First Dean called Larry and told him they needed to meet after closing where they could be alone. Larry didn't complain about the hour or the need to talk and Dean didn't think any more about it, there was way too much to do.

Dean shut Vettes down as usual, then ran everybody out, and cleared the parking lot. He drove off as if going home in case someone who had lingered after work might see him, but after leaving a couple blocks he circled back to Vettes and went back inside to wait for Larry.

After Larry heard Dean tell the story, he asked for a bottle of Bombay Gin. Dean got the bottle, Larry poured a shot, drank it down, poured another and lit a cigarette. Larry got up and paced around in a circle on the dance floor and cussed to himself but didn't seem mad.

Larry made Dean nervous and so he didn't usually deal directly with him when he could avoid it. However, he instinctively knew to straightened out this particular mess, Larry would be the one. Additionally, Dean wanted to protect Johnny as much as he could, so he really wanted to know what Larry was going to do. He also figured Larry was the only one crazy enough to send any narcotics in a shipment, or to have something going on 'on the side', Dean or maybe even Louis didn't know about.

Finally, Larry stopped and turned to face Dean. Dean had been sucking on Red Rockets and smoking nonstop while Larry circled in thought with his drink. Now Dean sat with four dead Buds lined up next to a full ashtray, the beer labels ratty from his nervous fingers.

"Listen you're telling me he thinks this guy OD'd on smack?"

"Well, we don't figure it was Huggy, and Johnny said he tasted some of the opened shit and didn't think it was Huggy. He figured it must be smack, because he knows how coke tastes. But who knows, the man could'a just had a seizure, I guess anything possible."

"F&A Salvage, are you sure?"

"That's what he said. He wrote down everything to keep it straight before he called. Look, he's scared and we gotta do something, he's freaking out. He's my brother, man. Fuck! I can't believe this...".

"You and me both. It's good he took notes. Ok, tell you what, Dean-O, here's what we'll do. You have him close up the packages best he can. Tell him not to mix any of the powders from the different packages that were open. Better to leave them short and clean up later."

"But Larry! What about the body?"

"I'm getting to that, be cool. Don't worry about the body, I'll send some boys over. They'll leave tonight. They'll get there in a day and a half. They'll take the body and F&A Package off his hands. Tell him to keep his cool, keep the body cool, and stay in his shop till they get there. No pick-ups or deliveries until this is done. Got that?"

"Yea, but that's crazy. You want him to keep the body for like forty-eight hours?"

"Calm down, man. Maybe they'll get there sooner. Tell him to sit tight, we'll make it worth his while. Trust me, I'll personally take care of him."

Dean took a deep breath, then a long drag off his cigarette, and shook his head as he exhaled.

Larry stepped very close and took an intimidating stance. His expression got very serious very quick.

"Do I need to fly over there and talk to him myself? Huh?"

"No! ...No, I'll talk to him. He'll take care of his end of things. Just promise me they'll get there as soon as possible."

"Don't worry, Dean-O. Larry's gonna take care of this. You wait, we're gonna laugh about this someday. I'm ready to laugh now! Ha-ha, haaa..."

Suddenly, Larry seemed to be reveling in the situation. Dean exhaled a long slow weary lung full of smoke out of both nostrils and sides of his mouth. He was very uncomfortable with Larry's current mood and just wanted to get it resolved.

"Yeah, ok, you let me know if anything changes right?"

"Sure, Dean, I don't want you to worry. You just keep pumping out these drinks here and I'll take care of this. No big deal. Really."

"Ok, let's get outta here, I'm beat. This is crazy."

"Hey, whaddya say you play The Diamond's *Silhouettes* for me one time while I finish my drink?"

Dean looked over at Larry in disbelief, but he saw the look on Larry's face, and knew it wasn't a joke. Unbelievable. Larry was crazy. He didn't want to argue with him, even with all the shit going on.

"Ok, Larry, but just once."

"Hey much appreciated. You know what, you're all right, Dean-O."

Larry started dancing around with an imaginary partner before Dean even got to the DJ booth. Dean figured he would have to drink more Buds because he knew Larry might have another request.

Larry was in a world of his own now.

I've got to find the hero inside me...
   I'll keep moving
though my wheels are slow.
And while the river races to the sea,
I'll keep the beat
and stay in harmony.

I don't know any more
Don't know any less,
Gotta find a way
out of this mess.

When I got to work, the visit from Angel and call from Eddie were still fresh in my mind, but Vettes' manager's shifts didn't give me time to ponder the past. Especially with another case of the Vettes 'DJ Flu'. Again I would have to step in as a DJ for a few sets.

I jumped in the booth and started Sweet Home Chicago by the Blues Brothers. The Vettes crew gathered around donning hats and wigs, and clutching plastic horns or toy guitars. We swung, swayed, shouted, and had a grand old time, until a hostess stuck her head in the booth, and grabbed my coat and tugged frantically.

"Mr. Max! Mr. Max! Fire Marshall's here! He says there's a bomb threat and we gotta evacuate!"

She was freaked out, her eyes about to pop out of her head.

"Say what?"

Barely audible over the song and mayhem in the booth I was pretty sure I hadn't heard what I thought I heard. Plus, I was beginning to feel a bit of that reoccurring Vettes' buzz and my sensory receptors were fuzzy.

"Mr. Max, the Fire Marshall's here. There's a bomb threat! He says we gotta evacuate!"

"No way! Let me talk to him."

Jumping down from the turntable platform, caused the needle to skip, and made the Blues Brothers sound more buzzed than usual.

"One and one is...- Skrichhibbit! - eight..."

I hit the floor and raced past the hostess to the front door.

"Hey Chief, I'm Max Wilson, I'm the manager on duty, what can I do for you?"

"Well, hello Mr. Wilson, I'm Chief Hadwhich and you've got a serious problem right now. There's been a bomb threat and we need everybody out in fifteen minutes! We need to search the place inside and out."

"You're kidding, right?"

"Max, let me save us both some time, and possibly several hundred lives. Either make an announcement, or I will. Get your head together and tell everybody to leave in an orderly manner. Hopefully nobody will trash your place. I'm gonna give you sixty seconds. I want the music off, and the lights up in a hurry. One of us is gotta address this crowd."

"OK, OK. I got it. I'll stop the song and turn up the lights. Just give me a second to let my staff know how to handle everything they got going. Okay?"

"My watch started. You do what you gotta do, I'm already counting down."

I turned to the door staff and had one guy take the door and had a hostess go for trash cans and bus tubs for any drinks the crowd might try to take outside. I sent doormen to both ends of the room to turn up all the lights on my cue when I got back on the microphone.

"Let's do this!"

"You got it, boss!"

I jumped in the DJ booth and let everyone know what was happening. I turned the music down slowly while letting the crew around me know what was going on and directing them to tell the rest of the crew. I asked bartenders to try and collect on their biggest tabs. As I faded the music off, the crowd noise rose in response.

"Ok, here goes, please listen up everybody! I'm afraid we have a problem! Listen up!"

The lights turned up throughout the room and the dance lights stopped.

"Please, we need everyone to listen up! The Fire Chief is here. He needs us to clear the building quickly and quietly. If you've paid up, please head to the door now. If you're not paid, we'll find you outside and you can pay then."

I made that last part up and could hear confusion and discussion. I looked over and saw the Fire Chief watching me impatiently, so I pleaded with the crowd again.

"Listen, we need everyone to leave as soon as possible. This is not a drill! Everyone exit in an orderly fashion, right now.

Everyone! Please, let's get out of the building. You can leave through Emergency exit by the Corvette if you're over there. Please everyone! Stop talking! Let's do this now! The sooner we do, the sooner we can come back in and start dancing again."

I had told the bouncer sent to the rear light panel to open the fire exit. I could hear the door's alarm buzzer going off and realized I'd forgotten to give him a key, but at least he'd opened it. I pulled the key off my ring and gave it to a Shady, to go shut it off.

After Vettes was cleared only the Fire Department remained inside. I stood among restless Vettes' employees hanging around the dumpsters behind the building. We did roll call, I didn't want to lose anyone in the chaos, then we started trying to piece together the unpaid bar tabs. Elsewhere, hundreds of Vettes' party guests scattered around the main lot and meandered among the parked cars. Some drifted off into the neighborhood and down the street to other bars unhampered by bomb threats and Fire Chiefs.

After the Vettes' crew minded the tasks at hand, I took my clipboard and headed back around the building to the Fire Captain who remained outside. He was on his walkie talkie with his Chief with the Bomb Squad inside. Since the Captain was not able to talk, I went back around the building to check on the Vettes crew, who were fine. I turned back to try to talk to the Fire Captain again. That's when I heard Lehigh.

"Pssst! Hey Max! Gotta minute? We need to talk."

He wasn't in the crowd. No, he was leaning against a van, in dark clothes, his collar flipped up and cap pulled down over his eyes.

"Lehigh? Can't you see I'm kinda busy here. We're in the middle of a bomb threat…"

I stopped and squinted. Wondering about his bad timing and weird get up, I wasn't sure what he wanted but walked towards him anyway. I noticed those little tickles in my brain reminiscent of my night gone amuck at South Mountain. He began to move towards me by sliding along the van, motioning with his head. His little finger in front of his chest, beckoning me like in a Spy vs. Spy cartoon.

"I just need a minute, Max. I'm sure you'll agree this is important. Come over here, I don't wanna be recognized."

I sighed and strode closer. He backed up and made room for me to slide next to him still flush against the van. His head swiveled back and forth as if looking for someone watching.

"Okay Lehigh, what's up?"

"Yeah, now be cool. Listen, Max, we need to talk after you get off work tonight. Can you meet me?"

"You can't tell me what's up now?"

"Well…a little bit. So, we haven't really talked about this before, but I saw a car tonight from Phoenix. I'm pretty sure one of their heavyweights is here. You might be getting involved in something dangerous."

"What the…? Who the hell are you? What do you mean heavyweight… and a car being from Phoenix doesn't make it a problem."

"Listen, just trust me, this could be serious. I'm just looking out for you, all right? I promised Chris I'd keep an eye on you and… I…, …listen, I called in the bomb threat."

"You what? Are you fucking kidding me?"

I did a three- sixty with my clipboard extended like an airplane wing and stopped it with a loud slap. I looked at him while I held it over my head as if I was ready to clobber him. I held off but continued my death stare and shaking my head.

"Are you for real?"

"Hey man, I had to get you out of there for a couple of minutes to talk. Look, I'm really sorry, but they'll be through in a few minutes, and let everybody back in. Don't worry...it, it was the only way. If they don't open you up soon, I'll call in an all clear from the same number."

"You do understand with all the bullshit this thing has caused I'll probably be here pretty late..."

My brain was still percolating, ready to boil.

"Yeah, sorry 'bout that. Look, I can wait. I'll come back after everybody's left. If you want, I can pick you up or meet you for breakfast. Look, this is important. Listen, Max, I wouldn't have done anything this drastic if it wasn't big, you know, something you need to know about."

I let out an unintended laugh of exasperation before I was able to talk. I dropped the clipboard and balanced my hands on my knees to take a deep breath. I was feeling residual drug and alchohol damage or exhaustion. Or maybe just too much Lehigh!

Finally, I put some words together.

"Ok, whatever! Come back after three. Come to the back door, I'll be out by the dumpster or just inside."

I shook my head, "Uun-fucking believable."

"Ok, see you then. Max, I, uh, ...again, I'm sorry...".

He slipped back between the cars and disappeared hurriedly into the parking lot with his head on a swivel. I picked up my clipboard and tapped at it. I remembered the Grateful Dead had a song for this kind of bullshit.

'Passenger' - *"Upside out or inside down, false alarm the only game in town...".*

With Dead playing in my head, the world made sense again. The conversation with Lehigh sparked new energy, even though it sprang from frustration. I strode up to the Fire Captain with a retooled attitude and sense of purpose, even if the world was "upside out and inside down."

"Hey Chief, how are we looking?"

"Max, the good news is there's nothing to report so far."

"Well, I guess that is good news, when can we get back in?"

No answer.

I nodded like the concerned manager but turned away and whistled the Dead's melody surveying the parking lot. I left to find my Vettes crew around the corner of the building now knowing what the bomb search outcome would be and there would be a lot of work to do when we got back in. Much of our crowd had dissipated and probably wouldn't return. They were on a party high and probably sought out a nearby spot to keep their groove going.

It turned out Fire Team gave us an 'All Clear' about ten minutes after Lehigh had slipped away and we got in and reset the club in another fifteen and let the remaining crowd inside. The momentum for the night was killed by the cold stop, and the remainder of the night was quiet. This allowed us to close down quickly. Employee check outs were going smoothly, and I had time to reach out to Eddie in Arizona, and was lucky enough to reach him on the first try.

"Hey man, sorry about cutting you off last time, what's up?"

Eddie started in on the details about overdosing at student parties referenced in our last conversation. He reeled off the symptoms: "Nausea, vomiting, fainting, muscle spasms, seizures, total black outs, hyperthermia, aggressive out-bursts..."

I cut him off.

"Ok, Eddie, I get it, but what else did you find out about Vettes?"

"Well, they pretty much fly under the radar. The partners are involved in some sketchy clubs but so far at Vettes they've kept their nose clean. Probably cuz of Vettes' shitty dress code!"

He started laughing.

"Yeah, well I guess it is a deterrent. So, what are some of the other clubs then? Any in Memphis?"

"Well, it looks like the guys Carter Benson partnered with had The Club Robot and some place called Candy Canes there... I think that's a strip club like the one here in Phoenix. They do have ties to several strip joints."

"Hmmm, okay good work, I'll let you know if I find anyone who knows Carter. It's weird. You're telling me he's connected, but then he's nowhere to be found. Say, you hear of anyone named Lehigh or Doomuch in your searches?"

"That's a negative Max, never heard of either one."

"Well, it's interesting, this guy Lehigh was referred to me by an old friend. Tonight, Lehigh called in a bomb threat on Vettes, just to warn me about some big wig, whose name he didn't even know. He said they were from Phoenix. It really pissed me off. It was a pretty crazy thing to do, don't you think?"

"Man sounds like everything that's happening there is pretty crazy. Better watch your step."

"Don't worry, I'm trying."

I had to cut our call short then because Shady began knocking on the office door. Turned out the Fire Marshall was back, and I needed to sign some paperwork. After securing everything in the office, and letting everyone out, I went to the bar for a much needed cold one. Pretty soon, I was sitting on a stainless-steel counter in the kitchen with a sweaty Heineken, and a shot of Cuervo. I had prepared for a talk with Lehigh with a handful of Heinies in an ice bucket. Eventually I heard a tentative knock on the kitchen back door. I let the alarmist in.

"Ok, what's up?"

"Well, I went by Ernie's tonight, remember that place?

I nodded.

"Yeah, well there was a car parked there with Arizona tags and I recognized it. I saw it there once before."

"You already told me about Arizona plates, so?"

"Well, I'm pretty sure it was one of the Etrusco's cars, and I hear they're trouble, especially Larry."

He stared at me like he expected a response, but I waited for more, so he continued.

"And they take care of trouble their own special way, Max. This is never good. And that's the thing."

"What? Larry and Louie are brothers, right? I thought Louie and Joey were partners? I mean how bad can he be?"

"I don't know what it is, but with Larry involved, trust me, it can be really bad. Sometimes his cure is worse than the problem. Know what I mean?"

"So, you're telling me he's some kind of hit man or something? I don't think Joey would be involved with something like that."

"Hey, Joey may not know everything that's happening, but I guarantee you Louis does. I figure he has to, he's Larry's brother."

"Ok, so I should call Joey, right?"

"Hell no! You just need to watch your step and your back. You understand?"

I realized wherever this was heading, it was picking up speed. From the day I sat down to interview with Joey I knew there had to be more than an audit involved. Lehigh probably wouldn't have called in a bomb threat just cuz some rumored badass was in town.

"So, what do you know about all this. What is it you're not telling me? You gotta know more than what you've told me. Come on Lehigh...".

"Look, Max, I don't know everything, but I know a few things. Ernie's Body Shop is a place I got Huggy. I think it's a distribution hub. I think Doomuch gets it there, too. Once Ernie told me to stay away and now I see this Arizona car there. There's something else, too...",

He put his hands in his pockets and walked around in a circle blowing air out of his mouth and I could hear a slight whistle through his teeth. In the background a sink dripped, making an ominous sound combination.

"Ok, what is it?"

"Look, Max, you can't tell anybody any of this...".

He took off his hat and rubbed his head before putting his hat back on tightly.

"I got this friend, who worked at Wetlabs when the company first started. They designed leaping fountains, you know, water art installations like those in Vegas and around the world. I met him in Detroit when they did the airport fountains. Anyhow, he broke away and started his own company. He called me last year and told me they designed a dispenser for Vettes' clubs. I didn't think much of it at the time. Later, he told me it was called an Octosperser. Vettes approved the design and ordered twenty-four units."

"Well, shit, Lehigh, that don't mean squat to me, so what?"

"He said they paid cash for the whole shipment."

"Ok that's pretty strange, but not illegal."

"No, it's not, but then we had some cocktails on Beale, he got kinda loose..."

"Again, not a crime, Lehigh."

"Well, when he got lit up, he told me how at the last minute, before Vettes actually paid him, they changed it. Instead of water going in the dispenser they went to his lab and showed him some gel that looked like stringy frog spawn."

"Ok, now that's strange, but what why was that bad?"

"I think it's part of the reason he told me. When he got the dispenser hooked up for trial they fed their stuff into the line and poured drinks from it to celebrate. Larry Etrusco was there and insisted they toast together. Larry poured a little gin on top, and they drank."

Lehigh took a minute to pause and get another beer out of the bucket, so did I.

"So, they had a weird cocktail, then what happened?"

"Well, my friend said he tripped his butt off for hours after the meeting broke up."

"I see... so why did he go through with it?"

"He said he had no way out. Larry gave him half their money before they even tested it! In fact, ended up he paid for the whole lot in cash, thirty-five large. My buddy had to sell;

he was stuck. He'd invested too much in the components to break the contract.

He thought he might have been the target of some kind of a prank, but later got scared. See, Larry had a private conversation with him and kept making a point of telling him he had such a nice lab. But Larry didn't stop there, he kept saying, 'Wasn't it a shame these labs have so many accidents?' shit like that. Larry was very weird. My buddy said even when Larry joked it wasn't in a fun way."

"Ok, ok, so there's some shady shit going on. You know, I keep thinking I'm having flashbacks at work. Now I'm thinking there's more to it than that."

"Oh yeah, I think so too. Vettes ain't my kinda place, but one time I was here just drinking casual you know. By the time I left I was too high to drive. I took a cab. At the time I thought it was the pot I was smoking but later I felt sure it was those Jell-O shots." Well, we do get Jell-O shots delivered that are made at the Phoenix headquarters."

"No shit? Okay, there you go. I wonder what's going on with the dispensers?"

"I guess I'll have to try and find out."

But I'd had enough for one night.

"Hey, it's getting late. We better get outta here, can you give me a lift? I don't feel like walking to my pad right now."

"Sure man, you ready?"

"Yeah, almost, let me clean up here, I know Nate'll be looking over everything with a fine-tooth comb tomorrow, especially after this bomb threat thing."

As he drove, I reflected on how Lehigh'd been so carefree when I first met him. Now his bombscare shenanigans and paranoia over Larry Etrusco and Vettes had me spooked. I couldn't help but wonder what other antics he might have in store.

R ace to the finish.
      Just go, go, go.
It's a fool's errand but it's what you do,
While the catfish howl
at the bottom of the stew.

Grind your wheels, hit the road.
A lonely voice wails and waits for you,
We toast any man due
to slip into the muddy brew.

Richard Boone looked in the rearview mirror and squinted into the slice of afternoon sun. He held an almost empty Styrofoam cup against the steering wheel, full of his cold remains of truck stop instant creamer and sugar loaded coffee. His elbow rested on a mini cooler full of Mountain Dew wedged between the front seats. His brother Danny dozed on the passenger side, his brother Dave out cold in the back, his limbs pointed at odd angles. It'd been a long time since they'd traveled together.

Larry had left Dean at Vettes around four, called Richard immediately and told him to drive to Memphis. He wanted him there in twenty-four hours and said to make sure to have his mobile phone for further instructions.

Richard was relieved, luckily he'd kept the phone charged, knowing Larry would get pissed-off if he called and Richard didn't answer. The phone was a hassle, and he knew Larry was going to be busting his balls on this job because he told him to get help, or he'd get it for him. He told Richard to consider it a two-man job. Richard sort of agreed.

"At least two, maybe more."

"Hey whatever, you figure it out but make sure it's locked down tight. This is your deal, Richie."

Richard was responsible for any loose lips or slip ups. It was probably going to be messy, so Richard packed light, making sure to grab clothes he could live without. He didn't bother to call his brothers to ask if they wanted to go, nor did he give them time to prepare, instead he drove to their place and knocked until they answered. He told them both to get ready and it wasn't negotiable. He told them Larry would make sure their supervisors excused their absences.

He knew he'd have to remind Larry to take care of that. Another hassle.

Once in Memphis the next morning, he checked them into neighboring rooms and told them to get some rest. They'd have to work through the night and next day, then hit the road back to Phoenix as soon as possible. The hotel rooms were only a place to crash.

Richard had Black Beauties for himself, but he wasn't planning on sharing unless it was an emergency. Once they got situated, he told Danny and Dave to stay in the room while he was gone no matter what, telling them he had to get supplies and meet someone.

He didn't mention he was going for breakfast before he met up with Johnny Unato, a man none of them had previously met. Larry warned Richard beforehand to use 'kid gloves with a hammer', when dealing with Johnny. Richard believed the job was big. A chance to prove himself. He would be taking care of something Larry wasn't able to. He didn't wanna screw it up, of course, but he wasn't starting on an empty stomach either.

Richard would've never guessed, based on what Larry told him, how big a mess he'd find when he got to Ernie's Body Shop. Larry only told him to get rid of a body. He had not provided any other details other than it was a mess.

"Fix it so nobody will find the body, and if they do, make sure it's too far away to be connected and can't be identified. Got it?"

Richard was glad it was just a disposal job; he wasn't going to off someone because Larry said to. Richard was a big guy, able to intimidate in his own way but he rarely resorted to violence. He'd mainly been a driver though he'd taken on jobs lately that were more involved. He was most comfortable being quiet, looking mean and acting mad. He'd roughed up a few easy marks, but they rarely had any fighting skills. For this job he had to be careful because of Dean and Johnny's connection. Larry thought the world of Dean and his club was a big-time money maker.

Richard announced himself as he stepped into the body shop as soon as Johnny opened the door.

"I'm Richard. Larry sent me. I hear you gotta problem."

Johnny looked like he had been pacing the floor all night. Richard surveyed the scene after introducing himself while Johnny ran his mouth.

"Hello Richard. Man, I'm glad you're finally here. This is bad, *really bad.* I don't know what to do. I put ice on the dude like Dean said, but I've been here by myself for what seems like forever and I'm freaking out. We gotta call somebody, what if somebody's looking for him?"

"Don't call nobody. We can handle it."

"I cleaned up the dope and repackaged it over here."

He scooted over to the table. He was unsteady and his hands shook. The shop smelled like a high school locker room after the game, where someone had pulled a V6 engine apart and scattered it on the floor. In addition to auto shop fumes and Johnny's whiskey breath, there was that post-trauma death blend of puke, piss, sweat, and shit.

Johnny needed rest and a bath. Richard would have to get him out of there to pull himself together before they started working. However, he had to make sure Johnny was back as soon as possible, in order to keep an eye on him. The boy was so freaked out he surmised he may have dipped into the Huggy. Then again, babysitting a corpse could have that effect on people, too.

Richard looked over the hastily sealed packages on the worktable. They looked sketchy as hell, and he could still see powder smeared on the floor. The body was covered with several half-melted bags of ice on top of lots of empty bags.

And there was something more, and Richard knew what it was, as he'd smelled it before. A man's fear oozed out of him like a ghost leaving its host. Richard was catching a whiff of the ethereal residue of Johnny's fearful vigil, the vapor rising from Johnny's weary pores. Pushed past their limit by his young heart and frazzled nerves, it settled around him like a wobbly horse harness.

He sensed Johnny was trying to speak, but instead made little choking noises. As he struggled even his exhales made strange sounds through his teeth and sides of his mouth. While Richard surveyed the shop, he heard Johnny holding back sad muffled moans. Richard didn't remark on Johnny's tribulations, he stayed silent. He knew if he waited his message to Johnny would have greater impact.

Richard didn't know Johnny's inner dialogue was stirred to a greater intensity by an old blues song. Though Johnny had dismissed it earlier, his mind played Leroy Carr's *Prison Bound Blues* in a loop, with every beat of his heart pushing its haunting sentiment.

Johnny's soul struggled for a way to escape the tune, but the song stubbornly stayed on. Not even the Jack Black could make it go away for long, the whiskey only quelling it momentarily, before the haunting lament returned again and again as he waited for Richard to speak.

Fully aware Johnny was suffering, Richard continued to stall and pulled out a piece of Juicy Fruit and slipped it in his mouth. He carefully folded the wrapper and put it in his shirt pocket. He chewed a little and surveyed the room one more time.

"Yeah. Hmmm..."

He stopped short of actually saying anything.

"What? What are we gonna do, Richard?"

The man Dean had sent had such a methodical manner; Johnny couldn't stand it another minute. His body's response to the situation was beyond shuffling his feet and hyperventilating. He began fidgeting uncontrollably, no longer able to care if he might initiate a heart attack.

Richard saw Johnny was ready to jump out of his skin. Even he couldn't stand the man's vibes any longer. He decided to wrap it up. He laid it out while staring at the ceiling.

"All right, Johnny. You go home, clean up and get some rest. Go get your shit together and be back by eight tonight. We're gonna take care of this for you, but you gotta be here. We don't wanna fuck up this job or mess up your place, so we all gotta be on same page and do it right."

He stopped and stared at Johnny with his hardest glare.

"Can you do that for me?"

"Yeah, I think so, sure. I mean, what are we gonna do with the body?"

"*You* ain't gonna do nothing with it. We'll handle it and take care of these packages, too. Get some rest, and don't call nobody. You hear me? Nobody!"

"Okay, okay, yeah...I got it, no problem. I'll be here."

He nodded in exaggerated wobbles.

"Good, now destroy your clothes...better yet just change here and give'em to me? You got some spare duds here, right?"

"Unh, yeah sure."

Johnny was a little puzzled by the request but was happy to finally get to leave.

"You do? Great, then when you come back tonight wear stuff you can do without and bring yourself another change, too. Got that?"

Richard's deadpan scowl told Johnny it wasn't a question.

"Yeah, yeah, I can do it, no problem. It's fine. I'm just worried about someone coming around looking..."

"Let me worry about that! Gimme the key to the lock on the front door and be back by eight. Don't answer your door or phone while you're gone. Understand?"

Again, the look let him know it was not a question.

"All right, yeah, I got it."

He struggled getting his keys out of his pocket then fumbled with his keychain till he got the key off. They both froze for a moment, then Johnny handed Richard the key to the lock. Richard never looked at the key when Johnny handed it to him, he stared into Johnny's eyes the whole time. After his hand closed around the key, he continued his stare. Johnny was mortified and his eyes grew wider. He tried to gather himself. He sighed deep and began nodding. Richard held up his hand to stop him from leaving.

"You know what? One more thing... before you go, bring that car that's in the alley into the garage. Tonight, you're gonna strip the VIN number so I see it's done right. Then you're gonna overhaul it so no one'll recognize it."

He nodded towards Johnny and motioned towards the alley.

"No problem, Richard, I won't let you down. You'll see. I got this."

"Good."

Johnny went in the other room and changed and dropped the clothes on the floor behind Richard who was looking over the dead man's body. Once Johnny opened the front door, Richard turned to watch him walk out. He stared at the door after it closed and waited till Johnny started the car.

He heard Johnny pull up outside, get out, open the overhead garage door and pull the car into the bay, get out and carefully pull down the door. He came in the room with Richard and set the keys on a worktable. He exhaled loudly.

"Okay, uh, I guess I'm gone."

"Don't forget what I told you."

"Got it."

He shut the front door and drove away.

Within seconds Richard relaxed, relieved Johnny was gone. Richard could now truly absorb what the room full of folly held for him and his brothers. He began making his mental checklist for the Boone squad. He sighed and pulled out another piece of gum. Finally, without Johnny bouncing around in a panic, he could smile.

He took time to appreciate his performance. Not bad so far. He had watched Louis, paying particular attention how he kept it together, never losing his temper. He was catching on to some of the finer points of how to deal with people in a jam. He didn't think he'd ever go all crazy on people like Larry. Well, maybe, if he had a football in his hand, and his helmet on with his old file-sharp cleats. The vision made him smile. But when he looked around Ernie's Body Shop, his gridiron fantasy faded quickly.

"What a bunch of crap! My brothers better bring their damn 'A' game."

And lucky for him they did.

Richard set the tone on the way from the hotel how things were gonna go.

"We're gonna wrap the body up tight and weight it down so it'll sink. We're gonna scrub the place so there ain't no trace of dope or blood. When we're done with the shop, were gonna dump the body, drop off the package, burn the clothes and go back to the hotel. Then we'll hit the road back to Arizona. No questions unless I ask'em. Just do what I say. I got all the shit we need in the trunk."

Fortunately, once he arrived Johnny also stayed relatively calm and out of the way. He covered the ground rules with him as soon as he arrived.

"I really don't want you to ask any questions. I think you're gonna see what's up real quick. Just get that VIN scrubbed. We may need to ask you some stuff about the shop, and if you gotta ask a question before you answer, I'm ok with that. But that's all."

Richard's brothers gave Johnny their best tough guy stares while he talked. It kept Johnny clamped up tight the rest of the night. When he finished with the VIN job, Richard put him to work clearing the equipment off the floor. Then he had him make sure the floor drains wouldn't back up. Richard had an industrial snake for the drain, as well as gloves, masks, goggles, bags of shop rags and lye-based, scented drain cleaner treatments.

With Richard in command the three worked in tandem and lifted the body out of the basin and put it on a wool blanket. None of them ever checked the corpse's dental work.

Initially, the body was difficult to wrap but got easier as the shroud took shape. They pulled one burlap bag over the head down to the waist and another over his feet up to the first. Once the face was covered Richard's brothers quickly got comfortable working with the corpse. It was as if it was a just some thing, not a person. They cut slits in the two bags and tied them together, then lashed enough burlap rope around the whole thing to keep it stable when picked up.

Richard asked Johnny for any old tools that couldn't be traced to his shop. Eager to be in Richard's good graces he dug around and brought him an armful of tools. They tied them together with cored out red bricks Richard brought as makeshift weights, and attached them to the neck, stomach, and knee areas of the shroud.

Richard instructed them to leave the back free of weights. When the other two hesitated, he explained.

"Look, I don't want none on that side! We're gonna have to toss him or slide him into the water. The body needs to be light and flat on that side, I want him to sink face down."

Once prepped to Richard's satisfaction, they set the shroud on a plastic tarp in the next room and scrubbed down the basin where the corpse had been iced down, then scrubbed the floor. While his brothers worked, Richard went through the packages. After inspecting them, he tightened up the packing job on those that had been opened. Once they'd finished the floor, Richard had them mop then scrub down the areas where dope and body fluids had been again then squeegee it dry. Afterward they applied detergent powder and grinded it into the concrete with their deck brushes.

He made Johnny promise to use drain cleaner every day for a week after they left, and to dump the engine fluid and all other automotive liquids into the drains every other day for a month. Richard told him to wait a few days till the floor completely dried out, then pour dirty grease on the area they triple cleaned.

"Let it sit, then grind cat litter into it, then leave it until you repeat a week later. And you best do it 'cause I'm gonna come back and check."

Richard's detailed cleaning process naively gave Johnny confidence regarding Richard's expertise. For the first time since he found the body, he thought he might be able to keep on working out of Ernie's Body Shop. It was good, he needed to relax and it gave him focus as he worked on the tasks he was assigned.

He didn't realize Richard was winging it.

When they were done cleaning, it was after two AM. Johnny changed clothes as ordered and got ready to hand them over when Richard asked him a question.

Richard faced Johnny as he stood holding the dirty clothes Johnny removed.

"Got any booze in this place?"

Richard's question caught him off guard.

"Uh, yeah, I keep some Jack Black here, sure."

"Good, get dressed. Then let's give this motherfucker a proper farewell."

"Don't worry I'm always ready for some Jack, don't matter what for."

Johnny hustled over to the recessed cabinets in the next room and came back with an open, but mostly full bottle in tow.

Richard started his spiel.

"I don't want nobody getting all fucked up, this here is just to show proper respect to the deceased. We ain't never gonna know what killed him, and he ain't never going back home, ...wherever home may be. So, it's only fair we give him a proper send off. Now, let's do the best we can. Gather round."

He looked at the other three and nodded sagely, letting them know they were about to start, and they better get in the proper frame of mind. His quiet intensity told them he was only going to tolerate the conduct such a somber ceremony required. His brothers had never seen such a performance. He'd always been a joker in the spotlight, the Adonis prima donna who thumbed his nose at his town and its traditional ceremonies.

Johnny found some Dixie Cups and Richard made him pour everyone a shot. They stood there looking at each other awkwardly for a moment. All of them tired and humbled by after having handled a corpse so intimately.

Finally, Richard looked to Dave. His countenance remained intense, and his voice didn't waver.

"Dave, you gotta verse that'd be appropriate at this time?"

"Uhm, let's see..."

Dave was caught a little off guard but didn't let it show. He squinted and took a whiff of his shot, then closed his eyes. When he reopened them, he spoke in a halting somber voice.

"There's an old Roger Miller song we used to sing when Papa was sad. I think it went something like this...

"*One dying and a burying, six people carrying...*

He paused before finishing.

...I'm crying with a six pack in me...

...Lord, please let me be free..."

They all froze then nodded in response. Richard and Danny were impressed, but Johnny was freaked out. He realized he may have to contribute and started searching his memory.

Richard turned to Danny.

"Your turn."

Danny cleared his throat.

"Um, mum, yep, I 'member part of an Oyster song,

"*Seasons don't fear the reaper,*

nor the wind, sun or rain...

uh, We can be like they are...umm...don't fear the reaper...
...Amen."

Richard was staring at him with his mouth open and a creased brow.

"Danny, what the hell was that?"
Danny shrugged, but before he could answer Richard turned to Johnny.

"Nevermind, very strange, but okay, at least you kept it short. How 'bout you Johnny, do you feel moved to say anything?"

The other three all stared at him doubting he'd respond, but then he surprised them.

"Well, I reckon there is one thing, I'm not sure who wrote it, but here goes:
"I didn't know you,

but I hope you's in heaven..."
He shuffled his feet.
"...half hour before the devil knows you're dead...".
They all nodded to that, and then he added,
"Whoever you were, God rest your soul."
He slugged down his shot, shocking the other three. Richard quickly reprimanded him.

"You weren't gonna wait for us? What the fuck? Jeez! ...Aw right...".

Richard turned away from Johnny while slowly shaking his head. This made Johnny nervous, and he regretted slamming his shot.

But then Richard nodded sympathetically, "Well, I guess it's been harder on you," then looked around to meet all three of their gazes, and Johnny relaxed just a little.

"Let's drink ours to Johnny here, then pour another one and I'll finish this up."

When they realized they'd be getting another shot, the brothers chimed in with earnest yet subdued enthusiasm. Johnny nodded in agreement but thought better of saying anything and let the younger Boones hold sway.

"That's my big bro! Sounds good, Richard."

"Now you're talking. Uh huh! Righteous."

Once they finished, Johnny poured a refill, and Richard raised his cup.

"Here's to a quick death, we hope it was an easy one.

Here's to a pretty girl, let's hope she was an honest one...

...and here's to tomorrow,

let's hope there's another one."

He pushed out his lips and bowed his head,

"That's all anyone can ask...".

After he lifted his cup and drank, they all followed suit. His was a more concerned look than the others when he lifted to drink. He was already thinking about what came next.

After they dislodged the back seat, they fit the body in the trunk. Richard sent Johnny back into the shop to straighten up and prep for his normal business. Once his brothers were in the car he told them he decided to dump the body in the Mississippi, explaining it was a simple but perfect solution being the closest and quickest way to get it off their hands and away from Memphis.

"We'll toss it out as far as we can from the riverbank. It'll sink into the channel current, then the river will carry it downstream and away from the city."

When they got close to the Memphis Arkansas Bridge, his brothers were cutting up. He stopped the car and turned off the music.

"Will you shut the fuck up!"

Their somber mood had disintegrated from the Jack Black, and gallows humor took over their entry-level-body-disposal-experience psyches. Perhaps letting off some steam may have been justified, but Richard couldn't stay focused and listen to it. Well, at least not without joining in, so he shut'em up.

He drove the car slowly down the dirt access road and got as close as possible to the riverbank, stopping on the edge of a gravel spill, south of the bridge, in a clearing which must have been used as a dump. The smell of garbage, engine fluid and dead fish hung in the air. They pulled the wrapped corpse out, pushing any loose edges of the tarp beneath the ropes binding it. They set three four foot-long two by fours on the back of the tarp and bound them to the shroud on the outside with small ropes, using shoelace bows.

Richard and Larry had planned how they would dispose of the corpse. Larry had agreed the river was a good burial spot, but didn't care to hear the other details, just wanted it done as soon as possible. If all went as Richard hoped, the bows would come undone shortly after submerging in the top rush of current and release the boards, freeing the weighted corpse to sink down into the current's undertow and carry it downstream.

Richard patiently directed and corrected his brothers as they proceeded to the water's edge. Finally, he decided they were ready to launch. Three astride, with Richard in the middle, they descended the riverbank slope. Richard kept extra cuts of rope slung over his shoulder, and his knife in his belt.

It was dark, but an after three AM dark. They could hear cars on the bridge and see random lights dancing on the water. It was awkward maneuvering through giant weeds, tree roots, and rocks, and every sound seemed amplified. They moved step by step in a sideways stance, when they stumbled, branches snapped. Without thinking they whispered profane apologies.

Suddenly, after getting within a few feet of the water's edge, the bundle fell from Dave's hands, and Danny lost his grip. The makeshift shroud with the flesh-filled center rolled and slid toward the water.

"Shit!"

"I got it!"

Dave scrambled to grab it but was unable to stop. When he finally got his hand on it, he somersaulted over like a cheerleader, his legs landing in water up to his knees though he managed to grab hold of a rope. The water's force and rope's tension caused the bow to untie, and he teetered, unable to recover quickly enough, fell awkwardly into the river.

The grip of the current tugged at him. Realizing its relentless power might win out, he panicked and thrashed around. His brothers quickly dropped their load and rushed to his aid at the water's edge.

Richard hollered, "Let go of the rope and get back on shore first, you dumbass!"

Dave flailed around, losing ground, and the water reached his waist. He'd never learned to swim, further hindering his ability to stay calm. Luckily, his survival instincts kicked in and he let go of the rope and began to pull himself towards the bank with bushes he could grab. Richard and Danny reached for the body again with one hand and extended their other to him while urging him on. Once he got his foot on the edge of the riverbank, he flipped over on his back and crab crawled to safety. Once he realized he was safe he looked back at the water in shock.

His brothers waited for him to catch his breath. Dave looked down at his feet near the water's edge and realized he'd lost a shoe.

"My tennis shoe... Hey!"

He pointed at the water.

Richard and Danny leaned forward, squinting at the murky mix beyond the Mississippi's edge. Mini whirlpools spun, the surface flecked with pieces of trash and wisps of light. Sure enough, over an arm's length out they saw his shoe bob up once, then slip under, quickly disappearing forever into the blackness.

"Shiiiiit, I ain't getting near that damn water again. No way!"

"All right, just take a minute and calm down. Look, I'm sorry I yelled... Listen, Dave, let's just take it easy. And come on now, y'all, we can't make all this noise."

Richard was intent on getting their heads together and finishing the job.

"We're the Boones! We can do this."

He looked at each of them.

"Let's just settle our shit down and brother up."

Danny pulled out a cigarette, but Richard stopped him.

"No, not yet. Not till we get back in the car, sorry, man."

He pursed his lips and gave Danny a sympathetic look.

"Oh yeah, right."

Danny didn't really understand, but knew there must be a good reason, and nodded as if he did understand. Once Richard heard Dave's breathing return to normal, he asked him the question.

"What you think, Hank? Ready to give it another go? I'll take your side and you can guide from the back."

"Yeah okay, I guess so. I was really spooked right then. It was like there were hands in the water pulling me down. I tell ya Richard, this damn place gives me the creeps!"

Dave shook his head, feeling more exhausted than any time he could remember.

Richard nodded at the bundled shroud.

"Well, sooner we get this done, sooner we can get rid of these duds and hit the road."

They repositioned the boards, retied the bows, then maneuvered themselves perpendicular to the water. They shuffled around to point the shroud headfirst at a forty-five-degree angle to the water. Richard was at the water's edge facing Danny, with Dave in the rear, holding it low at arms-length. Richard nodded and they began to carefully swing it back and forth, careful not to loosen the ties.

Richard counted them off.

"Let's throw together on the count of three. I'll say go..."

"One,"

"Two,"

"Three,"

"Go!"

They let loose at the highest point and looked on anxiously. It lifted through the air the same distance as its length landing with an unceremonious splash. It plunged then bobbed after it hit the water, moving haltingly as if snagged on a bush and Richard shook his head.

"Oh shit..."

Then as if a pinata swatted by a catfish from the depths below, it rotated towards the shore, then abruptly spun the other way, heading into deeper current. One would have to say good fortune smiled on the Boone brothers' efforts.

They watched thinking their ordeal with the unnamed corpse had finally come to an end.

True, they never knew the corpse also known as Hollywould before their shared adventure. They stared with lips parted, barely breathing, in ghoulish wonder, now bound to him by some innate otherworldly kindship. It was weird, they knew, but they shared in his misery and naively believed it would be his final journey.

As they watched their handiwork rock then sink, continuously moving, the end with the head descended first. As it went under the other end bobbed clumsily in the surface swirls. Then, as if in a farewell salute, the whole unwieldy bundle twisted back and forth before lifting briefly and finally disappearing without any further play.

In their hearts they knew the spasmodic manner of the cocoon's last motions were fitting; though they didn't know how much it echoed the chaotic final moments of Hollywould's life. As far as they knew his last gasps of air before he died were never witnessed.

Richard believed they took too long at the river's edge. He decided to go straight back to the hotel. They bagged their clothes and threw them in the trunk, as he wanted to hit the road as soon as possible. He figured they could find a place to destroy the garments on their way to Phoenix.

"All right boys, ya'll done good. I'm proud of you. But we ain't got time to celebrate. Let's get cleaned up and get the hell outta here."

"Damn fine by me."

Danny nodded in agreement and looked over at Dave who was definitely the most harried after the ordeal at the river's edge.

"Yea, no shit, I don't care if I ever come back, either."

"Ok then, let's do it."

Richard opened the trunk, threw in the rope and knife, grabbed a towel, and slammed it shut.

"Here Dave, clean yourself off and get dry before you get in. Then sit on it. I don't want none of that mud getting in my car on the way to the hotel."

He tossed the towel and Dave caught one end, but the rest landed on his head. When Danny looked up, Dave resembled a makeshift Halloween ghost for just a moment. Startled, he did a double take, but as Dave pulled the towel off the image was gone, so he shrugged it off, even though he couldn't help but feel a little bit spooked.

Johnny finished off the leftover Jack from the makeshift wake. He placed the empty bottle on a bedside table, and forced an expression of a job well done, and lay down. He was hoping he could sleep. After a minute that seemed like hours, his eyes popped open. He stared at the ceiling and began to hyperventilate. He jumped out of bed, went to the kitchen sink, and poured a glass of water. He drank it down, gulped and grimaced. The wail of the blues man crept up his spine and into his brain.

"When I had my trial, baby, whooo, you could not be found"

He would need a lot more Jack before he would get any shuteye.

Her thermostat and radar
      know you're ripe.
She's circling now,
And ready to harvest –
That's drama.

Your defenses are down,
Just consider it a compliment,
she's a picky bird.
She demands!
That's efficiency.

If you try to deny her,
It won't matter.
You will succumb –
That's comedy.

She'll make you sweat
Hotter than a roasted pig!
Beware, she'll tear –
the apple from your mouth.

After her meltdown at Hotel M, Angie tried to locate Beatri. She tracked down Maddie who had been the cook and care-taker and all-around Auntie at Miss Jackson's where they started in the life. She found her after contacting Doctor Smith, the aging physician who serviced them at Miss Jackson's.

The Doctor tended to Maddie, now bed bound and living with her niece. The girls had always referred to him as the 'Diddle Doctor' behind his back, though his medical services were courtesy of Miss Jackson. He'd earned the nickname, lathered in perfume and whiskey while carrying out his duties in an obnoxiously gleeful manner, especially during routine examinations. Though good natured, and commendably handling emergencies with serious care, he continually made overtures to the girls for what he called little favors.

At worst, the girls tolerated him like a distant relative, since he did keep them healthy, got most any pill requested without questions and performed private procedures on the side for any of their children. Certainly, having someone they could trust with their most delicate secrets was a small blessing and gave them comfort. This indebted them to his attentions, even if his style was occasionally bothersome.

Angie was reluctant to engage him again but knew he was the best way to find Maddie and planned her approach accordingly. The Doctor was very protective of Maddie at first.

"Miss Angie, please don't upset her. She's got high blood pressure, gout, asthma, a bad back, hell, I've lost track of what all. But she's still got a good heart and some days her memory's clear as blue sky. Promise me you won't stir up any of her contrary conditions."

"No sir, don't you worry about me. See Doc, I just want to visit and pay my respects. I want to let her know about dear Gloria's passing and so we can pray together, that's all. Maddie had a special interest in Gloria, and I stayed in touch with her. So, I promise I'll take care. If she ain't feeling well, I'll just pray beside her and leave flowers."

"Well, I'm glad to help you out. It saddens me to hear about Gloria. Tell me, Angie, are you still in the game, or did you get out and marry yourself a nice young man?"

"No sir, neither one, I'm a beautician now."

"Well, good for you, that's great. When was the last time you had a check-up?"

Uh oh, there he goes, she thought, and made up something on the spot.

"Well, see, I got a client whose husband is a doctor. He does my check-ups and I do his wife's hair. But thank you anyway, Doc, you're sweet to think about my well-being."

"Well, you come back and see me now, I mean it. After all these years, here you call me out of the blue..., Why I wanna take a look at you myself. I bet you're still a beauty."

"Oh, Doc, you're sweet to say that. I'll do that when I get back in town, thank you."

"All right darling, now are you sure you'll be all right, going there by yourself? I could pick you up and take you over my-self."

"No sir, there's no need, I'll be fine. Look, Doc, I'm sorry, but I gotta go."

She hung up before he could add another thing.

When she finally got to Maddie, the one-time House Mom didn't have a lot to say. When she spoke, she squeezed Angie's hand like someone living out their last days.

"Angie, bless you, bless you, you made an old woman happy today. God bless you child."

However, Maddie didn't actually give her Beatri's phone number. After Angie helped her sit up, Maddie shuffled through the drawer in her bedside table to find a business card. Clutching it as she fell back on her pillow, she asked right then they pray together. Afterward, she lifted her fist with the crumpled card slowly. As Angie reached out to receive it, Maddie reached over and pushed the card into Angie's pants pocket before she could stop her. Maddie cringed with a distasteful look as if the card itself was contaminated and wiped her hand on the bedspread. She looked at Angie sternly, then shut her eyes before speaking.

"Angie, you make sure you don't end up a Devil's Bride, now. Beatri don't pray at the right church, but she a Calico Girl and she means well. Keep your holy cross in your pocket when you go to her, and promise you'll come back and see me again."

With nostrils flared she opened her eyes again wide to demand Angie's solemn word.

"Promise me!"

"I promise."

After the look Maddie gave her, Angie was spooked. The realization she might never see Maddie alive again made her shiver. She also had not considered how much Beatri may have changed. After she got in her car to leave, she pulled out the card and examined it.

Parlour 16 * Spirit Health
> Fortunes – HOODOO – Vodun <
7935 * New Orleans

No street or phone number or even Beatri's name. Nevertheless, Angie was determined to find her. The card was a starting point, and she believed if Beatri meant for Angie to find her, more clues would follow. She took the train to New Orleans then started her search in Jackson Square. She watched and waited for any sign or signal from Beatri. She wasn't sure what she was looking for but felt certain it was nearby.

In their younger days, Beatri captured the other girls' attentions with her Louisiana stories. She referred to Jackson Square as a powerful place where unseen spirits and the powerful forces from beyond nature's visible boundaries visited regularly.

Angie planned to follow French Quarter Walking-Tour guides for clues. While they led their tours, she stayed just close enough to hear. After familiarizing herself with the different guides, she approached the one she felt most likely to know Beatri. Her instincts told her he was the one she feared the most and was the least money-driven of the lot.

The man was an eccentric little conductor of tourist groups who could have been anywhere between thirty and sixty years old. He was New Orleans through and through, a Crescent City mix of Creole, African American, Cajun, Haitian, and Native American. Though he made her uncomfortable, after only one day of following as he plied his trade, she knew in her heart he would know of Beatri.

The way he described The Quarter's darkest secrets creeped her out. When addressing his tour groups, he would stop short of the juicy bits, baiting them for extra cash to loosen his lips further. Due to his sketchy demeanor, few took the bait. When they did, Angie watched him revel in ushering forth the vilest of details. His behavior as he described these morbid details of death, sexual proclivities and graveyard horrors was too much for even the most curious. He invariably disgusted them, so they seldom tipped with any vigor or took his bait a second time.

She observed these tendencies, hoping she could gain an edge. She didn't want to become like one of the victims he seemed to relish. She was certain he could not be trusted for more than simple directions. The first time she approached him, he responded with belligerence.

"My name no important for you to know. Your name is all that matters."

"Well then, my name is Angorra."

She thought he had donned skeletal make up for tourists, but up closer it appeared to be his pigmentation. His green hair was rubber banded in ratty knots, jutting out beneath a weathered top hat. He smelled of cigars, sweat, and curry. His eyes never met hers directly. When she gave him a twenty, he turned away from her and simply stared down the street before speaking.

"Next day, meet me at de same place, same time."

He walked off without waiting for a response. When he arrived the next day, he refused to tell her anything until she gave him another twenty. Afterward, he handed her an envelope taped together and folded into fourth its size.

"You no open this until you get to the door."

"Ok, but how do I find the door?"

For another twenty, he impatiently talked her through a route while she wrote on a sandwich wrapper she picked up from the gutter. He injected syllables of nonsense, often muttering in gibberish about food and guides' territories in between the names of the streets she needed for her route. To her disbelief, he refused to take her, not even for another twenty, though she continued to tempt him, waving the bill repeatedly while jotting down directions.

Finally, for the first time since they'd met he stared directly in her eyes, though his focus seemed from another world. While he spoke she looked back into his yellow vein-streaked eyes, and watched the fluctuating luminous gray flare of his iris. There were unhealthy pink flecks on the edges and an infinite black depth in the pupils.

"No ma'am, I no go to Parlour 16. No! You go only by yourself, and don't be telling dem, neither of dem, that I give you the way."

His pupils enlarged and irises disappeared as he reached over and snatched the wrapper away on which she'd scribbled. He spoke unintelligibly as he folded it, staring at the sky and turning it over repeatedly, before pushing it back into her palm.

"No open dis map till I leave your sight. I want no more of your money. My help for you is done. Now is time I must go."

He quickly slipped into an alley and out of sight.

She unfolded the wrapper.

She was startled as crumbled rose petals fell to the ground. She then looked at her notes, no longer her scribble, the writing had turned into the tiny slanting strokes of a small child's first written words. She could only hope the instructions would help her locate Beatri. In addition to the mysterious penmanship, beneath the names of the streets were small columns of words written in tiny dots. She surmized they were the various items she would need to take to Parlour 16.

She squinted at the first column and decided she best buy these items first and look to find Beatri the next day. However, once she looked further, she realized it wasn't a grocery list. It was a gathering list of Vodun tithes and tributes. This would be tricky as she'd have to visit Pearlie and others to get the items. She'd never get to Beatri the next day, she'd have to leave New Orleans immediately and come back as soon as possible.

Angorra returned to Jackson Square a week later with the map and her offerings. After much walking and rereading of the map she found Beatri's lair. Parlour 16 was at the end of a short alley off St. Villare Street, the actual rear entry of a weathered two-story building. At first glance it appeared abandoned, the windows boarded up. She thought she might have been duped by the guide, but under closer inspection, she saw 7935 engraved under the mold covered stone above the door.

She turned and looked back down the alley where she'd walked. Should she leave, or did she want to go inside this seemingly condemned building? She recounted chickening out about using a gun after her dream, so why was using a hex to get revenge any different? After all, Pearlie's injuries were from an accident of sorts, and her condition had improved. It had been a while, but would Pearlie possibly make a full recovery?

As Pearlie's mother, posing as her sister she'd done a lot, but still hadn't told Pearlie the truth about their relationship and was increasingly consumed with guilt. She should've protected her better, instead of leading her to danger. When considering her role in Pearlie's troubles, regret added weight to her constant lie about their relationship. This grew heavier

every day though buried deep beneath her day-to-day concerns. She knew it would be increasingly difficult to reveal the
truth the longer she waited. Then again, she was determined
they get revenge. This was the strongest force in her mind. She
convinced herself to hold on to its power while she cleared her
mind, or her heart would unravel.

Squeezing her eyes shut, she swallowed hard, after looking
around the alley she stepped to the doorway. After wiping
away a tear with the back of her hand she looked down at the
doormat and unfolded the instructions. Though faded and its
edges tattered the doormat was full of signs. Indeed, an orange
'16' was painted in the middle and '4X4' stenciled in white
centered all its four sides. Per the instructions a small brass
bell sat on top of an oval basket next to the door.

She sniffled and tried to remember the last time she'd cried
when she hadn't been arrested or beaten. Instinctively, she
reached down to feel the Holy Cross she promised Maddie
she'd carry in her pocket. She finally allowed more tears to
run freely down her cheeks. She took a deep breath. As she
read the instructions further, she was surprised to find another message in different handwriting.

IN ORDER TO ENTER
YOU MUST ANNOUNCE
THIS WHICH IS WRITTEN

Though disarmed by this seemingly instant message, she
gathered herself and spoke the words.

"B-B-B-Bon Dieu, please grant me sit with you. I wish to
cross the threshold that you may feel my heart. I will open
my heart to you; and release my burden that we may share to-

gether. I humbly ask you accept my gifts and allow me to do your bidding. Now may it come to pass as I say: I will be your servant. I welcome you in my soul."

She returned the folded instructions to her purse and lifted the bell off the basket and rang it four times. Then lifting the lid off the basket, she set it on the mat over the number 16. Inside the basket was a well-preserved hollowed stump, its outer edges snug against the sides. She pulled her tithes from her purse in the order listed.

First, a pint of El Presidente Brandy, which she opened, took a drink, then drizzled some of the liquor in the stump. She crossed herself, put the cap back on and slid it down inside the hole. Next, she set down raw pork chops wrapped in Sunday's paper, tied with purple ribbon in three knots. She added the three chicken feet wrapped in cloth, tied in five knots with a red ribbon. Last, a diaper rubbed with catnip she chewed 16 times picked from a field behind Mawmaw's, and half an apple with four bay leaves pressed against. After inserting all into the hole of the stump she pressed down using both hands, until the basket lid rested level.

"Let it be so."

After her words, she picked up the bell and rang, set it on the ground, then reached in her purse to reassure herself with a touch she had the bundle of cash required. Her mind was a mixture of fear and curiosity, her emotions and thoughts itching like poison ivy, both in need of a scratch. She longed for whatever would sooth the tremulous itch binding her heart and soul, but forged ahead, determined to reach Beatri. She rapped with the door knocker and glanced around making sure she was still alone. She nervously tapped her foot, until she heard a woman's voice behind the door.

"You must set the bell back in its rightful place."

"What? ...Oh, shit, sorry."

Her voice came out a hoarse whisper. She knelt quickly and reset the bell on the basket lid, then stood up, pushed her purse beneath her arm, and folded her hands, bowing slightly in apology. In the old days she and Beatri had been good friends, but their paths hadn't crossed in a long time.

She'd never actually dealt with the Voudou Society Beatri currently lived among. Truth is, Angorra had never even had a palm reading. Everything she was about to do was new. She didn't have experience to build confidence. She believed she could trust Beatri but wondered if Voudou would upset her own easygoing lifestyle. Since the early days, she'd stream-lined her life, now seldom finding herself in any situation where she didn't know exactly what to expect.

The Parlour door opened slowly, and incense wafted through the air, finding her sinuses immediately. The vapors stopped her wandering, worried mind but as her body's con-trol relaxed.

Ten feet in front of her stood a woman, whose eyes were closed. Neverthelees, Angorra locked onto the eyes in a trancelike stare as she waited for them to open. A shawl cov-ered most of the woman's face, while her tall head gear created commanding height.

She knew she had found Beatri, though neither spoke. The only sound was the dimmed noise of the city, which drifted further away from her senses with each incense filled breath. The foyer was dark. Angorra's eyes strained, drawing past Beatri further inside. The interior resembled an opulent movie set. There, through the parted curtains, was a candlelit room and movement from another in attendance.

Beatri's eyelids slowly lifted. Angorra's attention shifted back to her friend, as Beatri began to speak.

"Please enter Miss Angorra, I have waited with a sister's heart..." she lifted her hands and covered her heart, "A heart longing to be reunited with its twin spirit. Follow me, we must allow ourselves a proper reacquaintance."

Beatri turned quickly and silently, breezing through the hallway and past the curtains. She turned around when she got to the candlelight, and spread her arms like wings, expanding her finery. The candlelight revealed a glittering priestess. She faced Angorra, following a few steps behind. She motioned for a hug, her eyes smiling but unfocused.

Angorra smiled back and noticed Beatri's face was more colorful than ever. She examined her old friend and tried not to look surprised. On Beatri's head was a red tignon with metallic sheen, a diamond brooch attached to the side. She had a royal bearing, her smile comfortably remaining in place as if time mattered not and it was natural to be admired by others.

In addition to the contrasts in her skin tone, Beatri now had tattooed arcs of dots above her eyes and triangles underneath. Her lips appeared sewn together from stiches etched into them like binding for a wound. On a reptilian silver necklace, hung a pewter skull engulfed by a green jewel covered snake threading the eye sockets. The snakehead perched on top of the skull, with its forked tongue extending down one side. Underneath her chignon were earrings, one a spider in its web, and the other a knuckle bone from which a green beetle wing dangled.

Angorra dropped her bag on the floor and drew into Beatri, reaching inside her Priestess garments and around her body as guided. Beatri's arms then wrapped around her and smothered her inside the royal trappings. Beatri, the 'Calico Girl', was indeed a Hoodoo Priestess.

She led Angorra to a large oval table covered with black velvet embroidered with celestial bodies and magical beasts. The figures portrayed real and imagined beings in dance. A worn coin purse lay open, the contents spilled on the velvet. Angorra sat down, and ready to finally relax, but was immediately startled by bodies moving in the shadows. In addition to Beatri there was another woman of similar age as well as a teenage boy. She squinted to meet their blood shot eyes but realized they only received Beatri's gaze and awaited only her commands.

Beatri directed the doors be locked and the young boy scurried to the task. The woman bowed to Beatri after the boy left and Angorra heard clinking from the rings adorning her thick leather choker. The woman then bowed to Angorra, and she could see the woman's open Tignon cradled long loops of multicolored dreadlocks sprouting from her head. Angorra was being fanned with a floral rainbow of hair bouquet. A brooch on the side of her Tignon was exactly like the pendant on Beatri's necklace.

The incense began making Angorra dizzy. As the rainbow haired woman moved silently back into the shadows, Beatri quietly spoke.

"Now we begin."

Beatri covered the burning cones of incense in the star shaped dish, then lifted a Churchwarden pipe from the table and held it to her lips. Angorra felt time slow down and found it hard to remain in focus. Beatri lit the pipe with a candle, casting shadows over the oddly shaped bowl. Little red gems glowed from the fire inside the bowl, and she realized they were eyes of a serpent, its tail wrapping around the shank and stem. Beatri sucked the lip, split like a serpent's tongue. She slid the end into her mouth. After two long draws she exhaled towards the ceiling and though Beatri's lips moved she remained silent, eyes closed. When the smoke stopped, she beckoned to Angorra.

"Come here, darling sister, receive the breath of the serpent. Open your mouth and your heart. Let go of the world you know. I petition you: Breathe in my smoke and my soul deep into your own. Do this now my love."

Beatri lowered her hand to a velvet covered stool sidled against her chair. Angorra moved quickly, opening her mouth. Beatri leaned toward her, eyes open but without pupils. Before Angorra could react, another set of hands calmly slid around her waist. In an instant, Beatri and Angorra's mouths were locked, in a long-lost lovers' kiss. Her body relaxed as she received the smoke, coursing down her throat into her lungs while the other set of hands caressed her body, soothing her stomach and chest, encouraging the vapors to ignite the will of the Priestess.

She heard an unfamiliar husky voice from behind but did not fear it.

"You are in the hands of your sisters. We will do your bidding. That which is in your heart we can and will abide. Hold the smoke we share deep. Hold it till you pass to the other side. Fear not, our spirits will be together when you arrive."

When Angorra came to, the three of them were on a round bed covered in pillows, surrounded by burning candles of varying heights. The other woman was fully dressed, while balancing on an elbow, singing, and humming, gently stroking the sides of Angorra's uncovered body with her fingers. Occasionally, Angorra heard the word 'Tingalayo' interspersed with her melody.

Beatri sat cross-legged in front of her, hands folded in prayer. Angorra's clothes and bag sat folded neatly in a pile. The cross Maddie asked her to carry forgotten. Beatri was wrapped in a simple black veil wearing only jewelry and her Tignon. Her skin patterns were barely visible in the candlelight, like shadows in a pond.

Angorra had brought the other necessary items pertaining to Pearlie: a picture, a letter in Pearlie's handwriting spotted with drops of blood, Pearlie's lip prints on Candy Canes' stationary, a lock of Pearlie's hair, and lastly the vial of liquid, a mixture of Pearlie's saliva and urine.

The other items needed were a picture of Danny Boone, and a copy of his driver's license and a piece of a towel he'd used; all things bartered from the bouncers and the valets at Candy Canes. The offerings were neatly arranged in a display on the bed with the bundle of cash, surrounding Beatri, who opened her eyes, smiled and stared directly into Angorra's. She lifted both arms and extended her hands. On cue, her assistant stopped her caresses and slowly pulled away.

"Let's get down to business, Angie my love. Come sit next to me."

Angorra moved to her, without giving a thought to their nakedness. It was as if they were back at Miss Jackson's; young, free and uninhibited. Sure, she harbored fears, but was not going to let them stop her as she'd acquiesced to the process, no longer concerned of consequences. Her mind and body were in unison, her intentions and actions on autopilot.

"Now tell me, Angie, who else do you want to bring into the circle for this spiritual transfer? I speak of a person who would help you if you needed. Please bear in mind I recommend adding a man's spirit into the circle, one you can trust with your heart, but who is not of your blood."

Angorra closed her eyes and scrolled through the men in her life and wondered. Not Harry or anyone from the dance clubs, who else might be able to get to the Boones, someone she could trust. Someone who could find their way around the path of her unusual lifestyle and fringes of perilous nightlife.

Max's image entered her mind.

He might work. She wasn't sure why, but he'd always been unquestioning of her intentions from the moment they'd met. Plus, he wasn't too close to the situation though loosely connected in design. And she felt close to him when together.

"Please Angie, let it be the first soul drawn to your heart. Let them be the one. Know your heart! I can tell - you know who it must be."

Beatri tried to urge her on, stern in her tone. She knew whomever Angorra fixated on as a conduit for the circle would most likely only encounter minor distractions, but she also knew they would not be shielded if things turned foul.

Angorra slowly opened her eyes and looked into Beatri's and began to speak.

"Max... it will be, Max, ...yes."

"Who is this Max you speak of Miss Angorra?"

...It was me, Harper Maximillan Wilson III, a man who had only tiptoed through the periphery of Beatri, Angorra, & Pearlie's world.

Without choosing, I was unwittingly woven into the tapestry of their Hoodoo spell. I didn't know it and sure, I continued my job at Vettes with the best of intentions. However, from that moment on, another force, with a separate point of view pushed me into the path of the Etrusco brothers. The power of their spell was a strong test of my sense of duty to Joey Spasula. I held the rudder to stay the course as the unforeseen storm now conjured broke loose.

Peace, all you hippies,
    and say,
Do ya' wanna dance?

Don't sell yourself short kid,
there's no telling how
much boogie might be in ya'.

When the sun comes up,
Count your eggs like days.
Once they hatch –
Count'em as hens,
Because the sun's gonna set again.

The bomb threat left me paranoid, I started looking over my shoulder expecting the leering gaze of a snoopy Vettes guest or employee.

I had to know what was in the locked room but didn't think it wise to investigate during a shift. On the other hand, I wasn't sure when there would be a safe opportunity. No matter when I did it, it could compromise my situation.

First, I thought it best to explore when everyone had already gone for the night..., ...unless there was a hidden alarm. If I set an alarm off while inside and it was after hours, it would be very suspicious. I'd be caught red handed poking around and the police might be notified. That would probably end my Vettes career or at least any chance of helping Joey. I decided if there was an alarm, it was better to set it off during normal business hours. That way it would raise less suspicion, and I could claim it was an honest rookie mistake.

My shift started off okay, but then things got weird. The senior manager, Nate, left about seven. Around nine, I had to step into the DJ booth and take over for Needles McGee, the DJ, apparently ill, who ran past me as I was getting a reading behind the bar. He had a towel draped over his head, and only lifted it long enough for a quick, "Sorry, boss."

I checked on him right away in the employee restroom. He told me he could get keep working but was curled up in a ball on the floor, and said he needed more time to get it together. I listened, but decided it was best to find him a sub for the night. I couldn't spare anyone currently working and when I tried to track down an off-duty replacement, I had no luck. There were only six hours left till last call, so I figured, why not pick me - Max the DJ?

I hustled to the booth and got started. Needles had the turntables set for a crowd pleaser, *The Love You Save* by the Jackson 5. When it ended, we would mix in a Vettes 'Team Feature' dance.

I chose *Ain't No Mountain High Enough* by Marvin Gaye and Tammi Terrell which included spotlight dances by the smaller bar bartenders and girls dancing in the Pink Corvette. As Marvin and Tammi wound down it was my job was to switch to

What A Feeling by Irene Cara, and give the main bar bartenders a chance to show their stuff. It was three minutes long, so there was time to run to the office and try another call. Next, I would fade into *I Want You Back*, by the Jacksons, which returned the spotlight to the small bar.

While in the office attempting to find a DJ, I heard the last verse – "*I was blind to let you go baby...*" – so I dropped the phone and sprinted down the hall, sliding sideways in my saddle oxfords down the waxy tile floor and around the bar into the crowd. Full of apologies, I passed through bouncing bodies, and pushed them aside as I made my way to the DJ booth.

I reached the second step and leapt, landing near the turntables without the necessary nimble touch which caused "*I Want You Back*" to skip just as it ended. I used the pause to fade to the next song, keeping my head down and looking for *ABC*. I found it leaning on a tambourine by the turntable and smoothed it in, brushing the props off the playlist to see what was next. I was in luck, there was a two-song slow down for the crowd to do some buckle polishing.

I pulled *You Showed* Me by the Turtles and *When A Man Loves a Woman* by Percy Sledge for the scheduled grope fest. As soon as the Turtles began, I got Percy set up. After all the rushing around I felt overheated and decided to reward myself.

"Hey Marni, could you please bring me a soda and a Cuervo?"

After her affirmation wink, I was off into the crowd to make my rounds. I encountered Shady carrying a case of Corona to the small bar and asked him to meet me in the booth, figuring I'd have him handle some spins for me. I couldn't worry any longer about the tight staffing situation. When I got to the booth, however, I found a revived Needles back at the controls, and though his pompadour was damaged, he was getting busy with his playlist. I gave him a thumbs up and leaned against the side of the booth to take a deep breath. When Marni showed up with my Tequila, I fired it down quick enough to set the glass back on her tray before she turned around to leave.

"You want another, Max?"

She encouraged me with the 'why not?' look of someone used to seeing a Vettes' manager in need of relief.

"No that was great, I'm good for now, thanks!"

"Ok, no problem if you change your mind."

Then Shady walked up and gave me the look of someone who'd been left out.

"Gee boss, you started without me."

"Change of plans man, just keep an eye on Needles and help him out if he needs it. If you can't, let me know. Ok?"

"You got it Max."

Things breezed along from there, the night seemed to be back on autopilot, so I got bold. I decided to score some points for Joey and check out the 'No Access' room behind the main bar and discover the secrets locked inside. First, I took the General Manager master keys out of the safe. No, I'd not gotten permission from Nash or Dean to use the keys or enter the 'No Access' room, but I knew the keys were in the safe and was certain one of them would unlock the door.

If there was 'Huggy' or anything else illegal stored in Vettes, that room had to be the spot. While carrying out my work tasks I'd pretty much stuck my nose in every other place in the building. All I'd been told about the secret room was how the water and beverage system lines went through it, so I thought the 'No Access' designation was strange. Since it wasn't the only way to access the lines, it stood to reason something else was inside, too.

A little after eight-thirty I unlocked the door after trying a half dozen keys. I slipped inside and closed the door behind, hoping no one noticed. Inside was dark, and I struggled to see, right away hitting my head. I'd incorrectly assumed the neon in the box glass behind the bar also illuminated the room but a thin sheet of metallic material behind it was cutting off the light. I couldn't turn on the overhead because it might attract attention from an employee or guest. I didn't want to risk that; I was too paranoid someone might be keeping an eye on me for Dean.

I slipped back out and went to the office to get a mini flash-light. But when I entered the office, I got delayed because Katy showed up and presented me with bar tab discounts need-ing approval. I took care of those and moseyed over near the 'No Access' door, looking over my shoulder the whole time. I waited till all the girls then at the well picked up their drink orders. Once everyone left, I slipped back inside.

Because of low ceiling beams I had to squat and hold the flashlight pointed at the floor against my hip, while I duck-walked in the narrow pathway between boxes of bar mix. This got me to the far wall where two metal cabinets with numer-ical displays were mounted below a panel of switches and in-dicator lights. What were they storing? One of the cabinets appeared to be connected to the CO_2 dispenser used to ser-vice the bars' soda systems. Interestingly, as if by design, the fifty-pound cannisters powering the system were on the other side of the wall where a purveyor could service them without entering the 'No Access' room. In the corner beyond the cabi-nets, I noticed an additional twenty-pound CO_2 cannister with dedicated timers and gauges on its line running to one of the cabinets.

There was a partially torn sticker on the cabinet, so I shined the light on it. 'OCTO-SP' was printed on the remains of a tag. Maybe this was the unit Lehigh's friend built. The way it tied into the system, it had to be driving something other than Vettes' beer, or sodas.

As I looked the cabinet over and considered how I could open it without leaving any trace, I heard a tentative knock on the door. I hurriedly duckwalked back to the entrance and stood up, smoothed out my coat, turned my back to the door, and slipped out as if it was part of my normal nightly duties. There stood Shady, who I'd asked to monitor Needles. I hoped he wouldn't ask what I was doing in the room.

"Hey, Shady, what's up, man?"

"Mr. Max, sorry to bother you, but I wanted to ask you... uh, who's supposed to be DJ right now?"

Apparently, Needles our DJ had bailed on his post again. It was nine-thirty and Vettes had just experienced 30-seconds of dead air, an inexcusable faux pas as well as a violation of the Vettes' policy. Thank goodness for quick-thinking Katy, who happened by the DJ booth during her stand-up rounds, and jumped in the booth, smartly fading in the song Needles had cued up and was waiting for him to return.

I didn't understand why Shady didn't get there first but since I'd been snooping, didn't want to cross examine him right then. Anyhow, Katy grabbed Shady and told him to find me. I of course, had wrongfully assumed he would have done this on his own, but no matter, my lesson learned, I needed to hurry.

I double checked the lock on the 'No Access' room and headed to the employee restroom to find Needles. Sure enough, he was in there laying on the floor. He was out cold, and the room smelled like he had spilled his guts. I wet some paper towels, put them on his head and tried to rally him by shaking him while dabbing his head with the towels. He reacted right away.

"Unnhhh, sorry, I'm not feeling well."

"Shit... okay, well, why did you even come in? I could'a found someone to cover you..."

As soon as I said it, I realized the evening DJ problems weren't gonna get solved asking him any questions and switched my tactics.

"Look, can you rally, or do I need to get you to a hospital? What do you want me to do here?"

"No! No hospital, I just need to take a day or two to get better. I'll call someone if you need me to..."

"That's all right, I'll get up there for now. I'm gonna send the cook in to help you clean up and get you home, okay?"

"I'm sorry, I'm just not feeling good, unh...".

He reached for the toilet again, he was done for the night. I rushed into the kitchen to get him help. Afterwards, I stepped in the office and put up the GM keys then raced down the hall past the bar and pushed through the crowd to the DJ Booth. After I stepped into the Vettes' music pulpit, I consumed more Tequila and Jell-O shots. I was gonna lead the congregation for the rest of the night wherever the music took us.

Shady came to let me know Needles had been taken home safely, but by then I had my groove on and was in party heaven.

"Yessss! I love this!"

Shady gave me a big thumbs up. I admit it, I had a buzz. It was true, I liked being the DJ, it was a lot more fun than the manager's job.

After more Jell-O shots from Vettes' party devotees, I engaged in a full dance floor feature with the Vettes crew egging me on. I was loving life and boogieing in the spotlight. While I moved my body in time to the music, I began seeing unusual images darting about on the edges of my vision. There were demonic images and celestial beings; a serpent with red eyes gave way to a skeleton in a top hat, a spider with sewn together human lips danced with a donkey and there were other creatures I have no words to describe. It reminded me of the time at South Mountain with the Bar Belles, except this time I felt good and wasn't disturbed by these odd hallucinations.

"Jamming like a salmon baby, and we're swimming upstream, I'm working at Vettes and life is but a dream..."

Celebrating my mood afer singing the Vettes' song, I put on the red bandleader coat with tails and the fancy black felt top hat with the purple sash. I got looser and more brazen as each song climaxed. Soon, I was leading the crowd in Johnny Mathis' *Your Love Keeps Lifting Me Higher and Higher*. When it ended, I mixed in the live version of the same song with its faster tempo. Indeed, this did take the crowd higher, and I perched atop the jukebox playing a toy guitar with frenzied enthusiasm as I overlooked the craziness. Streaming translucent rainbows arced out of the guitar neck into the crowd, as I waved it around like a submachine gun spraying the colors all over them.

If I followed the playlist, next was supposed to cool things off with a slow song, but after I scrambled back into the booth, I had an inspiration to slot in Bobby Freeman's *C'mon and*

Swim-Part 2, keeping the jam at high intensity. I ditched the guitar and grabbed a plastic trumpet to mimic the horns. When I looked above the dancers, the blinking color spotlights showered loops of shimmering colors onto them, turning them into humanoid rainbows. The place was like a swimming pool sized aquarium full of gigantic Paradise Guppies in a feeding frenzy.

I knew I should cool down the crowd and my kaleidoscopic state of mind. *The Limbo,* a group activity was next. I signaled Shady to get a volunteer to work the Limbo stick. He came into the booth right away, leaned over the side, and handed the Limbo stick to Kimmie 'The Shimmie'.

She was so excited, her voice intense, her squeaky squeal could be heard over the music.

"I love the limbo! Shady, sweetie, give me the fruit hat, too, willya? Pleeeease!"

He looked at me for help, and I pointed to the plastic pineapple, which topped the special-order Carmen Miranda prop. He handed the hat to Shimmie and she responded immediately, lip popping a mango sized bubble with a flirty wiggle and a wink.

"Max, you know I can lead the limbo if you want."

Suddenly I felt the need to move.

"Naw, Shady, I'm getting out of the booth. You take over! If you wanna cue up Ricky Ricardo's *Babalu* next, you can keep the booth as long as someone's working the Limbo stick with Shimmie."

"I got it, Max, don't worry!"

Pumped to show his stuff at the turntables, he dashed out of the booth and found a limbo stick helper in seconds, pointing to Katy who joined Shimmie on the dance floor. I bowed, motioning that the turntables were all his and I slipped down to nab myself another drink before *Let's Limbo* began to play.

Midway through the spirited back-bending promenade, I had a dance floor epiphany inspiring me to get on all fours as soon as *Babalu* began. The Limbo line followed me intuitively, we were on our hands and knees, in a boozy crawling snake dance, at the center of the dance floor. Our collective dressage swirled outwardly in an ever-expanding loop, stopping only to stick out alternating hips and legs with the song's hard stop beat.

Shouting out, "*Babaluuuuu!*"

I led us beyond the dance floor and around the standups among spilled cocktails and random stir sticks. Folks were on all fours on the bar tops as well, and though I knew that was a bad idea, I was too crazed to care. I'd reached a point void of any common sense and was intent on leading my club-sized, wiggling centipede of party maniacs into what was certainly an unattainable party nirvana. I maneuvered us toward Vettes' Pink Corvette, while feeling unstoppable, my mojo totally immersed in the holy buzzing bosom of an oldies altered euphoria.

Of course, if I had been consciously present, I would have known better, but instead I never even considered my condition. Looking back, I realize I lost touch with my playlist and Manager-On-Duty responsibilities several songs before I ever stepped out of the booth.

It wasn't long into our trek before many of the line crawler party girlfriends were riding on their partner's backs. We'd inaugurated a new horsey dance, and the riders lifted their cocktails high at the same hard stop their mount's hips shook and shouted "*Babaluuuu*"!

At the Corvette, I realized my hat was gone and the crowds' voices were echoing in phonetic layers in my head. I instinctively rubbed my ear because I felt a feather like tickle. Even through the cascade of voices, I realized it was more.

It was the intentional whisper of a woman.

Her voice grew larger than the moment, overshadowing all other sound. She began to sing words I didn't understand. I had to strain to make it out.

"Binga-bayou?" or maybe *"Tinga-layo,"* it was like in a canyon, an echo in response to *"Babalu."*

I froze, drawn to a stop by a powerful but unfamiliar force. I jostled the procession following behind which caused some to drop their drinks and I tried to listen more carefully.

I felt someone shake my shoulder.

At first, I thought it was a wanna-be rider set to climb on board, but it was Shady. He hesitated, looking nervous, as his adrenaline had him on high alert.

"Mr. Max, you gotta phone call. Umm... you want me to have them call back?"

"Hey! ...uhhh, maybe, who is it?"

I wasn't one hundred percent in the present, and many voices bounced around my brain.

"It's Frankie Fortuna!"

My Vettes' manager's internal alarm went off, shutting out everything else.

"Oh shit! Yea! Ummmm, I'll take it in the office. You go ahead, stay in the booth!"

He looked at me expectantly and I realized he was waiting for more instructions, he wanted me to tell him what to play.

"How 'bout...",

...I knew we should slow things down and searched my memory for a slowdown set. I remembered a Vettes' favorite go-to sequence.

"Play *When A Man Loves A Woman,* then *Son of A Preacher Man,* then after that play Bob and Earl's *Harlem Shuffle* to give me some extra time."

As soon as I finished talking, the echoes returned.

"Binga–playo, Tinga-layo..."

I shook my head and tried to clear out the woman's weird song. Shady looked at me curiously.

"You okay, boss?"

"Unhhh, yeah, sure, can you find the songs and hold things down till I'm done?"

"Yessir! You got it Mr. Max."

He saluted as I looked around. I was still on my knees, hoping to find my bearings and a way back on my feet. When he extended his hand, I was grateful to clasp it. I think he sensed I was on shaky ground.

"Okay, shit, don't worry, I'll be right back."

I stood up with his help and rearranged my coat and tails. My vision sparkled, and my knees stung. I stumbled to keep my balance but held up both hands when he reached to help me. I wanted to reassure him; I was fine. I was faking it.

"I'm good, Shady, are you? If you're up for it, you better get up there."

I motioned at the DJ booth and rubbed my eyes and ears while he waited to make sure I was ok. What he didn't know was I was trying to get the lady's voice singing *"Tinga-layo,"* to fade from my brain.

He reassured me he was up for the task.

"No problem, I been practicing with Needles in the after-noons, I can hold it as long as you need."

"Okay, fine..."

I continued rubbing my eyes and ears, turned, and pretended to step away. Over my shoulder I saw him bound through the chaos of the dance floor like a frog jumping through lily pads. Many of the revelers were still saddled on their mounts and singing, while others had progressed into more outrageous activities normally found on playgrounds or pool parties. I hoped for all our sakes they would revert back to a normal, PG-rated dancing when Shady changed the song.

I didn't have any more time to wait so I slipped out of the crowd but had to stop for some badly needed deep breaths. I was dizzy and sparkles were taking over my vision. I hoped for some clarity to hold me long enough to get me back to my desk. I had to talk to myself out loud.

"Max, you're flying high. It's all right. It's okay, you been through worse, but you gotta regroup right now! You gotta get it together..."

With the Vettes' music system, the woman's omniscient whispers, and whatever was coursing through my blood, I had trouble keeping it together. I resorted to bullshitting myself, and luckily no one else heard my pep talk.

"I can do this. I've done it before."

I grabbed a towel and filled it with ice. I was oblivious to employees hooting at me. They were only showing their approval for the 'Babalu' routine. I barely noticed. I attempted to regain my Vettes' manager state of mind, wiped off my dusty pants and grabbed a glass of water.

I rubbed the towel full of ice on both sides of my head while moving down the hall and once inside the office, grabbed a fresh towel and dried off. When I got to the phone, Frankie didn't beat around the bush.

"Hey Max! How's it going? I hear you're writing a helluva new playlist in Memphis tonight."

"Hey Frankie! Naaaaww, hey, I was just having a little fun, we're bringing it back down now. Needles tried to work through being sick but just couldn't make it. I've got it under control though."

"Are you sure, man? I sure do hate hearing one of my best men is ailing..."

He waited for a response that didn't come from me, so he continued.

"I called to speak to Needles, but they told me he was out, and you were tearing it up. So, I guess you're doing reeeeaal good, and you're pretty tore up too, huh?"

"Yeah... No! I'm fine, I got a little carried away for a couple of songs, that's all. Shady's there now."

"Sure, sure. I know it's easy to do, but you better keep an eye on our numbers. Go ahead and check'em out before you get back up in the booth. Shady can handle the tunes for a set, he's been in training before."

I was kinda dumbfounded I didn't know about Shady's training. I'd been so caught up in everything else with my situation, I'd missed this tidbit. I wondered what else Shady may have going on with corporate.

"It's great you've got confidence in him... I do too, he's a good kid. I'll get caught up on sales readings, don't worry. And I'll make sure Needles is okay before letting him work again."

"Good idea, Max. Tell you what, maybe you better sip on a little whiskey and lay off the Tequila tonight. Whaddya say?"

I wasn't sure but knew it meant he could either see me or someone told him I was buzzed. How else did he know what I was drinking?

"Hey, don't worry about me, I'm fine. You trained me right, Frank, and I won't let you down."

"Far out, that's what I like to hear. Just keep to the plan, my man, and everything'll be all right! Hey, that bomb threat really sucked the sales out of the place last night. How did that go anyhow?"

I certainly didn't want anyone, especially within Vettes, knowing I knew the culprit who called the bomb threat in, so I answered quick before he asked anything else.

"Yes, it was a shocker, but our crew did great, and the Fire Marshall didn't shut us down. Of course, he made us empty the place, costing us a couple hundred dollars in tabs we couldn't collect, plus the sales we lost when we were empty."

"That really sucks!"

"Yeah, it sure did, but we tried to keep everybody happy and did what we could once we got the OK to open back up."

"Well, I want you to know, if there is ever another call-in incident or if there is actually a fire, you gotta make sure to get the Vettes Top 25 collectibles out of the building. You got that?"

He wanted me to prioritize a couple boxes of records over the people and the other things inside Vettes!

"Sure, Frankie, you got it, no problem."

He hung up before I could find out any more out about other unusual emergency priorities. Maybe he was just calling around to all the Vettes' locations checking on things, but he could also have been keeping tabs on me.

Later, I found out the daily Vettes' reports are sent electronically to the main office, and they had sensors set up in critical areas of the operation. Unbeknownst to me at the time, the sensor in the Bar Prep room where I'd been snooping around indicated an intrusion had taken place. Of course, the only person on duty in Memphis with access to a key was me.

I don't know if the Vettes' world was closing in on me, but I did try sipping whiskey as Frankie suggested. I pondered how I sensed an urgency to report something, anything, to Joey or maybe Sarge, ramping up.

Let me be honest, I didn't stop with sips of whiskey as suggested. Instead, I took a fifth of Jack Black and two Jell-O shots into the booth after finishing the employee check outs and tried creating a few more playlists of my own. My sense of my work at Vettes and the purpose Joey hired me were on a collision course. It made me anxious, and I felt a need to escape into a world of booze and music I could only create on my own.

I must have gotten really buzzed, the next thing I remembered I was in a child's playground and the vision filled dream that was chasing me finally broke through...

We were kids, holding hands, dancing in a circle, but with grown up faces. The ground we stood on began to rotate like a merry-go-round. Looking around I recognized Mira and Effie, Will Campen and Raidyo Luv, Joey Spasula, Janet the counter girl, Frankie Fortuna, Dean, Nash, Needles, Olga and Darla. And there were other men I didn't know, one had a bloody, bashed-in head.

Inside the circle, Angel held hands with an attractive younger woman with caramel skin. They intently watched a woman in the middle wearing a turban, her arms lifted in the air while dancing in tandem with a donkey on its hind legs. Other than Angel and the girl, no one paid any undue attention to them. It was just as natural as any other couple dancing together.

As the lady motioned her arms, she began levitating, while we continued to move in the opposite direction around her, beckoned by her hands. Though draped with loose fabric and jewelry, I couldn't help but notice her calico skin. The air shimmering around her, particles rose in continuous streams from up under as if she the center of a magic fountain. The particles becoming cascading sparks sizzling and falling like spent firework debris.

I heard the song I'd heard before. Throughout the dream compelled to join the circle as I danced with the others, I found myself holding the donkey's hoof with one hand and Angorra's hand with my other. When we sang, our voices were as children...

'Tingalayoooo, Tingalayoooo
Come little donkey, come.
Me donkey fast, me donkey slow
Me donkey come and me donkey go

Tingalayoooo, Tingalayoooo
Come little donkey, come.
Me donkey hee, me donkey haw
Me donkey sleep in a bed of straw

Tingalayoooo, Tingalayoooo
Come little donkey, come...'

The donkey released my hand and danced back to the center with the woman conductor. The two began dancing and spinning together, faster than our outer ring. Darla took my free hand, and we sang "Babaluuuu" & "Tingalalayooo" alternating as if the words fit the song. I phased in and out of consciousness, sometimes just letting my eyes close and my form jostle along with the circle, while still totally feeling the buzz of my dancefloor performance.

Oddly, my dream world and reality had blended together.

Suddenly, our circle pulled us down to our knees. Once down, the Calico sorceress and donkey began spinning so rapidly, they merged into a single blur. As the blur evolved into a humming vortex, the sound seemed to bend us, and we bowed, still on our knees with hands extended, and our palms slapped the ground.

In that moment inside me came a powerful desire to hold the vortex's power close and I reached towards it, trying to harness its power by grabbing the swirling spiral in a bearhug.

As I moved, I was pulled away in the opposite direction. Somehow, something was interfering and pulled me away. I desperately tried to resist...

The Hatching Aftermath

I came to, with someone shaking me, and trying to wake me. Through the haze it looked like I was in a parking lot. On the pavement next to me was a box of records. It was reminiscent of my night on South Mountain, except instead of gale force winds there had been children singing.

"Max! Max! Wake up, Max, wake up, please!"

"Unhhh…".

At the time, I didn't really know if it was day or night, or what happened to the vortex I grabbed at or why I was sprawled on the pavement.

"Max, it's Darla! I been trying to wake you up. We gotta get you outta here. You don't belong out here in the parking lot! Come on, now. We gotta go somewhere safe."

She squatted next to me, straining her neck to see over the top of her knees and get a close look at me. She was worried, squeezing a handkerchief in her hand, and waving it around my face as if she meant to wipe something off. I vaguely remembered seeing Darla and Olga sometime before last call but was blank on whatever happened after that.

I guess I'd had another black out.

"Where's Olga, is she okay?"

"Max, she's fine, I took her to the airport, she had to fly back to Phoenix. I came back for you because you were so messed up. You said you needed a ride when we dropped by earlier."

"Oooohh, man. What's going on? Was there a party or something?"

I was propped up on my hands now and motioned with my chin at the boxes of records.

"I mean, why do I have these records out here?"

I was having trouble getting my bearings.

"Max! I don't have any idea. I was gonna ask you the same thing. I'm thinking you got too high. I mean, I was only gone a couple of hours. I don't have any idea how you ended up here. Were you here all alone when you closed?"

I shrugged to show her I didn't have any idea, while I pushed myself over into a sitting squat.

"Tell you what, Max, lemme help you take this stuff back inside. Did you already set the alarm?"

"I don't know..."

"Well, okay, let's just get you upright and figure this out."

She reached under my arms and her hair fell into my face as she struggled to get a hold of me.

"Wha? Okay, wait a second, lemme get my feet down first."

I pulled my legs around setting my feet on the asphalt while she relaxed her grip.

"Okay, thanks."

I bowed my head she had me sitting up and planted my feet with my knees in front of my face. She pulled her hair behind her head, though some of it immediately fell back in front of that intense gaze. She gave me a serious looking over, turning her head side to side and studying my eyes with care.

"Look, I'm gonna take these over to the back door while you get yourself ready."

She moved the records over by the kitchen exit then returned. She sat down next to me and had me do some breathing with her and gave me some water. She finally got me together and stood me up.

After we got inside, we put the music back in the DJ booth, sat down, and she made a pot of coffee. After several attempts to get me in a conversation, she went behind the bar. Without asking she brought a bottle of Bailey's and Kahlua to spike our coffee. She set the two liquor bottles down like sentries next to the pot and cups. It took a couple helpings of spiked coffees, but she finally got me into a human conversation.

"Why do you think you took the records outside, Max?"

"Well, tonight I was warned to save them in any future emergencies by Frankie Fortuna who called. That's if there was ever another bomb scare or a fire or whatever."

"Another *bomb scare*? Was there a bomb scare?"

"Yeah, last night, but it wasn't real."

"Whaddya mean it wasn't real?"

"I know who called it in, that's why."

"Did you have them do it? ...I mean how did you know who did it?"

"Lee... I mean, someone I know did it so he could warn me about something."

"Huh? Was it someone I know?"

I thought about it for a second.

"Well, maybe, it's definitely someone who knows Olga. I mean, we saw her playing at Rum Boogie the first night I got here."

"Yeah, I think I know who it is too, you gotta be talking about Lehigh. You know, Olga told me she saw you your first night in Memphis and that she'd already met you in Phoenix."

I nodded as if it made sense, but she wasn't through.

"She thought you were cute, too."

She smiled and crossed her legs, tossed her hair over her shoulder and gave me a coy smile as she swung her top leg up and down. She let the coffee and the moment play for all it was worth.

I wondered right then if I'd said too much. For the first time in a long time my shoulder began to throb, and I remember thinking I couldn't trust anyone even loosely affiliated with Vettes. But of course, I also felt of all the people I'd met so far in Memphis, I could trust Darla. Maybe even more than Olga. By then, I knew she was much less impetuous than her running buddy, roommate, or partner, or…

I decided to let her know how I felt.

"Well, I can't say I wasn't attracted to her, either."

I finished off a cup and reached for the Baileys, but she uncrossed her legs and quickly reached over and grabbed my hand.

"Here, let's put coffee in your cup first," and she poured it three quarter full of Joe before she let go my hand.

"Okay, have at it."

She smiled warmly. A kind twinkle shone in the corner of her eyes and her eyes got smaller as her smile swelled.

"Yeah, you're probably right about that. Darla, you know what? Thanks for rescuing me. I'm really not sure where I would have ended up if you hadn't showed up."

"Well, when I pulled in the far side of the lot, I saw someone over here grubbing around on all fours. I drove slowly, but as I got closer, I wondered if it was you. But Max, crawling around with that crate you had your arms wrapped around? I sure as hell didn't understand what you were doing. Thing is, you must have passed out right before I drove up."

"Well, I would've never known how long if you hadn't told me. I think there's something in the water, if you know what I mean."

"Yeah, maybe, I'm not sure about that, but tell me, what did Lehigh wanna warn you about?"

"Oh, he thinks the owners may be in some kinda drug ring, and maybe even spiking the drinks at the clubs. He said they had hitmen and one was in town. Maybe to do somebody, and for me to be really careful."

"Shit!"

She suddenly pushed her chair out and stood up, slamming her fists into her thighs.

"Damnit, I've been so worried about Olga, I kept telling her she needed to get out of this gig."

"Why? Did she piss somebody off?"

She came back over to the table and grabbed her chair by the back and leaned in over it.

"No, but there was some kinda mix up not too long ago and she ended up with a box with one of those weird pumps they have her install. She was curious about it and took it apart. She couldn't figure it out what it was, but she showed it to me, and I finally figured out what it was. I had to do some research at the library but turns out it was some sort of dispenser that worked off the same physics as those big water fountains on the Vegas strip and at airports and shit. It didn't make any sense, why they were having her install something like that at Vettes."

"How did you figure that out? What are you some kinda engineer or something?"

"No, I used to be a librarian, so research is kinda my thing. And there was something else..." She let go of the chair and started walking in a little circle. "...Olga, Olga, Olga..."

She was talking to herself, and I could barely hear her, but didn't want to stop finding out where this was gonna lead.

"Did you guys ever suspect drugs?"

"Ha! That's rich. We do drugs! Of course, we recognized the buzz we got at Vettes. You kidding? Sure!"

"So, it really is a thing..."

"Well, we didn't wanna admit it to ourselves, we were crazy in love and stuff, and it was such a good gig at first. They paid in cash and all. It was just like a big party that was never gonna end."

"So y'all been keeping this to yourselves all this time? Really?"

"Well, she travels a lot, and we've never really pieced it all together, but we had our suspicions. You know, we've dealt with a lot of unusual people, and we didn't wanna cause any problems for anyone. I mean, we never thought they were killers or anything..." She rubbed her hands like she was washing them, "...just people priming the party pump. You know what I mean?"

"I guess, yeah, I understand how you could see it that way. But my understanding now is, well, some people are getting sick and maybe worse."

I began to feel nauseous myself, with an inevitable headache coming on.

"Shit, this is too much to think about now. I need a clear head to deal with this and right now my head's starting to hurt."

She gave me the look of genuine concern again.

"Okay, maybe it's time to take you home. You know, I think it's best you come with me. I don't think you're gonna be a hundred percent for a while. I don't want you puking in your sleep or something. I won't be able to sleep, unless I see you're safely asleep with my own two eyes."

"Well, okay, if you think so. I did have quite the crazy buzz. You know, I haven't blacked out like that in while, not since..."

I remembered the South Mountain party with the Tempe Bar Belles, but decided not to mention it, instead thought I'd better clear the air with her and Olga.

"Will Olga be okay with this though?"

"Hell, she'd insist on it! ...Ummm, well you know, she might get a little jealous when I tell her."

She stopped and leaned over and whispered in my ear.

"We'll just have to behave, I guess."

She lifted a 'you understand right?' eyebrow and then gathered our cups and the coffee pot.

"Are you steady enough to put the liquor back?"

She glanced over her shoulder as she walked away.

"Sure thing, right on it."

Actually, it helped reduce my queasiness to move around. Then when I got behind the bar I took the chance to splash some cold water on my face. I realized she was right, someone should look over me for a while, as I had consumed way too much of everything.

When we got to their apartment, she took me in the bathroom and took my shirt off and sponged me down. Then gave me a quilt and took me in her bedroom. She went in her closet and came out with an old t-shirt with 'Georges' on the front, 'Drag Bar and Truck Stop' on the back.

"Here you go, you can sleep in that, a-a-and your undershorts, of course."

She gave me a flirty wink as she went back in her bathroom.

I don't remember falling asleep. At one point I woke up and we were on top of the covers. She had an arm wrapped over my side while holding on to the t-shirt but was sound asleep. I had to gently undo her fingers from the fabric and lift her arm, to slip out and use their bathroom. When I got back to the bed, I lifted her arm up and brought my knees up to snuggle my rear backwards into the warmth of her angled hips. Our impromptu spooning in place, I lay her arm back down gently onto my side.

As soon as I released her arm, I closed my eyes, and her hand gripped my shirt, a soft fist against my chest. I peeked down and saw her hand squeezing gently, stopping only once the wrinkled fabric was taut between her fingers.

CHAPTER

26

It's finally your time,
  You're next in line.
No exceptions,
even though
you fell off your moonbeam.

Suddenly you realize,
You're no longer a child
No matter if you still have the drive
and those dreams in your eyes.

Angorra offered Pearlie a place to stay in her Scottsdale, AZ, apartment after the blast at Louis' Birthday Party. Though Pearlie accepted she made it clear it would only be until she could get reset financially. She'd have preferred staying in Memphis, but still couldn't make ends meet on her own. She had to cope with her injury, rebuild her strength and work through the pain until fit enough to work steady. You see, in spite of everyone's suggestions to find a new career, she wanted to go back to what she loved. Dancing was the one thing she truly loved.

A complicated and emotional period ensued. Coping was hard for Pearlie. She made a lot of mistakes working back into shape. She changed her hair. She combed her bangs over her new wandering left eye. Guess what? Men thought it looked sexy. And though her eyesight had been diminished she realized people only noticed something was wrong when it went crazy. She figured it out, this only happened when she lost control, and she only lost control when she was partying. Those times she might drop her guard and lose her inhibitions. Once she realized the connection between partying and her crazy-eye, it made her more determined than ever to stay in control.

She learned discipline, stopped partying and having one-night stands. She gave up trying to live like Angie and her friends. She knew others who found financial independence living that way, but the path didn't work for her. She began to have days where she noticed her radiant beauty in the mirror and knew she could cause a stir with her old crowd, but no longer cared about going to their parties. She turned down any and all invitations.

As Pearlie regained confidence in her physical prowess, she let herself feel good. What made for her best life and more importantly, how she saw the world had shifted. This changed her mindset, she no longer considered the injury a misfortune, instead she believed it was an attack from unseen forces in the universe. She was now certain the men at the party had not intentionally attacked her or meant to hurt her, but instead spirits of nature acted through them and ambushed her.

She believed these spirits behaved like wild animals. When you entered their element, they struck at you when hungry or if they sensed you meant them harm. Why? Because they were just forces exerting their power in an ages-old battle for survival. Pearlie believed she had somehow stepped unwittingly right into their path.

She found great strength in this epiphany and was determined to be as tough as anything she might ever encounter again. She was still very young, and though her newfound strength went missing some days, it ebbed and flowed on others. When she felt good, she could work herself till she had nothing left to give. Those days, she knew she was ready to show the world her true spirit at its most powerful. She felt ready to prove she deserved a special place in the world, no matter what force might stand in her way.

She remembered how before getting hurt, when she danced, her spirit would be in a special place and the rest of her identity got lost in the song. Her body would naturally take over letting her spirit soar.

It was so easy then.

When doubt crept in, her confidence shrank, and made it hard to find her way. Trying to be sociable was frustrating, especially with her natural lack of patience. Being partially deaf made her feel clumsy, it affected her more than her damaged eyesight.

After getting hurt, she had to relearn to coordinate her body with music. It was like climbing a mountain; she often wondered if she'd ever reach the top. In the very beginning, she sometimes slipped into partying, wallowing in self-pity. There were times Angie came home and found her passed out on the floor.

But eventually, Pearlie learned to feel the beat of a song in her jaw and click her molars with the beat. With practice she found her jaw could take over and she wouldn't have to think; once again she could lose herself in the music, tune her body to the beat, and let her spirit soar. That trick also made her feel her hearing had improved, though tests showed otherwise. Once her confidence returned it didn't matter, she knew she was dialed in.

When Angie was out of town, Pearlie played music loud like at the club. She learned her neighbor's schedules to avoid their complaints so she could dance full throttle, whirling and gyrating throughout the entire apartment without worry.

As her confidence grew even more, she started to decline joining Angie for getting high or for cocktails. She remained polite and grateful but realized rooming with Angie cramped her style. Angie was pretty chill when relaxed, but the world she lived in wasn't chill at all. Too many crazy people, too much hustle and though Angie didn't really use them much as far as she knew, there were too many drugs in her circle.

As far as Pearlie was concerned Angie was too driven, going too fast, and doing too many things all the time. Pearlie didn't share Angie's fear of being financially insecure. She knew Angie couldn't help it, she just always wanted more. Pearlie knew in Angie's mind, no matter how much money was made; it was never enough.

It was tricky situation for Pearlie to sort, because her sister was so encouraging and supportive and had paid her bills. She'd bought the groceries and taken her to doctors' appointments. Through it all Angie never asked for money. Instead, she patiently supported Pearlie when at home, telling her she was smart and beautiful and could do whatever she put her mind to. Of course, Pearlie knew where Angie went and what she was doing but was still grateful she spent time with her when home.

This was a new dynamic for Angie and Pearlie's relationship. When Angie had a break from out-of-town appointments, she offered Pearlie jobs again and asked her what she was going to do once she regained her fitness. At first, Pearlie took a couple easy jobs but was hesitant to give an answer on her future plans.

The problem was, Angie's life hadn't changed, and when in town, she left at all hours of the night, hustling in order to keep living her life the way she was accustomed.

The truth was, as much as Pearlie loved Angie and was indebted to her, she knew it would be impossible to complete her own journey if she stayed in Angie's world. When she started to ponder this, she was conflicted about moving out. She was acutely aware of her early setbacks she first moved in.

Finally, Pearlie's attitude about going to live on her own changed. It happened after one of the gigs Angie found for her. She was dancing at a clubhouse party, when a young, drugged up member of the main guest's entourage got rough with her. It took too long for the bouncers to sort it out, and it left her frightened. She never wanted to feel in danger again. She never wanted to not feel in control again. Afterwards she declined any more gigs Angie offered.

In fact, she stopped socializing completely with Angie. At long last she found the confidence to tell her sister she was moving out in a nervously delivered announcement requiring all her power to remain under control. She even promised Angie she'd repay her generosity someday.

Angie remained calm, too, and instead of acting hurt or asking for justification, she filled with sadness. In that moment, Pearlie didn't understand the sadness stemmed from the guilt only Angie knew and continued to hold inside.

In fact, after Pearlie spoke, they cried and fell into an embrace. Though it seemed the longest one either remembered, they didn't feel at odds with the moment. Their faces were soon wet with tears. The reality was bigger than their comprehension. Bound by more than words or memories, only their eyes managed an exchange, their lips unable to contribute. They remained in a clutch long enough for the last sob to fade gracefully into awkward nods until they turned away.

After Pearlie moved out, she was pleasantly surprised Angie hadn't freaked, but instead became less of a friend and got back to being a big sister. This was of great comfort. They were more relaxed when together. As Pearlie's confidence grew, her desire to combat the spirits she believed had attacked her grew in intensity each day.

When Pearlie had first moved into her sister's place, Angie explained the guy who'd bounced the fireworks into the cake, put his foot through the side, and trapped her was Danny Boone, one of three Boone brothers. She told her how she'd seen them around and could find out more if Pearlie wanted. She even offered to help get even, whenever Pearlie felt the time was right.

Pearlie didn't know how to fight back against the spirits that had come for her, but she figured the man who brought them to her probably was the best place to start.

However, when Angie first suggested they use a spell to exact revenge, Pearlie certainly wasn't on board. First, she wasn't sure the spirit would still be in the man. But she also found it especially distasteful since she'd have to consume so many different potions and herbs. It was too bizarre, and she had worked hard to get in shape. Plus, when she considered the process, she feared what she might do, and where it might lead. She'd never experienced Black Magic or Voudou first-hand and didn't want to upset the delicate balance she'd finally achieved in life. She shared her fears with Angie, who only response was to not push too hard about it.

Angie didn't tell Pearlie she was keenly aware that Beatri's spell, already set in motion that day in Parlour 16, would not stay potent forever. They needed to act soon. Beatri stressed to her that spells were unpredictable in their strength and duration from start to finish.

Beatri indicated the spell was probably good for a season but couldn't state an exact length of time in which they'd have to execute. She also assured Angie the spirit world would win Pearlie's attention and sway her, and once she embraced the idea, Pearlie's power would amplify the spell's affect.

"There be no telling how it changes one who casts, nor the one who receives. The spell is already in dere hearts, and when you cast, de hex brings it from dere. You see our fears are greater than anything our Voudou allows me to bring from the darkness where they dwell...".

"How can I help her with the spell if she's afraid?"

"De spell already started and if de spirit opens her heart to it, the spell will rise to her lips, and she will tell you of the desire herself."

Angie'd dropped hints and took Pearlie with her to special shops that featured spell makings whenever possible. She'd even left magazines with articles regarding curses as well as Black Magic bric-a-brac around the apartment.

In a strange but fortuitous turn of events, after Pearlie had moved out and Angie was about to give up on Pearlie agreeing to take part, she called. It was the morning after a ferocious desert monsoon knocked out her power and power at Pearlie's new place, too. By the time their power returned, and Pearlie called she was so worked up, Angie couldn't get a word in edgewise.

"Angie, I'm ready, I wanna do it. My head went all crazy last night, and I couldn't sleep during the storm. Children were singing crazy songs in my dreams! I lived that awful night over and over, until my soul was on fire. And I'm angry! Angie, it's crazy! I still can't believe no one from that party ever apologized or offered any help."

"Oh Pearlie, I'm sorry you had a bad night, but are you sure?"

"Oh, I'm ready! I want to be the vessel! I want to be the one. I want to get even. I want to wave the wand... It *has* to be me."

Angie was excited Pearlie was ready. She prepared the potions Beatri had prescribed, and Pearlie drank them as directed. There were incantations and charms, and Pearlie rehearsed them as eagerly as she consumed the potions.

Pearlie wanted to get to it as soon as they could isolate her with Danny, even if meant making up a story. Angie, still popular with the Managers, DJ's and dancers at Candy Canes worked it out with key staff members to they'd let her know if the Boones ever showed up. Pearlie got on the Candy Cane's part time schedule, telling them she wanted full time eventually.

Pearlie was the one who got the tip. One of the girls who'd heard her queries, let her know Danny was coming in the next weekend to celebrate his birthday. Pearlie had been taking the potions long enough for them to work.

She was ready.

Angorra paid one of the dancers scheduled that night to give her shift to Pearlie. Then while Danny was there, Pearlie could lure him into the champagne room after her spotlight dance. Once inside she could kiss on him or lick him, or find some way to get herself on him and complete the spell.

The Boones Return
and
The Spell Slips Out

When the Boones finally pulled into Phoenix, the traffic was bad, and Richard decided it was time to have the talk. He pulled off at a gas station to fuel up. Once they were all back in the car, he pulled to the side near the air and water pump, parked, turned off the radio, and began.

"Listen, I wanna thank you both. You did good. I'm proud of our work. I know it was a really tough thing to deal with, and you both did a great job."

"Thanks Rich."

They'd replied in unison.

He quickly held up his hand to shut'em up.

"But...the job is only half done. The other half is the hard part. And that's to never tell *no one*!"

He just stared at them.

"...I mean no one. No bragging at work. No telling your buddies. No drunk talk to girlfriends, nothing. It was family business, and it ain't never gonna be no one else's. Got it?"

His brothers looked at each other then turned and Danny spoke first.

"Yeah, we got it."

Danny then looked at Dave, who agreed, "Yeah, I got it, sure. We'll be cool."

Richard wanted to drive it home.

"You see that you are. Fucking this up now would be worse than if you'd fucked up when we were in Memphis, you understand? Now I'm gonna take y'all home, then go check in with the boss. You got any questions?

He stared at them both and breathed.

"...Okay, then this is the last time we ever mention it."

His younger brothers sat in awkward silence. Richard considered what else to say. Meanwhile, the images of the last few days together tinkered with their brains like little mad elves building puzzling toys. Mentally spent, unable to add more, he never said another word, instead he turned and put the car in drive, and pulled into Valley rush hour traffic.

Richard dropped his brothers off at their apartment and went to C.B. Products, where Larry was still around. He was relieved he could finally get rid of the F&A package, though he fully expected Larry to be pissed because any hassle was reason enough for him.

Of course, as far as Richard was concerned, Larry was the reason for the problem, but then Larry wouldn't see it that way. At this point it didn't matter to Richard, he was too tired to care. Larry would just have to be pissed if he was pissed. Hopefully there would be some cold beer in the office to drink and he watch Larry blow his top.

"Richard, my main man!"

Larry seemed enthusiastic when he saw him approach the office. Everyone else must have gone for the day.

"Larry."

He set the package down on one of the chairs in front of Larry's desk. After shaking hands, Larry reached around his neck hugging his shoulders while chuckling.

"My man! Good trip?"

"Yeah. Everything in Memphis was taken care of."

"That's what I like to hear. That's why you were the man for the job. You know I could'a done it myself, but I knew you could take care of it."

"Yeah, well, thanks. We took care of things real tight like you wanted. All the trouble just washed away. No problem."

He looked around the room.

"Hey, Larry, you got a cold beer? It's been a long day."

"Sure."

He reached behind the desk into the cabinet and his minifridge.

"So, everything, huh? That's great, and no problem with Johnny. I'm telling you Richie; you got the touch. Yessir!"

He handed Richard an Old Style and kept one for himself, popping the top and looking for a response. Richard popped his and took a drink, then after wiping his lips he started with a little nod.

"Well, there's only one thing but you already know that, right?"

"Know what Richie?"

Richard pointed at the bag in the chair.

"F&A."

"Aww yeah, the fucking package."

Larry motioned for it and Richard grabbed it and set in on the desk and added his two cents worth.

"It was kinda nerve racking driving this all the way back, you know."

"Hey, I'll take care of it, don't worry."

Larry opened a bottom drawer, threw it in and slammed it shut and acted like it was no big deal.

"Hey, whatcha gonna do, huh? We make it work, right?"

He reached his beer across to click bottles, but Richard's was empty, and he'd set it down on the desk while looking at Larry.

"Sure, but I need another beer first. That ok?"

He smiled at Larry with a beer drinking buddy's grin.

"Absolutely!"

Larry was taken aback by Richard's assertiveness at first, but quickly smiled and pivoted, spinning in his chair away from Richard and grabbing another. Without missing a beat, he swiveled back around and put it in Richard's hand, picked up his own beer once again and waited with his eyebrows raised for Richard to click, making sure Richard knew he was still in charge of the conversation.

"Thanks."

"So other than what you just told me and what we discussed when you were in Memphis, anything else I need to know?"

"Well, I just want you to know that Danny and Dave did a hell of a job. You know they may get some flack at work for being gone with short notice...".

Larry was waving his hand like shooing a fly before Richard even finished.

"Not a problem, if anything comes up, I'll take care of it. Consider it done."

"Thanks, Larry. You know Danny's birthday is coming up and I ain't said nothing to him yet. We was all business for this job, but I'd like to show him some love by doing something special. Maybe another day off or...".

"Naw, no way. Let me handle it. Tell him his favorite uncle, Uncle Larry, is gonna fix him up. We'll do it up right. Take him out for dinner then down to Candy Canes..."

Larry paused and seemed to be getting an idea.

"Better yet, you tell him it's on you, but let me take care of it. How's that sound?"

"Well, are you sure, I mean that sounds like more than I would've expected...I mean you ain't gotta do all that."

"Sure I do, absolutely. He deserves it."

Suddenly Larry stood up.

"Look, I'll get y'all a limo so you can make a night of it. Tell you what, tell them not to even bother with work tomorrow or the next couple days. Yeah, let'em rest up after the trip and then he can even recover for an extra day after his party, too. It'll be great."

"Ok, boss, sounds good. That's a real nice thing you're doing, really."

Richard thought he should probably leave, as it was already more than he ever thought would come of it, and he didn't want Larry to somehow rope him into dealing with the F&A package. He got up out of his chair and stretched his neck before taking a swallow and finishing his beer. He set it down on the desk.

"Well, I'm gonna go get some shut eye. Thanks again, Larry you're a generous man. I really appreciate it."

"Hey, thank you. Tell you what, don't bother coming in till noon tomorrow ok? We'll get some of the other details together then for the celebration."

"You got it."

After Richard left, Larry picked up the phone and made a call.

"Yeah, it's me. We had a little delay, but I got you your package...No, I got it right here...What can I tell you, good help is hard to find...No, no, you come by here and call when you're close. ...Yeah, hey sorry 'bout that I'll take care of you...OK, no problem...Later."

Larry knew it didn't do any good to give ultimatums to Veda. He also knew he'd have to kick in some extra cash to smooth the deal. She'd wanted to take the package when she had her hands on it the first time, but Larry said no. He didn't realize then he'd have to use the damn thing to square things with her later. Now it was worth the extra expense not to deliver it to Vegas since she was already on her way through.

He wanted clear his books with her. He might need her again soon.

When the Limo dropped Danny at Candy Canes for his birthday, the cosmic radar in Pearlie's brain blipped. When she reached backstage to for her spotlight dance, she spotted him with a couple of buddies stage left. She requested Baller the DJ play the special bottom mix: Cliff Richard's *Devil Woman* and Santana's *Black Magic Woman.* Her outfit was too skimpy to hide a dime, so she tucked the old Mercury dime, a safety charm for the spell, under her tongue. Later she would try to put it in Danny's ear.

Baller the DJ made the announcement.

"And here she is, Miss Pearlie Pearl!"

Pearlie's dance began similar to many girls' routines. She twirled upright on the main pole several times, then while she gripped the pole with both hands, she flipped over, and spun upside down with legs extended. After several turns, while still circling, she slyly removed her top before returning to the upright position.

When her pole routine ended, her superior natural talent took over. Drunks were easy to hook, but she consistently hypnotized the sober ones in the crowd with enough taste to distinguish her talent, as she moved fluidly from one enticing pose to another. She dropped and rolled across the stage to rise in a sitting position. Without hesitation, her legs folded underneath, and she arched backward. Reaching down to push against the stage with her hands, she raised her thighs above her high heels. She reached underneath, grabbed her high heels with her fists and let her torso fall slowly, first as graceful as a swan landing on a pond, then by thrusting her body forward in delicate little hops. In time with the beat, she moved to the edge of the stage, to entice tips from the crowd.

At stage's edge, admirers stood with eager faces, bills dangling from their mouths, hoping she'd accept them, waving them tantalizingly close to her hips. Fans considered themselves lucky if they let loose their tribute and a girl snagged the bill with a snap of their G-string, inches from their gaze. However, despite the dancers and fans intentions, most of the money ended up scattered randomly around the stage.

Her focus was elsewhere as the spotlights strafed the faces in the crowd. Her body continued its well-rehearsed undulations, and she glanced side to side till she spotted Danny.

Once in her sights she worked her way towards him. Long simmering sensations blossomed from the center of her brain and middle of her chest. The feeling grew larger in scope and intensity until stirring down into her tummy. She held on tight to the bottom of her stilettos, flexing her body from head to toe. It was her distinct limbo-like move. The pearl drop jewel in her navel and fringe on her G-string flew in the air and popped against her skin while a growing wave of sensations rolled through her midsection.

Catching Danny's eye, she smiled and initiated her plan. She grabbed her right breast, and while maintaining eye contact, pushed it up, reached for it with her tongue, giving him a sexy wink and come-hither look.

She had his undivided attention.

He quickly pulled out a twenty and waved it. She ignored the other men, then rolled over once, grabbed some bills, tucked them in her G-string, and then lifted her torso again. Clutching her heels, she smoothly scooted over like a gliding spider. He licked his twenty-dollar bill and stuck it on his forehead like a drunk poker player.

In the depths of Parlour 16, Beatri sat surrounded by a cascade of veils. A pungent fragrance hung in thick swirls of smoke. Her semi-conscious attendants, bellies full of Beatri's spiced brandy, lay by her side, their eyes bound by scraps of Auntie Brake's burial shroud. Beatri clutched the tuft from Tingo's tail against her heart with Angie's sacred bag of coins. As she hummed her eyes rolled back in her head.

"Tingo... ...come, donkey come...".

Though vulnerable to earthen interference in this state, Beatri remained consumed by the forces she summoned and connected to the cosmic currents she sought to steer. She maneuvered her spirit to form a deep bond with her friend Angorra's daughter Pearlie, till intertwined with the primal fibers of Pearlie's spirit force. She went back to the moment Pearlie's energy was first realized, to the very moment it began to exist inside her body's core.

Pearlie sensed Danny was primed for the spell. She originally planned to get him in the Champagne room and seal the spell by mixing their sweat or saliva but was guided instead by instinct and a newfound sisterly bond. She turned and swung out her hip, allowing Danny to slide his sticky bill under the G-string against her hip.

So, now the die was cast, though not as planned.

She remembered Angie's repeated warning from Beatri, "Spells cast work differently on all who receive."

Regardless of the uncertain consequences, she was determined to make this worth her time and effort. She already knew revenge wasn't easy, and was learning as she went it was messy, to boot.

With her confidence and rhythm in harmony, it was time to finish. The realization created momentum, and a tickle moved down her throat. She only had a minute left in her song. She looked around for Angie but didn't see her. Without stopping, she made a fist with her left hand against her chest, lowering her butt to the stage for balance. She lifted her right hand, folding her hands together, fingers extended. Her head lowered; she quickly whispered the invocation.

"Spirit to spirit, let the change begin...," intertwining her fingers in a beggar's prayer, she breathed deeply. Her chin touching her collar bone until the end, "...bring forth Tingalayo, release him from his suspended idle state."

As soon as she finished, her body was almost completely under the spell's control. She flattened her right hand under her balled-up fist, lifted her head, and spread her elbows and legs to complete her pose. She looked down, focused on her belly button, and aligned it between her breasts like a rifle sight, aiming it at Danny, only a few feet away. Her body was a weapon, cocked and ready to fire.

At first, just barely a notion, an unusual sensation fluttered in her gut, and she intuitively mused she might have gas. Still slightly self-aware she clenched her butt cheeks to stifle any urge to fart and dropped back into her inverted crawl position. She decided to go with her original plan, finish her dance and get Danny to the Champagne Room.

Whatever her self's intuition tried to do mattered not, as she fell deeper into the trance. A concentration of energy burst from the center of her brain circled her scalp, ears, and eyes, then ricocheted to the base of her skull. Still humming, it rapidly clicked down her spine joint by joint. The vibration also shot through her shoulders into her arms and raced through her hips down the inside of her legs, through her ankles, all the way to her toes.

With scintillating effect, the force came rushing back up her body, and the energy gathering density then plunging into the center of her abdomen as if swirling down a drain. As the sensations repeated, she was helpless to do anything but undulate, clench her teeth and cheeks, while feeling her heart race. For a fleeting instant she thought she was having a seizure.

Just as she feared the worst, there came a gentle lifting sensation, where her thoughts cleared, her mind's eye was freed, her consciousness light as a feather. She was present but not in control of her body. The swirls in her gut condensed, migrating through her core to her pelvis and buttocks.

Danny had been waving his arms as she undulated, trying to get the crowd into to it, wanting everyone to feel as good as she made him feel. He was enthralled, bent to her will.

She knew she no longer controlled her butt cheeks or anything else. She didn't know if she was about to piss herself, poot out her G-String, or have some type of orgasm...

...and she didn't care. It didn't matter. She was part of the spell like the tide is part of the ocean. She couldn't stop it, and calmly embraced her point of view in the eye in the storm.

Danny transfixed like a statue, was held in place by her gaze. As they stared into each other's eyes, she had no feelings, instead, she was simply breath and gaze. He looked at her body, and she reflexively showed him her Million-dollar smile, bringing the spell to its peak.

She pushed forward, her crotch arched high, aimed towards his face. Keeping his gaze, he hastily jabbed another bill into his mouth and leaned in. The sensation in her guts intensified to a small spot below her belly button, connecting to her sphincter.

In an instant the sensation swelled to bowling ball size, and she grimaced. Danny thought her expression was intense passion. The spell quickly shrank to pinball size, carrying its connective intensity to every nerve in her body.

With the bill dangling from his teeth, Danny reached for the knotted bow of the G-String on her hip. Once the bill was under her thong, the pinball stirred, and she began her final undulation. As he started to pull his head away, the spell escaped, racing through the final few inches within her.

She stopped, spasming briefly at the apex of her stomach roll, her thighs flexing. The energy release seemed beautiful, like a fluffy donut of sparks from the abyss having passed through her core.

Her self-presence slightly restored; a thought percolated up into her mind; the spell felt like a poofy fart. Nerve cells tingled from her sternum to her lips.

Her voice was faint.

"Ooohhh..., ...come, I bid you."

In his DJ booth, Baller was the only one who noticed Candy Cane's house lights blink ever so slightly, like a candle flame's flicker. At the same moment, he heard a miniscule skip in the song, so brief it challenged his ability to measure. But more importantly he felt something that made the hair on his arms stand up. It was an interruption of the vibe, of shift in energy in the room.

As for Danny, when he saw her body shudder, he paused expectantly, but didn't realize why, as the spell was invisible to him. After her faint exhalation though, he responded instantly, his eyes widening like he'd seen a ghost. The next instant his face melted as if inhaling a chloroform-soaked rag and he collapsed on the side of the stage. Fortunately, for him his head landed on his hands.

Pearlie spoke quietly, "Spirit, do my bidding. You are free."

Believing she might finally be released from the spell; she was exhilarated but aghast. Had Danny buckled under from the smell of her fart? When she sniffed, she smelled nothing other than the seedy essence of Candy Canes.

The spell's form was invisible and odorless to the crowd, but Pearlie could see....

...and she marveled at it; circular, revolving and rolling like a smoke ring, moving towards Danny, stopping and hovering above his head. He was not fully conscious, but his head lifted. Much like a spinning hollow disc, the other-worldly halo of the spell paused, expanded, and fell like a lasso around his neck.

Enraptured, she watched Danny tilt his head while his face became confused, the lasso morphing as if a gemstone ring of sparkles circling his neck.

She took note; no one else in the crowd had reacted to her body's phantom emission. The vaporous lasso turned dense, reminiscent of Wonder Woman's lariat. Then like an animated cartoon sequence, the glowing rope tightened, the loose end falling to the side. Just as quick, the entire manifestation dissolved into his body like a mirage fading into the desert. Afterward, the edges of Danny's form seemed to shimmer. Pearlie felt high as she observed his glow, and an incredible body rush ricochet from her core out to her pores.

Without effort, the muscles in her voice box moved, and she uttered the final proclamation.

"*Me Donkey hee, me donkey haw...*

...now let it be so."

Danny gave her a euphoric but stunned look, oblivious to the fact they were the only ones presently experiencing a supernatural event. From the moment she'd gasped, "Ohhh...

come I bid you," to what was now his zombie-like state, less than sixty seconds had passed.

The crowd screamed and cheered like always when the DJ called for their approval at the end of any Candy Cane dancer's routine.

Pearlie collapsed on the stage and the crowd called for more. Danny tumbled onto the carpeted floor by the stage, unnoticed by most of the crowd except for his brothers, who exchanged disappointed sideways glances before leaning over to stir him.

When Pearlie opened her eyes, she found herself laying facedown, cheek flat against the dance floor with drool dribbling from her mouth. She was in a stupor, and at first only able to stare blankly about. She didn't noticed the dime slip out of her mouth and roll directly towards Danny who'd disappeared below the edge of the stage. The tiny silver blip was lost among the many spots and sparkles in her field of vision. The dime however, hopped the edge of the stage, and landed squarely on Danny's forehead. His brothers lifted him by his armpits, and he smiled a goofy, love-struck grin while they tried to talk him into a stable stance to avoid a visit from the bouncers.

Pearlie watched, immobilized, but slowly gaining consciousness, and waited for body control to return. She observed with calm curiosity as a smaller version of the luminescence appeared around Danny once again. As if traced by a cartoonist, it came out of his skull through his ears as a new pair of large extended ears, while his brothers tried to keep him standing. The luminous ears continued growing upward till they resembled donkey ears. Then she noticed her dime on his forehead. Suddenly his lips curled back, and his nostrils began to expand and flare. His teeth grew long and bucked out from behind his lips.

He seemed to be rallying and leaned back his head and appeared to attempt to shout.

Instead, he bellowed a full-throated barnyard call.

"HEEEE-HAAAW!"

The dime fell, rolled down his elongated snout and ricocheted off Richard's ample belly. Richard slapped at the coin like a mosquito, trapping it against his stomach and immediately felt a strange burning sensation swirl on the spot beneath his shirt.

Danny, however, continued to bleat like a barnyard donkey wanting dinner, so Richard dismissed the sensation and instinctively slipped the dime in his pocket.

Pearlie slowly regained control of her body, shook her head, wiped her mouth, and propped herself up on an elbow. She looked around to see if anyone else might have seen or heard the same crazy visions but decided none had. Confused, as it seemed over, Pearlie looked at Danny who now seemed to appear normal. It was a brief normal though. He stiffened again and collapsed, faster than his brothers were able to catch him, and as they lurched at him, she saw bouncers headed their way.

Well, he must have heard his own braying!

Her self-consciousness kicked in, and it brought slight embarrassment. She realized when the spell was cast, she'd farted on the main stage. To be fair it wasn't a first for a dancer and to be fair it was a perfect bullseye on Danny.

She knew it was very different from the normal poot in passing. She'd never felt anything like it in her life. No plate of sausage and beans ever left her in such a state. This supernatural poot had ignited her whole body and lit her like electric current. Her body and soul, indeed her very existence, felt transformed. It was as if she'd molted away her past states of mind like an old skin.

Oh well, she couldn't waste any more time contemplating the cosmic ramifications of her preternatural poot. She flipped on her belly in time with the music. Baller the DJ had graciously put on a transition song to give her time to gather herself and her tips. Urgently aware of the bills scattered around the stage, she tried to rally, but her physical prowess was slow in returning to normal.

Haphazardly clutching at the wrinkled bills, a bolt of confidence embraced her heart, and though exhausted beyond any normal dance routine, she surprised herself with an affirmation.

"I did it!"

Pearlie's routine had entranced Baller the DJ as well. Combined with the odd blips he witnessed; it was unlike anything he had ever seen by any dancer before. Since it looked like she was getting it together, he shook his head and returned his attention to the dance line-up with his typical zeal.

"Let's hear it for Pearlie, folks! What a Pearl, what a lady. Come on y'all, show her some love…"

Y ou took a chance then,
    Danced your best dance there.
You made water run,
and rainbows in the sky.

Tonight, laying by the runway
Watching the planes fly by,
Now you know for certain
You were twice as high.

Holding hands with your Sunshine,
It's just a matter of time.
Reviving tales of yesteryears.
You never forget, you never mind,
It's just a matter of time.

I settled into a welcomed night of rest, grateful to Darla for rescuing me from self-induced psychic depths. Lying next to her comforted by her nurturing companionship and nothing more, more of the odd dreams narrated as if from another's soul took me to another unusual setting...

I was hidden, squatting snugly inside a small turret atop a stack of hollow wood cylinders. It was dark, and I was reaching for my wallet. Apparently I'd dropped it somewhere beneath my perch. Something else was amiss too, I smelled gunpowder and began to feel sharp pricks of heat nicking at the skin on my arm.

Was I in a fire?

Instead of getting an answer, there was a flash and deafening blast around me. In that millisecond I saw the interior of my hidey hole. There were old carpenters' marks, blobs of used gum, a Candy Canes' Gentlemen's Club sticker, and indecipherable graffiti. When the flash subsided, my eyes struggled to refocus.

My hearing was sucked out of my body by the blast and a dull hum stuffed in its place.

I started to choke on Sulphur fumes, and my eyes burned. I began to experience concussive hallucinations as tiny particles glimmered, growing into bright colored creatures moving in stilted patterns. Then as if in a flashback from crib stage infancy, my focus returned in time to see these creatures in story book animal shapes slowly rotating on a mobile.

A donkey pinata among them began to move. He danced, leading the animals in song, but the words didn't sound quite right, my hearing was damaged. I could only pick up muffled phrases, indistinct words like nursery school class voices reverberating down an old corridor...

"...inga-ayo, lil' one...ayo, lil one...

...on-ey wal..on-ey wal..."

...inga-ayo, lil' one...ayo, lil one..."

In my odd, childish state of wonder I instinctively reached at the slow orbiting objects and grabbed the donkey. As I tightened my grasp, it burst open, spraying forth bright lights that settled in a glimmering noose. While the noose floated to the center of the circle, the other animals merged into a large donkey-like centaur beneath the noose. The newly formed donkey's face appeared frozen in mid-laugh and as if on cue, the noose slipped snuggly over its head and around its neck. Once the noose tightened, the centaur came to life, its mouth opened wide, braying cartoonishly.

As dreams often due, everything changed suddenly and a translucent mist enveloped me accompanied by the sound of a percolating coffee pot. I realized I might be regaining consciousness, the bitter aroma of fresh coffee entering the surreal scene. My senses tingled, and I experienced a deja vu.

Had I arrived at Cindy Masters kitchen's back steps? My heart skipped a beat.

Wait! I was still in a dream!

I cowered as the centaur's mouth widened, creating a cavernous void, the darkness covering my field of vision. I pushed inside the beast's ever-expanding gullet, searching for Cindy's screen door.

I thought I saw the door handle but as I reached, it faded into the abyss. Determined, I leaned further forward, squinting to find the handle. When almost in my grasp, I lunged forward, but only fell.

But not very far.

Instantly, the nursery crib and centaur disappeared, as I hit what I thought was the interior wall of the wood cylinder hiding place. Was I back where the dream began?

I woke abruptly to find myself face down, buoyed only by my forearms on the hardwood floor at Olga and Darla's apartment. When I'd lunged, I'd done so off the bed, and though my legs were still on the mattress, my torso now hung over the side. I looked up to see Darla making coffee in the kitchen.

For some reason the first question that came to mind was why had Cindy Masters slipped into my consciousness during the dream? Was she checking on me to see who I was having coffee with?

Could she do that?

Did she care about me that way?

Did she have a donkey?

Darla, as always, was a truly comforting presence.

"What's the matter Max? You look like you've seen a ghost."

Of course, I didn't believe Cindy was a ghost, only a fantasy summoned by my dream. I didn't know what to say to Darla, but I certainly wasn't ready to pin a donkey tale on her. Maybe we could handle some small talk. I was grateful she sensed I was too confused to speak and kept her greeting going.

"There's a cup of Community to set you straight."

She nodded to the counter where she'd set a cup full of steaming black coffee.

"Do you need help getting up?"

She tilted her head and her good morning, welcoming smile was turning into a look of concern. Understandable, as I was in the middle of an awkward maneuver pushing myself ass up backwards onto the bed with weight on my forearms and hands. She moved slowly out of the kitchen towards me while sipping on her cup.

"No, I can manage, just shaking out the cobwebs, that's all. It wasn't a ghost, just an unusual dream. I'm sure glad you don't have a raised bed! That might have been really painful."

She was the perfect hostess. I was beginning to appreciate her more each time we interacted. Her kindness made me feel welcome after such a disturbing dream. I gathered myself and rose stiffly to my feet and examined my borrowed night clothes. Though determined to be a gentleman and proper guest, I was truly fuzzy on the previous night's pre-dream details. I hoped to get some clarity before we went our separate ways.

"Thanks for the coffee, it's great.

The Community coffee was already helping clear out my hangover.

She stopped and turned to face me.

"Well, I'm glad you like it, and you're okay. Look, I got to get ready to go, but maybe you can share your crazy dream with me sometime later. It looked like it was getting interesting."

"Yeah, okay, hey, we didn't, uh, I mean…"

"Max, don't worry, I was a perfect lady, and you were quite the blotto gentleman. So, nothing to worry about between us, if that's what you're wondering. Keep the outfit I gave you for now. Your work clothes are in the bag with your shoes by the door."

She pointed to a red bag with a Voodoo skull design. It read, 'Tater Red's Lucky Mojos' and sat neatly on top of my Vettes' Saddle Oxfords. She disappeared into her bedroom, and I sauntered around the kitchen. I poured another cup, adding a large dollop of cream and two spoons of sugar then slurped my coffee while looking out the window above the kitchen sink at an overcast sky. Birds and squirrels were busy doing their thing in the trees.

After several swigs I got antsy and realized I should leave. I walked over to the bedroom and leaned in to say goodbye while pushing open the door.

I unintentionally almost knocked her down. She was right behind the door, bent over while digging in her closet.

"Hey, careful Max!"

"Oh, shit, I'm sorry. I didn't mean to intrude, uh, just wanted to say goodbye, that's all."

"Well, I'm glad you hit my head with the door, if it'd been my keister I would have had to make you kiss it and make it better."

"What?! ...damnit Darla, you're pretty saucy after your morning coffee."

I must have been leering because she was immediately dismissive.

"Ok, *goodbye* Max! I got to get ready. I'm gonna miss you, too."

"OK, Darla, you don't have to tell me three times. So, thanks for being my rescue angel, you're the best."

I picked up my bag, keeping the shoes on top.

"I owe you one, Darla."

I knew I better leave before saying anything stupid.

"Oh, don't worry, I'll collect...and by the way you're right, I am the best!"

I heard lighthearted laughter, as I descended the stairs.

Once back at my place, I spent time collecting thoughts and jotted down a few notes for a meeting I hoped to have with Joey Spasula. I tried to call Eddie but got no answer.

I wasn't late getting to Vettes, but my shift started with a cold reception. When I opened the office door, Nash stood there staring at me, keys in hand, as if he'd been waiting. He gave me the proverbial evil eye and started in on me.

"Well, Max, I see your *keys* seem to be working just fine."

"Hey, Nash. No problem at all. Why, what's up?"

"Nothing, I hope. I'm just thinking you don't need any other keys... since yours work so well, and all."

"No, it's all good, man. These keys are working just fine." If he wanted me to take the bait, but it wasn't going to work.

"I hope so."

So, he left it at that, and I did my best not to show I was sweating the situation. I knew there was a good chance he found out I was snooping around, but felt it was best for me to play dumb. If he confronted me about the 'secret' room, I'd tell him it was insignificant, that I was just looking for some bar mix and I'd already forgotten about it. I certainly wasn't going to let on I suspected there was anything unusual in there.

Other than the stare down from Nash, it was an uneventful, low-key night and that was all right with me. It still included a typical night shift at the club happenings. Like when I looked for a cook who wasn't at his post and found him smoking hashish in the freezer. And then later found a server making out with a bouncer by the dumpster. Hey, 'Jamming like a Salmon' was an appropriate theme song for the Vettes crew.

The next two nights, things went smooth enough, though Nash kept his distance. He was short-spoken and continued to glare from afar. He must have found out I'd been in the secret room. The second night, there was a note from Olga and Darla on my screen door when I got home.

Max – We have to go back to Phoenix tonight. Sorry, couldn't say goodbye in person - no time. Please be careful! We won't be around to pull you out of a twister game OR the river, Ha, Ha!

There's a crazy old dude who may be able to help named Chipson Smith. We call him 'Doc Whazzit'. He hangs after-hours at Beale's Endless Tavern. Find him & tell him Darla & Bongos said to tell you the 'Password'. He might be a <u>FOUNTAIN</u> of info. Beware cuz he's a crazy drunk.

Please use Darla's pager # if you get stuck in a Memphis jam and need us.

P.S. You owe us a dance!

XOXOXO

Olga + Darla

I didn't feel up to hunting down this Doc Whazzit right then, so I drank a beer and headed upstairs to call it a night. I took off my Saddle Oxfords and khakis and threw my shirt on the chair with the tie loose but still knotted and in the collar in order to be ready for my next shift. I lay on my bed a moment to relax before I brushed my teeth and crawled in the sheets.

Before I could get to sleep, I heard the familiar honk of Lehigh's VW, then his rapid knocking on my screen door. I realized my night wasn't over, only the sleeping part. The search for Doc Whazzit might still be part of the night's activities.

Lehigh was full of questions...

"Did you hear anything at work?"

"About what?"

"You know, the heavies from Phoenix. I told you about them the other night."

"Oh, you mean when you emptied Vettes with your fake bomb threat. Those guys?"

"C'mon Max, what's wrong? I told you why I did it, listen, I'm just looking out for you, man. We're on the same team here."

"Okay, look, you wanna help me out, let's go to Beale's Endless Tavern. I'm looking for a guy."

"Are you serious? That's too deep a dive for even me to hang out. Who are you looking for?"

"You probably wouldn't know him, some guy called Doc Whazzit. Olga, I mean, Betty Bongos told me about him."

"Hmmm, Whazzit...never heard of him, but I know Beale's Endless shows the Playboy Channel, is this Doc some kinda perv?"

"I don't know, never heard of him before. Just lemme get some jeans on."

Pearlie didn't maintain her cool very long after her self-awareness returned. As she collected her money, it finally sunk in she'd cast the spell.

She began to lose it.

She was too exhausted, and her tears started. She was unable to collect herself or her money, much less savor the moment. Baller the DJ sensed he was witnessing another dancer's personal internal struggle playing out in front of the crowd, so he extended the transition song to give Pearlie extra time to wipe her tears and clear the stage.

Angie had arrived backstage near the end of Pearlie's performance and watched through the curtains. Once she saw

Pearlie sob, she broke house rules and ran onto the stage to help.

"Pearlie!"

Baller shook his head, turned off Pearlie's spotlight and started to mix in Josie's introductory song. Josie had been pre-occupied getting herself ready, so hadn't really noticed anything unusual about Pearlie's performance. But now under the spotlight cue she saw Pearlie was upset, behind schedule and how the stage was still a mess.

Josie was fired up to start and knew it was to Pearlie's advantage with their boss if there was little delay between acts. Since she wanted to help cover for her she darted out and motioned Baller for a new spotlight to take attention away from Pearlie's situation.

Josie decked out in blue jean cut offs, wore a Bud bikini top and 'Kiss My Bass' trucker hat, none of which stayed on long. She strutted away from her fellow dancer to the ringing chords of *Hold on Loosely* by .38 Special, dancing as far away as possible from Pearlie to give her more time to collect herself.

Pearlie's mind fluctuated in and out of the present, a first unaware she'd sat back down. Embarrassed, as she became aware about plopping on her ass instead of getting off the stage she welcomed Angie's presence. Normally she would have been pissed if anyone, even her sister came on the stage, but after the cosmic fart and everything else she really didn't care about protocol anymore.

Angie didn't see the spell through Pearlie's eyes and thought the opportunity to take Danny to the Champagne Room had slipped away. However, Pearlie did respond to Angie's voice. She grabbed her top and rustled what money she could, cradling it against her breasts. She was physically drained but felt a strange touch of euphoric afterglow.

Angie, meanwhile, was down on her knees grabbing the remaining bills. She was panicky, regretting the whole spell idea in the face of what she thought was an apparent failure. Had she pushed Pearlie into it too hard? She stood up and put her arm around Pearlie, and they shuffled backstage avoiding Josie's stride. Fully wired in her routine, Josie just winked at the two of them from her patented one-handed grip pole rotation.

Angie and Pearlie ducked into the dressing room. Pearlie sat in a make-up chair, while Angie wrapped her in a robe, handing her a bottle of water.

"I'm sorry, baby what happened? Whaddya need?"

"I need Tequila, Angie. Can you get some?"

Flabbergasted, Angie had to ask,

"What about the Champagne Room, aren't you gonna meet Danny there?"

"Tequila, Angie! Tequila! Get me Tequila!"

Angie sensed a powerful confidence in Pearlie and rushed to the bar for the shots. Pearlie lay her head back and reminisced about when she was a youthful teenager and Angie worked in a brothel in Southaven, Mississippi. She smiled, recalling how she once dropped by on her way to school and the ladies shared funny farts at the breakfast table eating eggs, grits and sausage. They had so much fun being gross yet were gorgeous, and always treated Pearlie with respect. They let her hang out, though only briefly, like she was an adult, too. When at their house, she felt more special than in any club at school.

She returned her gaze to the mirror and saw the slightest smile trying to break through her beleaguered face. She looked up as Angie returned.

"Here you go baby, Gold Tequila in a snifter just like you always liked."

Though she'd pretty much given drinking up, she was disoriented and allowed herself some liquor satisfaction.

She didn't really understand how the spell came out and got in Danny. She reckoned she was like the girl who split the seat of her pants in front of the entire class. It might have been embarrassing, yet she somehow got the attention of the boy she wanted to notice.

She lowered her head and looked in her snifter, resigned to fact some things never made sense. She snuck a look at the mirror and saw Angie fidgeting around behind her like she didn't know what to do next. She probably didn't know the spell was cast. Pearlie allowed a big smile to break through and enjoyed a loving look at her sister for the first time in months. Angie took a hesitant sip from her snifter surprised to see Pearlie's big smile.

"You must be feeling better."

Angie handed Pearlie an open water bottle water to wash down her shot. Pearlie accepted it and drank without a word, but Angie pressed on.

"I thought you were gonna take him to the Champagne room," she whispered.

"Just a minute, Angie. Lemme finish my drink."

The water followed the tequila's path like a sunset streaking across the river. Once quenched, she reached her snifter towards Angie.

"Let's toast!"

"Okay, but we aren't finished yet, are we?"

"Oh, I think so, at least for now, I done put a bullseye on that Danny!"

They downed what remained of their Tequilas, while Pearlie told her what happened. She described how the spell felt like a power dryer at the car wash going through her body. She laughed as she described how she clenched her butt cheeks as hard as she could while she danced out her moves. She said she'd been afraid she was about to let loose the biggest fart of all time, but at the critical moment, it was a dainty little poof.

Angorra's face changed from worried concern to one of a proud mother who understood her beloved daughter did exactly what she needed to.

She finally got it. Pearlie didn't need to go in the Champagne room or risk being alone with that man. Pearlie used her cute little ass to cast the spell and it turned Danny into a Jackass.

"I love you, baby sister! I love you, Pearlie girl."

To Pearlie it felt like her older sister was finally and truly proud of her. Angie hugged her hard, turning her side to side until Pearlie had enough.

"Okay, dammit, Angie, you're gonna suffocate me!"

"I'm just so proud of you, Pearlie!"

Pearlie held out her snifter and cocked her head at Angie to indicate she wanted another shot of Tequila.

"Angie, what was in that potion anyhow? Y'all didn't put no donkey puck in it, did you? *Please* tell me y'all didn't!"

Veda woke to the desert sky in the moon shadows of ancient Joshua trees. Looking up she saw an abundance of stars, brilliant like backlit diamonds. She'd fallen asleep outside her tent, head comforted only by her sleeping roll against a boulder. A half smoked joint lay cold in the dust by her side.

She felt a sudden rush of energy course through her body. She pushed against the boulder to stand and survey the area, for signs intruders, human or otherwise.

She sensed a presence.

Unable to remain in one spot she began to pace in a circle around her site. The energy burst she'd felt was so strong, it was like she had huffed a spoon of meth. It wasn't necessarily pleasurable, more like a slap before a challenge to a fight. Instinctively a challenge she welcomed and foe she immediately sensed as a rival.

Something was different about this energy force, it spoke through the elements. First, she saw the twinkle of the stars flash. Then something else caught her ear. It was direct as if meant only for her. There, mixed in among the coyote howls echoing across the canyon, she heard a donkey's bray, like a bugle call to battle.

She knew at once this was from forces she held in awe. Rare to her, the feeling included a healthy dose of fear. She had only ever felt this way before in her darkest, most forbidden dreams.

Beale's Endless & Doc Whazzit

Lehigh and I arrived at Beale's Endless, and descended the short set of leaf covered steps, topped with crushed beer cans and cigarette butts. It took a minute for our eyes to adjust to the seedy den. Lit by a small TV, and a dimming Malboro Clock now permanently at three, the bar centerpiece was a tree trunk with a half-lit string of multi-colored lights wrapped around and protruding from the wall at one corner. The trunk disappeared into the ceiling while two limbs hovered over the bar stools. Odd knick-knacks and photographs were haphazardly strewn among the smallest branches, some tacked, others stabbed onto twigs.

A man with graying red stringy hair in a dingy dayglo orange stocking cap, sat on a beer cooler behind the bar and faced the barstools. His similarly streaked beard covered the top half of his red flannel shirt. He had a PBR tall boy between his legs and grinned at us in an unsettling manner as we looked around.

"Ya' know y'all should'a brought a camera, a picture lasts longer... Of course, my ugly mug probably would'a cracked your lens if you had."

He arched his eyebrows and squinted, pushing his round wire rimmed lenses up his nose as he had a good laugh while we stood speechless. Our numbed silence prompted him to continue.

"Well, if I don't break the lens, 'Lil Billy' could do it just fine."

He reached under one leg and pulled out a Billy Club wrapped with bright orange tape like a barbershop pole. He thought his joke about the peacekeeper was hilarious and slapped Billy in his other hand and laughed some more. We looked at each and wondered if visiting Beale's Endless was such a good idea.

"Is it too late to get a beer?"

That was the best I could come up with to break the weirdness. I didn't want to encourage show and tell with 'Lil Billy,' and Lehigh hadn't joined in yet. In fact, Lehigh needed motivation, so I nudged him with my elbow.

"Uh, yeah, we ain't carrying no camera here, we just want a cold one."

Snappy patter from Lehigh.

"Well, lemme see."

'Red' reached down between his legs, slid the cooler lid open, and leaned over to check his stock. His quick movements caused the pom-pom on his stocking cap to toss forward, landing below his chin atop his impressive beard.

"Whaddya know, looks like we have some beer in here. What'll it be?"

He lifted his head quickly, sending the fuzzball in the air back over his head. He pushed his wire rims back up his nose and resumed his routine of his sinister laugh and psychotic grin.

"The house favorite is good with me."

Lehigh and I nodded in agreement. Surprising us both, Red leapt down from his perch and pivoted towards the tree trunk with 'Lil Billy' extended, and we backed up anticipating the worst. Luckily there was no need, he was just moving to another cooler.

He reached down, pulled out two longnecks, popped the caps on the side of the cooler, then set them on the bar in one continuous motion. The beers foamed over but were very cold. In fact, there was ice on the bottles. They weren't PBRs, their white and gold label spelled 'Stag' in red letters.

I couldn't remember the last time I'd had a Stag beer. I didn't even know it was still being brewed or could still be legally purchased. To be honest, I wasn't looking for it either, but 'being in Rome,' I smiled and as if on cue, Lehigh and I simultaneously saluted the beverage situation.

"To Stag!"

The bartender didn't join our party, instead he countered with an announcement.

"Cash only, unless you wanna wash dishes.... Oh wait, we ain't got none! ...Hah, hah, hah! I guess you'll have to scrub the john if you ain't got cash... Haw, haw, hee, hee..."

He was cracking himself up.

Lehigh started digging for cash and I looked around the joint to see if I could find Doc Whazzit. It didn't take long to scope out the crowd, there were only two other people in the main bar that I could see from where we stood. There was also a dark hallway at the other end of the room which looked like where the bathrooms probably were.

The couple canoodling below the tree trunk occasionally glanced through the tree trimmings at the small TV. Indeed, it was showing The Playboy Channel or something similar and they alternated taking turns kissing and fondling while they watched the same happening on the screen.

No Doc there.

I nudged Lehigh again.

"I'll be right back, keep Ole Red busy, I'm gonna see who else is in here. Don't go anywhere without me."

I took a swig of my ice-cold beer and moseyed down the hallway. There was a door with 'Lad_e_' on my right, but nothing for the Gentlemen. I continued on until I noticed a small room with stacks of old, waxed cardboard beer cases filled with empty returnable bottles on my right.

That's where the hallway ended, and I stood in front of a noisy walk-in cooler. Due to my history with walk-ins, I wasn't about to look inside. I turned to go back and rejoin our unusual host, when the cooler's compressor cycled halted. Without its rattle filling the hallway I distinctly heard the sound of snoring suddenly stop, then a split second later heard the snorer gasp for air. Whoever it was cleared their throat and went silent. I waited a few seconds, and just as I started toward the sound, the snoring started again. It sounded like a man, though you can never be sure. I was determined to find out.

I heard our bartender call.

"Hey buddy, can I help you with something? Are you looking for the john?"

"No, I'm just stretching my legs."

I needed time to figure out who was snoring, but Ol' Red hollered back with another knee slapper.

"Well, your buddy here paid up so you ain't gotta clean nothing...hah, hah, hah."

I hesitated, stepped across the hall and poked my head into the small room behind the stack of beer cases.

"You got quite a collection of beer bottles here...".

I wanted a more time to explore.

I spotted a pair of dirty tennis shoes propped up on a sink table. The rest of the wearer was in the sink, except for their head, which lay on the sink table on the other side, face covered by an old bar rag. Stringy wisps of the rag fluttered each time they exhaled. Somebody had taken up room and board in the sink at Beale's Endless.

Well, why not? As Ol' Red pointed out, the sink was no longer needed for dishwashing. I decided to get back to the bar and check in with Lehigh and decide what to do next. I didn't want to get on the wrong side of Ol' Red's 'Lil Billy.'

When I got back to Lehigh, I whispered in his ear about the man asleep in the back. I asked if he could distract the bartender until I found out who they were. Lehigh had a plan. In fact, he'd already learned our bartender's name, Rusty.

Of course, it was.

"So, we'll take another round, and if you don't mind, I do gotta piss. Where's that men's room?"

"Well, you're welcome to go outside by the dumpster, but if not, I don't imagine anyone's in the Ladies either. If you're sure you can shoot straight, you can go in there."

Lehigh got another round and quickly engaged Rusty in a game of quarters. He moved over to block as much of the view of the hallway as possible, then flipped and slapped his first quarter on the bar.

"Gotcha!"

"You little weasel, I got a whole bag'a quarters, I hope *you* got plenty'a dough. I don't lose no flippin' flippin' game to no stranger. Not tonight... and not any night."

"Well, better rub it for luck cuz I feel like I might be red hot!"

Lehigh had Rusty pegged, so I probably had at least fifteen minutes. I took my fresh beer and the rest of my old one and slowly faded into the hallway. I opened and shut the 'Lad_e_' door, without entering, then backed into the little room full of boxes and the slumbering boarder.

I reached down and slowly lifted the rag off the face. I discovered a surprisingly baby-faced fellow, his haphazardly shaved face flushed, and his nose an extraordinary garden of gin blossoms. Drool ran down one side of his chin and sunburn lines went back from the corners of his eyes like racing stripes. He must've worn glasses, so I looked around for a pair, but didn't see any, too dark. One of his hands was in the bottom of the sink, so I reached for the hand resting on his chest in case he tried to strike and leaned in by his ear.

"Ready for another round, Doc?"

I pressed my cold Stag against his open palm.

He sniffed and snuffled but then settled back to rest. I could smell old beer and menthol cigarettes, enhanced by the room's cases of old empties and concrete floor, which was probably never mopped except with spilled beer.

"Doc... Doc! Here you go, let's drink another round."

His other hand came up holding a pair of glasses missing one temple. He rubbed his nose with them in tow. With his other hand he grabbed my beer like a life preserver, but never opened his eyes.

"Ummm, harrumm, yup. Un huh, yup."

He wiggled a little but was hopelessly stuck in the sink unable to extract himself. Only his arms and lower legs could move freely. He opened his eyes, squinted at me, then shut them again quickly. Suddenly the nearest eyeball opened and gave me a big once over while I straightened up.

"Hey Doc, Betty Bongos and Darla sent me. How ya doing?"

"Yup, ur, umm..."

He lifted the fresh beer to his lips, turned it upright, and guzzled down several gulps before he returned it to his lap. He mindlessly did this at just the right angle so even though the beer overflowed, the foam fell between his legs. Miraculously it only grazed the crotch of his pants, before flowing into the drain.

"Where's she at?"

He was beginning to regain his faculties.

"She had to go back to Phoenix, but she told me you were an 'Okay Guy.' She said you'd show me the secret handshake."

"Oh, ummm, the handshake, uh huh, hmmm..."

He repeated his beer guzzling trick and expertly wiped his chin with the hand holding his glasses. The glasses looked worn out. He lost his hold on them when he let his arm fall against the side of the sink and they clattered on the floor and skittered over to the wall.

"Naw, shit, they're no good, nope, unh-unh."

He shook his head.

"No really, Doc. They said it was 'Okay.' Betty Bongos and Darla, they sent me. Understand?"

"Nope, they're no good, nope. Gotta get some specs, yup."

I got it then; he wasn't talking about the girls. That was a relief.

"Yeah, we'll get you some more glasses, so what else you need?"

"Password!"

"Yeah, well you're supposed to tell me the password."

I was beginning to think I wasn't gonna get anything useful from this character.

"Password!"

This time he was adamant, shaking his bottle at me.

"Password!"

"Oh, I get it, some Bettie Bongo humor, huh?"

Sometimes I'm kinda slow, but it finally dawned on me Darla and Olga must'a had a drunken word play game with Doc, and as long as I provided him with a beer, he would engage me.

I clinked bottles with him.

"One password coming up!"

I headed back to the bar.

Lehigh and Rusty were engaged in high stakes quarters' warfare prompting Rusty to light a joint and dump a bank bags' worth of quarters on top of the bar. As I approached, I witnessed Rusty lower his open hand, quarter cupped in the middle of his palm, and from below his waist, he swooped his hand over his head and smacked it onto the bar with a splat and a click. He squinted menacingly at Lehigh who simply flopped his hand over from a couple inches above the bar to challenge.

"Even."

They held each other's gaze, then slowly lifted their hands to see the result.

"Damn it to hell. Lemme see that quarter!"

"Just like last time, Rusty? OK, here you go. See, it's good."

With his other hand flat on the bar, Lehigh maneuvered the winning quarter over his open fingers from one end of his hand to the other, the quarter smoothly turning over several times. Lehigh smiled, and stared at Rusty while performing the trick. Rusty snorted derisively and pounded the bar, shoving a palm full of quarters across to Lehigh.

"Your luck won't last, you little varmint!"

I felt time was slipping away with Doc, so I spoke up before their next round.

"Hey, hate to interrupt, but I ran into an old friend and need to get a couple more rounds."

"Yeah, yeah, get'em yourself. Can't you see I'm busy here?"

Rusty was pretty distracted alright. When I looked up after reaching into the cooler to fetch another double-fisted, double-handful of Stags, I couldn't help but wonder if Lehigh had Huggy'd old Rusty. Especially when I noticed the grifter's leer on Lehigh when he winked. As Lehigh's gaze returned to Rusty, he began nodding like he had it all under control. He was obviously more than comfortable with the way things were playing out. I was sure he had some kind of edge in play.

Doc had an amazing capacity for beer, considering he'd been roused from a dead sleep. Sunk into the sink, he guzzled his beer, then lay his head back so far on top of the metal sink table, where his speech became an unintelligible gurgle. So, first thing I did was convince him to let me help him out of the sink and onto a hastily made throne of beer cases against the wall, while I plied him with several rounds. Using my keenest drunk-deciphering skills, I was able to gleam a couple of loose facts.

'Huggy' was a vague term, as there were already several street names of similarly misunderstood substances around like Stardust and Sprinkle though later it became more commonly referred to as 'Molly' or 'Ecstasy.' In college, Doc and his pals acquired rare documents detailing the research of psychedelic drug makers Owsley, Stanley, Cargill, and Scully, and subsequently conducted their own separate research.

The papers they obtained were the two-year endeavor of an underground reporter known as Alius Berthouse from the River City Review, a free press publication in Memphis. Alius was a close personal friend of Doc's who went to Berkeley and relentlessly stalked, cajoled, and pumped the four infamous psychedelic makers for their story. According to Doc, Alius' self-indulgence of their home-made goods altered his course so much, he ended up cooking on king crab boats off the Alaska coast for years. Doc and the other friends never quite duplicated those recipes on their own after he left.

However, before his personal career compass went haywire, sending him sailing on his Alaska voyage of self-discovery, he mailed his treasure trove of investigative paperwork to his parents, telling them they were research for a term paper and to store them for his return. They dutifully squirreled them away in their attic for safekeeping.

They were forgotten by almost everyone, but not Alius. During his parents' estate sale a few years later, destiny's random wheel of fortune saw to it that Alius received an advance notification. Still in sporadic correspondence with Doc, Alius telegraphed money and at Alius' behest, Doc purchased every document of value to their mutual psychedelic endeavors.

Alius returned once Doc confirmed he had procured the Berkeley papers. Once back together, they teamed with a woman Doc simply referred to as Sunshine and threw themselves into their own chemical research and development. After all, Doc was a chemistry major drop-out himself.

The three delved deep into creating new Mescaline-like drugs, some of which hadn't even been identified as illegal perhaps to this day and definitely at the time. Most of these compounds had simply not been recorded by anyone previously doing this type of research. It should be mentioned, psychedelic research is notoriously full of gray area, probably because of the effects on those sampling their work. They finally settled on a tasty derivative with a bromide ring that could be enhanced with a little ketamine or caffeine for mainstream consumption.

The three became quite close, living out their own mini-Acid Kool Aid Test with Huggy traveling the train from Chicago to Memphis to New Orleans. With Alius' connections to seafaring culinary talent and diligent networking with passengers on the The City of New Orleans train route, they established connections to crews on the Gulf oil rigs. This was particularly fertile ground, loaded with clients hungry for their renderings. Most notable were the personal chefs of big rig bosses from the oil companies. These kitchen wizards were constantly flown around the world to temporary digs where oceans give temporary home to a bigshot's oil rig and his dinner table in need of haute cuisine.

Sunshine's organizational skills and charm helped them set up their network of clients around the world. They were able to find enough sufficiently charmed vagabond chefs to get the 'Huggy' to their desired destinations.

They didn't really have to sell it on the street, but they did, and when they did they called it 'Broccoli.' Broccoli became an easy term to work with. Chefs could simply add it to their shopping lists as they would say, "None of the bosses really eat much Broccoli but it looks quite natural on a grocery lists and manifest."

They were able to make their product potent. A portion the size a small pack of Juicy Fruit gum was enough for two thousand doses and easily waterproofed and hidden in the middle of a case of produce, perhaps even real Broccoli.

Doc worked on a portion control delivery system that suspended the drug in liquid. Glycerin-wrapped strands of the substance could be immersed for several minutes at a time without dissolving. This allowed him to create a device which calibrated and dispensed the Huggy in approximated doses. They planned to create a substance that would allow even longer suspension for bulk distribution. Then they could package it in gallon-size containers. Doc called this a pass around pump full of Rainbow Beads.

As the beers added up he blurted out phrases I couldn't make sense of.

"I spilled a batch of the 'Beauty Beads,' hee-hee."

He began laughing hysterically.

"They looked like a springtime pond full of Toad strands, ha-haw!"

As we drank, Doc's tale got sketchier, and he became less coherent. Then suddenly he became angry. Angry, because it turned out he and Alius both fell in love with Sunshine. She, however, refused to choose between the two, and remained content to ride the waves of their three-way courtship, enjoying the men's ever-expanding and increasingly expensive overtures.

Neither man could get her to agree to marriage, and in time the initially free love, good-natured aspects of their arrangement deteriorated. Once the fun-loving triad became contentious, Sunshine left, taking her structured organized chart of connections with her.

However, in a unpredictable move that increased the pain of the break-up, she didn't restart the old business model, instead she took up with a hot shot guitarist, or maybe it was a drummer. Doc's tale was murky. Anyhow she went on tour like some extraordinary groupie, with lots of mind-blowing candy.

I could tell from that part of his story Doc had no patience for anyone with music making inclinations. So, even though it was my go-to line of bullshit, I did not tell him of my musical journeys, and instead kept the focus on him.

Without Sunshine, the other two ended up in bad company and their project quickly taken over by a club-owning family of pizza makers.

The Etruscos.

I was getting used to hearing the name.

According to Doc, as soon as the Etrusco's learned the Huggy trade, they kicked Doc and Alius to the curb.

Ever since the two street-candy chemists kept a low profile in the illegal drug trade, though I deduced it was due more to their self-destructive lifestyle than any mindful intent. Doc said they eventually went their separate ways, rightfully sensing the forever danger the Etrusco brothers posed. Also I believe it was inevitable two hearts broken by the same woman must have led to unavoidable friction.

As for being a drunkard, Doc was all that, but I didn't judge him otherwise. If his story was true it'd been one hell of a ride with Sunshine and Alius. I wondered what other demons might haunt him. I mean, how could anyone comfortably settle in every night folded in half in an old dishwashing sink?

When Lehigh and I finally left, we headed to the Mississippi River by Tom Lee Park and parked with our beers. Lehigh wisely allowed Rusty to win back enough of his quarters to make him think he'd won, then he sold us six more Stags for the road.

We climbed up the levy to a spot under some trees with a clear view of both bridges. Once seated, Lehigh promptly surprised me with a joint. After we shared a couple hits, he handed me a small gum wrapper sized baggie of white powder.

"You might wanna little Huggy after all that beer. It'll help you enjoy the river's song…"

"Thanks, Lehigh."

I played with it but never put any in my mouth, instead I made a show of licking my fingers and slipped it into my pocket. I was determined to have it tested somewhere and somehow find out what the hell it was. After we finished the joint, Lehigh began to wax philosophical.

"On every corner in Memphis, in any available plot of shade, there's a guitar and a voice connected to a soul that's got the blues."

He inspired me and I joined in.

"And they're ready to sing them for you. Doesn't matter if you've heard them before…"

"It's like a fire glowing… a river flowing… It's a contagious sensation you just gotta move with… and move to…"

I'm sure he was pretty high, but I couldn't help but top the line.

"And just let it take your heart away…"

The next morning, hard pressed to sleep off that endless supply of Stag, I struggled to wake up. Meanwhile, at Vettes, Nash was in the office early on a long-distance call with Dean.

"What the fuck was Max doing in there is what I wanna know."

"Heh, heh, yep, looks like we got ourselves a naughty boy, ole Maxey is snooping around."

Dean had finally watched the footage of my visit into the off-limits storage room, printed a still shot and faxed it to Nash.

"You want me to fire him when he comes in tonight?"

"Hold your horses, Nash, it could have been an honest error, plus we don't hire choir boys, in case you hadn't noticed. He probably got tired of seeing it was off limits and wanted to check it out. You know how it is."

Nash was fit to be tied Dean wouldn't let him take any action.

"Yeah, maybe, but I specifically told him not to go in there. I told him I'd personally show him how to deal with stuff in there if it ever came up... He disobeyed a direct order!"

"Ok, Nash, I got it. You got your panties in a wad, but listen to me, you ain't firing him tonight. I think I'll just bring him back to Phoenix where we can keep a closer eye on him."

"Well, you're the boss, but I think it's bullshit!"

"Look, I know how you feel but I gotta balance these gorillas who own the joints, with their partners, and keep all you GM's out there happy, too. You understand we're all trying to make us some money. Heh-heh, you know I'm juggling chainsaws here every fucking day."

"Okay, whatever Dean, I'm pissed, that's all."

"So, I can get someone to Memphis to replace him in two days. How long can you go without him?"

"Send over his travel plan and I'll tell him he leaves tomorrow."

"Okay, let me get right on it. I appreciate you Nash, I really do. Now don't let on you know he went in there. Don't forget, you're the only one there who knows about the cameras."

"You got it, boss, I won't."

"Cool! All right, 'Jamming like salmon,' my man!"

"Life is but a dream!"

He tried to sound enthusiastic, but Dean knew Nash was still hot.

I got the cold shoulder from Nash until my Memphis Vettes' tenure came to a close.

It was less than a week after sneaking into the secret room when Nash handed me my transfer paperwork. I had to be on a plane back to Phoenix in twenty-four hours and go back to work with Dean. Nash wished me luck with attitude. I knew he didn't mean it. He wasn't sorry to see me go.

Regardless, I really enjoyed my time in Memphis and wasn't ready to leave, but at least I still had a job. I'd committed to Joey that I'd report to him whatever I thought was going on with his Vettes investment and it would be safer and easier to do so in Phoenix. So though disappointed to leave Memphis, at least I was going to back to familiar territory.

Once I got back, I could get caught up with Eddie, Cindy Masters and other old friends. I kept the 'Huggy' I'd gotten from Lehigh to get it tested there. After I got the results, I'd try to find out what Sarge knew, and decide what was safe to tell him in return. I could meet with Joey in person and report what I felt appropriate. Plus, I felt I needed to connect with

Darla and Olga who it now seemed might be in more danger than even they thought.

I was learning how complicated things got when you were swimming upstream.

This matter of penance,
    throwing dollars for laughs,
It's fogging my window,
Now I'm feeling a draft.

I'm getting slapped unhappy!
It's not a good dream.
I'm fighting in paradise
You know what I mean?

My return to Phoenix wasn't the celebrity's welcome I received in Memphis. At Phoenix Sky Harbor, I was just another guy with travel bags and a story to tell. My welcoming committee was my friend Eddie in his patched together Chevy Blazer, its unattached back seat and couch sliding around at every turn.

It had been a while since we'd met face to face, so we took the opportunity to catch up on things. He drove into Tempe on the back streets, and while he talked, I listened. He confirmed local authorities were looking for anyone involved with Carter Benson's final weeks. Carter's unusual demise was listed as a possible homicide, determining his messy, suicidal jump off an interstate overpass was staged. As far as Eddie was concerned, the Las Vegas Police knew more than they were saying, at least more than he'd dug up so far. Eddie found no mention of Carter having ties to companies like Vettes or any of the partners at CB Products.

However, in a drug task force memorandum concerning synthetic hallucinogenic drugs on the streets by the DEA, Carter was listed as a possible person of interest. His disappearance was noted before his body was found. Eddie emphasized things were pretty serious, and he felt I should stay vigilant at all times, perhaps consider getting myself a gun or a lawyer or both.

"Are you kidding me? Vettes is just a dog and pony show. Don't you think you're getting a little carried away about this?"

"Max, the DEA is not a dog and pony show! You need to take this seriously. Look, I'll get you more info and you best take heed. Right now, we got to meet someone."

We pulled into Tempe's 602 Lounge lot.

"They're very anxious to see you. I promised to bring you straight off the plane."

"Well, I appreciate you picking me up man, but it would'a been nice to get back to my place first... Hey, wait, is it Cindy? I wouldn't think she'd wanna meet here."

"Max, you gotta quit thinking with your little head. Have you forgotten who helped you get the Vettes gig?"

"What, you got Joey here?"

"No man, *Jonesy*'s here. Come on!"

He jumped out, then fastened the bungee cord to the driver side door. I followed him in after securing my door the same way, now a little on edge about all the uncertainty ahead.

"Bruuuthuurrr!"

Jonesy's bear hug greeting was a welcome back that put me at ease.

"Awww Max, my bruuthuuurrrr, you never were nothing but a hound dog! Ha haaa!"

"Jonesy my man, good to see you!"

He doubled up on the bear hug. Since I felt like I'd failed a career test with my Memphis Vettes' ejection, the love of an old friend who accepted me regardless of my title, success, or lack thereof, brought welcome relief.

I looked over his shoulder and spotted Sand the bartender, her well-worn PDR in hand. Leaning back, she watched with interest over her cheaters, while almost laying on her register, a leg propped up on a bar stool she'd drug behind the bar. I gave her a big wink and smile in mid hug just to get one of her patented eye rolls. It worked, and after Jonesy and I finished our greeting, I got reacquainted with her.

"Good afternoon, Sand, can I get a round of cold ones over here?"

I reached into my pocket knowing she'd get a kick out me sporting legitimate US currency.

"No, not gonna happen, your money's no good here. At least not yet. Sand, put those on my tab, and why don't you get one for yourself."

Jonesy had easily trumped my attempt to pay.

"Better luck next time, Max," Sand took off her glasses and smiled, tipping her chin to let me know how it was gonna go. Her expression emphasized how she wasn't surprised I wasn't paying. Then she turned her attention to who was.

"You got it. My pleasure, Jonesy."

She set the Dos XX's down on the bar with questions.

"What are we celebrating today boys, someone get outta jail or did one of you finally get laid?"

Without waiting for an answer, she stuck a knife blade tip-first in the cutting board and slammed the blade down loudly on a lime, chopping it in half. Then she flipped a half in the air, caught it on the blade, and sliced it on the board, splitting the lime again. She wacked the blade a couple more times, then reached down and produced three perfect lime slices between her fingers. Waving her hand ceremoniously over the bottles she inserted a wedge in each beer with a properly ordained bartender's silent blessing.

Jonesy, impressed by the show, whistled and pushed his hat back.

"Ooooweee, so precise, she's a wildcat!"

She looked me directly in the eyes and leaned forward on the bar in front of us, bending over just far enough to peak in her halter top, and pushed the beers toward us with a magician's assistant smile. Still the professional troublemaker I remembered, she was equal parts sass and sex appeal. It's kinda funny, even though she was the only woman in the joint, she was nevertheless compelled to show her dominance. Only fair to bask, I guess. After all, she was the reigning Queen of the 602 Bar.

"Thank you, Sand, you're as impressive as ever."

I reached for my beer.

"Sand," Eddie nodded with respect, grabbed his beer and stepped back.

"Smoooothhh, baby, smooth, Sand you're the best!"

Jonesy was impressed, his eyebrows high on his forehead. He grabbed his beer and raised it in a toast.

"To Sand!"

We clinked, saluting in unison.

"My, my, you boys gonna make me blush."

She fanned herself to show she deserved the attention, but her eyes showed she would also soon be bored by our best efforts.

"I best get back to my reading so y'all don't make me forget myself."

She batted her eyes, turned, and slid back into position like a cat in its den. She grabbed her cheaters then the PDR, opened it and let us know she was still in charge.

"Y'all just holler if you need anything."

Jonesy took over our group.

"Yes, ma'am. We're gonna sit over there at a table, not because we don't like your company, we just got business to discuss."

We meandered over by the jukebox and Jonesy held up a fiver.

"If you don't mind, why doncha play DJ, Eddie. You know all that hugga-bugga stuff better than me."

"Don't mind if I do, Jonesy, not at all. In fact, I prefer it that way."

Eddie grabbed the money and leaned on the jukebox as he slid the bill in the slot. He started punching in numbers he had memorized, and I got started on a report of sorts.

"Look, Jonesy, I don't really know all that much yet. I mean, I've been at Vettes less than two months, really just learning the basics. They got a great record collection, high energy staff, and a great formula for getting the party going and drinks flowing."

"Paaartyyy, they sure do that my brother."

"I mean as far as I can tell, Joe made a good investment with Vettes. I don't know enough yet to understand how all the money's being handled, but he should be making his investment back. At least from what I saw. There's only one thing…"

"What? Something's wrong? They got something going on under the table or underage girls drinking in there. I mean, here in Tempe that's normal…"

"No, that's not it. I'm not a hundred percent sure I know what it is, but I think some people are involved in dealing street drugs…"

I let it hang in the air for a moment. Before Jonesy could respond, Eddie came back over and scooted in next to me.

"Hey, y'all got awful quiet, am I interrupting?"

Eddie looked from Jonesy to me.

"I was just telling Jonesy there may be somebody affiliated with Vettes involved with some street drugs."

"Bruuuuthuurrrr, that's no bueno."

Jonesy continued speaking but lowered his voice to just above the level of a whisper.

"Joey's not like that, man. He gambles a little and got money in strip bars, but not drugs, not Joey…"

His head dropped and he groaned quietly to himself.

"Well look, I didn't say he was involved with the dope, in fact, I don't know for a sure how it's happening but something's going on." I looked around for emphasis, "…something's not right and I think somebody who's involved with Vettes is part of it."

I looked over at Eddie and wrinkled my brow to let him know I needed support.

"He's right, Jonesy, something going on, but it may be the partners who are in another businesses besides Vettes. They may have already been part of the Vettes organization before he got involved. It may have nothing to do with Joey. From what I can tell, he isn't one of the main players. He hasn't got any other business ties on paper with these other guys. Of course, I haven't been able to check on all the officers of the other businesses..."

"Yeah, Vettes is doing a lot of cash business. It would be easy for someone to launder their dope money in the day-to-day operations."

I couldn't let Jonesy know all I knew and was searching for what to say when Eddie chimed in again.

"Remember they have five Vettes' locations, too, and he's only involved in Phoenix."

"So, what are you saying?"

Jonesy wasn't sure of his point. Eddie continued while looking directly at me while he doubled down.

"You told us Joey's only investment is in Phoenix, and that checks out. If someone is using Vettes as a cover in some way, they got five operations to work with. So, it could be someone who's part of a single unit's investment group, or a sub-contractor or fake investment group who's involved in all five."

"Yeah, it might be tricky to figure out how they are connected. Something could be going on and Joey wouldn't know anything about it. After being on the inside, I can tell you that's a fact."

I gave Jonesy a calming look. The last thing we wanted was for him to do anything rash and of course we still wanted to talk to Joey in person.

"Well, let's go see Uncle Joey, you said you wanted to talk to him, right?"

"Uh, ok, when?"

I wasn't sure what I'd say to Joey, but things were moving fast, so the sooner the better.

"Let's go to Little Naples now and see if he's there."

Jonesy was ready to roll.

"You think he'll be ok with me tagging along?" Eddie was thinking ahead.

It was going be a touchy subject and it would be best if Joey was comfortable with the company present with this sort of conversation, Jonesy digested the hint.

"I see, hmmm..."

I already knew what needed to happen but thought it would be better if it was Jonesy's idea. I gave him an inquiring look hoping he would take the cue.

"Of course, it's best if I take you Max. Then we can rendezvous with you later Eddie. How's that?"

Jonesy looked from Eddie to me and nervously took a swig. His eyes went back and forth between the two of us again a few times. He caught on to what we told him but was still stunned his Uncle Joey might be in trouble. Jonesy didn't like being in charge of more than the next round of drinks. He was a loner, a freelancer who liked to hang with his drinking buddies, but at the end of the night usually traveled alone unless he had a woman in tow.

"Sounds good to me, I can try and get caught up on news about these other characters while y'all meet."

Eddie set down his half-drunk beer and stood up. He didn't drink much in public anyway, he preferred drinking at home, which wasn't that often.

"When do we meet? ...tonight?"

"Yeah, if you're gonna be home, we'll call you when we're done at Little Naples."

"Ok, sounds good."

"Hey, will you drop my bags off at the place first?"

"Hubba hubba, y'all got your big wheels turning for sure!" Jonesy was impressed, "we better get outta here then," but anxious.

I stood up, turned my bottle up, emptying it in a couple gulps. Jonesy turned to the bar.

"Sand we gotta go, can you total me up? Maybe we'll catch you later."

He started dug in his pocket, grabbed his bottle and headed to the bar. Once he got there, though he announced a slight change of plans.

"Aw, hell, Sand, line up a couple Herr-durras for me and Max for the road."

Sand already had the bottle out and was pouring by the time he set down his money. I shrugged at Eddie, but he waved goodbye like waving off an unwelcome suggestion while he was on the phone.

I smiled back with an upward nod goodbye, turned, joining Jonesy.

"Let's do this!"

"Bruuthuuuurrr!"

Turns out when we got to Little Naples, we were a little late. Joey was already gone, picked up by Larry's driver, Richard. After we bought them a round of beer, the cooks told us the guys went to Little Angels to see Janet's 'Dancing with Doves' show making suggestive faces and flapping their arms. We called Eddie as soon as we heard, who told us to meet him at my place. When Jonesy dropped me, Eddie told us his car wouldn't start so we took the Blazer and Jonesy took his truck to eventually meet us.

Most importantly Eddie gave me a printed note Sgt. Bob Growler had left at the place. There wasn't a lot of information.

'See Me ASAP – Sgt. B Growler'

Eddie drove us in the Blazer near the Tempe Police Station and dropped me off. He said he'd check back on Mill Avenue every fifteen minutes. This is the method we used in the Blazer to avoid tickets and we never parked on the street near the station, as the Blazer begged for a close inspection with its glaring infractions.

I went inside, but only found out that Sarge had stepped out and no one seemed to know when he'd return. It was a dead end, so I walked to Mill Avenue and played tourist for a few minutes, staying visible, with an eye out for the Blazer. I enjoyed the college town shenanigans on Mill. I got the beginning of an out of tune sidewalk performance of Neil Young's *Heart of Gold* when Eddie pulled up and honked.

I explained the situation.

"So whaddya wanna do now, Max?"

"Well, hell, let's go see Janet's 'Dancing With Doves' unless you got a better idea."

Eddie shook his head and punched the gas pedal as I tightened the bungee cord. It was another night that wasn't wild yet, but we were still playing it by ear. We were starting to chase our tails a little, or maybe a wild goose. Then again, it appeared we'd be doing some dove hunting first. The night was young.

When we got to Little Angels, we decided to park at the far end of the lot. I'd never been before, and Eddie didn't like the idea of parking near the door.

"I'd rather leave first and bring the Blazer around when it's time to go. Why are we here again?"

"We hope Jonesy and Joey are here. I tell you what, I'll go in, you wait here in the lot, and we'll just go with the flow."

"No, I tell *you* what. I'll cruise the front door every thirty minutes, and if you're not out by the third time, I'll call Sarge for you before I come back again."

"Ok, I guess that's a good idea. If you get a hold of Sarge, you gotta come tell me, though. But even if I'm not here, you tell him I'm here anyway."

"Hmmm, if it gets to that, we'll see…"

Birthdays are for desserts
    But you might wanna desert.
Birthdays are meant for sweets
That's not your kind of fix.

Oh, boys,
you just don't know,
but I know:
"Reap and sow"
But then you want to go low."

For you I ain't got
No more dirty tricks.
Like the man said,
"Nix Nix!"

Richard didn't like the direction everything seemed headed. Danny was still acting weird ever since his birthday. Now Richard began doubting taking his brothers to Memphis had been the right thing to do. He'd hoped his brothers would be helpful, and they were, but most importantly, he wanted them to become part of his work, his crew. He wanted the three to be closer as a family. He believed he was obligated to do something. If not, he feared the only family he had would drift apart and now they seemed to be doing just that.

Larry was getting to be a real pain in his ass, too. When they first got back from Memphis, Larry acted all proud, like he was their long-lost, rich uncle and insisted on sponsoring Danny's birthday party. But after Danny's episode at the club, Larry acted like the Boones had been unappreciative and said some hurtful things.

"You Boones lack the finer traits necessary to have what's known as class. You know, like in our family."

Reliving the conversation made Richard mad. "Maybe we're not all perfect like you, Larry, but we're going to learn..." Richard talked out loud when replaying Larry's words in his mind, "...you little shit."

He was tired of Larry's holier-than-thou ways.

On top of family anxiety and Larry's attitude, the cops were snooping around CB Products looking for information about Carter Benson. Richard's gut told him to prioritize that situation above all else.

Why? Because he didn't trust Larry one bit when it came to cops, especially now. After Larry's remarks about Boone's family lack of class, he suddenly announced something else Richard thought was very shady.

"With these cops snooping around about Carter, well, if it messes up the Vettes' deal at all..." he shook his head, "that would be really, really, bad for every one of us."

And while Richard nodded in serious agreement to what was said, he realized Larry was staring accusingly at him.

"You all better keep your nose clean."

Then he wiped his finger down his nose. Maybe that was Larry being dramatic but sometimes it was his way to give a warning. Richard had seen him do it plenty of times.

In spite of Larry's dangerous words, Richard continued to agonize about Danny. He knew it was part guilt and part his own loneliness. He really wanted his family to be close again, but it was hard while Danny was being looney. They were closest in age, and Danny had always tried to follow in Richard's footsteps. Danny had been a good football and basketball player in high school, and always credited Richard for teaching him. Working at Vettes and other jobs where Richard observed him work, he'd always been reliable.

But now Danny was acting like a damn fool. Richard thought his brother was turning into a maniac, some sort of weird donkey man.

On his birthday, after the bouncers got Danny out in the Candy Canes parking lot, in deference to Richard they willingly left Danny with his brothers instead of beating the shit out of him.

After the bouncers went back in the club, Danny proceeded to kick out one of the headlights on Richard's Lincoln, hitting it with his bootheel while doing a crazy backwards kick. Danny laughed loudly as if possessed.

"Haw, haw, haw, heeee! Haw, haw, haw, heeee!"

He was completely crazy, throwing his head around, while bent oddly at his waist, his jaw pushed to his chest, jumping backwards, like bucking to shake off something. Then after acknowledging his brothers as they tried to calm him down, he jerked all around again as they tried to get him in the car to leave.

His bizarre behavior change came on so quick, he thought Danny must've done Huggy on his birthday and was suffering from side effects. Did someone sell him drugs at Candy Canes? Danny denied it, but who knows if he really remembered, with all the tequila they drank.

The damaged car, however, wasn't Richard's, it belonged to Larry and Louis. He couldn't risk Larry finding out, so Richard had to take the Lincoln to a body shop the very next day. Also, it had to be a place none of them ever used, so word wouldn't get back to the Etruscos. It had to get fixed before any of them saw it damaged. On top of that, he had to pay for it on his own, and on the down low.

Richard remembered seeing Angel, one of the party girls, come out on the stage and help Pearlie at the end of her dance, right after Danny fell down. He'd seen her around and found out Pearlie was her little sister. He knew Angel once worked at Little Angels and Candy Canes, as well as the Clubhouse parties.

He'd only seen Pearlie work at Candy Canes but remembered her at Louis' party. She left early with all the drama going down. Afterwards, there was a rumor Pearlie tried to scam some money for what happened. It was the same damn night Danny hurt his leg playing with Cherry bombs. Talk about *stupid*. Of course, Danny wouldn't talk about the details, just said it wasn't a big deal, just a party foul.

Richard decided since both Danny and Pearlie were part of what went down that night, there might be a connection, but until now he never put it together. When quizzed, Danny said the only time they'd been around each other was his birthday. Richard didn't know for sure and hated getting involved in gossip about these girls. But now this whole situation with Danny convinced him to make an exception.

When he was calm, Danny would say Pearlie showed him the light, and after a few beers say she was sent from heaven to touch his heart. However, later the same day he would be cursing her for putting a demon inside him. Either way, since Danny couldn't seem to get Pearlie off his mind, Richard wanted to try to get the two of them together so they could sort it out.

Richard wasn't personally acquainted with Angel or Pearlie, but decided it was time to get to know them better. He asked around but no one knew how to get in touch with Pearlie. He decided the quickest way to put his plan in action was to find her sister.

He suspected Angel knew most everybody in both clubs' organizations. Including who was doing who and what they were up to when they set up parties. He reckoned she might even have something to do with Danny's wacked out condition, too.

Larry called and told Richard he wanted to be picked up and taken to Little Angels later to meet Joey. Then changed his plans, saying he'd drive himself, but first Richard had to get Joey. Larry mentioned Janet would be doing her Dove show and since Richard had the night off, maybe he'd enjoy it too, Larry's treat. Richard was thinking maybe something fishy was up, but thanked Larry and decided to bring Danny, too.

He didn't care about Janet's show, but Danny wasn't working, so he could pick him up after dropping off Joey. Not only would he be able to keep an eye on his brother, but he could see what Larry was up to. Plus, even though the shit with Danny happened at Candy Canes, while he was there he could check around to see if anyone knew Angel's whereabouts. If he got lucky now and found the girls, he'd already have Danny with him.

Richard picked up Danny and on the way to Little Angels, they stopped in downtown Phoenix and got food at Lolo Belles Chicken & Waffles. It was Richard's favorite place and was sort of on the way. They ate their waffles then Richard drove them to the club. His left hand hung over the steering wheel, while his right dug around in his to go box of chicken, shoveling whatever he found toward his mouth. They both munched merrily on their chicken with napkins stuffed in their shirt collars. Danny hadn't been enthusiastic about the food at first, but after a few minutes he was smacking along noisily. Richard was relieved to see Danny acting normal for a change.

Once inside Little Angels, the brothers looked around for Larry and Joey. They spotted them in the back of the club with some other bigwigs and went to say hello. After handshakes, the bosses acted like the Boones had interrupted something private. Larry explained they were going into the meeting room in the back to talk and the Boones should stay out in the club and enjoy the show.

Since Larry had invited him, Richard asked for a table where they could see things up close. Larry called a girl over and she set them up by the stage. Then Larry and the others disappeared into the back.

Richard was hoping the show would grab Danny's attention and take his mind off Pearlie. Richard made a point to try and engage Danny, explaining Janet's routine. As he talked, she slinked around in a silverish cape among her stage props`, wearing a modest sequined Danskin and white shiny latex boots. An ornate pearl tiara with feathers on her head was reminiscent of a Vegas showgirl, only Janet showed a lot less skin. Occasionally, she'd pause at her small staging table, do a few wiggles and wave her cape, and a white dove would fly from her hand while she completed a pirouette. The audience sort of paid attention, but the effect was more like a bunch of horny guys being polite, while they waited for the next hoot-hungry and hooter-heavy stripper to take the stage.

"She's pretty good, huh? Who'd'a thunk Janet could do this stuff?

"Uh-huh."

Danny nodded but seemed uncomfortable, bouncing his knees nervously while he looked around the room. Richard used a comforting tone and hoped he'd relax.

"Yeah, you know one night I was driving Joey around and he told me all about it. Turns out she's got this tube leads up from under the stage into her boot. Damn birds shoot up the tube on back of her leg into her gloves some kinda way. Then she reaches in her cape and pulls out the dove. Hell, it looks like they just appear in her hand!"

"That's pretty cool, I guess."

Danny strained his eyes as he watched Janet, trying to discern the set-up Richard had explained.

"Yeah, it's *real* cool, you ask me."

Richard looked at Danny's reaction and was satisfied he'd given Danny enough to chew on for a few minutes. He felt he could finally leave him by himself while he went around and asked about Angel.

"Hang loose, Danny, I got to check with some folks about something."

First, Richard went up to the door. He recognized one of the bouncers.

"Angel, yeah, I know her, haven't seen her around tonight, man."

So, Richard strolled over by the stage where the girls accessed the dressing rooms, but knew better than to go backstage uninvited. He hung there a minute and surveyed the room until he spotted a bartender he recognized and strolled over to try his luck with him. The music was loud, so he had to shout to be heard. He called for the bartender's attention, while he spotted another man approach the other end of the bar waiting to order.

The other man was Harper Maximillan Wilson III. He wasn't on Richard's radar at the time. Richard didn't even look at him twice as Max waited quietly for a chance to order a beer.

Max, meanwhile, watched Richard. He heard him ask about Angel.

That got Max's attention and he stepped up on the footrest, leaned over the bar and tried to hear the conversation. He wanted to look casual, so he turned his head to continue looking toward the stage. It was an awkward pose. He didn't want to stand out but couldn't stop from snooping. At first, it sounded like the bartender was playing it cool.

"Sure, I know her, she been around town a while. You know she doesn't work regular hours and she's not here tonight."

"Look, I know that. I need to get in touch with her though. It's important!"

"Sure buddy, we all need to get in touch with her. I know what you mean." He smiled patronizingly at Richard.

"You want another beer?"

He nodded at Richard's hand holding a beer. Instead of nodding back, Richard waved the bartender to come closer. Then he leaned over the bar as if he was going to tell him something important. The bartender who seemed to recognize Richard, leaned in respectfully. When he did, Richard's free hand shot out and grabbed the bartender by the front of his shirt.

"Look, you know I work with Larry and Louis, right? I don't want no trouble with you, and you don't want no trouble with me. Just tell me where she is, and everything'll be all right."

Richard let go of his shirt and the bartender looked around like he was trying to catch someone's eye, but Richard kept talking.

"Don't even think about it, man. Not if you care about working here. All the bouncers are friends of mine. I don't wanna mess with you, I just need to get a message to her, that's all."

The bartender tried to decide what to do. Sure, he'd seen Richard around, but except to owners and managers, employees weren't supposed to give out any girl's information. Resigned to an unfavorable resolution to the jam he was in, he pressed his lips together and turned away. He grabbed the pen from behind his ear and wrote on a pad. He tore off the page and handed it to Richard. Richard looked at the note, shook his head and handed it back.

"Her *address*, too."

The bartender frowned and creased his brow then went over to a cocktail waitress, who stood waiting for her order. He spoke to her, and she pulled a notepad out of her garter, flipped through some pages and read to him. He wrote it down, turned and walked back over to Richard, during which Richard noticed the man at the other end of the bar slip ungraciously down off the bar footrest.

"Here you go. Listen, don't tell her it was me please, unless it's good news."

"Don't worry, brother, I won't mess things up for you with her," Richard raised his chin.

"Here, I'll have another beer," he threw a twenty on the bar.

"Keep the change, thanks."

He turned and walked away without waiting for his beer, putting the paper in his pants pocket. He walked at an angle towards the door but decided he wanted to follow up on the dude at the other end of the bar.

Max tried to hide his surprise at Richard's action but didn't hear every word. He flagged the bartender down right away.

"What was that all about?" Are you all right?"

The bartender squinted at Max.

"Look pal, none of your business. I don't know who you are but I ain't no pimp and I know you ain't no regular, so why don't you scram!"

He started to look over at the bouncers by the door, so Max slipped off to the side and headed for the exit in a roundabout route. He didn't realize Richard watched his interaction with the bartender.

When Max finally got to the door he left quickly, stepping out with a cordial "Good night gentlemen," and looking for Eddie. He walked out about twenty feet from the front door, and stepped off the sidewalk onto the pavement, and nervously waited for Eddie. It was just enough time to rock from heel to toe a couple of times.

He suddenly heard a voice behind him.

"That dude? Hell, he's a manager at Vettes!"

Max started to turn and see who was talking, when he was grabbed. Richard easily locked both of Max's arms behind his back.

Max was trapped against Richard's chest and beer gut.

"Where you headed, Max? My brother here says you should be working at Vettes, not hanging around Little Angels. Whad-dya doing snooping around?"

"Hey man, what's going on? Are you trying to hurt me, shit. Look, what did I do? I'm off tonight, and just trying to have some fun. What's it to you?"

Suddenly, Danny came flying around in front of Max, swinging his leg while as he faced him. Instead of kicking directly, he wheeled his leg out awkwardly, spun around and tried to kick backwards at Max with his heel. He made a crazy noise.

"Hee-yaw, hee-yaw!"

Richard jerked Max away from Danny's strange rear leg thrust and yelled at his brother.

"Danny! What the fuck? I got him, chill out!"

"Hee yaw, hee haw, hee-haw..."

Danny started off loud but began to get winded. He almost fell as he jerked and pirouetted around on the pavement, finally bumping into a parked car. He stopped and wheezed on his final bleat. Then he bent over and put his hands on his knees.

"Man, I'm sorry, I don't know man, I don't mean to fuck up. Whoa, yeee-hah... Man, I'm outta breath."

"Calm down, man. Just relax."

Richard regained control of the situation and whispered in Max's ear.

"Listen, Mr. Max, we're gonna go for a ride and you're going too."

At the same moment, Eddie in his Blazer pulled around a row of parked cars and headed towards them. Eddie sensing the need for caution, , didn't wave or show he knew Max, instead he wisely gave them a passerby's casual 'how's it going?' expression while looking out the driver side window. He looked at the entrance expectantly, and only appeared to glimpse at Max.

Regardless of what the two Boones had in mind; I knew Eddie would hang back. If we left, he'd follow. Further out in the parking lot, I spotted Jonesy walking through the cars. I thought it best to take some initiative to keep him out of the mess I'd gotten in.

"Hey Jonesy, glad you finally made it!"

"Bruuuthurrr! Whasssup?"

Richard relaxed the hold on my arms in a double nelson but pushed what felt like a gun still in his coat pocket against my back.

"Make it short."

He held it there and switched his other hand to a grip on my bicep under my shoulder and squeezed hard to show he disapproved of starting a lengthy conversation.

"Who's that?"

When he leaned in beside my head, his breath smelled like cheap beer, fried food, and syrup.

"Just a friend. We're meeting for the Dove Show."

"Get rid of him, tell him you'll be in in a minute."

"Hey Jonesy, I'll join you inside in a minute."

I tried a convincing smile as Richard turned me to continue facing Jonesy and moved to my side with his hands still in position.

"Okay, Max, are you doing some kinda double-oh-seven on me?" Jonesy laughed.

"Ha-ha, you're funny! Naw man, we're having a little business discussion, that's all. I'll catch up with you inside."

"Oh…" He seemed puzzled but took the hint.

"You got it my Bruuuthurrr, but y'all better hurry you wanna see them doves!"

He tipped his brand new Peterbilt cap, hitched up his pants, and squared his jaw at us. I could tell he didn't approve of the arrangement but strutted inside anyway. I knew he'd follow up on us, too and was anxious to talk business. Plus, Richard and I had to look ridiculous the way we stood together, him looking over my shoulder.

As soon as Jonesy disappeared, Danny pulled the Lincoln up and Richard pushed me in and across the back seat then slid in facing me. The doors locked once we were in, but I couldn't see the gun, his hands were now in front of him, one squeezing a paper napkin. I looked him over but couldn't tell if his firearm was in a shoulder holster or his pocket.

He was a big dude. His oversized coat was wrinkled with bulging pockets, and the car smelled like fried chicken and beer. I didn't want to make my situation worse but did want to find out what they were up to. Despite jumping me, they didn't give off the vibe of professional killers. I wanted to figure out an angle to get away. However, it's true I wasn't really confident about my radar for what a killer's vibe was.

I plowed forward.

"I recognize you," I nodded to Danny in the front, "but do we know each other?" I turned to look at Richard.

"Shut up! Danny, drive us to Angel's place. Here!"

He handed the slip of paper up to Danny.

"Hee-who, hee-haw, you g-got it, Ri-Ri-Ri-Richard!"

Danny snorted and cleared his throat. His unusual stutter sounded almost like a horse's neigh.

"Hey! No crazy shit, not now!"

Richard was obviously pissed at Danny. Since there was some tension, I decided to try and unnerve them.

"Hey, you know what, I know both y'all."

I beamed over at Richard.

"Yeah, well fuck you, what do *you* know anyhow?"
"Well, I might know Angel, for one."

I smiled like what I'd said was an important piece of information. As I said it, I wondered what'd happened to Danny. Since last time I saw him at Vettes, he'd developed a speech impediment. I remembered him as a little weird but not with a stutter, or such a strange laugh.

Richard interrupted my thoughts.

"Oh yeah, smart guy? Ok, why don't you tell Danny up there where to drive to and we'll just enjoy the ride. Danny, give my paper back, I'm gonna double check his directions."

I realized my big mouth backfired and I better think fast.

"Sure, is she having a party tonight or something?"

"Or something."

Richard reached into his jacket pocket sitting on his right hip and pushed the pointed bulge at me. It got my attention, though I couldn't actually see a gun. I'm not a gun grease connoisseur or anything and the car smelled like fried chicken and a touch of petroleum, but I really couldn't tell if there wasn't also a whiff of gun grease mixed in.

The only thing I was sure of was I didn't know what he might be capable of and didn't want to tempt him to use a gun as he threatened. I had no desire to get shot again.

Since he made me the navigator, I decided I'd take the longest way possible and hope he wouldn't get suspicious. If we could catch more traffic lights it would give Eddie and Jonesy a chance to catch up. I was desperately hoping they'd trailed us.

"Danny, don't worry, I got your route covered. Now don't speed, the cops got a lotta speed traps here in Scottsdale. That's how they get everyone. It's ok though, I know the best way, because I know all the cop's favorite hide outs."

I winked at Richard hoping to annoy and distract him, and it worked. When I stalled as I would decide where to turn next I cleared my throat. We took our time and proceeded in a round-about way to her condo. It took about fifteen minutes, including some key indecision on my part, which allowed us to catch several extra stop lights.

We eventually pulled across from her condos which were on Miller near Indian School Road. It's a weird layout with parallel access roads on both sides of Indian School going into the neighborhood. It meant we had to do some back tracking to get to her parking, delaying our arrival. There was no security gate, so after we passed through the entrance to her condos, we got to her building quickly.

Richard took over. "Danny, stay in the car, if I don't come out in thirty minutes, go get Dave and come back."

He looked at me and pointed his chin my way.

"Okay, Max, let's go see Angel. You get out first and don't try anything funny."

He raised his pocket for emphasis.

I looked at his face then at his pointing coat pocket.

"Okay, whatever you say, but why don't you tell me what we're doing here, anyhow?"

"Me to know, you to find out. Now get out."

Danny got out first and waited. I got out next and he had me flanked next to the car. After Richard got out, closed the door, and turned to me, I looked him in the eye.

"Has it got anything to do with why the cops are looking for you?"

"What do you mean cops? Where do you get off asking about the cops? Just do what I tell ya. Now let's go."

His pocket pointed to the right, but I had more and decided to give it to him.

"I happen to know how the cops are looking for you in connection with Carter's disappearance...".

He squinted at me.

"You know a Carter Benson?"

That really struck a nerve. He stopped and grimaced, and told Danny to get back in the car. I waited while Danny got back in, then Richard circled around me.

"What do you know about it?"

"Well, just enough to get me in trouble, I guess. I know the Tempe cops are looking for a Huggy dealer around ASU. And I hear the Nevada cops might be looking for you....",

I had his attention, "...yep, you and some guy Larry? It's in connection with a missing person. A certain Carter Benson. I'm betting he's a very unlucky guy, too."

"The hell you say! Listen, who knows anything about that crazy bastard Carter? I don't know nothing about it."

But I could tell he did know something, and whatever he knew was upsetting him.

"What does Angel have to do with it?"

"What? How the fuck do I know. That's bullshit, you don't know nothing. You know what? She put a fucking hex or something on my brother and now he ain't right... Don't you see?"

"A hex? You mean like a curse or something? Really? You gotta be kidding me. Wow!"

I struggled to produce a laugh, so I shook my head trying to show how stupid I thought blaming a curse was. He wasn't impressed.

"Hey, you don't need to know nothing. Why don't you shut up and just keep moving."

He pushed his pocket toward me. He was trying to stay cool, but I could see glistening beads of sweat on the ridges of concern lining his forehead.

"Listen, Richard, I don't think it's worth taking a fall for someone, and I'll bet you anything Carter's dead."

I turned to face him again.

"What do you think?"

"I think you'd better keep moving if *you* don't wanna be dead. You gotta big mouth and I prefer you kept it shut unless I tell you otherwise."

"Alright, but I don't think Angel's a witch doctor, so I think you're wasting your time here."

"Well, fat lotta good your thinking's gonna do you, cuz you're gonna tell her that *you're* here to see her."

I stopped and turned around.

"Me?"

I pointed to myself and looked at him, trying to think how I could make a break for it. Her condo door was just around the corner from where we were standing.

"Yeah, you. You said you knew her and that means you must'a done business with her. So, you're gonna tell her you're back for more, got it?"

"Unnhhh, I'm not so sure that's gonna work, man, I'm not really what you call a client..."

I wasn't sure how I could alert her to his presence, or what I could do to stop him. I wanted to do both, so I stood my ground.

He didn't stop.

"Just keep moving."

He stepped right up to me and pushed the pocket into me as I backed away from him just a little. He smelled lousy when he got close, even more fried and beery than in the car.

I decided it was safest to play along a little more.

"Okay, no problem, I'll see if she's home, but I never come over this way, I mean unannounced. So she's gonna think somethings not right."

"Oh, I think it's gonna work out fine. I'll be standing right behind you. Go ahead and ring the bell. Don't say nothing, 'less I say."

I rang the bell, knocked and turned to him quietly.

"I always announce myself. Is that okay?"

I noticed she had a peek-hole, so I hoped she could see us when she looked through.

"Just your name and cover the hole and I don't want no funny business."

I shuffled up to the door and rang the bell.

"Hello? It's Max, anybody home?"

Nothing.

I balled my fist and banged hard a few times on the door and once on the frame. I turned to the patio on our right and called out towards the sliding glass doors.

"Angel, it's Max are you here?"

"What the fuck are you up to? Keep your ugly mug in front of that peep hole!"

He raised his coat pocket at me again.

"Hey, I ain't up to nothing man! You know she could have on headphones, that's all."

I raised my hands up in the air to show they were empty and thought I heard a noise from inside.

What I didn't see was Angel.

She had glanced through the upstairs window curtains and saw Richard behind me. From her vantage point she'd only heard me call out and couldn't actually see me. After what sounded like someone moving around in the condo, I heard her voice.

"Max? What are you doing here? Are you by yourself?"

"Hey, yeah, it's just me, ...uh, myself and I. Just wanted to see if you're open for business."

I tried to sound as unnatural as possible. It wasn't hard.

"You know I don't take clients this late! You wanna haircut, you gotta call for an appointment first."

The tone in her voice let me know she was stalling. She'd never called me a client and had never cut my hair.

She knew something wasn't right.

Richard pushed me out of the way, took two steps then lifting his leg, shoved his foot into the door with all his might. I didn't expect it and could only watch as his heel landed below the doorknob. He immediately followed with a second smash, and the door gave a little.

I moved out of the way and leaned back against her side entry wall.

"Whoah! Are you crazy?"

The door's interior had crushed inward, but the edge was still intact. The door still hadn't opened. He took another quick step back, and put a little hop in his next try, and stepping into it with all his weight and hitting it right below the doorknob.

The door gave way with a crash and a clattering of broken wood scattered.

Inside, Angel started hollering.

"Wait! Noooo! You ruined my door! ...Don't you dare come in my house!"

He kicked out wooden shards to widen the hole.

"Now listen, Angel, I'm not here to hurt you, I just wanna talk."

He'd announced himself in a very matter of fact manner, then while he ignored me, he stepped through the door's remains with his left hand in the air to protect his face from splinters of wood, his right hand still in his pocket. He acted as if he'd done nothing unusual. For a moment he forgot about me all together.

Angel went ballistic.

"You're fucking crazy! You kicked my door in! Stand back!"

I moved back to the door to get a look.

Angel was livid, but also terrified and hyperventilating. I could see her standing in her living room, holding her position, her arms fully extended in front of her. She had a pistol in a two-handed grip pointing right at him. Her eyes were open wide, full of tears and fear. She stood on unsteady nervous knees; her head was shaking.

I decided it was my cue.

I slipped through the door and leapt from behind. As I jumped forward I reached for Richard's right arm with the hand holding his gun.

That's when she fired.

He was hit somewhere in the midsection, but I didn't catch anything. He twisted his body to clutch his stomach with his free hand and fell to the floor. His hip landed first, but once on the floor, he rolled over onto his stomach, his free hand underneath.

I scrambled on top of him and put a hand on the back of his neck and pushed his head into the floor. He groaned in response, and I reached into his jacket pocket to grab the gun.

Instead of a gun, I found something greasy. Clutched in his hand was a drumstick wrapped in napkins. I rustled around the pocket and felt a biscuit in there, too.

No gun.

I checked his other pockets.

Still no gun.

Who would have believed it? The whole time he'd been threatening me with a late-night snack. Damn guy didn't have a gun on him.

And now he had a bullet in his gut.

I tried to stand but slipped awkwardly, falling against the entry wall with his blood on my shoes. Angorra screamed and threw her gun on the floor like it was on fire. It went off again then I heard something crash in the kitchen.

"Holy shit!"

Just when I had relaxed!

"Maaaaxx! Are you okay? I was only trying to stop him!"

"I think so. Yeah, it's okay, I'm okay, I just slipped. Are you ok?"

"No! This is awful!"

"Angel, we need to call an ambulance right now!"

"Oh shit, lemme get rid of the gun..."

She fell to her knees and started crawling towards her gun, when we both heard the sirens.

It was a party all right.

ook out,
to look in.
Out of order and out of turn,
Losing track,
feeling the burn.
Without a Prince or a palace
The world is full of malice.

Then trouble whispers
in your ear,
and they carry you away.

"Everybody, freeze!"

The cops arrived immediately after the sirens as if transported in from another dimension. A half dozen cops from the Scottsdale Police Department scrambled into position around us, setting up in 'Charlie's Angels' poses in the condo. A silver haired officer with his gun drawn who wasn't posing took charge.

"Hands up! Now!"

I lifted the drumstick with my right hand as well as lifted my left hand, while slowly pushing up the hallway wall with my back. Angel's sobbing got louder as she raised her hands in the air.

"I didn't mean to hurt him, I just wanted to stop him. He kicked in my door! ...and he had a gun ...I mean, I thought he had a gun."

Meanwhile, the silver haired officer barked orders to his squad and demanded an all clear from the ones who went upstairs. One officer inspected the back patio while another rustled through a closet in the downstairs bedroom. Even with the all the commotion around us, I heard the familiar sound of Jonesy outside the condo.

"Oouuweee Bruuuthherrrr! Hey Max, are you okay?"

Then I heard him greeted by Scottsdale's finest.

"Stop right there! Put your hands up!"

I heard Sarge from Tempe work his way through the entry.

"Excuse me, officers, Sargent Robert Growler, here on official police business and already on this case."

When he finally got to the end of the hallway, he spotted me, and I smiled timidly, my arms and hands pressed against the wall. His expression quickly changed from the commander taking charge to a cop jinxed by a reoccurring glitch. He shot me his 'not again!' look, then shook his head with a grimace of resignation. After he surveyed the room, he lifted his hands to the other police at the scene.

"Officers, stay calm. I know the one with the drumstick. Crazy as it sounds, he actually called this in."

Richard couldn't respond to any of the hands up commands, instead he lay moaning and bleeding on the floor. He was curled on his side holding his stomach. The first Scottsdale officer in went from holding a gun on him to kneeling beside him. Then he used his walkie talkie to call an EMT, then tried to calm Richard down before hollering for help to stop the bleeding.

"Somebody, throw me a towel!"

While Sarge explained how he was working the case to the Scottsdale silver hair, the other officers' hand cuffed Angel and me. In the process the officer handling me found the bag of Huggy I was carrying.

I tried to nip the usual domino effect of being-busted in the bud.

"Look that's evidence for an investigation, just ask the Sargent over there, he'll tell you."

"You shut up. Let us sort this out."

I looked to Sarge for help, but he just gave me a stern look indicating I better shut up, and he'd handle things his way. I tried again anyhow, since the officer was adamant on giving me several thorough pat downs, checking all my pockets and crevices.

"Look I'm telling you, that's not mine, it's just evidence I was bringing in for testing. You gotta believe me."

"I said to shut up and keep still or we're gonna strip and hogtie you."

Sarge had his back to me and was patiently waiting for the Scottsdale officer in charge to finish a conversation with dispatch. They sat me and Angel down on her couch facing her backyard with an officer standing over us. I could hear them shooing Jonesy away by threatening to arrest him if he didn't clear out.

We could only see the action going on behind us through the reflection in the patio's sliding glass doors. I noticed my shoe had left a footprint of Richard's blood on our way to the couch. Angel's anxiety continued to climb. Though I had never seen her anything but calm before, she was increasingly concerned about his condition and what it might mean for her.

"Please don't let him die, please, please, please…".

I didn't hear anything about the where abouts of Eddie, or Danny, much less Jonesy's final status. Instead, we watched while the ambulance lights flashed through her front door's remains. The medics showed up and hustled Richard onto a gurney, then outside to an ambulance. Angel pleaded with eyes closed that he would live.

Then he was gone as the sirens blared before finally fading away. We were relieved hearing the silver hair talk to Sarge.

"He was lucky, his beer gut was like a pillow, he should be ok."

But then we heard the bad news.

"We're gonna take these other two and lock them up in Scottsdale for now."

Unfortunately, jurisdictions being what they are and the situation being what it was, Angel and I spent the night as guests in Scottsdale City Jail holding cells, though in separate wings of the jailhouse. We both got out the next day but were not processed at the same time or by the same desk. When I got outside on the sidewalk, I saw her get into a tricked-out Mustang convertible driven by a tan bleached blonde bombshell, who wore a pink bikini top, a backwards Cubs hat and a wraparound, a typical Scottsdale hottie uniform.

"Hey Angel, wait! We need to talk!"

I ran down the sidewalk towards them to get their attention. They heard me and screeched to a halt. When I caught up to their car, Angel reached her hand out to me to give me a business card, but I had already started talking before stopping to get my breath.

"Geez, don't you think we better talk about this?"

"Yeah, I know, baby, but you gotta understand, I gotta go take care of some things right now. Call me tonight!"

"No! You can't leave me here right now! We got too much going on with all this shit!"

"I'm sorry baby, I gotta go. I'll explain later, but I gotta go now. This here's Hattie. Don't worry, your friend is around here somewhere waiting for you in a Blazer. We already talked to him."

Hattie gave me an air kiss greeting before turning back to the road ahead and Angel gave me the full hand-launched air smooch. They drove off in a hurry, Angel's hair fluttering around her head as they turned the corner. The engine roared as Hattie put it through its gear changes like a high school show off. I felt like I was screwed, but it turned out they weren't lying about Eddie, he pulled up right away in the Blazer.

"I thought they'd never let you out. Angel told me she'd heard you were getting out any minute."

He undid the bungee cord to the passenger door and pushed it open for me.

"Well, I guess Sarge had to go through some bullshit to get me released. I never talked to him personally, but when they let me out, they told me I was lucky, told me I wasn't getting out on their account. They would'a much preferred to keep me. They told me to thank the Tempe Police Sargent for the quick release."

"Get the door secured and let's get out of here."

Eddie was all business and looked tired. I was tired, too, and had him take me home so I could get cleaned up. I had to work at Vettes that night and felt fortunate I remembered my job after all that had gone down.

"Eddie, did you see Jonesy? I thought I heard him at the condo, he's not in jail, is he?"

"No, he got out of there when they told him to. I stayed loose just cruising by the condos' parking lot from time to time. It looked like Danny took off as soon as he heard the first gunshot. Did Richard take both bullets?"

"Just the first one. He got one in the gut and was bleeding a lot. The other shot happened when she threw down her gun. It just went off. I guess we're lucky nobody else got hit."

"Why'd the police take you in?"

"I had some Huggy in my pocket I'd brought back from Memphis for Sarge. I figured it was the same stuff they're using here. It took'em all night to decide I wasn't lying."

"What about Angel?"
"I haven't had a chance to find out, but I guess since she pulled the trigger, I knew they were gonna hold her, too."

I shook my head as I considered the confusing way things played out.

"Yeah, well I'm sure she knows her share of lawyers and bondsmen."

Eddie nodded with his lips pursed while working the steering wheel around a corner.

"I'll call her tonight from work and find out. She gave me a card."

I pulled it out of my pocket and looked it over. Good thing I already knew her number.

ANGEL'S TOUCH
Hair Styling and Massage –
Scottsdale, AZ & Las Vegas, NV
(602) 689-63??

When I got to work at Vettes everything was still the same as before. Murray welcomed me back. I had a good night, but the previous night's adventure and accompanying lack of sleep left me dazed, in a dreamlike state.

Funny, no one seemed to notice.

At one point we got the crowd worked up doing *What'd I Say Part 1* by Ray Charles with some cool call and response with the crowd. I cut the volume right after "*Tell your mama, tell your pa-*" and the crowd shouted back, *"I'm gonna send you back to Arkansas!"*

There was a moment when I felt like another all-nighter was coming on, but then I ran out of steam. After finishing check-outs, I managed to find the correct brains and willpower to decline the crew's invitations for a welcome back cannon-ball leaping party into the deep end at Freddy's in Tempe.

Of course, there was another reason I didn't go anywhere. Sarge called during the course of the night to talk about the Huggy. I told him I was busy, but he said I could either talk now or he'd come down and cuff me and converse right there in his cruiser. So, I told him what I knew, that it came from a ship-ment of CB Products sent to the Memphis Vettes. I told him I didn't know for sure if there was a connection to the Phoenix Vettes, and of course I didn't tell him about Lehigh.

He said it looked like it would check out to be the same stuff sold on the street in Arizona. Also, he wasn't going to interrogate Richard any time soon because the Feds were already talking to him about turning state's evidence in an ongoing investigation. So, he'd be off limits till a decision was made. If Richard took the bait Sarge might never get a face to face with him.

He also mentioned I might not be in the clear but possessing the Huggy wasn't the problem. He thought with the Feds involved, there may be issues with whatever I'd done while working at Vettes. When I asked what he meant by that, he declined to advise me, instead told me to keep my nose clean and hope for the best. He said he had to cut it short, warning me not to share our conversation with anyone.

When I called Angel, she couldn't talk but agreed to meet me the next day. After work, I went to my apartment and had a hard night's sleep until morning. After I woke, I left for my lunch with Angel hoping to make some sense of the nonsense.

We met in the back room of AZ Union Jack's, a pub in a strip mall in a less glamourous part of Scottsdale than our last lunch date, though perfect for two citizens freshly sprung from jail. Dark and mostly empty but for some hard-drinking British expats in the front room, it was the perfect place to tell secrets and lies.

I'm not someone you would seek to explain Voudoo and spells. I guess what works for me is whatever helps us make sense of the unexplainable. But the Voudoo wasn't my priority anyhow.

As soon as we got our fish and chips, we shooed the bartender away. I wanted to talk to Angel about why Richard pursued her and what else she might know. I knew of course, I'd get a roundabout answer.

"So, what about the gun you shot him with?"

"Oh, it was mine, licensed and everything, but you see I had some...," She looked around the bar with a touch of paranoia before continuing, "...some umm, parking tickets and stuff, and of course then they had to mess with me about arrests from my young and crazy days working the streets."

"Well, you don't have to explain all that, you already told me you had lots of shady stuff happening. I'm just glad you got out right away. Do you still have more legal matters to clean up?"

"Oh Max, let's not worry about that, my lawyer's taking care of everything for me. He's *really* good to me."

"Must be nice."

"Yeah, he's sweet, but I feel bad about Richard. He didn't even have a gun and I shot him. Course he smashed in my door, and I was scared, of course it was self-defense..."

"Of course. You and me both were under attack!"

"...I uh, I gotta go to the hospital and see how he's doing."
"You think that's a good idea? I mean he works with some dangerous people."

"Yea, I know. I been around them before. But you see, I know he's not in charge of nothing. He's just a 'BC' and a driver, you know, a big size errand boy. He's never done anything mean to me and I've never seen him do nothing cruel."

"He's a 'BC'? Whaddya mean?"

"Oh, it's short for bonecrusher, it don't really mean nothing."

"Well shit, sounds pretty serious to me. I guess you're more familiar with them than me, I'm just starting to learn, and they don't seem very trustworthy. Please be careful."

"Oh, don't worry I know better than to trust them or even turn my back on them."

"Ok, well, hell... maybe you can you do me a favor?"

"What's that, Max? You know I'll do what I can for you." She pushed back in her chair with some attitude.

"C'mon baby, haven't you figured that out already?"

She smiled provocatively, tilting her head in anticipation of a request, but before I put any words together, she leaned forward again, continuing to explain her experience with Richard's people.

"You realize of course, I've relied on his boss for work from time to time. They extend offers, and if they good I accept. I know sometimes they up to no good and I also know they don't always play fair, *especially* with someone like me...".

She looked around again to see if there was anyone wandering around she should beware of, "...even though they should trust me by now. So anyhow, as much as I'd like to walk away from them for good, I still ain't satisfied there's been the proper atonement, so to speak, for my sister Pearlie's..."

She uncrossed and recrossed her legs before pushing back in her chair to finish, "...situation."

"Uh-huh. Well, you better tread carefully there. Look, why don't you ask Richard if he knows anything about the Memphis Vettes connection to Phoenix? Can you do that?"

"I'll try to work it in if I do get to see him."

"Ok, that'd be great, let me know. So, tell me, what happened with Pearlie and Danny anyhow? Why was Richard so hot and bothered to find you because of all that?"

"Well, my sister Pearlie was hurt by their carrying during a party for Louis, one'a Richard's bosses. This Danny was the main dude screwing things up. Shit, afterward, she couldn't hardly see out'a one eye and couldn't hear proper either. We *had* to get even."

"How'd Pearlie get hurt? I mean, what happened?"

"They were setting off fireworks, cutting up, and throwing them around. Some went in this big cake box she was inside of and exploded before she could get out."

"Cake? I thought you were talking about firecrackers?"

I know I gave her a strange look. I was confused.

"Max! It was a fake cake, and they were playing with M-80's or something. Hell, might as well have been dynamite! Them boys were outta line! Look, you gotta understand they didn't ever offer to help her out and didn't even apologize. Maybe they were too high that night, I don't know. But even after, and much later on when she still wasn't better, they didn't do nothing! I let them know about it through our chaperone that night, a guy named Harry. He said not to worry about it, they'd help her out, but I swear they never did nothing. Then they stopped calling me for gigs and they cut back Pearlie's hours at 'Canes cuz she took so much time off. But she had to, they knew she was hurt."

"Well, if Pearlie worked at 'Canes, why didn't she go to them herself?"

"She had too much pride to ask for help. She's hardheaded! She's my baby...".

She reached up with her hand, wiped her eyes and kept talking, "...my...my baby sister. By the time she was ready to work again she got pissed about it too. She just figured out how to hide it."

"Okay, well, is she better now?"

"She gets a little better all the time, but she's still hurt and still hurting inside. Me, too, see, I got her that gig. I told her I'd do anything I could to help get even."

"So, you know witchcraft or something, did you put a curse on him, or something?"

She was shocked at what I said, but quickly regained her focus, shifted gears, and laughed at me.

"Lordy, Max, you must think I'm a lot more than I am!"

She slapped her knee and nervously pulled her hair back from her face.

"Well, Richard said y'all put some kind of spell on Danny, least *he* thought y'all did."

"Max, listen, I got an old friend who's like a Voudoo Queen down in N'awlins. She tells fortunes and stuff. She taught us how to mind trick him, that's all. It's all in his mind, he'll be okay after a while."

"Are you sure 'bout that, I mean Richard tracked you down and seemed damn serious...", I felt serious too, even talking about crazy spells and stuff. Still, I had to smile, "...though he was only carrying a loaded drumstick!"

"Ha-haaa! Max, you tickle me. I sure do miss you! ...sure do."

"Angel, you got to tell me the truth now, what's going on with this?"

"Max, listen you gotta trust me to handle this my way. If I tell them everything then they may go after Pearlie. As long as them boys think we got some kinda power over them, we're safer. Don'cha see?"

"OK, so they might stay away, but what about the guys they work for? You think any kinda mumbo jumbo is gonna stop them?"

I looked her square in the eye.

"...Because I don't."

"Hey, so far, they ain't involved, so let's leave it at that. Look, if it'll make you feel better, I'll check with my friend Beatri and see what she says can be done to make that Danny boy better, if need be."

"Well, ok, you may be right. You know that Tempe Sargent says Richard probably gonna go into hiding, but if Danny doesn't, or gets in with them and takes his place, you might have a problem."

She got up quickly.

"Max, I'm sorry, baby, but I gotta go."

She left me in a hurry, and I left with only a little light shed on the whole mess. Now I knew we were lucky our stories stood up with the cops.

At least so far. We both told them Richard acted like he had a weapon. Then kicked the door in and didn't halt when she told him to stop. It's too bad they still had to jerk our chains with a complimentary night of incarceration.

At least it was only one.

I was still able to go to work at Vette's. Considering everything that happened I felt lucky to remain gainfully employed. I was rested and ready to give it another go at 'swimming upstream, life is but a dream' but I was starting to wonder if their idea of a dream might be my nightmare.

That night, I was proud of my music mixes. I worked the crowd step by step down memory lane with songs with increasingly higher BPM's and guided them into a frenzy. I took them from Tom Jones' *It's Not Unusual* up to Question Mark & The Mysterians' 96 *Teardrops* then Roy Orbison's *Oh Pretty Woman* then Stevie Wonder's *Uptight* before cooling them down with The

Five Satin's *In The Still of The Night*. After that, anyone who didn't get their belt buckle polished with the Satins got another try with *Cherish* by The Association.

I was full of myself and ignored the eyerolling of the cocktail servers and the bartenders when I stepped down from the DJ booth. I wore my smuggest look and went about my business attending to the Vettes' snafu of the moment. Just because they were tired of the old songs, didn't mean I couldn't enjoy a flashback every now and then.

I got another invite for an afterwork soirée and accepted, even letting Olga and Darla know when they dropped in to see me around midnight. They suddenly seemed a little uneasy in Vettes, and tried to wave me over, but I was too busy at the time. When I was finally free enough to visit, I couldn't find them. They had left. I wondered what they wanted and why they left without leaving a message. When I did my closing rounds, I found one of Olga the Plumber's business cards at the Hostess stand. There was a message on the back.

"Max - Come see us ASAP! XOXO"

It pissed me off the staff forgot to give me the note. Oh well, I let it go, I knew how their young hearts get distracted. They were probably going be at the afterwork party, so I could tell them how disappointed I was when I finally got there.

After locking up, I headed to Olga and Darla's to check in with them. After all, they looked serious, and I knew it was important since Olga left her card. There was weirdness in the air as I approached their street, but I shrugged the feeling off, as it had been several strange days all around.

When I pulled around the last corner, flashing red and blue lights lit up the street. Cruisers quickly pulled up to block my vehicle. I was surrounded by what I thought were cops.

I was taken completely off guard. At first, I thought maybe I had a headlight out, or maybe Eddy had incurred some horrible traffic sin and not told me about it. If I'd paid better attention, I'd have remembered the city cops used blue lights, but the Sheriff Department used red and blue.

When I realized they were Sheriff's vehicles I was puzzled. I did a quick inventory of what I was carrying and relaxed a little since at least I was clean. But, still, there I was, on a quiet Phoenix residential street, not out on the highway where they usually roamed in packs. Right away they cranked up a megaphone and began broadcasting for the whole neighborhood's enjoyment.

"Get out of your vehicle with your hands up."

I did, but really didn't think anything would come of it. I was still in my blue sport coat and button-down shirt, khaki pants and saddle oxfords, my tie only slightly undone. I appeared more professional than I'd ever looked during any previous stop by any authority. It made me feel kinda cocky.

"Hey how's it going, y'all? How can I help you tonight?"

"Keep your hands up and your mouth shut!"

The Sheriff's Deputy had his gun drawn on me while the other in their car talked to headquarters.

"Yessir, Joe, we got'em, we followed him right here like you said. We're ready to bring him in."

Interspersed in the conversation were the same crackling sounds you hear on the TV cop shows, and it added to the entertainment for the neighborhood as a few people came out on their steps to watch.

"Now wait a minute, this has got to be a misunderstanding. They cleared me of everything the other night, you can check."

"I told you to shut up, so *shut up!*"

Another Sheriff's deputy came up to me from behind pushed me against the Blazer and handcuffed me.

"Mr. Wilson, you're under arrest..."

I didn't pay much attention to the rest of his spiel until I heard, "and for suspicion of aiding and abetting the distribution of a controlled and dangerous substance. Now get moving!"

"What?"

He poked me with a nightstick and directed me to the back of his car. After he pushed me in, he slammed the door shut. The deputy in the front seat turned his wide brimmed hat towards me and smiled.

"You ever been to Tent City, Mr. Harper?"

"No sir, why do you ask?"

"Because, you got a first-class reservation there, my friend."

He pulled out while screeching his tires, the siren blaring and lights flashing. The neighbors held their children and watched, and we headed to the special place they claimed they'd reserved for me.

Olga and Darla, meanwhile, watched in shock from their bedroom window as the last of the Sheriff's cars sped down their street and into the night.

I remember sunsets,
   When you were smiling.
Helped me forget
You were lying.

Trying to get ahead
Without getting lost,
It's a long way since yesterday
Where did we put the time?

There's no sense crying
over senseless games.
We cheered for tomorrow,
but lived for today.

Angorra walked into the hospital determined to see Richard Boone a day after her lawyers wrapped up their plan for her trial. She hoped the plan would clear her of any wrongdoing in the incident culminating with her shooting Richard when he broke into her condo. However, she still wanted to make sure she was clear on why he broke in. Did he only want to confront her about what happened to Danny?

Richard heard the nurse announce a visitor though his TV was really loud. He was enjoying, "Francis Goes To the Races," an old movie about a talking mule, a friend of Donald O'Connor's character, who mixed it up with racehorses and the mob. He begrudgingly turned down the sound after the nurse interrupted.

"Yeah, yeah, okay, come in."

He sighed and looked to the door, nervously thinking it might be Larry or one of Larry's other guys. Though the Feds said he'd get 'round the clock' protection if he took their deal, he knew better. He had until the next day and wasn't going to feel safe until he was out of town. Right now, there was just a rent-a-cop outside in the hall watching his door. He wondered who got by him to visit and hoped it was one of his brothers.

He was confused when in walked a strange woman wearing oversized sunglasses. He tried to straighten up a little. He was stunned. He recognized her. It was Angel, the woman who'd shot him.

She quickly took the sunglasses off and started talking.

"Hey baby, are you doing ok?"

She set a plastic wrapped plate of cookies on the table by his bed.

"These are for you. I hope you like chocolate chips, I baked'em specially for you."

Richard pulled the covers further up above his bandaged midsection and looked at her slack jawed and eyes bulging. His first instinct was to reach for the nurse call button. Last time he saw her, her pistol flashed, and he buckled. He didn't remember her showing any remorse that night as he laid on her floor.

She watched him recoil and grab the button, waiting for her next move. His furrowed brow showed his concern about her intentions.

"It's ok, baby. You know I didn't know you weren't pointing a gun at me, and I had to protect myself. I never meant to shoot you. I thought just showing you the gun would be enough. But when you lunged at me..."

"Yeah? Is that right? Well, if that nosey-ass Max hadn't jumped me I could'a explained it to you. I just wanted to find you to help Danny."

He relaxed his hand holding the call button and raised his head to sneak a better look at the cookies.

"That's all I wanted. I wasn't asking for no trouble...," he inspected the cookies some more.

"...So, you made these for me?"

"I sure did, baby. My Mawmaw's recipe. Mmm, sure is, they're really good."

She unwrapped and lifted the plate to his free hand. He carefully lifted a cookie, examined it, then sniffed it, before taking a little nibble. She started working over in her mind how best to handle his mention of Danny. She knew of course, it was about the spell. It must have worked pretty well to provoke Richard to such drastic action. She didn't know much about him really, but he never struck her as a real go-getter. Something crazy was happening in order for him to have taken the initiative to track her down like that.

"Well, how's Danny doing?"

She sat down and put her hand on the bed by his thigh and looked at him, trying to ooze sympathy. He was munching away on his cookie with increasing satisfaction, so she continued.

"You know, it was just a little prank. We didn't mean no harm. And it was my idea. You see, I sorta look after my little sister Pearlie. She's all I got 'cept my Mawmaw."

Richard had to look away, he realized she had the most beguiling eyes he had ever looked in.

"Well, to you it might be a prank, but there were some very serious side effects."

He looked again at the cookies but wanted to regain the initiative in the conversation. She resisted mentioning Pearlie being hurt, instead responding by leaning over him and guiding the plate closer. Her breasts grazed his legs slightly and she made eye contact and smiled.

"You not gonna be able to eat just one."

She coyly tilted her head, then backed up and eased back down into a chair beside the bed. She rearranged her purse and hair, then looked back up at him with an innocent smile. He realized he'd been staring at her with a cookie in his hand and his mouth open. As soon as their eyes met, he stuffed the cookie in his mouth. As he chewed, he bobbed his head in agreement.

Suddenly realizing he had taken on too much cookie, he mumbled and pointed.

"M-m-m-milk!"

There was a small carton on his tray, and she leaned over again, lifting it and moving the straw to his mouth. He'd been a real cocksman in high school, but those days were long gone, and he knew he'd never be much of match against the wiles of a good-looking street wise woman like her again.

However, he did realize earlier in this hospital stay while he interacted with the upbeat nurses, he found himself interested in a woman's company for the first time since those wanton high school days. As he lay in his hospital bed he'd considered maybe if he went in WITSEC he could find a woman that wanted someone like him to protect them, and in turn share their charms with him.

Yes, maybe he could pursue that after he got out of his mess. It occurred to him the pain medications must have had his mind wandering. He shook his head and returned his attention to the present. He needed to try and help Danny.

"Listen here, I don't know much about this stuff, but seems to me y'all pulled some kinda Black Magic Voodoo shit on Danny and now he can't hardly put two words together. He's always talking about how Pearlie put a spell on'im, then he has these spastic attacks where he wants to kick everybody. He ain't right."

He stopped talking and tried to look as serious as possible while chewing a little less energetically on the second cookie. Angorra stood up and closed her eyes for a second before turning to face him and launching into her spiel.

"Well, look, I want to help, I feel like it's the least I could do. There probably ain't nothing happened to Danny that he can't fix all by himself. This Voudoo stuff's all in our minds anyhow, there ain't no real magic going on. Trust me, he's just infatuated. It happens to young men all the time. Y'all ain't got the same smarts as us women regarding laws of attraction."

He'd cocked his head while trying to digest her words. She looked at his confusion and decided to keep going.

"That being said, I know a little bit about such matters and these so-called magic spells. I'd be willing to bet, with just a little work, I can set him at ease, and he'll be fine in no time."

She smiled at Richard, who had slowed his chewing down considerably, and continued.

"I certainly don't want you to worry. My understanding is you got enough to worry about. Max says you told the Sarge you might be willing to strike a deal…"

"Ain't none of your business. I might and I might not. It ain't nothing for you to worry about. Your only business in this is Danny."

She could see she wasn't getting much out of him regarding his plans, but the way he said it, she knew something was happening and Max's guess was probably right. She wasn't going to worry about the Memphis connection, but she couldn't let him finish the conversation by dismissing her either.

"And Pearlie…".

She bent her head down to look at him nose to nose.

"Now let's be honest with each other. None of this would'a turned out this way if the boys hadn't been so stupid with them fireworks at Louis's party."

She turned away to calm herself and took a couple steps, then turned back around to see him on the defensive again, maybe thinking she might pull out her gun or something. She waited for full effect then changed her expression to a kindly smile and walked over to his bed and gently put her hands on the covers.

"Look baby, I'll do what needs to be done, but I don't want nobody even talking to my Pearlie. You understand?"

She gave him a dead serious look and once it registered that he'd seen it, she relaxed into a much kinder expression and began to smooth the cover on his leg. He looked down at her hands and felt a rush in his thighs up to his groin. He realized he was truly afraid of what she was capable of. He knew he'd be powerless to stop her no matter what her intent was. Whether she meant comfort or harm, it didn't matter, he'd be at a huge disadvantage.

"Hey, look, don't worry, ain't nobody gonna mess with Pearlie. You just do what you gotta do and let me know if anybody messes with her."

With that, she left the cookies and his room after they exchanged some insincere goodbyes.

Without ever getting tired enough to shut his eyes, after she left, Richard lay uneasy in his bed knowing he would begin his indoctrination with WITSEC for a new life in Kansas the next day. He never actually fell asleep. Uniformed and plain clothes cops were exchanged outside his room to make sure he was safe and secure.

The night passed and turned into day and Angorra boarded the train for New Orleans to visit Beatri again.

Meanwhile, Eddie and Jonesy slept well thinking they'd be meeting me for happy hour.

In a few days Larry Etrusco would sit in a maximum-security cell while his attorneys plotted his defense. Larry knew Louis would already be working on ways to undercut or eliminate any witnesses the prosecutors arranged. Surely it wouldn't be that hard to figure out who the nose was who'd flipped on them.

In Las Vegas, Veda reviewed her newest request from Louis. She lit up a joint to preempt the rough edge she'd feel from her chunky mixture of meth and coke she'd prepared. She had been waiting for this day since the night she heard the donkey braying in the desert. She arranged the drugs in the shape of a heart on the skull shaped mirror topping her coffee table. She slowly rocked back and forth in anticipation of the hunt, and reread Louis' telegram.

Meanwhile Lieutenant Delmonico of the MPD slowed first, then parked his Chevy Impala in the gravel on the side of Arkansas State Road 131. He was near Horseshoe Lake, and as close to the Mississippi River shoreline on the Arkansas side as you could get in a car.

He was there to view a body that washed up on the spillover from Cat Island Number 50. Luckily, he'd gotten a head's up from somebody who'd actually paid attention to out of state bulletins. The Arkansas DPS officer who called him had remembered reading a description in a report of a missing man with a gold star in his teeth.

Delmonico wondered if he just might be his missing informant. The bulletin was put out weeks before but stated the man was of special interest to the Memphis Police. Delmonico, grateful for the call knew he'd have to reciprocate somehow in the future, especially if the body was his man. But for today he'd skipped breakfast to prepare for something gruesome. According to the call, bones and teeth showed where skin once covered the skull.

Of course, I didn't know anything about Delmonico or the beached corpse with the gold tooth, I was detained.

My current status was as inmate Maximillan Wilson III in Tent City, Phoenix, Arizona.

While Delmonico skipped breakfast, I woke up in early morning heat of ninety-five-degrees, the coolest part of said day. A Pigeon, looking for some breakfast, picked at my ragged wool blanket on the end of the dilapidated two-inch-thick pad which masqueraded as a mattress. I shooed the bird away and looked through the tattered tent flaps to a dreary desert yard full of miserable meandering inmates scrounging for cigarette butts. In my tent were two rows of six bunks with an aisle down the middle just large enough to disturb each other when negotiating our way in or out of our own personal slice of hell.

If working at Vettes was the 'swimming upstream, life is but a dream' life, then this was 'dying destitute would be okay, compared to another night of tent city living'. I already lost my only sheet to an unidentified thief, leaving me with only the one nasty wool blanket for bedding.

But I wasn't letting it out of my sight, damnit.

Breakfast was probably gonna be as disgusting as anything anyone could imagine but I had to check it out anyway. I'd lucked into a tiny box of Fruit Loops on the first day. It was a relatively easy catch, because a snaggle toothed, young wannabe thug who couldn't have weighed ninety pounds, stared hungrily at the lonely piece of bologna on my tin plate and I simply traded him straight up for the Fruit Loops. I threw in my cold lumpy grits and stale piece of bread as a bonus.

Today it looked like more barely identifiable slop. I was guessing powdered eggs and fatback which the kitchen prepared with careless indifference. Uninterested, I drug my blanket back to the tent and tried reading my copy of Kurt Vonneguts' *Breakfast of Champions* while it was still quiet. To get the book on the first night I traded my greasy raw chicken fingers, along with a bar of soap and my socks, just to give me something to read. It helped stave off insanity.

The tent's elder statesman was in the corner. He hoarded paperbacks under his mattress and had a 'bodyguard' who slept below. I was lucky, I happened to be standing minding my own business staring at the sky when the meal truck backed up nearby and started dishing out food. When I saw the commotion the fingers caused, I figured they'd have some value. I wrapped the chicken fingers in a napkin as I wasn't about to eat them. I'd already decided I wasn't eating anything they served that wasn't a piece of fresh produce or something still in its package.

After my tentmates moseyed back from breakfast, they started their midmorning shenanigans, and my reading session was over. I rolled up my blanket and strolled over to the TV canopy. Might as well see if there was anything worth watching. So far it had been slim pickings; the mob rule committee that held sway bowed only to viewing tastes of the lowest common denominator possible.

They had *Gilligan's Island* on when I arrived, and all the benches were full, so I found an unattended post to lean on. It wasn't a great spot, as from that angle, the sun hit the old tube TV set directly on the screen, bleaching out half the picture. That being said, it was the first time I'd even found a place to lean.

Gilligan had the Skipper flabbergasted when someone seated in the front row announced he was going to watch the news and changed the channel without warning.

Only minutes into the local broadcast, I saw a reporter stating he was in front of the CB Products building. I thought I heard her say something about a federal investigation. Unfortunately, that's when a scrum broke out. Probably some cigarette deal gone wrong or someone who didn't know the Gilligan episode by heart. Things quickly escalated into a full-scale brawl, revitalizing hostilities that smoldered just beneath the Tent City surface and always waited for the proper spark to turn them into a blaze.

The bruhaha spread like a desert wildfire through nearby tents drawing dust-covered men to the TV area or dashing into their desired tent d'jour, yelling finely honed obscenities as they entered the fray. Like a swarm of flies on an animal carcass, it was instant chaos. I did my best to become invisible and slink away, steering clear of the paths of all and steadfastly avoiding eye contact.

Eventually I got back to my dingy, rusted springs, while the siren and the megaphones and whistles of the jailkeepers rang out as part of their response. Certainly, more pain would be inflicted by their peacemaking methods. I wished on any lucky star listening to keep me from a more dire situation after the jailers' bone crushers sorted things out. So far it seemed to be the unfortunate way the community here worked.

With my first phone call I paged Olga since no long distance was allowed, but I misdialed and had to use my second and last free call on a second try. I left Olga the only Tent City number they allowed for call backs. There's no telling what someone would be told by the persons who answered Tent City phones, or what they'd encounter at the front desk if they came in person.

Once the TV melee lockdown was over, I got in line for the pay phone, in order to call Eddie. While waiting in brutal midday sun, I heard the synchronized stomping of boots and the sounds of chains dragging. It was the Tent City women's chain gang. I turned to the sound beyond the fence, and there a stone's throw away, passing in their prison stripes, women marched in the desert.

I could make out the first words to the song they chanted, their only source of relief.

> *"Black and white we wear with shame,*
> *The prison guards, they know our names,*
> *We work hard and march for hours,*
> *If we don't, we don't get showers*
> *5AM is when we rise..."*

...their voices faded into the heat, and I looked at the half-dozen Tent City derelicts in front of me while clutching my quarter tight in my fist. I'd only been inside forty-eight hours, but it was forty-seven hours and fifty-nine minutes too long. So far, I only managed a half hour of sleep, and that in pieces.

I had to get out.

I needed to clear my name.

And it couldn't happen too soon.

E pilogue

Meet Leonard McAntired.

Leonard, 'Lenny' McAntired walked along the banks of the Sand Creek in Newton, Kansas and approached the dam. This dam, an inflatable rubber bladder used as part of Harvey County's watershed project fascinated Lenny. He'd never heard anything like it until WITSEC placed him in Newton. The area didn't offer a lot of diverse activity, but Lenny took great joy in the small pleasures it did allow. Plus, the dam looked surreal, kind of like a big gray calzone, when you stood right below it.

As he looked it over, he reached down and felt the scar on his abdomen.

"You and me, we gotta watch ourselves, not too much sun or too much snow."

He laughed. His innards took a long time to heal after the bullet from Angel's gun put him in the Scottsdale hospital.

For now, he had a part time job as a groundskeeper. It basically meant he rode a mower around and cut grass at sports fields and parks in the Newton Parks district. He didn't socialize and didn't go to bars. He preferred to drink his beer in his apartment.

He usually spent free mornings walking around the Newton Railroad Station, a grand old depot built in 1929 and modeled after William Shakespeare's Stratford on Avon. Once an important stop for the Santa Fe line it still harbored the ghosts and mysteries of people on the move. At one time it had essentially been America's geographic bullseye for the railroad system.

Lenny didn't learn much literature or history in his early life as Richard Boone. In fact, Richard Boone always dismissed the educational portion of the curriculum schools offered as unnecessary. However, now he looked forward to visiting the library, often researching the history of the place he'd ended up as Lenny. He attempted to read plays by Shakespeare but mostly preferred watching movies and listening to spoken word renditions of the Bard's works. When Lenny read lengthy plays and poems they usually put him to sleep.

He took to smoking on a regular basis and loved to leave the butts on railroad tracks on top of a penny, then track them down later for a collection he started. The only thing he knew for sure about his future was it had been shaped by the past. He gave a deposition and signed the papers that in all probability would be the driving force in sending Larry Etrusco to prison.

Those actions dictated pretty much everything else that followed. Lenny was on his own for the foreseeable future.

He didn't have the goods to give the Feds to lock up Louis or Joe. In fact, when he thought about it, he wasn't sure Joe had really been part of their racket. Sure, he'd partied with them, and he understood Joe was partner in some of their clubs, but he didn't know any more than that about the guy and he kind of liked him, too.

Lenny never had to admit to anything in Memphis that happened with his brothers, so maybe they didn't know about it. If they did, what else could they tag him with? In his mind, he hadn't done anything that caused anyone who was living any harm. Of course, like all of us, he remembered things in a manner convenient to his cause.

He'd looked it up and the statutes varied. Even with what else he read he wasn't certain, but he didn't think there was too much more they could charge him with at this point for simply throwing a dead man's body into the Mississippi.

Sure, he knew the law would say he should have notified the police instead of doing Larry's bidding. However, he now believed if anyone figured it out, the impetus to file charges still probably depended on who it was they threw in the river, and what that person was involved in when they'd died.

The whole thing was better left alone. It made his head hurt while researching and considering the possible consequences. It was bad enough he had to go to anger counseling as part of his deal. Naturally, he knew better than to discuss anything with the counselor concerning his job with relation to the Etruscos that wasn't already on the record.

He promised himself he'd never admit to anything that could possibly bring his brothers into the picture. As for WIT-SEC, they told him his brothers were offered the program simply because they were his brothers, and someone might harm them in order to get back at him. Maybe his siblings didn't know anything other than the Memphis job. He sort of thought WITSEC lied though. The Feds probably offered them a deal to find out the other stuff they might know.

He did wonder how the other Boones were doing, and wished they'd seen fit to join him, instead of going their separate ways. He was told Dave split for northern Arizona after turning down the pitch WITSEC made, and never looked back. Anyhow, that's what Lenny's WITSEC officer told him in confidence a couple weeks after he got to Newton, but who knew where Dave was now.

Danny joined WITSEC, but Lenny was told he left the program after a couple of months and headed to Memphis. The exact place he'd said he'd never go again. He was probably looking for Pearlie, but you never know. Lenny still felt pangs of guilt about Danny's condition as he last witnessed. He liked to think maybe he got better, though. Angel told him he would get better, she even promised to make sure. But then, she probably would have said anything to save her own ass and get the Feds off her back.

Yep, that's how he figured it, everything came down to whatever helped the Feds get what they needed to put Larry away.

Lenny was lonely, but alive. He didn't have to run from anyone or anything as long as he stayed put. He really didn't have any worries, though occasionally, he wondered what could possibly go wrong.

Author's note:
'Too Good Fountain'
Story line Consulting & Editing by
Anne Metcalf.

Please stay tuned for
Harper Maximillan Wilson III memoir and
conclusion to ***"The Too Good Fountain"*** with:
"The Costume Kiss of Death".

Acknowledgements –
In Memoriam: To Ellen Drewry Adams,
my wife of 34+ years who supported my endeavors.
Her spirit lifted me to the greatest heights I'd ever known,
and allowed me the voice of a life well lived.

Thanks to Shihiayah 'Ellie' Young my granddaughter,
who has continued to support my creative endeavors
as well as be a constructive sounding board
and encouraging consult for the Max series.

My parents Mary Adams-Smith and Thomas H. Adams
for creating a loving family foundation
and life of support from which I grew.
My sister Avis and brother John –
their spouses Sheila and Stan respectively
and families for their support.
Our family foundation has been a blessing
that gives eternally.

Neil DeTrana & Dayna
and my grandsons David, Matthew, & Chris.
Their love and support and ever-expanding lives
are inspiration to me daily.

My Drewry family, in laws in name only
as they are a truly loving family.
I can never be thankful enough to them
for accepting me as one of the family:
Bill & Ruth, Elizabeth, Ruthie, Polly, & Rice.
Theresa, Tom, Rachel, Lauren, Daniel, & Zach.

For the Too Good Fountain cover art, many thanks to Ral20.com

Nancy Austria for your support of this Novel. I love your appreciation of the written word and for storytelling. I am forever grateful for your love, friendship,
company, family, and more.
All I hold dear to my heart.

Andrea Valenzuela who joyfully assisted in supporting this project, reviewed the first book, and assisted with editing this story arc. Andrea, thank you my dear special friend.

Jeff and Missy special friends who support this process with love, good times, and unwavering focus on the written word and life's truth is stranger than fiction ways.

Victoria Young is an inspiration and dear friend
held close in my heart – Vickie, I love you.
You still have to write your book!

Michael & Rosie Elliott, Katherine & Guy Rose, Roger Wyer,
Paul McNeese, Randy Breen, Jake Guzman, Donelle Gradi-
jan, Gretchen & Laurel Long,
AJ Saum, Star & Micey,
Mark Edgar Stuart, Marcella Simien, Rice Drewry Collec-
tive,
Jaci & Chuck Redding, Jody Hallihan, Kathy Katz,
James Page, Ray Hill, Bill Godley,
Jennifer Marshall, Judy Vandergrift, Miss Jeeraporn Chom-
chuen.
And special shout out to Thomas Wilkinson
for his kinship & support.

To all those who keep Manna House going, both volunteer
and guests.

And here's to all soulful friends and associates.
<u>Humans.</u>
Those known and yet to meet.
Who don't judge others at a glance.
To all the spirits able
to hold forth with strangers,
and keep an open mind,
greet others with a smile
and receive one in return.
Who take joy in the comaraderie shared.